MW01469651

ZENOX

ZENOX

Alex Walker

Deeds Publishing | Atlanta, Georgia

Copyright © 2015—William A. Walker

ALL RIGHTS RESERVED - No part of this book may be reproduced in any form or by any electronic or mechanical means, including information storage and retrieval systems, without permission in writing from the authors, except by a reviewer who may quote brief passages in a review.

Published by Deeds Publishing
Athens, GA
www.deedspublishing.com

Printed in The United States of America

Library of Congress Cataloging-in-Publications Data is available upon request.

ISBN 978-1-941165-67-6

Books are available in quantity for promotional or premium use. For information, write Deeds Publishing, PO Box 5903, Athens, GA 30604 or info@deedspublishing.com.

FIRST EDITION, 2015

10 9 8 7 6 5 4 3 2 1

In memory of my maternal great-grandfather, Colonel Robert F. Patterson, who is introduced as a main supporting character in this book and also my paternal great-grandfather, Captain Elijah F. Walker, who appears as a main character in my three novels, Toltec, Cuzco, *and* Zenox *from the* Toltec Series.

PROLOGUE

At the edge of the Amazon Basin
1325 A.D.

THE TWO DARK FIGURES SLOWLY MADE their way through the entrance and along the narrow corridor of the building supporting the crumbling temple. The older man, a chief of high status, was deferentially carrying a pouch made from the soft hide of a jaguar. His companion, a young priest, carried a wooden bucket filled with mortar, a primitive stiff paste mixture of finely ground lime made from river shells, powdered fly ash, and water. The flame from his torch cast eerie apparitions along the stone walls, reinforcing the chief's belief that his mission was truly directed by the sun god Inti. The dancing shadows terrified his young companion who could feel the cold walls pressing in on him. Unawa was a war chief of the Chibcha tribe whose ancestors had built the lost city. It was later briefly occupied by Incas during the Spanish invasion and it had been uninhabited for several centuries. The ruins the chief had entered were located at the edge of the ancient city, a short distance from the village. The building was considered to be a gathering place for the original inhabitants. Rarely did any of the tribe members visit the old city as it was considered a sacred and haunting place where spirits of their ancestors dwelled. This belief was embellished by stories of warriors who had ventured into the ruins and never returned—it was well known the spirits did not welcome intruders into their sanctuaries.

The contents of the pouch were simple—a small rectangular box and a thin scroll made of a metal-like material. The scroll contained rows of strange images and glyphs, the meanings mysterious and unknown, but that was unimportant as it was the symbolism of what the images represented that made these items so sacred and honored to the Chibchas.

The contents of the box were even more puzzling. It contained a small, oval shaped, metallic-like object inscribed with more strange glyphs and symbols. The chief knew the items were once given to his people as gifts from ancient visitors and it was his self-imposed mission to secure the strange articles in a safe place deep within the depths of the temple. They had been handed down from generation to generation and now it was time to put them to rest. To the chief, this mission was a holy endeavor sanctioned by the gods.

As the two men proceeded along the corridor, they passed several dim, shadowy doorways leading into darkened rooms, many containing tombs of ancestors from years past and others filled with contents unknown. The whole haunting scene took on a sinister and threatening feeling, causing the young priest to shudder—he wanted to leave this place of evil and get back to the sunlight. Unawa sensed his fear and assured him, "We are almost there. As soon as we secure the pouch we will hurry back to the outside."

Soon they reached the end of the corridor abruptly ending at a blank wall. With little effort, the two men removed several blocks of stone revealing a dark cavity backed by another wall facing them within a stretched arm's reach. A recess had been carved into the inner wall, obviously prepared by their ancestors in ancient times to receive this sacred article. Unawa leaned through the opening and gently placed the pouch and its contents on the narrow shelf and respectfully backed away. Turning to the young priest he said, "Take a good look as you will see where our gifts from Inti will be hidden for all time."

The unsuspecting man peered into the cavity. With a sudden thrust, the chief plunged a dagger into his back and twisted the blade upward. The priest uttered a loud moan, stiffened, and slammed against the wall. His lifeless body then sagged to the floor.

The chief took a firm hold under the arms and, with some difficulty, pushed the corpse through the opening and whispered, "Now, my young priest, you and I are the only ones to know the location of these treasures and you will have the honor of guarding our gifts forever."

With the bucket of mortar and a small trough, the Chibcha chief carefully fitted and cemented the blocks back into place to conceal the opening. Satisfied that the wall was fully restored, he picked up the bucket and turned to make his way back to the entrance high above. He smiled...our sun god, Inti, will be pleased.

1

Richmond, Virginia – Late March 1865

CONFEDERATE PRESIDENT JEFFERSON DAVIS KNEW WHAT was coming. He had heard the faint rumble of distant cannon in the distance, giving further evidence that the Union Army was probing the outermost defenses and closing in steadily toward the capital city. His apprehension was further heightened knowing General Robert E. Lee and his Army of Northern Virginia were retreating toward Petersburg in a desperate attempt to prevent the Army of the Potomac from marching into Richmond. The capital of the Confederate States of America was on the brink of collapse and, although the citizens knew it, no one had the courage to admit it. Several days before, President Davis had evacuated his wife, Varina, and daughter Winnie on the Richmond and Danville railroad to Danville, Virginia, where he planned to meet them a few days later, depending on the fate of the capital. He wanted to stay as long as possible. Some of his cabinet members had already departed the city but Davis still remained, accompanied by the Secretary of the Treasury George Trenholm, Secretary of War John Breckinridge, and a few other diehards, who, with nervous attempts, were trying to show their loyalty. Trenholm's wife, Anne, had already left the city on the train with Varina.

Knowing the occupation of Richmond by the Union Army was inevitable, President Davis hastily devised a plan to save the accumulated wealth of the Treasury Department and hide it for future use. He reasoned if he and some of his cabinet could escape to another country, he could later recover and use the money to build and equip another Confederate Army and perhaps resurrect and continue the war at a more favorable time. The plan was to gather up the dying country's treasure from the three local banks and transport it to a safe location much further south, perhaps in a remote cache in the Appalachian Mountains of western North Carolina. He needed a trusted military officer to oversee and carry out the mission, someone familiar with the area.

It was a blustery and overcast day in the capital city and the weather seemed to match the mood of the citizens. Early signs of chaos and panic could be seen as the Union armies moved ever closer toward Richmond. The president turned to his private secretary, Burton Harrison. "Burton, please fetch the Secretaries of War and Treasury for me. You may tell them it is most urgent and come with all haste."

Within the hour John Breckinridge and George Trenholm entered the president's office with anxious looks on their faces. Davis greeted both warmly and motioned them to take a seat.

"Gentlemen," he responded with a foreboding look on his whiskered face, "As you know, the Union Army is knocking at the doors of Richmond and I fully expect it will be occupied within the next one or two weeks. General Lee is hopelessly stuck somewhere around Petersburg and faces a Union Army over twice his size. I seriously doubt if he'll be able to provide us with any help. Our meager forces guarding the approaches to the city are mere boys and old men, all exhausted and unfit to fight off a superior Union assault. The fact is, we must make immediate plans to evacuate the city and move our seat of government to a safer place…and if our new nation is to survive, we will need all of our remaining financial resources to see to it."

The room became silent as the enormity of the president's words sank in.

"In other words we're finished," an exasperated Trenholm mumbled.

"Hell, no, we're not finished!" Davis shouted defiantly. "We just have to move our seat of government and transfer our financial resources to a safer place until we can build our armies back to full strength. I'm hoping Lee can move his army south and link up with Johnson in North Carolina."

"You're dreaming, sir," Trenholm replied.

"You are wrong, Mr. Trenholm," Davis snapped back. "I have devised a plan. We're going to move the gold and all the contents of our treasury from the banks of Richmond to a safe haven much further south."

Breckinridge, showing a perplexed look, asked, "But sir, I was under the impression that all the funds in our treasury had been depleted and our country was broke."

"Mr. Breckenridge," the president assured him, "We have ample funds secretly held back that were planned for this possible contingency."

"Then why didn't we use some of this money to buy more arms from England and rearm our troops in Lee's and Johnson's armies?"

Davis answered annoyingly, "Because, Mr. Secretary, all our ports of entry have been fully blockaded by the Union Navy and besides, Great Britain's support for the Confederacy has waned. The British and French governments no longer support our cause."

"Our currency is now worthless. How and where do you plan to move this treasure you speak of from Richmond?" Trenholm interrupted, as he reached into his coat pocket to retrieve a small silver flask, downing a healthy sip of apple brandy. The Treasury Secretary was a nervous wreck and as of late, frequently consumed a sip of alcohol to calm his nerves.

President Davis ignored the brief interruption and continued. "The Minister from Brazil, Ricardo Ferreira, departed for home three days ago but told me the government of Brazil had given us approval to seek refuge in their country. There are some very pleasant settlements along their eastern coastline to consider or we could even find sanctuary in Rio de Janeiro if we wish."

"Never even thought of leaving our country," Breckinridge confessed.

"You'd better start thinking about it now," Davis reminded him, "because if you or I end up in the hands of the Yankee Army, we'll be dangling from the end of a rope just like ole' John Brown in sixty-one."

Breckinridge nervously rubbed his neck, indicating the comment had registered.

"And the gold and money left in our treasury?" Trenholm repeated sheepishly. "What are we supposed to do with it?"

"The first thing is to gather it up from the banks and then pack it securely and load it on to wagons. We'll send the wagons south and hide it somewhere safely and securely in the Appalachian Mountains, preferably somewhere in North Carolina. All our remaining wealth cannot be allowed to fall into the hands of the Union Army. With the remaining wealth of our treasury we can finance and rebuild another large army and regain our country and preserve our way of life."

Before either of the cabinet members could respond, Davis specifically addressed his Secretary of War. "John, I want you to find a trusted officer intimately familiar with the mountains of western North Carolina and bring him to see me quickly. We'll also need two good wagon drivers and a complement of at least fifteen to twenty armed men to accompany the wagons. We're running out of time and need to move fast if we're to make this plan work."

Breckenridge threw Trenholm a quizzical glance but knew better than to press the issue further. "I'll go find General Ewell immediately," he responded and left the office.

Turning to Trenholm, Davis continued. "George, I want you to contact our three banks and have them pack up the ingots, coins, and all other tangible items of wealth in sturdy boxes, ready for immediate transport. Don't worry about the paper script—I know it's worthless. Advise them to have the cargo ready to load in the wagons by tomorrow afternoon. Also, gather heavy wagons and mule teams to move the treasure south. I expect two wagons should do it."

"Yes, sir, Mr. President, I'll get on to it immediately," Trenholm answered as he nervously swallowed another hefty swig of brandy.

2

LIEUTENANT COLONEL ROBERT PATTERSON WAS CHECKING the outposts along the northern defense line defending Richmond. He was appalled at the poor condition of the few soldiers left guarding the perimeter. Our soldiers are only boys and old men, he anguished. There is no possible way they can hold off the Yankee Army. Many had no shoes and most of them were starving—they had not eaten a decent meal in days. If the Union Army only knew the true condition of these poor souls they would merely walk casually through the lines to Richmond. Patterson knew the end was near and the hopes for a new free and independent country were crumbling all around him.

He glanced to the rear and saw a horseman fast approaching from the south along Four Mile Mill Road. "Must be something big happening. That fellow is sure in a mighty big hurry."

The courier, a young lieutenant, trotted along the lines asking for directions and stopped to ask a youthful sergeant the whereabouts of Colonel Patterson. The soldier pointed directly to the colonel.

The officer trotted over to Patterson and quickly saluted. "Sir, are you Colonel Robert Patterson of the 16th North Carolina?"

"I'm Colonel Patterson."

"Sir, I am Lieutenant Caldwell and I have orders from Richmond to fetch you and bring you back with all haste."

"And who might be requesting my presence with such urgency?"

"The orders come from the Secretary of War, Mr. Breckinridge himself, and I was instructed to take you directly to the office of President Davis."

"My goodness man, what is this all about?"

"Sorry sir, I don't know. All I know was my orders were to find you and bring you back to Richmond as fast as possible."

Patterson turned and shouted to the young sergeant standing on a cannon platform nearby, "Sergeant Mann!"

"Yes, sir," the soldier responded.

"I've been summoned back to Richmond, so go and tell Major Carroll I said he is to assume command while I'm gone."

"Yes, sir, I'll tell him."

"And Mann?"

"Yes, sir," the sergeant replied apprehensively.

"You will accompany me as my aide."

Sergeant Parks Mann was the unit's youngest sergeant, having been transferred to the capital from a former Alabama cavalry unit that had once operated in the western campaigns. Although he was a bit perplexed at the sudden interruption, he turned to go find the major. He wondered, what the hell is this all about?

The two officers, accompanied by the young sergeant, mounted their horses and galloped back toward the capital city. As the men dismounted in front of the White House of the Confederacy, the citizenry seemed to be in the midst of a mildly controlled panic. A state of urgency hung in the air and some citizens were leaving the city with their buggies loaded with an assortment of possessions. There were two large carriages parked to the side of the building and servants were observed carrying a silver serving set, two large paintings, and several large trunks to the carriages. Someone was about to leave in a hurry.

Patterson was met at the front door by Secretary Breckinridge, who seemed to be one of the few portraying a sense of calmness. "Mr. Secretary, I am Colonel Robert Patterson and I believe you summoned me here with a sense of urgency."

"Correct, Colonel, please follow me quickly. We have an urgent meeting with the president in his study."

The introductions were hasty and informal. The president was a bit nervous but well in control of the conversation. "Colonel, you come highly recommended by General Ewell for a most unusual mission. I am told you are from the mountains of North Carolina and know the area well."

"Yes, sir! My home town is Asheville, located a few miles from the Tennessee border."

The president hesitated for a moment to collect his thoughts then continued. "You presently hold the rank of lieutenant colonel, is that correct?"

"Yes, sir."

"Then I am immediately promoting you to the rank of brigadier general and entrusting you with a most urgent mission, perhaps the most important mission of the entire war. As you are aware, the fortunes of our new country are in great jeopardy. It now appears that the capital is about to be overrun and occupied by Union troops, and General Lee seems to be hopelessly pinned down somewhere near Petersburg. It is doubtful that he will be able to defend the capital. Most of my cabinet and staff have departed Richmond and I plan to leave the city very soon to join my wife and daughter. I will try to make the Georgia coast and gain transport to another country where I will continue to keep our government alive and functional while in exile. In order to do this, we will need a great deal of money to finance the building of a new army and retake our homeland at a more opportune time. Your country urgently needs your help."

Patterson was dumbfounded. He couldn't imagine what could possibly be done at this late and hopeless stage of the war to save the southern cause. The Confederacy was doomed and everyone in the army knew it. "Yes, sir, I will do what I can."

The president continued. "Two sturdy wagons and mule teams are awaiting you at one of our banks. The entire treasury of the Confederate States is now being loaded with gold bullion, gold and silver coins, and a few boxes of precious stones, mostly diamonds, sapphires, and emeralds from South America. The coins consist of U.S. gold eagles, double eagles, Mexican gold pesos, and bags of various other assorted gold coins. The bulk of the deposits will be the gold coins and ingots. We estimate the total value at about ten to twelve million in U.S. dollars."

"My goodness, sir," Patterson gasped. "I can't imagine such a sum of wealth. And what am I to do with this large amount of money?"

The president hesitated and glanced over to Breckinridge who was sitting quietly in a rocker. "General, we want you to transport the shipment to a secret location deep in the mountains of North Carolina and hide the treasure so no one will find it. You will have some competent wagon drivers and a small contingency of cavalry to help transport, protect, and handle the cargo. You can also hand pick anyone you wish from your own command to accompany you. When you complete the mission you will prepare a detailed map with explicit directions as to the treasure's location, hopefully in an obscure cave deep in the mountains. I am counting on you to find a suitable place."

"I do know of some well hidden caves near Asheville that might be considered."

"Good," Davis answered with a glimmer of satisfaction. "I understand there is a small town near the eastern coast of Brazil where several members of my cabinet and I might take refuge for a while. We have been offered sanctuary there by the Brazilian government. The town is named Santa Barbara d'Oeste Bracil, not far from the city of São Paulo. You and your command can meet us there as soon as you complete the mission or, if that is not possible, you can travel there when things settle down a bit after the war. General, as you can see, this mission is most vital to the preservation of our country and the protection of our way of life."

Patterson couldn't believe what he was hearing as thoughts reeled through his head. How does the president, while living abroad in exile, think he can raise and equip an army from a generation decimated from four years of war? What complete madness, he thought. On the other hand, maybe a treasure of this magnitude could help rebuild the south after the war. It would certainly provide some bargaining power with the United States. "Yes, sir. I will undertake the mission."

With an expression of relief, Davis shook his hand. "General, you will proceed over to the main office of the Trader's Bank of Virginia where you will assume command of the loaded wagons and accompanying troops and immediately depart Richmond for your journey to North Carolina. As I said, after you select a safe and secure hiding place and cache the treasure, you are to prepare a detailed map of the treasure's location and deliver it to me in person in Brazil as soon as you can arrange a safe passage. Godspeed and remember the future of our country is now entrusted into your hands."

Patterson thought of his new rank of general as he trotted the few blocks south to the Trader's Bank. Hell of a way to get a promotion.

The two covered wagons were awaiting him and in the process of being loaded when he stopped in front of the bank. A contingent of seventeen cavalry troopers and one officer from the famed 19th North Carolina Light Horse Brigade was awaiting his arrival. The young officer in charge introduced himself as Captain William Stafford from the western North Carolina town of Hendersonville, located not far from Asheville.

"Captain Stafford, have you been told as to the nature of our mission?"

"No, sir. Only that I was to accompany you to North Carolina with the shipment in these wagons and we were to hide the contents somewhere in the mountains."

"Do you know what the shipment is?"

"No, but I have a pretty good idea since we're parked here at the bank."

Patterson nodded. "I will inform you of the contents at the appropriate time. Meanwhile, prepare the troops and wagons to move out on my command. We should be able to depart by mid-afternoon, as soon as the wagons are loaded."

Turning to Mann, he said, "Sergeant, you will accompany me on our journey. We're heading south—at least you'll be traveling closer to your home in Alabama."

"Actually I'm really from Georgia…a small town near Atlanta."

"Well, then, Sergeant, you'll be even closer to your home."

The small caravan left the city around five o'clock, turned to the southwest, crossed the narrow Appomattox River at Scott's Fork bridge, and then rolled through the small hamlet of Amelia Court House. The faint thunder of heavy cannon could be heard far to the southeast.

3

KNOWING THE UNION ARMY WAS PRESSING Lee at Petersburg, located just a few miles south of Richmond, Patterson knew he would have to take a more westerly route skirting the small towns of Farmville and Darlington Heights and bypass the advancing Federals directly below him. His window of escape was narrow, knowing Richmond would be completely surrounded within a couple of days. At this late and final stage of the war, he knew Union cavalry units were scouring the countryside everywhere, especially throughout the Shenandoah Valley to the west. Hopefully, he could slip between Martinsville and Christiansburg undetected and work his way south into North Carolina and follow a route secured by the remote valleys of the Blue Ridge Mountains. From there he was certain he could locate some back roads and trails through the mountains to Asheville. He knew that area well.

The trip to Darlington Heights was uneventful except for the trickle of refugees who had made an early exit from Richmond and were seeking refuge at any pro-southern, unoccupied town they could find…one that might offer a safe haven from the advancing Union Army. So far, the small band of wagons had miraculously avoided any enemy patrols. Patterson knew he was pressing his luck and sooner or later they would have to skirmish their way south. He spurred his horse forward and trotted beside Captain Stafford. "Good afternoon, Colonel…I mean, General," Stafford acknowledged embarrassingly.

"Don't feel bad, Captain, I haven't got used to the new rank myself—happened pretty suddenly. I told you I would tell you about our mission and the contents of the wagons. You need to know in case something happens to me."

"Yes, sir, I understand."

"Regardless, Captain, you need to keep this information to yourself. Understood?"

"Yes, sir."

"President Davis has entrusted upon us the ambitious task of transporting and securing the entire treasury of the Confederate States of America—mostly gold bullion, various gold coins, and some gemstones. The money will be used at a later time to re-equip a new and stronger army to regain our country back from the Union."

The astonished expression on Stafford's face mirrored his own feelings. "Sir, I thought the Confederate government was finished and totally out of money."

Sensing the captain's thoughts, Patterson replied, "I did, too. I know what you're thinking—I had the same reaction. President Davis told me they had sufficient funds secretly hidden away to use at a future date in case the government fell. I doubt if he could ever re-equip another army as he suggested, but my feeling is this money will be better used to rebuild our homeland—at least that's what I'm hoping. It might give the South some bargaining power. In any event, you and I are supposed to bury or hide this cache to make sure the Union Army, or any one else for that matter, never finds it."

Captain Stafford was speechless for a few moments trying to grasp the enormity of the situation. All he could utter was, "Well, I'll be damned!"

"All the men need to know is that we are carrying a load of new rifles and ammunition to be hidden in the mountains and later distributed to a new army being formed from remnants of our armies in the Carolinas and from the western campaigns. Realistically, I would imagine some of them have already figured out our true cargo since our departure from that bank."

"I'm sure they have and I can assure you they all know we can't possibly raise and equip a new army. Even the thought of that possibility is absurd."

"You're right, Mr. Stafford. We both know that. But we also know the South will need all the financial help she can get after this war has ended…which I suspect will be in the next few days."

It was a cloudless Saturday morning with a slight morning chill in the air. The small band had traveled three days without any signs of enemy troops. The wagons skirted around Smith Mountain and crossed over the Roanoke River at a little crossing called Sandy Shoals, reaching a seemingly isolated location well to the south of the small town of Christiansburg. A light rain had fallen throughout the night and the dirt road was slippery with pockets of mud. The once thriving fields they passed had not been farmed in months and were overgrown with weeds and tall cinch grass. The large field to their left sloped up to a large grove of hardwoods and nestled at the crest was an old dilapidated barn that leaned dangerously to one side. The graying color of the wood planking indicated the structure had weathered many decades of wind and rain.

Patterson had earlier detailed three scouts to ride ahead and look for any signs of Union infantry or cavalry patrols. So far they had been lucky in their journey—no sign of the enemy. In the distance a lone rider galloped toward the column at breakneck speed. "It's Corporal Simmons!" a man shouted from the front. "Looks like he's seen the devil himself!"

The young trooper reigned in his horse and stopped next to Patterson's mount. "Sir!" he shouted anxiously, "I spotted a small detachment of mounted Union cavalry ahead!"

"How far, Corporal?"

"About two miles east and headed this way."

"How many men do they have?"

"Hard to tell—I'd guess about twenty-five or more."

Patterson glanced to either side and then pointed toward the barn. "Captain Stafford, get those damn wagons up that hill and run 'em into that old barn—and move the men and their mounts into the woods behind the barn so they'll be concealed from the road."

Everyone jumped at once. The drivers slapped the traces to the mule's backs and turned the wagons toward the hill. Loaded with the heavy boxes of gold, the wagons strained and creaked but slowly rolled up the slope to the rear of the barn. Both were pushed through the rear double gates while the front doors were closed and secured with a heavy timber dropped into rusted U clamps. Seven of the soldiers trotted into the barn with the wagons while the remaining troops led their horses into the concealment of the woods to the rear. One of the teamsters was heard to mumble, "Sure hope this rickety son-of-a-bitch don't fall down on top of us and save those Yankees the trouble of having to shoot us."

Patterson and Stafford climbed a sagging ladder into the loft just in time to see the leading elements of the Union cavalry detachment appear in the distance. From a crack in the planks, the general observed the soldiers approaching on the road below and momentarily come to a halt. What if they spotted our wagon tracks coming up the hill, he thought with concern. He observed the Union commanding officer glance up toward the barn then turn to give a command to someone behind him. Four mounted troopers broke off from the detachment and trotted up the hill to inspect the area. Turning to Stafford, Patterson spoke softly. "Captain, they're coming up to check out this barn—must have spotted our tracks. Have someone slip out the backdoor and warn Sergeant Mann and the men in the woods to be ready. We might have to fight our way out of here."

"Yes, sir," Stafford responded as he motioned to a man behind him.

"What are they doing now, sir?"

"They've dismounted and one of em's coming round to the back. Got stripes on his arm—a Yankee sergeant."

"When he comes through that door have someone stick a gun to his head and tie him up and gag him. But be quiet. No shots."

The Confederates concealed themselves behind some hay bales as the Union sergeant opened and entered the door.

"What do you see in there, Sarge?" one of the men shouted from the front.

"Only a couple of wagons and some mules in here. Come on back."

The three soldiers strolled to the back of the barn and passed through the door. Six of Patterson's soldiers arose from behind the hay with rifles pointed at the Federals. "You boys drop those guns quick or we'll blow y'all to hell."

"What the devil!" the sergeant groaned as he assessed his situation. It was hopeless. "Drop 'em boys. They got us outgunned."

"Sergeant, you or your men make one sound and you're dead men," Patterson threatened.

The Union sergeant was shaken, "We got a whole detachment waiting for us down that hill and if we don't come back soon they'll come up here looking for us. If you rebs are smart you'll just surrender peacefully and you'll live out this damn war. War's about over anyway."

"That's mighty generous, Sergeant, but I'm afraid we got other plans."

"Good grief! You're a reb general aren't you?"

"That's what they told me in Richmond, so shut the hell up." He then turned to his captain. "Get these Yankees tied up and gagged…quickly."

Patterson walked back to the front doors. "What are they doing down there?"

"It looks like they're getting mighty restless, sir. I figure they're looking for these men to come back down and report."

"Are our men in the woods ready? I think we got a fight brewing for sure."

"Yes, sir. They're waiting for my signal."

"Get some hay bales stacked to the front and under those two windows. They might slow down some Yankee slugs. We'll use the windows and that opening in the loft to fire and catch them when they top the hill. Bring the others to the edge of the woods and tell everyone not to fire until I give the order."

"Here they come!" a man shouted from the loft.

"How many?"

"About fifteen."

The Union detachment broke into two columns and started up the hill, fanning out to both sides of the barn. There was a clear field of fire from the two windows and loft. The concealed Confederates patiently waited at the edge of the tree line and then split into two flanking groups. They swiftly moved into position to get a good frontal view of both sides of the hill.

"Easy now boys, we'll let 'em get to the top of the hill."

As Patterson watched the situation unfold, the words of President Davis kept ringing in his head. This may be the most important mission of the war. No pressure here, he thought. Although he was sure rebuilding a new Confederacy would never happen, as a general in the Confederate Army he was determined to follow the orders of his president. He assessed the men around him and instructed, "Wait for my signal, boys, and make every shot count."

His hidden troops had been directed to wait for the initial volley then provide supporting fire from their concealed positions in the trees. Patterson surveyed both approaches from the two advancing columns and realized the two advantages he had. In addition to the element of surprise, the riders advancing up the hill were moving directly into a late easterly morning sunrise angling over the barn. The bright glare in their eyes would ensure the Union soldiers would have a difficult time locating their targets once the skirmish began. He also knew they would be approaching the dilapidated barn more with curiosity than caution to find out why the earlier detachment had not returned.

The two columns advanced toward the barn from both sides while the officer in charge, a lieutenant, approached from the middle. Patterson held up his arm to refrain his men from firing until the last second. He knew the Union troops would attempt to encircle the barn once the skirmish started but was counting on the concealed men in the woods to open up and secure his flanks.

Armed with captured .54 caliber Sharps carbines, the Confederates held their fire until the Union columns had advanced to within twenty yards of the barn. The young lieutenant reigned in his horse and shouted, "Sergeant, you boys inside that barn?"

No sooner had he uttered the last word when a .54 caliber slug ripped through his chest and hurled him backward from the saddle. The Confederates opened up from the barn and dropped five more men from their mounts. All but one of the remaining startled soldiers spurred their horses around each side of the barn only to be met by deadly fire from the woods that dropped three more Federals. A lone trooper turned his horse and galloped back down the hill in an effort to escape the onslaught. Captain Stafford spotted the retreating rider and shouted to the man next to him, "Drop that man before he gets away." The shots went wide.

Sergeant Mann was a crack shot, earning him the reputation when he served with the 7th Alabama Calvary in several of the western campaigns. He had lifted a fine rifle off a dead Union sniper he had shot out of a tree while on a mission in a remote place in west Tennessee. It was an Austrian-made, model 1863 rifle, often called a Lorenz. It was mounted with a scope and fired a .54 caliber slug. It was deadly accurate. This was Mann's prize possession and he had kept it with him since the Tennessee incident. At this moment, he clasped it tightly in his hands. Hearing Stafford's loud command, he hefted the Lorenz to his shoulder and took careful aim, concentrating on the image of the fleeing horseman framed in his scope. He slowly squeezed the trigger. He watched the image as it jerked forward, threw hands in the air, and tumbled heavily from the saddle. Mann had hit his target with the first shot—he rarely missed.

The remaining seven Union soldiers dismounted and ran for a small cluster of trees scattered to one side of the barn. The Federals had a small advantage of carrying newly issued .52 cal Spencer repeating carbines that fired seven tube magazine-fed rounds before reloading. Turning their carbines toward the Confederates in the trees, the unexpected fusillade from the Spencers hit one soldier in the chest, one in the head, and another in the neck, killing all three instantly. A fourth man sustained a severe wound to his shoulder while another over-zealous trooper rushed from the woods and charged the Union position. He was cut down before he had taken ten strides. Four of the Confederates in the barn slipped out of the rear doors and eased around to a concealed position behind the Federals. Taking careful aim, three men in blue were killed and another, seeing the hopelessness of the fight, turned and ran down the hill in full stride. Two shots from the Confederate carbines brought him down before he could reach the cover of a nearby tree. Realizing they were outnumbered and out-gunned, the remaining three Federals dropped their weapons and threw their arms in the air shouting, "We surrender!" The skirmish was over. The officer and two remaining Federals at the bottom of the hill retreated back along the road from the direction they had come.

Patterson and Stafford emerged from the barn to survey the situation. "What's the damage?" Stafford shouted to Mann who was busy counting heads.

"Sir, we have four men dead and one seriously wounded."

"Place them in the wagons and we'll bury them somewhere along our route. We need to get the hell out of here fast."

Patterson turned to his captain. "Move these wagons out of the barn and gather all the Union weapons, ammunition, and horses. We can sure use those Yankee repeaters…and their horses. These carbines must be something new and their horses look to be in a lot better shape than ours."

The survivors were moved into the barn and bound and gagged tightly with the other prisoners. Patterson looked down at the hapless Union sergeant and spoke reassuringly. "I'm sorry it had to come to this but you gave us no choice. I'm gonna leave all of you tied up here but I'm sure one of you will work his way free soon. We'll leave some water so you won't die of thirst. Good luck to you." He turned and walked to his horse.

As the detachment and wagons headed southwest, Patterson knew they needed to get away from the area quickly. The remaining Federals on the road below had departed quickly and he knew other Union troops in full strength would soon be searching for the lost detachment as soon as the escapees reached reinforcements.

He wanted to avoid any more contact with the enemy—he had seen enough death for one day.

4

THE SMALL BAND TRAVELED SOUTHWEST AND forded a creek a few miles east of Hillsville. Patterson halted the group for a brief rest and called for a conference with Captain Stafford. Reaching for a map that had been given to him by a staff officer for General Ewell, he unfolded it and spread it on a flat rock. "We've got to get off this road and find an obscure back road where we'll have less chance of running into Feds. What do you think?"

Stafford studied the map and offered his assessment. "We sure can't go west into the Shenandoah—that whole area is crawling with Yankees. Seems to me we need to move a little further southwest and find a track on the eastern side of the Blue Ridge range." The heavy woods and foothills there should give us plenty of cover." He hesitated and pointed to a spot labeled Indian Valley. "Maybe we can cross the state line somewhere down around Mount Airy and try to pick up a road that travels southwestward toward a secluded little town called Blowing Rock. I know that area pretty well—used to hunt up there. I'm sure the good folks will give us some food if needed. We shouldn't have too much trouble with the wagons if we stick to the flatter highlands country just east of the ridgeline. We'll be getting into familiar country and I know of several back roads that can take us close to Asheville."

Patterson nodded in agreement. "I want to avoid Asheville—too many people there. We don't need to be seen."

Having been raised in Asheville, he knew this country well. He closely scanned the map. "There is a split about a mile up ahead and we need to take the right fork towards Indian Valley. What do you think, Captain?"

"Sir, I remember a place just south of Blowing Rock that is honeycombed with caves. There is a waterfall there that would give us a good reference point. A few years ago a friend and I were deer hunting near Grandfather Mountain and got caught in a terrible storm. Somehow we stumbled upon a cave and sought shelter there. The entrance was pretty obscure, but once inside, the cave opened up into a larger room. The place is pretty remote and I doubt if anyone would ever find it if we properly conceal the entrance. Seems to me this would be a good place to stash the boxes. I reckon I could find it again when we find that waterfall."

"Sounds good to me, Captain, you take the lead."

Partially concealed by trees, the small convoy rounded a bend where they were suddenly surprised by a small Union patrol consisting of seven mounted troopers led by a second lieutenant. The Federals were just as stunned as the Confederates. The heavy vegetation and dense woods on both sides of the narrow road prevented any sudden turn or retreat so for a few brief moments each column stood facing each other, trying to assess the situation and how to react. The Federal lieutenant broke the standoff by drawing his .44 caliber Colt and blindly firing into his adversaries. Stafford miraculously escaped the volley but one Confederate was hit and rolled from his saddle, dropping heavily to the ground. The Union patrol charged blindly into the Confederates, engaging them at point blank range. One trooper in gray took a shot in the chest and another in the head before they could react and return the fire. The Union officer was lifted from his saddle by a .54 caliber carbine slug and three other Federals rolled from their saddles with lethal wounds. Another Union trooper spotted General Patterson on his horse and leaped from his own saddle and wrapped his arms around the general, dropping him heavily to the ground. The impact knocked the breath from the general, momentarily stunning him. The soldier pulled a knife from his belt and raised his arm for the killing thrust when Sergeant Mann saw the movement and dove from his saddle in time to crash into his arm and deflect his aim. The knife dropped to the ground and Patterson recovered in time to pull his Colt and shoot the trooper in his chest. The short encounter was over but the cost in lives was horrific. All eight Union troopers lay dead, including their lieutenant, and four Confederates were killed and one seriously wounded in the groin. He died within minutes from bleeding. Patterson shouted, "Drag those Yankee bodies into the woods and let's get our boys buried quickly. We've got to get out of here – fast!"

The general was distraught. He had buried his dead soldiers from the barn skirmish a few miles back and now he had five more dead comrades to bury. *When will it end? This is insanity—so close to the end of this senseless war. I've got to finish this damn mission—quickly.*

He was now down to ten men. "Thanks for your help, Mann—he nearly had me. Now I know why I brought you along."

The column came to the fork in the road and turned toward the southwest. The road was heavily overgrown, an indication it was seldom used and hopefully offered more protection.

Patterson called for a brief halt. He motioned to Stafford and directed him to a nearby cluster of trees where he could speak in private. "We've lost nine troopers and I don't want to lose any more. I want to release some of the men and keep only enough to get this treasure to the cave near the Grandfather Mountain waterfall. We need a few loyal followers who we can entrust with the cache's location…and keep their mouths shut. They'll have to be willing to travel with us to Brazil. How many do you think we need to finish the job?"

Stafford pondered this for a moment. "I believe your Sergeant Mann is with us and most likely Corporal Roper. We'll need two more to drive the wagons so I'll pick Radford and Dunn.

"Good," Patterson acknowledged. "Why don't you talk to each man individually? Between the six of us we should be able to carry and secure the boxes into the cave."

Stafford explained the situation to each of the selected men, confirmed their allegiances, and then had Mann summon all the men for a meeting. "Boys, the general has a few words to say to you."

Patterson stood silent for a moment and observed the tired war-weary faces standing before him. He thought, how much more can they endure? The general had to be very careful how he worded his message because he could not afford to reveal the true nature of the mission or location of the treasure cache. Only those who followed him to Brazil would know. He smiled and then spoke. "We've been through a lot together getting this far. I know all of you are wondering what this mission is all about and why it's so important to our homeland. Let me just say that our new country is finished and hopefully this mission will help us survive the tough years ahead of us. I think we all know it's useless to continue fighting any longer and I don't want to see more of you men die—we've had enough death in the last four years. Our mission here involves the future and rebuilding our homeland. To complete our work, Captain Stafford has selected four of you who have agreed to accompany us."

A corporal from Virginia spoke up, "General, I ain't got much family left so I'll drive a wagon. Hell, I grew up on a farm driving wagons."

"How old are you son?" Patterson asked.

"Seventeen, sir."

"Where are you from?"

"I was raised near Charlottesville, Virginia. My ma lives on a farm with my younger sister and my pa was killed at Antietam in sixty-two."

"Well, son," Patterson reassured him, "I want you to return to your farm. Sounds like your ma could sure use your help about now. Besides, I think we have two drivers that will handle the wagons."

"Thank you, sir. I'll do that."

Along with Stafford, Mann, Roper, and two privates named Dunn and Radford, Patterson had his team.

"With the exception of those of you who are staying with me, the rest of you men are hereby discharged from the army and free to return to your homes. There are lots of Yankees roaming around these parts so be careful and try to avoid them as best you can. Good luck to all of you."

The departing men said their goodbyes and then mounted and rode away in different directions, all relieved the war was over for them.

The small convoy continued on the derelict road until it abruptly ended at a large field heavily overgrown with weeds. They were now in the foothills. "What now, sir?" Stafford asked. "It sure looks like this road ends here and I don't see how we can take these wagons through that forest on the other side blocking us."

Patterson rose up and peered across the field. "I sure hope we can pick up some kind of a passage on the other side—I sure don't want to do any backtracking." He turned to Roper, Dunn, and Radford. "You men scout ahead and see if you can find a road for these wagons to pass through. The way I figure it, we shouldn't be too far from Mt. Airy and our destination is just to the south of that. Sergeant Mann, you check to our rear to make sure we aren't being followed while you other men scout ahead for a road."

Patterson and the wagons stopped under the shade of a large oak tree. The brief respite seemed like an hour but within fifteen minutes Radford was spotted galloping back across the field. The grin on his face betrayed that he may have found something. "Well, General, I think we found us a road back there," he shouted pointing over his shoulder. "Ain't nothing but two ruts but they lead out through those trees."

Radford didn't exaggerate. The passage was nothing but two dirt ruts barely wide enough to allow the wagons to pass through. They proceeded slowly forward. The road was narrow as expected and in one instant a wagon became tightly wedged but a firm slap of the traces urged the two mules to wrench it through. The dense forest was so thick that if it had ended it would be impossible to turn the wagons around. Luck was on their side. The procession inched slowly forward without any serious mishaps. Patterson was thankful it had not rained for a few days or the ruts would have been impassable. Dusk was fast approaching when one of the forward scouts trotted up to the general. "Sir, the woods stop just ahead at the edge of another big field. And just beyond that I spotted a pretty good sized mountain."

Grandfather Mountain, Patterson thought with a sense of relief. "We'll make camp for the night at the edge of the field… and keep the wagons concealed in the woods."

"You know where we are?" Patterson asked his captain.

"Yes, sir, I do now. That big hill you see over there is Grandfather Mountain. Our destination is along that line of hills just south of the mountain. I think I can remember where the cave is located, but first we have to find the waterfall. When we get across this field, we'll look for a stream that will lead us to the falls. This is when the hard part begins because we'll never be able to get these wagons close to the entrance to the cave. We'll have to carry all the boxes up there by hand."

Dawn brought a cloudy sky with possible rain showers in the distance. "Let's move these wagons out," Patterson commanded. "It looks like some some rain coming and I don't want us to get stuck out in the middle of this damn field. Make toward that tree line to the south and be looking for a creek."

The column moved out of the woods and slowly rumbled across the field. Luckily, the dirt was packed and dry and the passage went relatively easy. Patterson saw Corporal Roper trotting toward him. "You were right, sir. There's a small creek down along that tree line and it meanders off toward those hills you see in the distance. The good news is there's a narrow road that follows the creek. Don't look like it's been used for a while though."

The group crossed the meadow and picked up the dirt track along. *This road and creek sure look familiar*, Stafford thought. *I've been here before and this creek should lead us to the waterfall.*

As they moved further south, the terrain became more rugged and the trees more densely scattered along the roadway. The creek bed increased in elevation and the rush of the water became more pronounced as the flow spilled over rocks and tumbled into small pools. It was a pristine setting that seemed to provide a relaxing mood for the battle-hardened men wearied by the toils and stress of four years of war.

To the left was an old deserted barn that had once provided shelter for animals and a place for crop storage from the overgrown fields nearby. The weathered pine planking displayed a sad, tired look, much like the faces of the few people that inhabited this war weary country. Captain Stafford broke the serenity of the moment. "I think I hear a waterfall up ahead, General."

The falls tumbled about fifty feet from a spring flowing from the face of the small mountain looming before them. It gathered in a crystal clear pool at the base and then formed the small creek they had followed along the road. Patterson gazed upward and asked, "Captain, where's that cave you were telling me about? Looks like a pretty stiff climb up that hill from here."

"Best as I can remember, about a third way up the mountain—over there to our right. You can see the path that heads up toward the cave and on around the side of the mountain. The entrance is not far from here...about a quarter mile walk. I remember it was hard to spot because of all the undergrowth covering it—should be a perfect hiding place. I figure it will take two men to haul each box up and into the cave. Those damn boxes are heavy."

"Go check it out, Captain," Patterson instructed, "and make sure we got the right spot before we start moving those boxes. We got a full day's work ahead so let's get started."

Stafford and Roper followed the path until they came to a depression concealed with rocks and undergrowth. His memory served him well—he recognized the entrance. Carefully moving rocks, vines, and brush aside, they lit a torch and entered the small opening into a passageway just as the captain had remembered. "There is a larger cavern ahead adjoining this corridor. We'll store the boxes in that room."

Roper nodded his understanding.

They returned to the wagons and confirmed their findings to the general.

The men unloaded boxes and worked in pairs. Each crate

was carried by each team and lugged up the narrow path to a spot below the entrance. They manhandled them through the passageway and back into the storage chamber. It was slow and grueling work requiring frequent rest breaks. Nightfall came and only half the job was completed.

Gathered around the campfire, Mann posed the question to Patterson. "General, what happens after we get all those boxes stored in that cave? You mentioned something about us going down to South America. "

The silence was deafening as the men waited for the general's answer. He knew it was foremost in each man's mind. He hesitated long enough to fully captivate their curiosity and attention. "There is a place down in Brazil where many of our soldiers and citizens are escaping to and I'm told welcomed by the citizens and the local authorities. I was informed our government will continue to function in exile until we can safely return home. I can't tell you the exact location until we are enroute at sea."

He paused again briefly to let his words sink in. "After we finish loading the boxes in the cave, we'll leave the wagons in that deserted barn we saw back there and then proceed to the Georgia coast together by horseback. We'll bury our uniforms and find some civilian clothes to wear while traveling. This way we won't be too conspicuous if any patrols stop us along the way. We'll just tell them the war is over for us and we are civilians. We're going home to plow our fields and attend to our families. I'll think of something. Best thing is to avoid getting seen and stopped. The worst thing that can happen is we have to shoot our way out and run like hell."

"When and where are we gonna end up in Georgia, General?" Mann questioned.

"There is a small seaport town on the coast named Darien, just north of the town of Brunswick. I'll show you on the map before we leave. I'm sure the locals can direct us there if we stray off course. I don't want to go near Savannah. The place is crawling with Yankees, mostly occupying soldiers from Sherman's army. Before we left Richmond, Secretary Breckinridge arranged for a blockade runner from Brazil to meet us in Darien and carry us to South America. The ship goes by the name of VALDEZ and the captain's name is Silva. We'll all stay together and we need to be there in six days…believe that's next Saturday." There were no more questions.

The next day all the boxes had been safely stored in the cave. Patterson realized they would need to have enough money on hand for necessary food and supplies and asked Stafford to open a box containing U.S. gold eagles and double eagles. They filled four saddlebags full of gold coins and passed out several handfuls to the men. The entrance was then covered by rocks and the overgrowth was carefully pulled back to fully conceal the cave. The cache was now secure.

Stafford motioned General Patterson to one side and away from the others. "Sir, I found a curious looking medallion in one of the boxes. I think you should see it for yourself."

He opened a small leather pouch and handed Patterson a large gold coin inscribed with strange glyphs and carvings. It measured about two inches in diameter and was very heavy. Patterson hefted it and remarked, "This is made of pure gold. I wonder what the writing and symbols mean and how something like this ended up in the Confederate Treasury?"

"I don't know, sir. It sure looks out of place with the other coins."

"I'll just hold on to it and we'll try to figure it out later," Patterson replied, slipping the heavy coin back into the pouch and into his pocket.

"Sir, there is something else I found in the same box you need to see…very strange looking document." He handed the general a thin metallic copper-like tube.

Patterson extracted and unrolled a single thin rolled up paper…more like a thin metallic sheet. It was inscribed with rows of strange symbols and what appeared to be rows of hieroglyphs, some similar to those on the gold coin. "What the devil is this?" he asked.

"Sure looks strange to me. I never saw anything like that

before. The document doesn't feel like paper…more metallic-like…perhaps copper."

Patterson glanced at the document again. "I'll hold on to this as well and maybe we can find someone who can interpret the darn thing. No telling how old it is."

It was the general's plan to travel in a southerly direction, staying within the hill country of western South Carolina, bypassing to the east of Greenville, and then moving across the northeastern corner of Georgia through sparsely populated Rabun County. From there the party would shift to a more southeasterly route and stick to the highly rural countryside to the west of Augusta. They would continue on a straight line to Darien, located on Georgia's southern coast. He would get there in six days or kill all of them trying. Now the toughest part of their mission was just beginning—their survival.

5

Washington D.C. – February 1873

Professor George Scott stood at the front of the new exhibit and looked into the hollow cavities positioned on either side of the massive skull. He had never seen anything like it before. The fossil remains had been recently brought in by a team of archeologists and assembled within the past five weeks. It was the remains of a monster. Nothing like this beast could have possibly lived on earth, much less in the remote area of the Mississippi Delta, he thought, but here was physical proof that it did once actually exist. The report said that a kid digging along a secluded riverbank recently discovered the partial skeleton. He asked himself, what had the eccentric scientist from New York University called it…A dinosaur head? He had even put a scientific name to the skull and the exhibit sign before him labeled the fragmented skeleton as TYRANNOSAURUS REX—King of Beasts"

"Pretty awesome sight, huh Professor?"

Scott turned to find his anthropologist friend and business associate, Robert Drake, standing behind him, gazing at the exhibit. The arrival of the pre-historic skeleton had recently piqued Drake's interest in the new expanding field of paleontology. "Well, yes. I guess you could say that. How old did that guy from New York think it was?"

"He guessed probably a few million years old although we don't have any scientific way to tell."

"I wonder how anything that old could possibly leave a well formed skull and other bones behind. You would think anything a million years old or more would be dissolved by now."

"Maybe it was trapped in a sand pit or mud and protected from the air and weather all these years," Drake speculated.

Professor Scott had joined the Washington National Museum in 1871, soon after the expedition to Peru in search of the Golden Inca. His friend, Professor Robert Drake, had been appointed director of the museum and had convinced Scott that his unique talents would be of great service to the institution. Scott had accepted the position mainly because he could participate in the many archeological expeditions funded by the government.

He had achieved worldwide fame and accolades through his work with the copper scrolls of Lythe, located on the sunken continent of Atlantis. Major Elijah Walker had given him the scrolls and a display of bronze coins as a token of appreciation for his contribution to the Peruvian expedition in 1870, and the subsequent journey that had carried them to the lost continent.

Scott had spent months deciphering and interpreting the hieroglyphics and symbols written on the Lythean scrolls and had presented his findings to the West European Archeological Society, headquartered in London. His first reports were met with skepticism and ridicule from a collection of old scoffers and cynics who demanded physical proof that Atlantis ever existed. Scott had provided the society the actual artifacts and allowed a physical examination of the copper scrolls and bronze coins. All doubts were laid to rest. The artifacts were certified as authentic and the existence of ancient Atlantis became the hot topic of the world wide scientific community. The professor became a well-known household name throughout the eastern United States, Western Europe, and especially Italy and Greece, where the theory of the lost continent was born through the writings of the Greek philosopher, Plato.

His findings revealed that two Atlantean scholars named Platius and Domicia, from the city of Lythe, inscribed the copper scrolls and gave a detailed accounting of the history of the city and many facts about Atlantis itself. The scrolls described how Lythe was founded as a coastal town and used as a port of trade for shipping and shipbuilding. The city was one of the earliest settlements on the island-shaped continent of Atlantis and later became an important cultural center in the western Mediterranean region. A vivid description was given about every day life in Lythe and the people and customs of a typical thriving Atlantean city. One scroll gave a description of the wars with Egypt and various warlike tribes along the southern Mediterranean.

Of special interest to the members of the Historical Society was the one scroll devoted to the ancient empire itself. Referred to as the Lost Continent of Atlantis, the scrolls explained how Atlantis was once connected to the extreme northwest tip of Africa near present day Casablanca, by a narrow strip of land believed to be an extension of the Atlas Mountain chain. Scott theorized the land connection could have extended as far as Tangier and the Straits of Gibraltar, and perhaps even as far north as the southeastern tip of Spain. No wonder Plato described the location of Atlantis as "Beyond the Pillars of Hercules, known now as Gibraltar."

The society members were also interested in a brief narrative by Domicia describing how the land bridge suddenly disappeared and the continent experienced a massive upheaval. "There came upon us a sudden and violent shaking of the ground. This brought about massive waves of water from the sea that covered much of Lythe and killed many of our people, but new land rose from the seas and enlarged our kingdom twofold."

The eighth and last scroll had been only partially inscribed. An unnamed scholar, long after Domicia and Platius, was able to record a few last lines before the scroll abruptly ended.

"The ground shakes with the violence and vengeance of angry gods. The earth splits open before my very eyes and spews heavy smoke and fire into the skies. The great Poseidon spits forth his anger and his fury is upon us."

Scholars believed Atlantis was eventually sunk by another massive earthquake. In those days, people believed catastrophic events were caused by the anger of the gods. In actuality, the quake was a result of a sudden shifting of the African and Eurasian tectonic plates. It is possible, some scholars further offered, that the present day Madeira and Canary Island chains were all that was left of Atlantis and these islands were sunk and then uplifted from the ocean floor hundreds of years later.

Professor George Scott was a competent and experienced archeologist but the infant fields of geology and paleontology was a little out of his realm of expertise. He was an expert on ancient ruins and civilizations, especially the Indian tribes of North, Central, and South America, but bones and fossilized remains of long extinct animals and reptiles were still a mystery to him, and for that matter, most people in the nineteenth century. The museum had a few broken samples of unidentified fossilized bones and skulls, but none as well preserved and defined as the fragmented beast that stood before him.
"Look at those jaws and teeth," he muttered. "That mouth could have ripped an elephant apart in seconds."
"That's probably what he ate," Drake answered, "that is, if elephants even lived that far back."
"By the way, George, I have something interesting to tell you. Do you remember General Caleb Kirby from the Army testing and procurement group?"
"Yeah…haven't heard that name in a while."
"He sent me a message yesterday. Kirby wants you and me to meet him for lunch this afternoon at two o'clock."
"I haven't heard much about him since the Peruvian affair a few years ago. Wonder what this is all about?"
"I don't know but I told him we'd meet him at two at the Capital Cafe."

The Capital Cafe was a lunch hangout for local military officers and officials who worked in the expanding government offices. It was only four blocks from the Capital building and easy walking for senators and representatives who wanted a quick and relatively good lunch. By two o'clock, most of the lunch crowd had eaten and returned to work, leaving an abundance of empty tables. General Kirby chose one in the back corner where the conversation had less chance of being overheard. The two professors spotted Kirby and made their way to his table.

"General," Drake acknowledged as he offered a firm handshake, "so good to see you again."

"And good to see you gentlemen…it's been a couple of years. I notice you both have been doing pretty well with the expansion and growth with our National Museum program."

Drake smiled. "With the support of the government and some additional funds from a few outside benefactors, we've been lucky to have the resources to add to our collections."

"And you, Professor Scott, I see you've done well with your deciphering the Atlantean scrolls you received from our old friend, Elijah Walker. I've read reports in a couple of archeological journals. You seemed to have created quite a stir in the scientific world."

Scott chuckled. "Guess that's true, General. The scrolls opened up a lifetime of new knowledge that substantiates the writings of Plato…seems he was right about Atlantis after all. At first there were a lot of skeptics and cynics but one look at the scrolls made believers of the old fogies. The most difficult were some of the members of the London Historical Society and a few Italian scholars, but they finally came around."

Drake intervened. "General, I don't think you called us down here for a social lunch to discuss the museum project."

Kirby hesitated for a moment. "Actually, you're right. I didn't call you here for a social lunch. I have something very interesting I want to show you."

He reached into the inside of his coat pocket and pulled out what appeared to be a well-worn letter. He looked at the document and then continued. "This letter was addressed to President Grant and arrived at the White House six days ago. It was postmarked from São Paulo, Brazil and dated August 25, 1872. In other words, it has been either bounced around in transit or hidden for over eight months. In any event, the president wanted me to show it to you since both of you were involved in the Peruvian affair a little over two years ago. He seems to think you two are pretty good at solving mysteries and treasure hunting."

The general handed Drake the letter. "This was written by an ex-Confederate general now residing in Brazil. "Perhaps you had better read it for yourself," Kirby suggested. "It is very interesting and confirms some of our suspicions about the Confederate government in its final few days. As you know, Richmond was occupied early April, 1865."

Drake carefully took the letter and held it to the side so Scott could read it as well. It was written on ordinary white stationary and indicated signs of wear with a few water stains. He began to read it aloud.

> 25 August 1872
> The Honorable President Ulysses S. Grant
> The White House
> D.C.
>
> Dear Mr. President,
>
> First let me offer my congratulations for your successful election to the Presidency. Your military accomplishments in bringing a costly American war to an end were exemplary and Confederate officers and men throughout the former Confederate States of America Army appreciated the kindness and generous terms you offered General Lee at Appomattox.
> I am writing on behalf of the Confederate Government in exile and submitting to you an exceptional offer in exchange for a safe return to our homeland. I am General Robert F. Patterson of the Confederate Army of Northern Virginia, 5th North Carolina Mountain Brigade, and formerly assigned to a unique mission by President Jefferson Davis and the Confederate Treasury Department in Richmond.
> Mr. President, I was the officer in charge of transferring

all the Confederate gold bullion and other valuable government treasure from the Richmond depository vaults to a secure and secret hiding place within the southern states. The treasure cache still lies within a secret chamber and is today estimated to be worth perhaps fifteen to twenty million U.S. Dollars.

On March 31, 1865, the fall of Richmond appeared eminent, therefore Confederate Secretary of the Treasury, Robert Trenholm, on orders from President Davis, authorized the transfer of a secret Confederate gold deposit to an obscure hiding place far to the south. Of the small detachment of soldiers that transferred the gold, nine died in skirmishes along the route and the others were discharged to return to their homes. Only five members of the unit helped me secure the treasure and accompanied me to Brazil. Of those men, one recently died of jungle sickness and two are unaccounted for, having traveled into the Amazon jungle in pursuit of rumors of a lost city. There are currently in excess of 1500 Confederate ex-military personnel and 2000 civilians with families living here and other parts of Brazil.

Now that peace has returned and the country is reunited, many of us in exile would like to return to our homeland as productive United States citizens and with a full pardon from your government. In exchange for our safe and honorable return, I am prepared to reveal the location of the Confederate treasury cache and turn it over to the United States government since we are now one united country again.

With respects, I graciously await your reply through your personal emissary or representative.

Your obedient servant,
Brigadier General Robert F. Patterson
Confederate States of America in exile
Santa Barbara d'Oeste, Brazil

Both Professors Drake and Scott re-read the letter carefully then looked up at Kirby with expressions of bewilderment. "Incredible!" Scott replied, glancing up at the general. "This is really interesting. Twenty million dollars in gold? Do you think the letter is real?"

"Our State Department checked through captured Confederate military records and did find an officer, a colonel of the same name, listed on a captured roster file for the 5th North Carolina. The officer is still unaccounted for. The president thinks it's real and I have to agree. When Richmond fell in April 1865, and our troops occupied the city, there was no gold to be found anywhere, only stacks of worthless Confederate currency notes and useless bonds."

Drake was still perplexed. "I was under the impression that the Confederate government was broke and had no reserves to expand the war."

"We thought so as well. From this letter it appears they were storing and holding gold reserves back in event of their collapse. Perhaps Jefferson Davis believed he could rebuild his army and resume the war at a later time. In any event, there seems to be a great deal of Confederate treasure hidden somewhere in the south…most likely in the Appalachian mountains since that region would be more accessible and quicker to reach from Richmond. Most likely Patterson and his men escaped to Brazil soon after hiding the gold. President Davis was captured in central Georgia in early May of 65' and spent the next two years in prison at Fort Monroe, Virginia, so it's very unlikely he and Patterson ever communicated about the whereabouts of the treasure. We're pretty sure Davis was also trying to escape to Brazil when he was caught."

Both Drake and Scott were getting a bit apprehensive and glanced at one another anxiously. "General, what does this letter have to do with two archeologists like us?"

General Kirby paused as to heighten the suspense. "Well, actually it pertains to you, Professor Scott. You have been selected as part of a team to go down there and fetch the good colonel and his band of "homesick" rebels. We especially want to learn of the location to the gold cache and recover it, therefore, we need to bring General Patterson back here in one piece. Based on his letter, there are only four Confederates left, including Patterson, who know where the treasure was hidden and unfortunately, it appears they are all down in Brazil. The president wants that Confederate gold badly to shore up our Federal treasury. We're still paying for that damn war, you know."

"And who was kind enough to select me?" Scott countered suspiciously.

"The president thought you to be a good choice along with a couple of others. After all, you do speak some of the native Indian dialect and certainly know about their culture and customs. Also, I happen to know you are a crack shot with a rifle and pistol."

"General, you do realize the language in Brazil is Portuguese, not Spanish or some ancient Indian dialect?"

"True, but remember the Confederate colonel and his exiles speak English but many of the native Indians there still speak their original languages and I am sure by now some of the Confederates have picked up enough Portuguese to communicate with most of the locals."

"What about Mr. Drake?" Scott asked, nodding toward his companion. "Will he be accompanying me?"

"I'm afraid not. Professor Drake is needed to oversee the new museum project. Also, I believe he still has problems with the leg he injured in Peru. I have already sent out a telegram summons for the rest of the team."

"Well, thank goodness I'm not going by myself. And who might they be, General?"

"None other than our old friends Simon Murphy and Elijah Walker…although they don't know it yet if they haven't received the telegrams."

Scott took a deep breath, taking in this sudden surprise. "I haven't heard anything about them for a couple of years. Any idea where they might be?"

"As a matter of fact, yes we do, or have a pretty good idea. Murphy remained in the Navy for a six months stint then resigned his commission. He decided naval ships weren't for him, especially since most of his military career was spent on horses. Besides, he gets seasick easily…not a very good attribute for a navy officer."

"Do you know where he is now?"

"We believe Murphy is back in Battle Creek, Michigan, peddling hardware. We heard he finally married that pretty newspaper girl he met here in Washington but I don't believe they have any children yet. Anyway, we want Murphy on the team."

"What about Walker?"

"Walker resigned his Army commission right after the Peruvian affair. Seems that our good ex-major owns some land in a little town in North Alabama called Gurleyville. He does some cotton farming and I also hear he's involved with a small timber business. The president happens to like Walker and is aware of his unique ability to smell trouble and get out of difficult situations. Plus, having been an officer in the Confederate army, we think he would have no problem gaining the trust of General Patterson and his companions in Brazil."

"How and when do we get Murphy and Walker to Washington, and how do we know they'll even come?"

"The president is prepared to give them a handsome sum of money for their services, and you as well, Professor…of course after you recover the treasure."

"And how much would that be?"

"One hundred thousand dollars each, provided we get our hands on the Confederate gold."

"That ought to convince them—it certainly has my attention," Scott conceded.

Kirby paused a moment to collect his thoughts. "At first, the president insisted we send you to Michigan then down to Alabama to pick both men up and personally escort them back to Washington. I suggested we send each of them a telegram signed by the president. I would imagine the state of Alabama has some telegraph offices in operation by now—the State Department is checking it out. Although the president doesn't believe a telegram would be persuasive or confidential enough, he finally agreed to it because of the expediency of a telegram compared to you taking a train ride halfway around the country."

I wonder what Murphy and Walker will do when they receive the telegram? Scott pondered.

"With Murphy now married, and perhaps Walker as well, and with all the harrowing experiences they had on their previous expeditions to the Yucatan and Peru, they might be reluctant to go back on some wild goose chase to South America. What if they refuse to come, General?"

"Oh, they'll come alright. I know those two boys pretty well by now and I can't imagine either of them will turn down a good chance for some adventure, especially with a fifteen to twenty million dollar treasure at stake. If that doesn't work, I have a letter for you from the president making this assignment a direct order from the president to each of you plus a hundred thousand dollars. I mentioned that in the telegrams. This will entice them here. You can count on it."

"Does the president want to re-commission them back into the military and give them an officer's ranking like before?"

"No, not this time. We'll let them remain civilians on this expedition. Like I said, we figure the ex-Confederate soldiers in Brazil would trust a Confederate ex-military civilian rather than a U.S. military officer. Walker's former Confederate officer's ranking should help gain the confidence of the exiles."

"Okay, General, guess you got me hooked. Based on my last experience with Murphy and Walker, there won't be a dull moment on this trip."

"One more thing, Professor," the general said as he reached into a leather satchel and pulled out a pistol and holster. "I have a little gift for you. This is a new 1872 model Remington single action revolver. Late last year the Remington Company provided us a few of these guns to test for them. This little piece holds six shots and shoots a .44/40 caliber bullet. In other words, it has plenty of punch to protect you if you need it. The gun proved quite successful in our field tests. I chose the 5½-inch barrel because the shorter barrel will be easier to conceal and maneuver if you have to have quick access. I also have one for Murphy and Walker when they arrive. You'll have a chance to fire them at the Washington Arsenal before you leave."

Scott took the gun and pulled it from the holster and hefted it up to the height of his eyesight. "She's a real beauty, General. Hope I don't have to use it."

Kirby then reached under the table and pulled out a sleek looking rifle. He held it in one hand to demonstrate the light weight. "And by the way, Professor, your team will also be carrying this newest rifle made by the Winchester Repeating Arms Company of New Haven, Connecticut. It's a big improvement over its predecessor, the Henry, and the earlier 1866 Winchester. This is a Model 1873 and also chambered for a .44/40 center-fire cartridge, much more dependable than the older rim-fire shells. Just remember the .44/40 shells for these rifles are different than those for the revolvers so don't try to interchange them. The rifle is built on a bronze-alloy frame with an improved 15 round tube magazine and a wooden forearm for better stability. The rifles you and your companions will be issued will be the carbine type with a 20-inch barrel for easier portability. The company provided us with several Model 73 prototypes and we've put them through extensive tests with excellent results. The rifles you'll receive will be the actual stock release models. Winchester tells us they're going to announce a full release of the rifle later this year—and I hope you don't have to use them either, but it's good to be prepared. I believe you and your companions will find this new rifle to be an incredible weapon."

Scott hefted the rifle, sighted down the barrel, and then nodded and smiled approvingly.

6

Battle Creek, MI – March 1873

LOCATED AT THE CORNER OF VAN Buren and Division Streets, the Murphy and Fox Hardware store occupied a two story wooden building with a wood plank portico covered by an overhang that provided the entrance slight cover from rain. The store was opened in 1856 by Thomas Murphy. When his only son, Simon, left for the war in 1862, Thomas took Howard Fox in as a partner, mainly because he was unable to manage the store all by himself. Fox died in 1871 and the elder Murphy retired in January 1872, leaving the management of the store to Simon and the two Fox brothers, Sam and Howard Jr. Simon got along well enough with Sam but thought Howard Jr. was an arrogant idiot. In 1872, Simon found himself back in Michigan and reluctantly back in the hardware business.

After the Cuzco expedition in 1870, Simon had remained for a while in Washington and in the Navy. He tried, with great dissatisfaction, to conform to the strict rules and regulations of the military establishment. The post Civil War navy went through a period of downsizing and the only officer's jobs available to Simon were mundane and boring staff duties, providing no hint of excitement, adventure, or advancement. While in Washington he met a beautiful young newspaper reporter named Maggie Patterson. Maggie accomplished something that no other woman had been able to do before—she captured his heart. After a brief engagement, they were married in September 1871, and along with the few possessions they had, Simon carried a beautiful new bride back to Michigan.

"Got a customer up front," Howard Jr. shouted to Simon from the back of the store.
 "Okay, Okay! I see him."
 "Hello, Mr. Potts. Can I help you?
 "Yep," Potts answered. "Need a wood burning stove."
 "We have several in the back. These are new cast iron stoves that burn coal or wood."
 "Don't want a coal burner–only want to burn wood. Coal's too damn dirty and I hate to clean the floor."
 "Well, Mr. Potts, as I said, these stoves will burn both coal and wood."
 "Don't want to burn both. Only want a wood burner."
 "You don't understand, Mr. Potts. You can burn coal or wood. You can also burn rags, or paper, or dried horse manure if you want."
 "Said I don't want to burn all them damn things…just wood!"
 "You don't have to burn anything if you don't want, Mr. Potts," Simon explained, feeling exasperated knowing this was going nowhere. "You can let the darn thing just sit there and look at it or use it as a table if you like."
 "Forget it, young man!" Mr. Potts shouted angrily as he turned toward the door. "I'll go get one from Mr. Pennington down at the general store. Know he's got some wood burners."
 Simon gritted his teeth as Potts left the store. "Dumb son-of-a-bitch," he mumbled.
 Howard Fox Jr. walked up to the front of the store. "What's old Potts so upset about?"
 "He wanted a wood burning stove so I told him we had some new stoves that would burn most anything, including wood. He didn't want any stove that would burn anything so the old geezer left all pissed off. That old goat has the brains of a bag of rocks."
 Howard was getting annoyed. "You should have told him our

stove only burned wood. That's twenty-one dollars we could have made in profit on a stove."

"Yeah, yeah, I know," Simon mumbled silently. Damn this stupid job. I hate to deal with dumb customers like old man Potts and arrogant jerks like Howard Jr. who think they know everything.

Otis Jeter worked at odd jobs around town. Today he was a runner for the local telegraph office. Simon looked up as Otis walked into the store.

"Morning, Otis, what can I do for you?"

"Morning, Mr. Simon…I got a telegram for you. Mr. Pope sealed it in an envelope. Fraid I'd read it."

"What would you want to read other people's mail for, Otis? A telegram is like private mail. You can't go around reading other people's mail—that's the same as stealing. You don't want folks to think you're a thief, do you?"

"Nope. Didn't think reading telegrams was stealing. I ain't taking nothing."

"Thanks, Otis," Simon answered as he rolled his eyes and handed him a fifteen cent tip.

He walked through the front door, took a seat in a wicker chair on the front porch, and then tore open the envelope.

"TO SIMON MURPHY BATTLE CREEK MICH STOP YOU HAVE BEEN REQUESTED TO COME TO WASHINGTON IMMEDIATELY FOR A MEETING AND SPECIAL ASSIGNMENT BY THE PRESIDENT STOP MOST URGENT STOP PRESIDENTIAL ORDER STOP CATCH QUICKEST TRAIN AND TELEGRAPH ARRIVAL DETAILS TO ME AT WASHINGTON ARSENAL TELE OFFICE STOP GEN C KIRBY US ARMY COMMAND STOP.

He had to read the telegram three times to make sure he understood the contents. Wonder what is so urgent to make the president want me to come to Washington so quickly.

Simon had experienced all the adventures and dangers one could imagine from the recent Yucatan and Peru expeditions, having, on several occasions, come close to losing his life. He promised himself he would not be caught up in another dangerous enterprise. After all, he had survived four years of Civil War and two hair-raising adventures. Lady luck couldn't protect him forever. Besides, he was now married to a beautiful bride. He could always take her with him, he thought. Her parents still live in Washington. Yet, the telegram sent shivers of excitement through his body. He hated the hardware store and the telegram gave him a way out. Besides, I can't ignore a presidential order, he reasoned. Simon walked back in the store and confronted Howard Jr. "Howard, you and your brother will have to mind the store for a while because I have to travel to Washington."

"How long will you be gone?"

"Don't know for sure, probably three or four weeks—maybe longer."

Howard, who considered Simon more of a hindrance than asset replied, "Okay, Simon, we'll watch everything while you're gone. By the way, we've wanted to talk to you about buying your half of the store out. Would you be interested?

"Possibly, Howard, we'll talk about it when I get back."

"You have to go back to Washington!" Maggie blurted out, exasperation ringing in her voice. "Why Washington? We just moved here from Washington."

"I'm sorry, Maggie, but the president has ordered me back for some reason."

"Why? What's so important to get you back to Washington so soon?"

"The telegram didn't say. The telegram said urgent. I have to leave in the morning."

"Well, I'm going with you because I sure don't intend to stay in this place all by myself. Besides, we can always stay with my parents in Washington."

Heaven forbid, he thought. "I was planning to take you anyway, so start packing your bags."

With a small case of essentials and three changes of clothes, the following morning Simon and Maggie boarded the Grand Trunk Line to Climax Prairie, Michigan, changed to the Grand Rapids and Indiana Railroad to Fort Wayne, then boarded a Baltimore & Ohio train to Washington. The trip would take three and a half days.

Gurleyville, Alabama

The large cornfield, bordered by Flint Creek, stretched several hundred yards across and ended where the creek made an abrupt change in direction to the north. Broken pieces of last year's corn stalks still remained on the ground, awaiting the plowing and spring planting. Elijah Walker was sitting on a small stool concealed in a patch of weeds on the northeast side of the field. His good friend and farm boss, Santos Lopez, sat fifty paces to the west, also concealed by dried stalks. Santos, the former Mexican guide, was an American citizen now, thanks to a presidential order issued by President Grant. This act was a partial reward from a thankful president for his participation and services rendered in the Yucatan and Peru expeditions. Santos saw no future in returning to California so he chose to remain in Alabama with Elijah and help him manage his farm and timber business.

"Here they come!" Santos shouted.

The three beaters were spread out and walking the field from the east side. Fifty yards to their left, a covey of six doves flew up with a flutter of wings and began to circle over Elijah in a weaving pattern, attempting to gain height. Elijah raised his new Parker Brothers 12 gauge double barrel shotgun and took a lead on a fast moving dove passing over. The loud commotion to his front caused him to flinch and miss the easy shot. "What the hell!"

No less than fifty doves flew up in front of him and scattered in all directions. Elijah threw his Parker up to fire but hesitated when an object to his immediate front caught his eye. It was Possum Potter standing there in the middle of the cornfield waving a piece of paper in his hand.

"Possum, what the hell are you doing out there? You've scared up every damn bird in the county. Are you trying to get your ass filled up with bird shot?"

"Got a telegram for ya, Elijah."

"Can't you wait till I get home?"

"Nope…Mr. Joplin said it was important and I should find you and give it to you in person."

"Okay, Possum, Thanks. You go back now and tell Mr. Joplin I got it." Elijah looked at the small yellow envelope and carefully tore it open. "Might as well read the damn thing since Possum fouled up bird shooting for the day."

TO ELIJAH WALKER GURLEYVILLE ALA STOP PRESIDENT REQUESTS YOUR PRESENCE IN WASHINGTON FOR IMPORTANT MEETING AND SPECIFIC ASSIGNMENT STOP PRESIDENTIAL ORDER STOP MOST URGENT STOP YOU ARE TO CATCH QUICKEST TRAIN TO WASH AND TELE ARRIVAL PLANS TO ME AT WASHINGTON ARSENAL TELE STA STOP GEN C KIRBY US ARMY COMMAND STOP.

Elijah read the telegram four times.

"What's this telegram supposed to mean?" Matilda grumbled when she read the telegram Elijah sheepishly had handed her.

"It means the President of the United States has ordered me to come to Washington for an important meeting."

"You're leaving on another wild goose chase for God only knows where. Besides we've been talking about getting married."

"It doesn't say that, Matilda. All it says is for me to go up there for an important meeting. It doesn't mention anything about going anywhere else."

"Well, it says special assignment and this can only mean trouble."

"I don't know that. All I know is I've got to go to Washington for a few days."

"How about Santos? Are you taking him with you?"

"Yes, I'll take him along. If there's any trouble brewing in the wind I want him along."

"With both of you gone, who'll run the farm?"

"I'll get Frank McClendon to watch things while I'm gone. I know Frank and you can manage it for a few days."

Matilda was distraught. Elijah knew she was a nice, well-mannered southern girl who came from a good family. He was certain she would make him a fine wife. On the other hand, he was having a hard time forgetting Rosita, the young girl he had met in Mexico who had accompanied him and Simon on their treasure hunting expedition in the Yucatan in search of the ancient Toltec city of Xepocotec. She was Santos' younger sister. He remembered the brief romantic encounter with her in the temple of Xepocotec and again, their meeting on a beach in California en route to Peru. It was on the beach she confessed her love for him. Rosita had a way of stirring up feelings he had never experienced before. He remembered marveling at her naked body as she swam under the waterfall in Mexico. The images were branded on his brain. But there was a problem—she was married, with twin sons. Elijah was very confused…he just couldn't get her out of his mind.

The next morning, Elijah and Santos caught the morning Memphis and Charleston train to Stevenson, Alabama, switching to the Nashville and Chattanooga line to Chattanooga, again switching to the Louisville and Nashville line north to Bristol, and switching again to the Virginia and Tennessee Railroad to Lynchburg. The Chesapeake & Ohio Railroad would take them on the final leg to Washington. "Shoulda rode my damn horse up here," Elijah grumbled, annoyed with all the train changes. He stopped at the telegraph office at the Chattanooga station and sent a telegram to General Kirby, advising him of their schedule for a hopeful Thursday afternoon arrival. With the president involved, he knew the general would be there in person to meet them.

The trip through the rolling wooded Virginia countryside was peaceful and relaxing, certainly a far cry from ten years earlier when a great Civil War was raging through the land. Elijah had spent those war years in the western campaigns as a cavalry officer for the Confederacy. Although most of his tenure of duty was spent in smaller skirmishers, he had seen some major action at Shiloh and Vicksburg.

The Virginia countryside was healing now but the scars of an occasional burned out house or building were vivid reminders of the dreaded horrors of war that had taken place on this soil. Many of the small towns were in the midst of rebuilding but the remains of that abysmal war were still evident. Santos sat next to Elijah in silence as they watched the northern Virginia landscape pass by. "The destruction here seems to be much worse than what I saw in Alabama," Santos reflected.

"Sure looks that way," Elijah answered, fighting back his own memories of death and destruction. "There were a lot more battles fought up here than in the Deep South. I understand some of the towns in Georgia and South Carolina caught it pretty bad though—burned to the ground. Sherman really had a burr up his ass when he went through Georgia."

They were interrupted by the voice of the conductor as he strolled down the aisle. "Folks, we're going to stop the train here in Charlottesville for about an hour and a half so the locomotive can take on water and coal. Give all you folks a little time to stretch your legs and get some refreshment."

Although still in the process of rebuilding, the historic town of Charlottesville was comprised of narrow streets filled with shops, inns, taverns, and well-maintained houses, many in various stages of restoration. Monticello, the home of Thomas Jefferson, was located nearby. It was Jefferson who founded the University of Virginia there in 1819. The university opened for classes in 1825. The Union army had left the town mainly unscathed, most likely because it was the third president's home place.

Jefferson Street appeared to be the main street in town. They strolled along and stopped so Elijah could gaze through the front window of a quaint colonial-style building. "I'll bet we can get a beer here," he remarked as they stood before a small establishment called the MECKLENBURG TAVERN AND INN. "Place looks friendly enough."

The tavern was to the right of the main lobby where the reception area and check-in desk for the inn were located. It consisted of a long, intricately carved bar and ten small tables. Five of them were occupied by an assortment of neatly dressed gentlemen engaged in various subjects of conversation. One common topic was Reconstruction, which was looked upon by these Virginia gentlemen as akin to the bubonic plague. A hush descended as Elijah and Santos took a seat at an empty table near the front window. A beefy man with a rusty beard stood up and walked over to the table. An eerie hush came over the crowd. "You must be strangers in town. Wouldn't be carpetbaggers would you?"

"Nope," Elijah answered, "just passing through and stopped for a quick beer."

"Your friend there, is he an Indian?"

"Nope, my friend here is a Mexican-American with a United States citizenship."

"We don't allow any Mexicans in here. And who the hell are you anyway?"

"Name's Captain Elijah Walker from Alabama and formerly of the 7th Alabama Cavalry that served under General Nathan Bedford Forrest, Army of the Mississippi, Confederate States of America."

"Well, I'll be damned," the man spouted between laughs. "Sounds like you're one of us."

"No carpetbaggers sitting here," Elijah answered bluntly. "And this man is my friend."

"Well, Captain Walker, how about a couple of beers on the house," the man responded as tensions relaxed and the tables of isolated conversation resumed. "Name's Lieutenant Maxwell Penn, formerly of the 10th Virginia Light Horse Brigade, under ole General Jeb Stewart's command, Army of Northern Virginia. Pleased to meet you, sir."

The locally brewed ale was cool and refreshing.

"Thank you, gentlemen…we must be on our way," Elijah announced, as he and Santos finished their beer, stood up, and headed for the door. "Appreciate the beers."

"Come back any time, Captain," Penn shouted.

Elijah turned to Santos. "Good thing they didn't know that right after we returned from the Peru expedition I was commissioned by President Grant as a major in the United States Army. All hell woulda broke loose."

By his friend's expression, Elijah knew he didn't fully understand what all the conversation was about but Santos smiled and nodded his appreciation anyway, understanding that somehow Elijah had avoided a nasty confrontation.

They stopped at the station long enough for Elijah to send another telegram to General Kirby, telling him the train was expected to pull into the station by seven o'clock this evening. The train departed Charlottesville and continued through Culpepper and then on to Washington. Elijah remembered the last two times he traveled into Washington on a train. He ended up getting involved in two implausible and highly dangerous expeditions that had nearly cost him his life. *What the hell am I getting into again*, he thought, with a deep feeling of apprehension.

7

As Elijah had advised, the train pulled into the C&O Train Station at seven-fifteen in the evening. On hand to meet him was his old friend and companion from the Yucatan affair, General Caleb Kirby. "Good to see you again," Kirby said as he met Elijah with a firm handshake. "Glad to see you brought our old friend Santos along."

"Yes, sir, General. Your telegram smelled like trouble and when trouble is around I want Santos nearby."

"I understand. Nice to see you again, Santos."

"Thank you, sir."

The General betrayed his secret with a slight smile. "I didn't tell you in the telegram but I also invited another friend along."

With a sly grin, Simon stepped out from behind a column. Elijah gasped, "I can't believe it." The two cousins embraced with a big bear hug and slap on the back.

"And you brought Santos with you," Simon shouted as he also gave his former young Mexican companion a big hug.

Kirby was all smiles. "Elijah, you don't think I was going to let you grab all the glory from the president without your cousin Simon along. Also, you'll be interested to know, another old friend of yours will also be joining us at the meeting with the president—Professor George Scott."

Both Simon and Elijah were pleased to hear this news. They liked the eccentric professor and his many unique talents, especially his skills with a rifle.

As predicted, Simon, Elijah, and Santos found themselves back at their favorite Inn, the Burlington House. They were shocked to learn the former hostess, Louise Parker, had retired for health reasons, but were pleasantly surprised when they discovered her daughter, Fannie Whittington, had taken over the Inn and was well trained to deliver the same delicious meals her mother used to serve. They were confident Mrs. Parker had taught her daughter well.

As usual, the meal was delicious, consisting of roast beef, mashed potatoes, green beans, yeast rolls, and plenty of roast brown gravy, Elijah's favorite. Simon just shook his head in disbelief as Elijah slathered the entire plate with gravy. "How the hell do you find your food under that pond of gravy you created?"

Elijah just grinned, "I just go fishing for it."

"Unbelievable!" Simon muttered in astonishment.

Elijah then leaned over to his cousin. "Hear you married that pretty newspaper girl that had you all starry-eyed last time we were here. I remember her name was Maggie."

"Sure did. Matter of fact I brought her with me to Washington. She's staying with her parents. How about you?"

"Not married. I have a girl back in Alabama who wants to get married but I haven't asked her yet. We've been talking about it though."

The meeting the next morning with President Grant was scheduled for 10:00 o'clock. General Kirby met them at the Burlington House at 9:30 AM to escort them to the White House. The two-block walk only took fifteen minutes. The party was escorted to a meeting room in the east wing where awaiting them with a big smile was Professor George Scott. After a few bear hugs and back slaps, an aide stepped through the door and announced the arrival of the president. He was accompanied by the newly appointed Treasury Secretary, William Richardson of Massachusetts, who had been thoroughly briefed on the group's previous expeditions.

"Gentlemen," Grant boomed, "how nice to see my favorite band of treasure hunters again. It seems like only yesterday we sat in this room discussing your trip to Peru." He introduced Richardson and then went around the room shaking hands and exchanging a few words.

"Let me get directly to the point for this meeting. Recently, I received a letter from an ex-Confederate general who claims to be living in exile with other former Confederates in a town in Brazil." He turned to General Kirby. "Please let Mr. Murphy and Mr. Walker read the letter."

Kirby reached into his coat and pulled out a well-worn envelope. He opened it and handed it to the two men who silently read it together. Simon had to read it twice, the expression on his face revealing a look of astonishment. It was noticed by the president, who responded. "You seem to know something about this letter, Mr. Murphy?"

"It's the name of the writer. I believe General Robert F. Patterson is my wife's uncle."

"Please explain, sir."

"My wife was a Patterson and her father, William, had two brothers. His older brother, Charles, lives in Philadelphia and fought with one of the Pennsylvania regiments. His younger brother was Robert Patterson and lived in a small town in North Carolina. I believe it's called Asheville, located in the mountains."

Kirby interceded, "Captured Confederate records do show a Colonel Robert F. Patterson on the rolls of the 5th North Carolina Brigade. He was probably promoted to general just before his mission."

"And that mission was to remove the Confederate treasury from Richmond and secure it in a safe place somewhere in the Appalachian Mountains," Grant added. "Information to its whereabouts is what he is offering us for a pardon and safe return to the United States."

Simon was perplexed. "Mr. President, I thought the Confederate government was broke...it's hard to believe they would have a treasure to hide."

Grant nodded. "That's what we thought as well but apparently they had secreted a sizable amount of gold away to hopefully refinance the war at a later time. Anyway, it appears our ex-Confederate friends are homesick and ready to return home."

"President Jefferson Davis spent two years in prison and is now retired in Mississippi," Richardson injected, "so we know that any resumption of the war is not going to happen."

"Gentlemen," Grant continued, directing his comments to his three visitors, "This is precisely why I want you to travel to Brazil—to bring Mr. Patterson and his party back so we can retrieve that treasure for our own treasury. We're still paying for that damn war and we need the money. This time you'll be traveling as civilians. With Mr. Walker's ex-Confederate ranking and now, ironically, with Mr. Murphy's family connections, I'm sure Patterson and his group will welcome you with open arms."

"Yes, sir, Mr. President, we'll do our best to bring him back in one piece," Simon answered as Elijah glanced at him shockingly.

"Thank you, gentlemen. The secretary and I must leave the meeting for another appointment so General Kirby will provide you all of the details for your departure. Godspeed to each of you." Grant nodded as he turned and left the room with Richardson trailing behind.

Elijah was annoyed. "You damn sure agreed to volunteer us for this trip without any discussion or input from me and Santos. What's Maggie going to say about this?"

"How am I going to turn down a personal order from the president? Besides, we're getting paid well and the trip sounds like an easy and quick journey to Brazil and back."

Maggie was in a joyful mood as she and Simon sat on the small sofa in his Burlington House room. She held his hands and smiled as she looked softly into his eyes. "Simon, I have some exciting news for you. I just found out today. My mother and I visited our family doctor this morning and Dr. Taylor confirmed my suspicions. I'm pregnant. We're going to have a baby."

Simon hesitated for a second to absorb the news then he swept her into his arms, "I can't believe it! I'm going to be a father. That's wonderful news, Maggie." He hugged her and kissed her lightly.

"Good grief! I'm squeezing you too tight," he added as he relaxed his grip.

"Don't be silly," she laughed, "it's early—you're not going to hurt anything."

Simon took on a more serious look. "I have some news for you, too. We had our meeting with the president this morning and found out what he wanted. He has asked Elijah and me to travel to Brazil and bring back an ex-Confederate general in exile who was instrumental in removing the Confederate treasury from Richmond and transporting it to a hidden spot we believe somewhere in the mountains of North Carolina. He's going to tell us where the treasure is hidden in exchange for a full pardon for him and his men and a return to the United States. We should be back in three or four weeks."

The frown on Maggie's face displayed she was obviously upset. "I understand. I wish I could go with you but Dr. Taylor said I should take it easy for awhile. We don't want to lose the baby."

"And there is something else you should know, Maggie. The general we're bringing back is your Uncle Robert."

Maggie gasped. It took a moment to process this information and catch her breath. "We thought he was dead. My father heard he had been killed at Gettysburg in 1863."

"We've checked captured Confederate records and he is very much alive. He was listed as a colonel in the 5th North Carolina Brigade but we think he was promoted to a general prior to his mission."

"Oh my goodness! I can't wait until I tell my father. Simon," she said with pleading eyes, "please bring Uncle Robert home safely."

"I will do my best," he reassured her as he took Maggie into his arms again and kissed her lightly on the lips.

The next day was spent at the Washington Arsenal where the team listened to instructions for the new Remington revolver and the new Winchester Model 73 repeating rifle. The group was impressed with the new rifle that held fifteen rounds in its barrel magazine. It was operated by a cocking lever in the bottom of the chamber and easily loaded through a side-loading gate. It was both fast and accurate. Professor Scott was especially impressed when he placed a neat pattern of fifteen rounds in a six-inch bull's-eye. "She sure is a beauty," he announced proudly.

The next best was Elijah who managed twelve bull's-eyes and then Simon and Santos each with ten. The team was now confident that in a scrap, they could hold their own—they were a small army.

General Kirby held up the rifle and announced, "Each of you will have one of these new Winchesters and three spares in case you need them."

Kirby also explained the plans for their transportation to Brazil. "You will gather your personal belongings and equipment and be ready to depart in the morning. We will provide you transportation to the Washington Arsenal. From there you will board a small skiff that will transport you down the Potomac River to a docking station called Point Smith. It's located on the Virginia side at the mouth on the Chesapeake Bay. A military steam propelled sloop-of-war will carry you on to Brazil. The name of the ship is the USS Halifax and the captain is a man named John Whitmore. I've met Whitmore and he's a capable officer. Your departure from the Burlington House is 7:00 AM sharp."

"What happens when we get to Brazil? How do we locate Patterson?" Simon asked.

"The Halifax will transport you to a town called São Paulo on the southern coast of Brazil. From there you will seek your own transportation to a small town a few miles to the northwest called Santa Barbara d'Oeste. This is where you will find General Patterson and his Confederados."

"And when we find him?"

"Bring him home…back to Washington. Captain Whitmore has orders to standby in São Paulo and wait for you to return to the ship. He will transport you back."

They now understood their mission.

After another fine dinner from Fannie Whittington, each member of the group returned to his room to make final preparations for the early morning journey. Bags were packed and weapons secured. Elijah picked up the Post to catch up with the news when he heard a soft rap on his door. Who could this be? He opened the door and was totally stunned at what he saw. "Could I come in, Elijah?" the soft voice asked.

"Rosita! What are you doing here?" he answered, pulling her gently into the room and closing the door.

"I had to see you Elijah…I just had to see you."

"How did you know where to find me?" Elijah questioned with a bewildered look on his face.

"Santos sent me a telegram the other day and told me he was going with you to Washington for some big meeting. I knew you would be staying here. I remember you talking so much about the Burlington House and the good food there."

"How did you get here?" He asked, knowing the answer.

"By train…from San Francisco."

"Does Don Diego know you are here?"

Rosita hesitated and then softly spoke, "I have no husband, Elijah. He died in an accident seven months ago. He was thrown from a horse and broke his neck."

"I'm so sorry, Rosita. And your sons?"

"My aunt and uncle are watching them in Capistrano. They will be well taken care of until I return. Since the ranch now belongs to me, I plan to move my aunt and uncle there. They will enjoy living at the Rio del Viejo."

She stood there, tears welling up in her eyes. "Oh, Elijah," she gasped and threw herself into his arms. The tears now streamed down her cheeks. "I could not forget you…I love you. I just had to see you."

All the doubt, questions, and confusion evaporated as he gazed down at this beautiful woman in his arms. He whispered, "I love you, too." He cradled her face in his hands and kissed her tenderly. Then the pent up thoughts and emotions he had concealed for many months engulfed him. The kisses became more passionate.

Their hands touched and fondled and explored until a wave of passion and desire burst wide open and an uncontrollable surge of lust overcame them. Then, as if some unknown force descended upon them, their clothes hastily disappeared.

Embraced in his arms, their naked bodies entwined, Rosita whispered, "Elijah, you don't know how much I needed this. I don't know where you and my brother are going but I wish I could come with you…but…my boys need me…I must return to California. I want you to come with me. We could have a good life together at Del Veijo…you would love it there."

"I would if I could, but Simon and I have to complete our journey for the president. I should return in a few weeks." He kissed her tenderly. "When I return I'll come to California to see you…I promise. I've thought about it many times. Tonight you will stay here with me but I have to leave early in the morning so you can stay in this room until you go to the train station. The room is all paid for…compliments of the government."

The Washington Arsenal was located just south of the city on a tip of land overlooking the Potomac. As Kirby had explained, a small skiff awaited the group at a short pier. The skipper, a sea weathered Irishman named O'Keefe, welcomed them aboard and cast off for the journey down the Potomac River. They would reach the mouth by late afternoon. The expedition group was small, consisting of Simon, Elijah, Santos, and Professor Scott. The mission was underway and, based on their prior experiences in the Yucatan and Peru, this seemingly routine journey could easily turn out to be another wild and dangerous adventure.

8

Paris, France – Late March, 1873

PRESIDENT ADOLPHE THIERS SAT AT HIS desk overlooking the Seine River. The day was cloudy and misty. His mood was much the same. The Republic of France had just been through several years of heavy turmoil, especially after the resounding defeat of the Second French Empire's armies in the Franco-Prussian War and the subsequent disposal of Louis Napoleon Bonaparte (Napoleon III) in 1870. Thiers had been heavily involved in the bloody removal of the short-lived succeeding ruling faction, the Paris Commune, and in 1871, he assumed the position of Head of State, a provisional title for President of France.

Sitting in the room with him was Rene Poullard, the head of his renowned secret intelligence branch, Le Guarde. He had brought Thiers a packet of documents and sensitive information that he felt the president needed to know…and fast.

Thiers sat quietly as he read through the secret documents and reports recorded by his predecessor, Louis Bonaparte and the former Minister of the Interior, Leon Gambetta. He occasionally glanced up at Poullard to show his shock and concern. As Thiers completed his examination, he was now aware of the bizarre events that had taken place with the startling discovery the Americans had made in 1870. He was also informed as to the names of the Americans who had made the discoveries while on an exhibition to Peru. He vaguely remembered reading an article in the

Washington Post about Simon Murphy and Elijah Walker. The Le Guarde files contained a well-documented dossier on the two men that revealed their discoveries of the huge Toltec treasure in the Yucatan and the astounding discovery of the amazing hidden contrivance in Peru that had sat dormant in a cavern for several centuries.

The discovery was something France desperately wanted in their armory, especially during these tumultuous times. "Sir," Poullard said, addressing the president, "a reliable French informant in the American War Department has advised one of our Le Guarde agents that the two Americans, Murphy and Walker, had recently checked into the Burlington House in Washington for a meeting with President Grant and they are supposedly embarking on a journey by ship to Brazil…the city of São Paulo, near the southern Brazilian coast, to be exact. The report further states they are seeking a band of Confederate exiles in a nearby town. The exiles are referred to as Confederados. We haven't determined the reason for their mission but the whole thing seems a bit odd. We think they are on to something big, perhaps relating to a lost treasure or perhaps the American discovery we were unable to secure three years ago."

President Thiers curiosity was aroused…he needed to know more as to why they would be making the trip to a remote jungle covered country like Brazil. When he thought of Brazil, the first thing that popped into his mind was the Amazon River. Strange, he pondered. With these two treasure hunters involved, this could only mean something big was in the wind and Thiers wanted to know what it was. In addition, the reports clearly revealed the identity of the Frenchman, who in 1870, had been dispatched to follow the Americans to Peru with a mission to secure the device for France in an effort to destroy the invading Prussian Army and prevent a Franco-Prussian War. The report indicated the Frenchman was also an agent for Le Guarde and was named Paul Devereaux—he had failed in his mission.

Thiers called for his private secretary and instructed him to fetch his Prime Minister, Jules Dufaure, and Minister of War, Ernest Courtot de Cissey, with haste.

The two new arrivals took their seats next to Poullard. Both men were apprehensive at such a brief summons but at the same time most curious. The president did not waste any time and came directly to the point. Thiers handed both men a summary copy of the reports. "Gentlemen, I want you to read these reports recorded by my predecessor, Napoleon III, and tell me what you think. Then we'll discuss our plan of action."

The next several minutes were silent while both men absorbed the astounding information before them. Thiers appeared to look busy as he fumbled with some unimportant paperwork while Poullard sat quietly observing the two ministers and their curious expressions.

"Well?" the president asked, probing the two men's reaction.

Both Dufaure and Cissey appeared dumbfounded. "This is incredible," the war minister finally admitted.

Poullard broke in to explain the role of the two Americans and told of their recent meeting with President Grant and the subsequent mission to Brazil. "What do you make of this?" he asked, directing his question to the prime minister. "What should we do about it?"

Dufaure answered without hesitation. "I think we need to pursue this matter and send a team to Brazil to find out what the Americans are up to."

"And who do you recommend we send on such an undertaking?" Thiers asked, now directing the question to his agent, Poullard.

"Paul Devereaux," he answered.

"But he failed in his first mission," the president reminded him.

"True, but under very unusual circumstances as I remember. Louie Bonaparte was very upset with his failure of the mission and was going to have his head chopped off with a guillotine but changed his mind, mainly because Devereaux had so much vital information about the American's discovery and also an intimate knowledge of the two treasure hunters, Murphy and Walker. The French president exonerated him."

"Where is Devereaux now?"

"He lives with his wife in a small town called Compiègue, just northeast of Paris."

In deep deliberation, Thiers walked over to the large window and looked out at the skyline of Paris spread before him. He could see the Eiffel Tower looming to the front.

"Poullard, I want you go to Compiègue and bring Devereaux back to Paris. Also, select three of your best agents to make up a team. Our Monsieur Devereaux and your agents are going to Brazil. And if he refuses, tell him it is a presidential order."

"I think he will be willing to go…I believe he has a big score to settle with the two Americans."

"I'll leave the team up to you, Poullard, but make sure they understand the importance of the mission. You may contact our Minister of the Navy, Louis Pothuau, and tell him to commission a fast ship to carry the expeditionary team to Brazil. From there they can pick up the trail of the Americans. I would suggest they start in São Paulo and then the other town where the Confederados reside."

"I'll see to it, sir."

Washington, D.C. - On the Potomac River

The most exciting part of the cruise down the Potomac was the brief glimpse of Mount Vernon, the historic plantation home occupied by the Washington family for more than forty years. Professor Scott was quick to explain. "The original name for the property was Little Hunting Creek Plantation, purchased by George Washington's great-grandfather. His half-brother, Lawrence, inherited it in 1743 and changed the name to Mt. Vernon. Upon his death in 1754, George Washington inherited the property and started his family there five years later when he married Martha Custis."

"Where did you get all that information?" Simon asked, impressed with the professor's detailed knowledge.

"History books my good man…history books."

Late that afternoon the skiff reached the mouth of the Potomac and pulled into the dock at Smith Point, overlooking the Chesapeake Bay. O'Keefe recognized the place by the crumbling lighthouse that was once erected there. As Kirby had informed them, the steam powered, three masted sloop-of-war, USS Halifax, was anchored and awaiting their arrival. Simon thanked O'Keefe and assembled his small group and equipment near the gangplank of the Halifax. Captain Whitmore, a middle-aged man supporting a thick grey moustache, stood at the rail.

"Permission to come aboard, sir," Simon shouted.

"Permission granted," Whitmore called back.

Introductions were made and Whitmore commented, "Well, Mr. Murphy, you and your men are the only passengers on my ship for the ride down to Brazil. You must have some strong connections in Washington to commandeer my ship for such a journey for only four men."

"You might say that, Captain…how about the President of the United States. I have a letter of introduction signed by President Grant if you would like to see it."

"My goodness!" the captain responded curiously. "That's not necessary, Mr. Murphy…my orders came directly from the Secretary of the Navy and by all means, welcome aboard. We'll make sure all the comforts of home are provided for our honored guests."

"Thank you, Captain."

The USS Halifax had served in the Civil War and had performed service in the blockades of Savannah and Charleston harbors. She was heavily armed with four 11" Dahlgren cannons, twelve 80 pound Parrot guns, and a smaller 12 pound rifled Dahlgren swivel deck gun set both on the fore and aft decks. The USS Halifax was certainly ready for a fight if need be.

The journey from the Potomac to the mouth of the Chesapeake Bay was smooth sailing, allowing the men to relax and explore the ship. Professor Scott, in his imposing scholarly manner, explained, "This ship is classified as a sloop-of-war. They were used by the British Navy in the 18th century and most of the 19th century.

One of the most famous American sloop-of-war ships was the USS Constellation. Most of these ships now are steam powered."

Simon looked at Scott sarcastically, "The history books… Right?"

Scott returned his comment with an annoyed look.

Captain Whitmore approached the group, his outstretched arm pointing to a distant shoreline. "Gentlemen, we are now passing around that point of land called Cape Henry and the water you see before you is the Atlantic Ocean."

Professor Scott couldn't stand it. He blurted out, "In 1607, colonists first landed here prior to their moving on to establish the settlement of Jamestown, and at the end of the Revolutionary War, this is where the French Fleet blockaded the bay to prevent the British from receiving reinforcements in Yorktown."

"Good grief!" Elijah groaned, "I feel like I'm sitting in a history class. Do you know everything, Professor?"

He replied with a smirk. "Well…almost."

"You'll have to admit it," Simon added approvingly, "it's a pretty interesting bit of history."

Scott nodded his appreciation and then gave Elijah another exasperating stare.

Whitmore chuckled and then continued. "Our journey will generally follow the U.S. coast until we reach the Caribbean and then we'll head due south to the top of Brazil and a port town there called Fortaleza. I want to stop there to take on water for the boilers and a few food supplies. Our water tanks will also need a fresh supply. The journey from there to São Paulo will take another three days. Brazil is a very large country. This early in the year I expect a fairly smooth journey, but there is always the chance of a tropical storm along the way."

Elijah groaned. "Oh no…not again," referring to his earlier sea faring trips to the Yucatan and Peru. He remembered his past experiences of seasickness with a shudder. Whitmore smiled with an understanding of Elijah's implication. "I can tell the sea does not agree with you, Mr. Walker."

"No, sir…being seasick is not one of my favorite pastimes."

"Whitmore understood his anxiety. "Well, maybe we can arrange a calm trip for you."

"Thank you, sir…I hope so."

The next day was smooth sailing. Whitmore approached the group lounging on the foredeck and cheerfully announced, "We passed the Florida Keys about an hour ago and now we are well into the Caribbean. Weather permitting, I expect to approach the coast of French Guiana in a little over two days and then we'll change to a more southeastern course around the upper tip of Brazil and on down to our first stop at the port of Fortaleza."

Whitmore turned and left to attend to other chores, leaving Simon and Elijah alone, leaning on the starboard railing chatting and watching the rolling and hypnotizing swells of the waves. Elijah turned to his cousin and in a low voice said, "I've been meaning to ask you. By chance did you bring along that communication contraption we had in Peru."

"You mean the zenox?"

"Yeah, I think that's what Commander Ahular called it."

"I brought it along…thought it might come in handy. Based on our trips to Mexico and Peru, this trip could always turn out to be a little more complicated than just returning some homesick Confederates back to the United States. If you'll remember, Ahular advised me to carry it with me—that they would be back in touch someday."

Seven years ago in the Yucatan jungle, while on their expedition in search of the lost Toltec Indian city of Xepocotec, Simon and Elijah had made a remarkable and startling discovery. Deep within a cavern beneath the lost city, they found a strange device that led them to an ancient flying ship that had been hibernating there for nearly nine hundred years. Incredibly, it had been kept alive by an inexhaustible fuel source called tracx. The device turned out to be a communication module that allowed the Americans to communicate with the ship's mechanical intelligence. It was a spaceship from another galaxy and it had lain there all these years in need of repairs. The original travelers had long since died out, leaving the ship dormant in the cavern. Through the use of a talking device, or head set they later learned, Simon was able to communicate with the strange machine and awaken it from its hibernation state. With instructions from the ship's computer, they were able to use parts stored on the ship and make the necessary repairs to enable it to fly again.

The ship's intelligence, or computer information storage bank, appointed Simon as the new ship's commander and, through his voice commands, was able to fly the craft out of the cavern, barely escaping hoards of vengeful Indians who were nearly upon them. The Americans, now joined with General Kirby, Professors Robert Drake and George Scott, flew the craft to Washington and scared hundreds of people who observed it soaring across the sky.

After realizing they were not being invaded by an unknown alien enemy, President Johnson and General Grant welcomed the former deserters back to civilization and re-commissioned them back into service to command the strange new craft. Named the TOLTEC by Simon and Elijah, President Johnson and top cabinet members decided to press this new machine, with its deadly laser guns and incredible unknown power, into the U.S. arsenal under the direction and command of the Navy. Some of the cabinet and top military officials suggested some very aggressive intentions for the ship, not realizing the potential dangers it could impose upon the human race. Voicing their strong objections, Simon and Elijah were relieved of command and ordered back into civilian life.

Both sensed the potential dangers and destructive power of the alien ship and the cataclysmic damage it could inflict on the earth's populations. So, while departing Washington, Simon ordered the Toltec to fly over the Atlantic Ocean and self-destruct. Distraught over the loss of their newly acquired powerful weapon, the president and other officials believed the ship had been ordered back to its own world by an unknown source. Prior to its departure, the Toltec planted a strange capsule into the ground, only to be found by a construction worker two years later. The device, called a zenox, was used by Simon and Elijah to communicate with another hibernating ship hidden in the Andes, leading to their harrowing expedition to Peru five years later. A third ship, designated the X326, and buried under the ice pack in the Arctic, was awakened by a signal from the dying ship in the Andes. With its inexhaustible fuel element tracx, the ship re-energized itself and broke through the tomb of ice where it had been hibernating for several centuries. The ship flew to the Andes, enabling the Americans to board and fly it from Peru to Washington. While on a test run, Simon, now the new designated commander named the ship CUZCO after the ancient Inca capital and their harrowing expedition in Peru. They were confronted with a frightening experience when they found themselves under the sea, in an airtight bubble, on the sunken continent of Atlantis. There they would meet an alien senior commander named Ahular who would befriend them and help them save the planet by thwarting a devastating underwater earthquake and cataclysmic split in the Eurasian and African tectonic plates. The earth was saved from blowing apart by a coordinated concentration of laser power from the alien craft to weld the splitting plates together.

As Captain Whitmore had suggested, the weather cooperated and remained calm during the voyage across the Caribbean. Elijah was relieved when he heard a shout from the foredeck, "Land Ho!" Simon overheard him mumbling a short prayer of thanks.

9

The Halifax had reached the coast of French Guiana and altered their course to sail around the top of Brazil. They would now stay close to the coastline. Captain Whitmore informed them they had just passed the Equator and were now in the Southern Hemisphere. Also, as he had advised, the first stop was the port town of Fortaleza to resupply the water tanks and bring on some fresh food and drinking water.

Colonization of the town of Fortaleza began in 1603 when the Portuguese reclaimed the settlement from the Dutch and constructed a fort there. In the 19th century, the settlement flourished with the growing and exporting of cotton. Strategically located on the northeastern tip of Brazil, Fortaleza became a key navigational port. It was there the USS Halifax docked to take on water and fresh produce.

The five-hour layover was just enough time for Simon, Elijah, Santos, and Professor Scott to go into the town and have some beer—a cool cerveja would be welcome after five days at sea. Simon turned to Santos, "Do you speak Portuguese?"

"Bits and pieces. I had a college friend in New Orleans from Brazil and he taught me a few words. The language is similar to Spanish but many of the word pronunciations and spelling are different. I could probably understand enough to get by."

"Can you order us a beer?" Elijah asked.

"Poderiamos nós comer alguma cerveja? …Could we have a beer?"

"I'm impressed."

"That's one phrase you need to interpret in any country. I have a better idea though. One of the crew I met is from Brazil and speaks Portuguese fluently. His name is Benedetto and you could ask the captain if he could accompany us."

"I'll ask him right now," Simon agreed.

Benedetto recommended the Pescadero Tavern located on Avenue Dragão do Mar, three blocks from the wharf and in easy walking distance from the ship. He had been there before. Pleased that he had been relieved from duty to guide the Americans, the young Brazilian smiled as he repeated, "Meninas bonitas...menitas bonitas!"

"What does that mean?" Elijah asked curiously.

"Pretty girls," Santos interpreted.

"My kind of place."

The front of the tavern was decorated with bright yellow stucco and pastel blue shutters framing a large open front window. The bold letters above the door read PESCADERO TAVERN E BARRA. The place looked clean and inviting with calypso like music drifting from the window—a perfect spot to relax with a beer.

The group walked in and arranged themselves neatly around a round table near the outside front wall. The tavern's inviting appearance was deceiving as several of the tables were occupied with some very unsavory looking characters—seamen no doubt, drinking their way through shore leave and always looking for trouble. The sudden appearance of the strangers was quickly noticed, producing several loud murmurs from some rough looking patrons. A shapely dark haired girl drifted over to get their order. As she turned with the drink order, she gave Elijah a cursory smile and passed by him with a suggestive swing of her hips.

Elijah leaned over and whispered to Simon, "Did you bring your revolver? I smell trouble."

"Yeah, I got it...and you?"

"In the back of my belt."

A large brawny man stood up, a bottle of clear liquid in his hand. His unsteady swaying revealed he had consumed far too much libation and was drunk enough to take on the entire bar. "Well, what do we have here," he boomed raucously. "A bunch of Americanos. And the one sitting in front looks like he is trying to steal one of our women."

Benedetto nervously interpreted.

Three more seamen stood up, obviously inebriated as the other, and started shouting more insults. They were looking for a fight.

Simon turned to Benedetto. "Ask the big hulk what is his name?"

The young Portuguese sailor looked at Simon apprehensively and shrugged.

"Ask him," Simon repeated.

Benedetto nervously turned to the big man. "O que é seu nome?"

The giant roared, "The Americanos wants to know my name. My name is Estevo and I'm the meanest son-of-a bitch in Brazil."

This brought a rumble of laughter and a few more shouts from the restless crowd.

"Estevo!" Simon shouted, "We want no trouble. We are only here for a friendly beer. Tell him that, Benedetto."

In his drunken state this only infuriated the big man as he pulled a long knife from his belt and staggered toward the Americans like a roaring buffalo. "I'll feed you Americano bastardos to the sharks today!" he screamed, totally out of control.

In an instant, Elijah pushed his chair to one side and slammed his boot heel into the seaman's kneecap. A loud crunch was heard throughout the bar as the knee shattered and the man's patella and upper femur disintegrated. He pitched forward and crashed heavily into the table, breaking it in half and slamming to the floor. He lay still. Scott and Santos turned him over—the man was dead, the knife protruding from his chest. He had somehow turned the knife inward and fell heavily on the blade, impaling himself to the hilt.

Three of the incensed seamen surged forward, determined to

avenge their comrade—they screamed for blood. One man pulled a dagger from his shirt and drew back his arm to throw it but at that instant a shot exploded and a .44 slug tore his left ear off. The drunk grabbed the side of his head and fell to the floor whimpering. Professor Scott stood calmly holding his Remington, a smile on his face. "Benedetto, please tell the mates that the fight is over and the drinks are on me." He reached into his pocket and tossed a double eagle to the barkeeper. As several seamen rushed to the bar for a free drink, the Americans quietly slipped out the front door and hustled back to the Halifax.

"Some quiet and relaxing beer we had," Elijah grumbled. "By the way, nice shooting there Professor. Took the bastard's ear clean off."

"He had big ears. They reminded me of that bull's eye at the Washington Arsenal."

The earsplitting laughter could be heard a block away.

10

Captain Whitmore briefly glanced at his map and then ordered his helmsman to make a slight turn to the southwest. The Halifax rounded the eastern-most tip of Brazil and maneuvered to the new direction toward Rio De Jeneiro. Their destination was the city of São Paulo, a short distance beyond the capital city and a few nautical miles further down the coastline. To Elijah's relief, the good weather held fast. The four Americans were standing by the stern railing chatting, fascinated with two bottlenose dolphins rolling and frolicking in the ship's wake. Scott turned to Simon, "What is our plan when we arrive at São Paulo?"

"We'll need to find a guide and transportation to the Confederados' town. The map shows the settlement to be about fifty to sixty miles inland from São Paulo—about a day and a half ride. We can find a hotel and spend the night in São Paulo. I'm guessing we shouldn't have any trouble finding a guide. The letter said Patterson and his Confederados live in Santa Barbara d'Oeste. If he's still there we'll find him."

The town of São Paulo was founded by Jesuit missionaries in 1554 and officially became a city in 1711. Located 43 miles from the Atlantic Ocean, it is served by the port town of Santos. It was here the USS Halifax docked on a clear Tuesday morning. Captain Whitmore stood at the gangplank to wish a farewell to his guests departing on their mission. "Well, gentlemen, my instructions are to wait here for your return. I understand you were sent here to escort some other Americans back to Washington."

"That's true, Captain," Simon responded. "I would imagine we'll be returning with our guests within a week. Thank you for your hospitality and safe voyage down here."

Whitmore smiled and nodded his response.

As they walked down the gangplank, Elijah turned to his Mexican friend and joked, "Hey Santos…I'll bet they named this port town after you."

Santos laughed. "Probably so…Captain Whitmore told us it was established in the early 1700s so I must have been a famous coffee planter back then."

"Not bad," Elijah laughed back. "That makes you about 160 years old."

With all of their baggage and supplies assembled, the group departed the gangway and stepped on to solid ground. They were in Brazil. A young Portuguese guide named Carlos was quickly employed as he was waiting at the foot of the gangplank peddling his services.

Aside from the export shipping business in bananas and oranges, the port town of Santos thrived on their biggest export crops…cotton and coffee. It was a busy seaport and a wagon was easy for Carlos to locate to transport the group the short trek inland to São Paulo. They arrived in the city late afternoon. The young guide seemed to know his way around town and he escorted the Americans to an eye-catching building near the center of São Paulo. The name over the door read HOTEL JARDIM ENSOLARADO. Like many of the buildings in the city, it was brightly colored in pastel blue stucco. Carlos explained, "The name, Sunny Garden, comes from the large garden in the rear where the kitchen gets much of its fresh vegetables."

Simon handed Carlos a gold double eagle and asked through Santos' interpretation, "Do you know of a good guide here that will take us to Santa Barbara d'Oeste?"

Carlos, pleased with the generous payment Simon had just handed him, further volunteered his services. "Yes, I know the area very well—I will take you there in the morning. I was raised in nearby Campinas. Barbara d'Oeste is only a short distance from there. The town and another larger settlement nearby called Americana is the home of many Confederados. They settled there soon after your great war."

"Very well, Carlos, meet us here in the morning and you can lead us to Santa Barbara d'Oeste. We will need five horses. Can you arrange it?"

"Sim meu amigo."

That night the four Americans enjoyed a fine meal in the hotel dining room. The kitchen served a plate of sliced mango and papaya as the first course followed by a dish called moqueca capizaba, a slow cooked fish with tomato and garlic. The popular rice and bean dish, bobó de camarão, accompanied the meal, topped off with a light tapioca desert and a shot of cachaca, a native liquor distilled from sugar cane. Elijah was in food heaven. "I'm not sure what all of that stuff was we just ate but it sure was damned good."

Simon laughed, "You never had a meal you didn't like."

Carlos awaited the group in front of the hotel at 7:30 the next morning to pick up the horses he had arranged. Packed and ready to move out, Simon and the group accompanied Carlos down the street to a nearby stable where three fine greys and two chestnut Anglo-Arabians awaited them. A sixth chestnut was secured to carry the packs and equipment. Simon paid the stable three double eagles and the group was ready to depart.

"Great looking horses," Professor Scott commented. "Sure better looking than those nags we used in Peru." Santos agreed.

Carlos smiled proudly. "These Arabians come from Portuguese stock, not Spanish-bred like many other South American countries use. They are strong horses."

The young guide led them on a northeasterly route, passing the small settlement of Jundiai. The well-worn road allowed them a steady pace and, hopefully, they would make Santa Barbara d'Oeste by early the next day. By evening they passed the town of Campinas, a quiet, sleepy place consisting of a few low sheds, fences, and some small casas. "This is where I grew up," Carlos proudly announced, pointing across a worn looking cotton field. "My parents and younger sister live in the house on the far side. We can spend the night there if you wish."

Deep shadows were stretching further across the road, signaling a fast approaching sunset. "It is getting late," Simon confessed. "I suppose we could camp there for the night if your parents don't mind. We can bed down in the barn."

"My parents would be honored to have Americanos as guests. My father's name is Miguel and my mother, Angelica."

The Caldera family lived in a small white stucco casa nestled in a grove of pau brasil hardwood trees. A few brazil-nut trees were also scattered nearby. Miguel Caldera farmed the adjoining field currently filled with cotton. The well-kept garden behind the house supplied the family with fresh vegetables. It was a pleasant and cozy looking place. Angelica was tending a small flowerbed when she spotted her son leading four strangers toward the house. She greeted Carlos with open arms and cautious eyes trained on the newcomers. Strangers were a rare sight in this small town.

Carlos introduced the Americans and explained the reason for the unannounced visit. The woman smiled, "You are most welcome here Americanos, but I am afraid our casa is too small to accommodate all of you." Carlos interpreted.

"We will be happy to stay the night in your barn with your permission," Simon offered.

With a warm smile, she answered, "Then you are most welcome amigos…to sleep in our barn and enjoy a Portuguese dinner."

The dinner was delicious…a beef stew served with the popular rice and bean dish, bobó de camarão. As usual, Elijah was enthralled and filled his plate three times. Angelica smiled proudly…it was a huge complement to her cooking. After dinner Miguel passed around a bottle of cachaca, the local liquor they had enjoyed in São Paulo. It had been a most pleasant evening as the guests thanked the Caldera family for their kind hospitality and retired to the barn.

Early the next morning Carlos led them away from Campinas, continuing their trek to the northeast. In a few miles, as they approached the small town of Americana, he veered to the left onto a narrow side road that meandered through overgrown fields and wooded areas. Buildings appeared in the distance indicating they were approaching another small town. The first thing they noticed was the bright red flag fluttering high on a flagpole—the stars and bars of the Confederate battle flag. They had arrived at their destination, Santa Barbara d'Oeste, home of the Confederate exiles—the Confederados.

11

As the group approached the town, Elijah handed Carlos another double eagle and sent him on his way. "Thanks for your service, Carlos, and please thank your parents again for their hospitality and fine meal and please give your mother this as payment." He handed the young guide two more gold coins.

"Mim senhor da vontade, I will, sir," he answered, proudly clutching the coins.

People could be seen milling around in the street attending to their normal chores. A young lady first spotted the Americans and nudged the man next to her. "Go get the general!" she cried. "We have visitors and they're dressed like Americanos."

As Simon and the others entered the main street, Scott noticed a tall distinguished looking man exit a doorway with three other companions close behind. The man eyed the strangers warily as he stopped and extended his hand to Simon. "I haven't seen you folks here before…what brings you to our small settlement?"

"My name is Simon Murphy and my associates and I represent the United States government…we are seeking a gentleman named General Robert Patterson."

"Well, sir," he responded, "I happen to be Robert Patterson. I presume you are here in response to a letter I sent to your president several months ago."

"That is correct, sir. The letter was received by President Grant about three weeks ago."

"My goodness, the letter must have been lost in transit to take that long to reach the president. General Ulysses S. Grant is a good man. He treated our General Lee with fairness and respect at Appomattox. Glad to hear he was elected President." He paused briefly to evaluate his new visitors. "Let me introduce you to my associates. This is Captain William Stafford, Sergeant Parks Mann, and Corporal Sam Roper." Patterson glanced around to be sure he was not overheard. "We are the last of the team involved in the situation I referred to in the letter. Two of our other members disappeared into the Amazon and have not been seen for several months. Mr. Roper here was able to escape a harrowing journey and by a miracle, he was able to return and tell their story. You will find it most interesting."

Simon made his introductions and replied, "General, is there someplace we can all talk in private? I'm sure you don't want our conversation overheard."

"Yes, we can retire to my house at the end of the street. I have some very good local brewed beer there."

Seated comfortably, the travelers settled in to enjoy the cool beer Patterson served. "It's a local brewed Bohemian type beer we call Arbusto Arene," he explained. "That means burning bush in Portuguese. Don't know how they came up with the name… maybe from the Bible. Perhaps the guy who invented the recipe called himself Moses…who knows?"

"It's very good," Elijah chuckled. "Sure beats any of the beer I've had back home."

Simon had many questions to ask the general. "Tell me, General, how did you end up here in Brazil? Most Confederates were given full pardon after the war when they signed an oath of allegiance to the United States."

"It's a long story. Right before the occupation of Richmond, we were picked for a special mission by President Davis to transport the Confederate treasury, or what was left of it, to a secure location in the south. The government had been secretly hoarding gold and gemstones away in the event the South lost the war. I was ordered to come to Brazil to meet with President Davis and reveal the location so he could later retrieve the money to raise a new army and revive the Confederacy. The plot was insane but we were under orders. A blockade runner was commissioned to transport us from the Georgia coast to Brazil. As it turned out, we heard Davis was captured in Georgia and placed in prison by the Federals. I'm sure the treasure is still secure in its hiding place in a very isolated place. The exact location was what I was offering President Grant for a full pardon and return to our homeland."

"Very interesting," Simon remarked. "We were sent here as the president's emissaries to agree to the bargain and take you home. He wants the money to help pay for that damn war. I'm sure some of it will be used to rebuild much of the South."

"I must ask you, sir, what was your role in the war, and that of your companions?"

"I was a captain in a Michigan cavalry unit while Elijah here was a captain in the 7th Alabama Cavalry. We both served in the western campaigns and met in a small skirmish in West Tennessee. Turns out we were blood cousins. We met Santos in Mexico a few years ago—he guided us during an expedition in the Yucatan. Professor Scott is an archeologist and anthropologist associated with our national museum project. He accompanied us on another expedition to Peru."

"Sounds like you've been very busy after the war," Patterson remarked inquisitively. He then turned to Simon's companion. "So Elijah," he said, obviously pleased with this revealing information, "I'm happy to see you were one of us."

"Yes, sir…born in Kentucky and moved to Alabama right before the war."

Elijah paused and then turned his attention to Mann. "Sergeant, you look very familiar. As I recall, I believe you served briefly in my command, the 7th Alabama. Do you remember when you shot that sniper from the tree up in Tennessee…and soon after, we had the skirmish with the Yankees near that creek with the funny name…Cockelberry Creek?"

Mann remembered the connection. "I do, sir, I had just joined the unit in Memphis. I remember you halted the skirmish and we called a truce with the Yankees. Then you sent us home. I ended up with the general defending Richmond those last few days but you were my first commanding officer. What happened after we disbanded?"

"It's a very long and complicated story, Mann. When we get some time I'll have to tell you. Mr. Murphy here was the opposing Union officer who commanded the Federals that day. Turns out the good captain is my blood cousin."

Mann was stunned. "Unbelievable!" he muttered, "Unbelievable coincidence!"

Simon addressed Patterson again. "General, how do you like to be called? General? Robert?"

"Most folks around here call me General but the war is over so why don't you just call me Robert. President Davis promoted me just before we left Richmond so I wasn't a general long enough to get used to it. I think we would prefer first names anyway."

"I have something very interesting to tell you, Robert," Simon disclosed. "Please sit down." He hesitated long enough to give Patterson time to get seated and then continued. "You have an older brother, William, who lives in Washington and a younger brother, Charles, in Philadelphia. They both fought in the Union Army. Correct?"

"Well, yes," Patterson admitted, his expression disclosing total surprise. "How did you know that?"

"Also, I believe William has a beautiful daughter named Maggie…your niece…correct?"

"You seem to know quite a lot about me. Yes, and I'm sure she is all grown up since the last time I saw her."

Simon continued, knowing this would be the biggest shock of all, "Your niece, Maggie Patterson, is my wife and we're expecting our first baby."

Patterson was speechless…his quizzical look betraying complete astonishment and shock. "Oh my goodness!" he finally mumbled. "My little niece Maggie all grown up…and married. Guess that makes you my nephew. Please excuse me for a moment…I need something stronger than beer." Patterson hurried to the cupboard to retrieve a bottle of brandy. He forgot to grab a brandy sniffer so he just tipped the bottle and downed a big gulp. "I just can't believe it…my niece's husband standing here in Brazil… in the middle of nowhere." Patterson tilted the bottle and took another huge swallow. "And you're my nephew…by marriage of course. That's incredible! " A third swig went down.

Patterson had a chance to settle down a bit, the alcohol aiding the process. "What a strange turn of events. I didn't expect to see a family member come down here to fetch me."

"I only found out myself just before we left Washington—Maggie confirmed the connection."

Patterson continued. "I have something very interesting to show you." He stood up and left the room, returning shortly carrying a small wooden box and a slender tube. He opened the box and retrieved a 4-inch bright shiny metallic cube.

"Is that what I think it is?" Professor Scott asked…"Gold!"

"Yes. A cube of pure gold…and that's not all." Patterson retrieved a small leather pouch from the box and pulled out a gold medallion. "This coin was found in a chest containing some of the gold coins from the Confederate Treasury. I have no idea how it got there but you can see it is very unique with all the inscribed symbols."

"May I see it?" Scott asked, inquisitively taking the coin into his hand. "The inscriptions look very old. The pre-Columbian Indians had no written language but this medallion appears to be similar to something I've seen before."

"But there is something else. The most fascinating thing we found is this scroll." He removed it from a narrow tube and unwound a thin piece of paper. It was filled with rows of symbols and hieroglyphs.

Simon took the scroll and felt the texture of the paper. He gave Elijah and Scott a curious look. "This is not paper…it feels more metallic-like. We've also seen something like this before as well."

Both Elijah and Scott spoke up at the same time. "The logbooks aboard the Toltec and the Cuzco!"

"Yes, and the ciphers and glyphs look very similar," Simon answered.

Scott was ecstatic. "I can't wait to try to decipher this document," he said, with an expression of exhilaration. "There may be a connection."

"What is this all about?" Patterson asked curiously.

Simon answered. "It's an incredible and very fascinating story. Something we encountered on our expeditions to Mexico and Peru. I'll tell you later."

"Where did you get the gold cube?" Elijah asked, mesmerized with the brightly glittering cube lying on the table.

"Have you ever heard of the lost city of gold—El Dorado?"

"I have," Santos answered. "It is an old legend started by the Spanish Conquistadors. In Spanish, El Dorado means the Golden One…actually the Gilded One."

"That's true. Many believe the city was built by the ancient Chibcha civilization that migrated down from North and Central America. Others think perhaps it was built by the Incas or perhaps the Toltecs or Mayans. No one knows for sure but my guess is the city was later occupied by the Incas. Mr. Roper brought the cube back from an expedition he made with the other two members of our detachment. They disappeared into the jungle and were never seen again…and I doubt if we ever will know what happened to them. The Amazon is unforgiving. Many conquistadors and treasure seekers have ventured into the jungle in search of the lost city. The most notable was Gonzalo Pizarro, brother of Francisco Pizarro. Also, the Englishman, Sir Walter Raleigh, tried to find it. Fortunately they returned, but hundreds of searchers never made it back."

This news piqued Scott's interest fast. "El Dorado…the ancient lost city of gold. I could have a field day there…but you do realize El Dorado is nothing more than a myth…a name and legend conjured up by the conquistadors."

"But this cube of gold and the medallion had to come from somewhere…they are believed to be hundreds of years old," Patterson contested.

"Let me tell you an interesting story." The professor was on a roll. "Around 1532, a Spanish conquistador named Francisco

Pizarro conquered the Incas of Peru and captured Atahualpa, their leader. He was imprisoned but told Pizarro if he would release him, he would fill his prison cell with gold and silver. Pizarro agreed so Atahualpa sent runners throughout the realm to gather gold and silver for the ransom. The Inca chief did as promised and gathered a large amount of gold for Pizarro but also included a secret message to his runners to pass along to the other Inca leaders. It instructed them to gather all the remaining gold, silver, and gemstones of the realm and secure the treasure in a hidden city to the south, most likely in the mountains near the Peruvian-Bolivia border, somewhere south of the Inca capital of Cuzco. Pizarro later deceived the Inca chief and executed him in 1533 and the city's whereabouts has been lost for over three hundred years, presumably in the jungles of the Madre de Dios. There is another legend about a lost city called La Ciudad Blanca located somewhere in Central America, presumably in the jungles of Honduras. Some have referred to this as El Dorado but most scholars agree these are not the same."

Patterson smiled. "Based on the information Mr. Roper discovered, we concur that the city is most likely located in the area you say, near the Andean Foothills, in the Madre de Dios region somewhere in southern Peru." He stood up and left the room momentarily and then returned with a rolled up piece of paper...a worn looking map. He opened the map and pointed to a spot well to the west and in southern Peru. "We are reasonably sure the cube of gold came from the lost city and the location of the city is the real prize I have to offer the president, far grander than the Confederate treasure we hid—but first we have to find it. Our guess is that it is somewhere near this location in the southern Andes, well hidden from the Spanish invaders but not too far from the Inca's capital city so they could keep an eye on the empire's remaining wealth."

Simon's interest was also stimulated. "Do you think we can find it?"

"Yes, I do. The journey will be long and hazardous but we can navigate the Amazon River and some tributaries for half the distance and then trek southwest to the Madre de Dios. Based on what an Indian told Roper's guide, who relayed the information to him, I think we can find it."

Professor Scott's aroused interest was focused on exploring the city but Simon's immediate thought was, what if we could present President Grant with a massive treasure from this lost city of El Dorado as well as the Confederate treasure…this would make Grant a hero and our country wealthy beyond imagination. It would provide Elijah and me, and even our kids, enough money to last a lifetime.

One glance at the excited expressions from his three companions told Simon everything he needed to know. Turning to Patterson, he replied enthusiastically, "Robert, you have our attention."

12

Patterson smiled, knowing he had fueled some very serious interest. He took another sip from the bottle and turned to face the group. "Several months ago, Mr. Roper, accompanied by Dunn, Radford, two other companions from the original detachment, and three locals, set out on an expedition to find El Dorado. They traveled up the Amazon deep into the interior and several weeks later Roper somehow returned to the coast, shaken and in rough condition—he was the only one that made it back. The others disappeared. His story is quite interesting. I'll let him tell you."

Roper stood up and began his fascinating story. "It all started ten months ago. We had heard of the legend of El Dorado and all the stories of the heaps of gold and emeralds located there. There have been many expeditions by the Spanish Conquistadors and later others trying to find the city, but none ever found it. We mounted an expedition of our own and found a young Indian guide named Mapi. He came from an east Peruvian tribe called the Kayapos. Earlier, Mapi and some of his tribesmen were deep into the interior of the Amazon basin on a hunting trip when they stumbled upon another Indian near starvation. He told them he was a descendent from the Chibchas who once lived near the border of Brazil and Columbia and had been wandering lost in the jungle for several weeks. He also spoke of a city filled with gold he had stumbled upon in the region near the borders of Peru and Bolivia. He became delirious and before he died he pulled this cube of gold from a leather pouch and told them it came from the city. Mapi had the cube with him when we hired him for our expedition. He was killed by a poison arrow and that's when I got it."

"And you think it came from the lost city?" Scott questioned.

"All I know is what Mapi told me. He said it came from a hidden city filled with gold just south of the Madre de Dios."

"You really think we could find it?"

"Yes, I think so. We have a good idea of the general location…a much different place from the sites where previous expeditions searched and found nothing."

Patterson could sense the growing attentiveness from his guests. "Gentlemen, I think we should go find that lost city filled with gold…are you with me?"

Simon glanced at his three companions and again noticed their enthusiastic and eager nods of approval.

"Looks like we're in, Robert."

Professor Scott was ecstatic.

Simon asked Roper, "How do you suggest we proceed…what route will we be taking? Robert mentioned the Amazon River."

Roper pondered the question for a moment. "Yes, the quickest and best route across Brazil would be the Amazon River. They say the Amazon is nearly 3,000 miles long and meanders from the Andes highlands and across most of Brazil. The river has many tributaries that branch off in many directions. We can travel by boat a few days and well into the interior. We would need to veer southwest just beyond a village named Itacoatiara onto another river called the Madeira. It leads deep into the interior jungle, mostly unexplored by white men. This is where things get risky. There are villages along the way inhabited by some very fierce tribes. This is where Mapi was killed…well up river on the Madeira. Some of the inhabitants along the river are headhunters—very bad people. Most have never seen a white man and consider outsiders enemies. Properly armed though, we should be able to work our way past them…if we're lucky."

"Why the Madeira?" Simon asked. "Wouldn't it be easier to continue due west on the Amazon? I've heard it travels all the way to Peru."

"Because we think the city lies much further south… more toward the Peruvian and Bolivia border. This is most likely why the earlier explorers couldn't find it. Earlier Spanish maps show the lost city well to the north and it's most likely they've explored most of the areas along the Amazon."

"How far does the Madeira take us?" Scott asked.

"The primary river ends near the border between the Pando and Rondonia regions where we can pick up another tributary and a series of native trails that will take us just south of the Madre de Dios region to the hill country between Bolivia and Peru. When we finally run out of river passage it will take several days to walk through some very inhospitable jungle. Several miles inland, into the Madre De Dios, we were attacked by hostile Indians and luckily, Mapi and I escaped and backtracked to the river where some friendlies carried us back in a canoe to the Amazon. It was also where I got separated from both Dunn and Radford, and never saw them again—probably killed by the Indians. Mapi was later killed on the Madeira before we reached the Amazon. I was just lucky, I guess."

"What will we be looking for…what landmarks will show us the way to the city?" the professor probed.

Roper walked to the window and glanced out at the trees dotting the rolling hills, remembering the horrific events of the expedition. "Well…according to the Chibcha, we'll be looking for a series of mountain peaks called Os Três Diabos. He said the jungle begins to thin out a bit here but hidden in front of the three peaks is a small valley covered with more jungle growth. This is most likely where the city is hidden. Mapi believed it lies further south, just inside Bolivia, but we have concluded the city is in Peru between Lake Titicaca and Cuzco."

"What does Os Três Diabos mean?" Elijah asked inquisitively.

"The Three Devils."

Elijah mumbled quietly to himself. "Besides headhunters and poison arrows, now we also have to contend with three stinking devils…how comforting is that?"

Patterson cut in. "Gentlemen, I believe we all can agree that we want to undertake an expedition to search for El Dorado. Is that correct?"

Everyone nodded affirmative.

"Then there is a lot of planning to be done and supplies and equipment to be gathered."

Elijah turned to Simon. "Haven't we forgotten something?"

"What?"

"Captain Whitmore and the Halifax anchored at the port of Santos. He's expecting our return with these men and has orders to transport us back to Washington. I'm sure the President won't take too kindly if we go wandering off into the jungle and happen to be several weeks or perhaps a few months overdue…that is if we ever get back."

Patterson and his companions watched curiously as Simon pondered the question.

"Whitmore doesn't know anything about our mission except to transport us back to Washington. I can take him into my confidence and tell him about the Confederate gold and our primary assignment from the president to secure it for the U.S. Treasury. Except, I'll change it a bit and tell him Mr. Patterson and his men need to guide us into the interior for a few days to secure it. We'll tell him the Confederates actually transported the gold to Brazil and didn't cache it in the Appalachian Mountains as the letter indicated. We can say that story was just a ruse to protect the exiles and treasure. We'll have Whitmore transport us as far as the mouth of the Amazon and I'll tell him Mr. Patterson has the contacts to secure a ship to bring us home with the gold."

"Think he'll buy that story?" Elijah questioned, a bit skeptical about the whole idea.

"He will, with Mr. Patterson's help to back it up."

Patterson grinned and nodded, "We'll convince him."

Aboard the French ship Bernard – Atlantic Ocean

Paul Devereaux stood by the starboard railing, staring at the monotonous roll of the waves. He had boarded the French ship,

Bernard, in Nantes, accompanied by a Le Guarde agent named Pierre Allard and two other agents, Jacques, and Bruno. They were ruthless men especially trained in stealth and assassination—hired killers. Minister Pothuau had arranged transport on the 216 ton, iron-clad steamer powered by twin screws. Her eight coal fired boilers gave her plenty of horsepower. She was a fast ship.

Allard approached Devereaux with questions. "Poullard gave me a briefing on the mission and told me about the Americans, but I'm not sure what we are trying to accomplish."

"My instructions are to find the Americans and see what they are up to. I was briefly aboard that flying ship back in 70' when they found it in a cavern in Peru. I was able to commandeer the ship and make them fly it to Paris. Bonaparte wanted to use the damn thing to destroy the Prussian Army but things didn't work out."

"Poullard briefly mentioned a flying machine to me but I didn't understand what the hell he was talking about. So what's the plan?"

"Captain Lavelle will take us to the southern coast of Brazil and we can start in São Paulo. I understand there is a town just north of São Paulo called Santa Barbara d'Oeste. This is where many Confederate exiles live. I was told the Americans were headed there to meet up with some of the Confederados. Our illustrious president thinks they are up to something big and wants us to find out what it is. It could either mean a big treasure somewhere or that damn flying contraption. In any event, we have to find them and find out what they're up to."

"Mon Dieu," Allard responded, "We have totally lost our minds. I hope we are armed properly," he added. "This could turn out to be a bit dangerous. The Americans might not take kindly to us stealing one of their secrets, especially after your failure in Peru."

"You don't have to remind me of that debacle, Allard. As far as weapons, our armory in Paris considered several newer guns, including the new Chassepot rifle made by Saint Étienne Arms. They deemed the rifle too long and bulky for our purposes. They are more suited for the army. An American company, Winchester, has a new Model '73 coming out this year but our people were unable to get them in time so they secured the next best thing… the Winchester Model 66 that takes fifteen .44-40 cartridges in a tubular magazine. The good news is they were able to requisition five newer Model 1873 Chamelot Deluigne revolvers that take 11mm cartridges. These guns should be adequate enough for our purposes.

Port Town of Santos, Brazil

Captain Whitmore was sitting at his desk thumbing through some papers and waiting patiently for his passengers to return when the first mate knocked on the door of his stateroom. "Sir," he reported, "Mr. Murphy and Mr. Walker have returned with some other men and ask for permission to come aboard."

"By all means, show them aboard." Whitmore was relieved the waiting was over. He put on his jacket and hurried topside to greet his passengers.

Simon and Elijah met the captain on the foredeck while the other members of the party lingered nearby. "Good to see you again, Captain," Simon greeted him cordially.

"Glad you're back. I've been wondering when you'd show up. I assume this is the group you came for," he said glancing at the four newcomers. "If so, I would like to set sail as soon as possible."

"Yes, Captain, you may depart anytime you wish, but first a private word with you, sir." Simon motioned for Patterson to join them at the starboard railing. "You were not privy to information about our mission, so I need to tell you more details. Mr. Patterson was a general in the Confederate Army and just before the occupation of Richmond he was placed in charge of moving the entire Confederate Treasury to a secret place somewhere in the south. He told me they initially planned to take it to North Carolina but changed plans and carried the gold to Brazil instead and then moved it to a secure location along the Amazon River. The cache consisted of gold and gemstones and is worth several million dollars. Our mission was to secure the gold and transport it to the United States Treasury in exchange for the restored citizenship and safe return of Mr. Patterson and his associates."

"Is this true, Mr. Patterson?" Whitmore asked curiously.

"Yes, sir, I sent a letter to President Grant offering the location of the Confederate treasury in exchange for a return to our homeland and a full pardon for me and other Confederate exiles in Brazil. I believe the cache is worth at least ten to fifteen million dollars and I believe your president would like to have it. We transported it to a secure location along the Amazon River for safekeeping. We felt it too risky to leave it in the States."

Simon continued, "Unfortunately, we must take a side trip up the Amazon so we can secure the gold and return it. We can arrange guides and boats for the trip and Mr. Patterson has contacts in Brazil to arrange for a ship to return us to Washington when the gold is retrieved."

Whitmore was a bit puzzled. "And what would you have me do, Mr. Murphy?"

"Take us to the mouth of the Amazon and we'll handle the rest. As soon as we arrive, you may depart without us…we'll arrange our own transportation home. Mr. Patterson says there is a suitable docking area in the town of Belém in the Bay of Marajó and his man, Roper, can secure suitable guides and boats to transport us to the Amazon River and inland."

Believing the story, Whitmore agreed, but with a bit of skepticism. He was concerned what the reaction would be from his navy superiors and the president if he returned home empty handed, but he had no choice but to believe their story.

Early the next morning the USS Halifax pulled anchor and departed on the high tide. The journey to search for the city of gold had begun.

Port town of Belém, Brazil

The return journey back to the northern coast of Brazil took two days of sailing to reach the small town of Belém. It was established as a colonial shipping port and the gateway to Amazonia. The Halifax easily navigated the bay and docked at a well-weathered, but suitable, wharf overlooking the town. A few other ships were moored nearby, attesting to the busy shipping activity that made Belém thrive.

As the expedition team gathered on deck with their equipment and supplies, Simon and Elijah approached Whitmore. Simon nodded appreciatively. "Captain, we wish to thank you for all your hospitality and assistance in getting us here. We had a most pleasant voyage both down to São Paulo and back here to Belém."

"My pleasure, gentlemen. I was glad to be of service. Are you quite sure you will be able to secure and transport the Confederate treasure to the United States without our assistance? My orders specifically instructed me to bring you back to Washington."

"Unfortunately, we have no idea how long it will take us to travel inland and retrieve the gold and bring it back to Belém. Mr. Patterson assures us he has some very reliable shipping connections that can arrange transport to bring us home with the treasure. It shouldn't take more than a couple of weeks."

"Very well," Whitmore conceded with a slight feeling of uncertainty, "in that case, I wish you Godspeed."

13

With the group of eight men, Simon and Elijah needed to find four rooms for the night. Luckily, with the help of Roper and Mann as interpreters, they found a saloon with suitable rooms on the second floor. Both men had learned to speak passable Portuguese in the few years they had lived here. Patterson and Stafford were a bit less conversant in the language but understood enough to get by. Simon suspected, having observed the few ladies roaming the floor below, the rooms were used for more than just sleeping quarters—but they were suitable for their purposes. Turning to Roper at the dinner table, Simon asked, "Do you know where we can rent a good guide and some boats to take us upriver?"

Roper hesitated as he swallowed a big slug of beer. "Yes, I do know a place…a couple of blocks from here. That's where we hired Mapi a few months back. There is a building on the waterfront that advertises boat trips to the Amazon. There are some very unsavory characters that hang out there, all claiming to be the best guides on the river. Actually, I suspect most of them would slit your throat if they thought you were carrying gold coins, but there are also some reliable guides that know the Amazon and interior pretty well. All we have to do is find the right one. Drop the proprietor a couple of American eagles and he'll find us a good guide. Everyone in South America will take a bribe…it's a tradition."

Early next morning, the group wandered down to the waterfront. Everyone had a specific assignment. Santos, Stafford, Mann, and Scott were designated to gather essential food and supplies while Simon, Elijah, Roper, and Patterson paid a visit to the guide shop. The building faced the wharf area and the windswept, tattered grey planking revealed the old building had faced many past storms. They walked through the door.

Facing them was a shabby looking counter filled with disheveled stacks of papers and old magazines. A few empty glasses were scattered about. A heavyset man with tousled grey hair sat lazily behind the counter nursing a brownish looking liquid in a glass…dark rum perhaps.

Seated around two round tables were several scruffy looking men who most likely called themselves guides. One man in particular gave the group a hard stare with cold grey eyes. This guy could be trouble, Elijah thought.

Roper walked over to the counter and spoke in Portuguese to the grey haired attendant. "Is Luiz here?"

"In the back. What do you want with him?"

"I want to talk to him about a boat and a guide to take us into the Amazon. I hired a guide from him a few months ago."

This caught the attention of the table loungers who began to buzz with conversation. Cold grey eyes stood up. "You need to hire me…I'm the best damn guide in Brazil."

"Sit down, Claudio," one man shouted. "You wouldn't know what the Amazon looked like if you fell into it." The others laughed.

"You would stay so damn drunk you'd get everybody lost and we'd never find you again," another yelled. More laughter.

Claudio turned and threw a roundhouse punch at the second heckler but missed and threw himself off balance, crashing onto the table. He and two others slammed to the floor in a heap of arms and legs, emitting more laughter from the other table. This really stoked his temper and he arose and turned toward the Americans, his cold grey eyes burning with hate. He lunged at Elijah but the southerner was too quick. He spun out of the way and slammed his heel into Claudio's foot. The brute fell to the floor in extreme pain, subdued for the moment. "Enough, Claudio," the older grey haired attendant screamed. "Sit down or get the hell out of here."

"This isn't a guide shop," Elijah chortled. "Damn place is nothing but a shop full of drunks."

Luiz, the proprietor, arrived from the back. "What the hell is all the commotion?"

The grey haired man behind the counter answered, "Just Claudio all drunked up and showing his ass again."

Spotting the strangers he said, "You men customers or trouble makers?"

Roper spoke up, "Luiz, you remember me? I hired a boat and a guide a few months ago. His name was Mapi."

He thought for a moment, "Yes, I remember you were one of the Confederados who hired Mapi. What happened to him?"

"Mapi was killed by Indians on the Madeira. Poison arrow got him."

"Damn shame…Mapi was a good guide and knew the river well."

"Do you have any more like him?" Roper asked.

"I might…all depends."

Roper interpreted the conversation in English. "He wants some money to loosen his tongue."

Simon reached into his pocket and handed Luiz an American gold $10 eagle. "Maybe this will help."

The quick flash of the gold coin did not escape the onlooker's eyes seated at the table. A big smile appeared on the proprietor's face as he spoke to Roper. "Your friend seems to speak my language. Let's go to the back and we can talk."

Luiz led the American's to a back room and closed the door. "Can't trust those cutthroat bastards back there…they'll try to rob you in a second and cut your throat for one escudo."

Like the front desk, the back office was much the same; a jumble of papers cluttering the desk with stacks of old magazines and newspapers stacked in the corners. "I know of an excellent guide that knows the river well—his name is Raphael. In the interest of your security, I won't ask you where you're going or why, but I need to know about how far so I can give you a price.

The Amazon is the longest river in the world…over three thousand miles."

Roper continued to interpret as Simon laid out the necessary information and filled in the gaps.

"We need to travel up-river as far as the Amazon will take us. Mr. Roper mentioned the Madeira River as a possibility. We can decide the direction when we get there, but when we reach the headwaters we'll have to go on foot."

"Hell of a trip you're talking about there, amigo…about eighteen hundred miles. Sounds like you're headed for Peru. Be a lot easier to take a ship around the Cape…longer but much safer. The river and jungle is a dangerous place. Many men have never returned from the Amazon. They just get swallowed up. That place has sixteen foot caimans that can swallow a man in one gulp… and piranhas that can reduce a man to a skeleton in seconds…very bad place to go."

"We'll take our chances," Simon assured him.

"In that case you need Raphael. He is one of the best, but it's going to cost you. You will also need a small paddle driven steamer for the trip up the Amazon and switch to dugouts when you hit the Madeira. Let's see," he said pondering the situation for a moment. "With Raphael and your eight men you'll need three of the larger dugs…they can hold up to four men. All of you will have to paddle, of course."

"We can handle that," Simon reassured him.

Luiz went over to his dilapidated desk and thumbed through a dog-eared notebook. "I see the Caribe is available. She's a tough old steamer…been upriver many times. The captain's name is Leandro Cadiz…crusty old bastard but knows the river well. We'll load the dugouts on top and you'll carry them with you." Luiz scribbled some notes and added up some figures. "The guide, steamer, and dugouts will cost you $500…in American gold eagles, of course."

"That's too much money," Simon complained, "We'll give you $300 in gold."

Luiz grumbled as he made more notes on his pad, pretending to make some calculations. "$400 and you have a deal…no less.

The Caribe is difficult to charter," he added. "Big demand for her. She is one of the best steamers on the river and Captain Cadiz knows it better than anyone. Also, I'm giving you the best guide on the river."

Simon hesitated for a moment. "Done!" he agreed. "We have a deal. We would like to depart day after tomorrow…that should give you and I time to get everything together."

"Be at Pier 2 Saturday morning and be ready to shove off. I'll expect full payment when you depart…in American gold eagles."

Simon nodded.

Friday was spent gathering food and a few necessities. Each man had his assigned duties and a list of specific items needed to outfit the expedition. Once completed, most of the day was leisure, allowing the men to catch up on some rest. Elijah suggested to Simon, "Let's go get a beer."

The idea was appealing so Simon, Elijah, Santos, Professor Scott, and Mann began walking the waterfront in search of a bar. Santos eased up to Simon and Elijah and whispered, "We have a man behind following us. He looks like that big drunk that was causing all the trouble in the guide shop yesterday."

Elijah stopped to look into a window and took a concealed glance behind him. "Yeah, and he has another man with him… one of the drunks who was heckling him. The one with the cold eyes named Claudio has a bottle in his hand and just passed it to his friend. They're probably half-drunk again from rum…looks like more trouble to me. Also, it looks like the cold-eyed bastard is limping where I stomped on his foot. When he sees me I know that's big trouble."

"Don't worry, he's already seen you," Scott reminded him.

Just ahead was a dull looking building with an overhanging sign that announced the name of the bar as Tibarão Com Fome. "What does that mean?" Elijah asked.

"It means Hungry Shark," Mann informed him.

"That ought to be a nice quiet place for a relaxing beer," Elijah answered sarcastically.

"Don't count on it. 'Ice Eyes' is still following us."

They strolled through the door and took seats at a small table near the window. A few patrons were scattered about nursing glasses of clear liquid, most likely tequila or rum, and some were tilting pints of locally brewed cerveja. A couple of regulars were seated at the bar but most of the customers at the tables resembled rough seamen enjoying some libation before sailing off to sea in some old weathered cargo ship. Moments later, Claudio and his companion ambled by the bar and looked through the window, spotting the Americans sitting there. Stealth seemed to be no concern. They walked in and nosily took a seat at the next table. "Going to buy me and my friend a drink, Americanos?" he growled. "You seem to have all the money."

Mann answered brusquely, "We didn't invite you along…you can buy your own drink, you miserable drunk bastard."

This was enough to enrage Claudio and ignite the explosion again. He and his companion stood up, hatred burning in their eyes. A shout erupted from another table. "If you Americanos have all the money you can buy the whole bar a drink." A few "aye mates" and cheers sounded off and four more seamen stood up, egging Claudio on. Dark Eyes and his mate hurled themselves from their table and crashed into Mann and Elijah, fists flying. The table collapsed with all of the occupants crashing to the floor. Two more seamen rushed over to join the melee and the fight was on. Mann took a glancing fist to his jaw and felt like his head was going to explode while Elijah took the full crushing weight of Claudio on top, arms and legs thrashing. A third medium-built seaman charged at Simon, unintelligible words sputtering from his mouth. Simon kneeled and as the man hurtled over him Simon pivoted upward and launched him through the glass window, shattering it with the impact. Mann was getting the worst of it when Santos kicked his assailant in the head, knocking him senseless. He collapsed as Mann pushed him to the side. A fourth seaman assailed Professor Scott and threw a roundhouse punch that glanced off his shoulder…no harm done. He took another punch that skimmed Scott's jaw. The professor sidestepped and slammed his knee into the seaman's groin—he fell like a rock, screaming in pain as he writhed on the floor. Meanwhile, Elijah was having a tough time as Claudio pummeled him with flying fists. A punch to the stomach sent Elijah reeling and the big man raised his fist for the kill. Simon reacted and slammed a chair into Claudio's face, stopping the charge. He then threw a solid punch to his kidney that stunned him and then Elijah stopped the fight by smashing a heavy table leg into his head. A loud shot erupted as Scott pulled his Remington and fired a single slug into the ceiling. The patrons slid back into their seats and the Americans withdrew, slowly backing out of the door. "Let's get the hell outta here," Simon shouted, "before these animals really get pissed off."

The shot from Scott's revolver apparently ended the fight because no one seemed to be following them, knowing they would be confronting armed men. Elijah warned, as he rubbed his aching midsection, "I don't think we've seen the last of Claudio… that drunk bastard is crazy." He continued his grumbling aloud with a tone of aggravation. "Why is it we have to get into a fight every time we go into a bar? I don't recall ever starting one."

Professor Scott was quick to answer. "Because, my good friend, we pick the worst sleazy bars in the worst imaginable places, full of the worst possible drunks who all think we have lots of money to hand out. From now on, perhaps I should select the next bar… one that serves cognac and fine wine instead of beer and rotgut." And glancing accusingly at Mann, the professor added, "And we always seem to say the wrong things to the wrong people at the wrong time."

Elijah just rolled his eyes in resignation. "Yeah…and maybe we should wear our best coats and ties to the next bar so we can fight like gentlemen."

14

Early the next morning the expedition group met at the wharf where the small paddlewheel steamer, Caribe, was docked at the second pier. Luiz was standing by a large wood pylon that secured one of the boat's mooring lines. He was talking to a slightly built man supporting a thin grey moustache and Balbo type beard. He wore a seaman's front-billed cap…no doubt the captain, Leandro Cadiz. A young, nice looking Hispanic man was sitting to one side chatting with one of the deck hands named Fabio. At least Luiz is prompt, Simon thought. Maybe that's a good sign that says he knows what he's doing.

Simon and the group approached Luiz who introduced them to Captain Cadiz and Raphael, the guide. Mann and Roper, who spoke and understood passable Portuguese, interpreted the introductions and were soon engaged in a friendly conversation with Raphael concerning the plans for the trip. The young guide seemed enthusiastic.

Simon and Luiz withdrew to finalize the hire. He handed the guide shop proprietor a small pouch containing twenty American gold double eagles. Luiz opened the bag and smiled when the flash of gold crossed his eyes. He shook Simon's hand, walked over to Cadiz, and handed him six gold coins. He would pay the guide his commission upon their return. On the other hand he thought, most likely he won't return, which meant the money would be his to keep.

Cadiz returned the handshake and Luiz departed the wharf… the transaction was completed.

The Caribe had a crew of five deckhands aboard—one Oriental and the remaining four of Portuguese descent. Two of the crew withdrew the gangplank and the steamer slowly pulled away from the dock. The Caribe was a small side paddle-wheeler driven by a steam engine consisting of a fire box and two wood-burning 75 gallon boilers. The steam generated from the boilers propelled the drive shaft that turned the wheel. The whole drive mechanism was a bit clumsy but it worked as long as the boat was stocked with wood and fresh water for the boilers. The sturdy little boat measured sixteen feet wide by sixty-eight feet in length and consisted of a main deck containing eight small bunkrooms and mess area for cooking and serving meals. The top deck contained a half size wheelhouse from where the boat was commanded. It was adequately fitted for Amazon River travel and suitable for relatively comfortable quarters. Captain Cadiz seemed likeable enough and Simon was pleased that at least they wouldn't have to paddle for a few days. He thought, perhaps the trip up the Amazon wouldn't be so bad after all.

Belém, Brazil

A dark-skinned man entered the back office of the guide shop where Luiz was sorting through some disheveled papers. "It's about time you showed up, Marcel," Luiz growled.

"Got held up by some coffee traders," the man answered. "Bastards tried to cheat me…they will never do that again. What the hell did you want anyway?"

"I have a special job for you and some of your men. I have a hunch that there might be a lot of money involved."

"I'm listening."

"Some Americanos came in yesterday wanting a guide and a boat to take them up the Amazon."

"So…what's wrong with that? Men travel up the Amazon all the time."

"These men are different. One hired a guide from me several

months ago—he was the only one that made it back. One of my best guides died on the trip."

"Men die all the time on that filthy river."

"The interesting thing was they loaded three large dugouts on the top of the Caribe. They planned to leave the boat at some point and take the dugs up the river. They mentioned the Madeira as a possible route."

"Why would anyone want to travel up the Madeira River? That's one nasty son-of-a-bitch. The head hunters along that river don't allow strangers in their region."

"That's what I was wondering…unless they plan on turning more to the south toward the Bolivian border. I overheard the one whisper something to another man about a lost city and gold."

"You mean the legend of El Dorado?"

"Yes…they may be onto something and we need to find out what it is. They boarded the Caribe about three hours ago heading north to the Canal do Sul. From there they'll most likely take the usual canals past Island Caras to the big river. That's normally the route Leandro will take. With your boat you should be able to catch them easily, but just follow them and see where they're going. Don't confront them…just follow them."

"What if they actually lead us to the city?"

"Then do what you do best. You and your men kill them and grab what gold you can find. And Marcel, take Claudio with you—I believe he has a big score to settle."

"Claudio is a drunken animal and the bastard will only get in the way. Probably fall off the boat in a drunken stupor and get eaten by a caiman."

"Then he will no longer be a problem for us, will he," Luiz responded with an evil smirk.

"I get the message," Marcel acknowledged, mildly amused.

Early the next day in the Guide Shop

Luiz had an uneasy feeling when the four strangers walked into the guide shop. They looked like trouble. Devereaux had been informed the proprietor spoke decent English, a language the Frenchman knew well. "You are the owner of this shop?"

"Yes, I am Luiz, the owner. How can I help you, gentlemen?" he asked, trying to appear as calm as possible.

"We were told you rented a boat to some Americans a couple of days back. We want to know where they were going and will need a fast steamer to follow them. Cooperate with us and you will be well reimbursed."

"You are French?" Luiz asked. "Your accent betrays you."

"That is correct," Devereaux confirmed.

"How did you know they came to my shop?"

"We know they are traveling with some Confederados from a town near São Paulo. With a bit of persuasion, we were able to get information as to where they were going. Belém is the gateway to the Amazon and we understand your shop offers the best travel arrangements for the river. We found out a steamer left dock for the Amazon yesterday and the passengers were Americans. We also found out your shop arranged the passage."

Luiz knew he couldn't lie his way out of this one. "You say I will be well paid?"

"That's what I said." Devereaux replied with some annoyance. "You will be well paid for both the information and rental of a boat into the Amazon.

"They left the dock yesterday on a steamer named the Caribe. The captain is a seasoned sailor named Cadiz who knows the river well. One of the Americanos mentioned the Madeira River as a possible route where they would probably have to transfer to dugouts. I have no idea why they would want to travel that river…it is very dangerous."

"We'll need a shallow draft boat that is both fast and one that can navigate the Madeira if need be."

"And my payment?" Luiz asked greedily. "Steamers are not cheap these days."

"This could cover it." Devereaux placed a bag full of gold francs in the proprietor's hand.

Luiz replied with a sudden change of heart. "You happen to

be in luck, my friends. I have an associate named Marcel who happens to be leaving this morning for the Amazon. Perhaps you have the same mission."

"And what is that supposed to mean?" Devereaux asked suspiciously.

"My associates are also following the Americanos. Perhaps you can join them and ensure you have a formidable team. Marcel has a fast boat and also knows the river. The gold francs should cover the hire and I can secure space for you on his boat, but we must hurry."

The Frenchman agreed. "Then by all means do it."

"Be ready to embark within the hour. I will arrange it."

Aboard the Caribe

The Caribe rounded the point at the head of the Bay of Marajó that put them back into the Atlantic Ocean. The calm ride in the bay was replaced by heavy rolling of the lighter vessel caused by the constant swells of the deeper water. The motion had not been as noticeable in the larger USS Halifax, but the smaller side-wheeler tossed up and down like a cork. Elijah, Mann, and Stafford felt the effects of nausea coming on. "When do we reach that damned river?" Elijah groaned. "I feel like I'm back on that miserable skiff near the Yucatan."

Patterson assured him. "Captain Cadiz said we'd be reaching the Sul Canal by late afternoon. The ride will be much smoother then."

"Sooner the better," Elijah groaned, "I feel like I'm gonna throw up anytime."

He hurried to the bow railing and stood facing the front of the boat and, holding tightly to the railing, he stared steadily at the horizon. This seemed to help a bit. The time passed slowly until he finally heard one of the deckhands shouting, "Sul Canal ahead!" The smoother, calmer water of the entrance had a miraculous effect and his color returned.

The captain steered the Caribe past the Llha Mexicana Island

and maneuvered into the center of the canal where he turned the helm over to the first mate. The small boat passed through the narrow passage around the north side of Caras Island into the main stream of the Amazon. The water was a brown murky color attributed to the tons of mud picked up on its 3,000-mile journey. Captain Cadiz joined Simon, Elijah, and Patterson along the starboard rail as the boat drifted by the village of Sãn José de Macapa. "That town was founded and claimed by the Spanish in the mid-fifteen hundreds but later occupied by the Portuguese in the mid-seventeen hundreds," Cadiz informed them.

He pointed to a formable structure along the river. "The fortress you see over there was laid out by the Portuguese in 1764, but took eighteen years to complete."

"Why so long?" Simon asked.

"Many of the Indian workers died of sickness and other workers just ran away. We've a long way to go before we reach the Madeira so I would advise you and your men to relax and enjoy the ride."

About 2,000 yards behind the Caribe, a smaller boat kept a steady pace, careful not to close the gap. Appropriately named Amazonia, it was powered by a steam driven engine that drove a single screw. The 100-gallon boiler provided plenty of steam power. Carrying less tonnage, the boat was noticeably faster than the craft they were following. Marcel stood at the helm, careful to maintain his distance when Claudio approached him, a heavy bruise still noticeable on the side of his head. "Why the hell are we just following them? We can overtake that boat anytime—I want to get my hands on that Americano that hit me in the head. I'll crush the pig into little pieces and feed him to the piranha. And why did you allow those damn Frenchmen on board…we don't need their help."

Annoyed at the sudden intrusion, Marcel responded, "Calm down, Claudio…you'll get your chance for revenge. Right now all we want to do is follow them to see where they are going and for what purpose. As far as the Frenchmen are concerned, I am being well paid to take them with us. Besides we may need the extra help along when we confront the Americans. Why the hell did I bring this stupid animal along?" he grumbled.

The big man, displaying hatred in those cold grey eyes, reluctantly nodded and ambled back to the foredeck where he picked up a spyglass and scanned the horizon ahead. He caught a glimpse of the stern of the boat ahead steaming toward a bend in the river. Two men were leaning on the rail talking. Claudio recognized Elijah chatting with another man. He tensed and gritted his teeth…I will tear you apart, he swore.

The Caribe steamed smoothly along and rounded the bend at Urucuricaia Island as Simon, Santos, and Patterson watched in fascination at all the heavily vegetated marshlands along the river. Thousands of birds flew from the undergrowth and clouded the sky as the boat passed by. Captain Cadiz strolled by and stopped by the railing and stood next to Simon. "Beautiful sight isn't it, gentlemen?"

"Quite amazing," Simon responded, gazing at the panorama before him.

"If you will please gather the other members of your group, I have something I would like to discuss with you…in the wheelhouse."

Simon sent Santos to fetch Elijah and the others while Patterson and he followed Cadiz up the ladder to the second deck. The other expedition members arrived shortly.

Cadiz spread a large map out on the table. "I do not know the purpose of your trip up the Amazon and on to the Madeira but if you are like most other foreigners who have come before you, I would suspect you are in search of a very special place…a place full of old legends and perhaps immense wealth."

"You are most perceptive," Patterson conceded.

"I wish I could accompany you but I'm afraid these old bones aren't up to it…maybe twenty years ago. Anyway, let's take a look at the map," the captain suggested. "This is the latest chart of the Amazon Basin. We still have a long journey to where the Madeira River forks from the Amazon, a four-day ride to be exact, but my biggest concern is for you to attempt to paddle the length of the Madeira. I'm afraid this will be too much of an undertaking, even for young lads like you. The Madeira is very dangerous, especially with some of the tribes along the river like the Jivaros, Camayurás, and Yunomamös. The Jivaros are savage headhunters and well known for their ability to shrink their victim's heads. Paddling against the current is bad enough, but trying to paddle dugouts past these villages is almost certain suicide."

"The Jivaros are the ones who killed our guide, Mapi, with a poison arrow on our return trip down the Madeira," Roper informed him. "They are a very bad lot."

"What do you suggest, Captain?" Simon asked.

Cadiz paused, tracing his fingers over the map following a thin winding ribbon—the Madeira River. His fingers stopped at a tiny spot on the map. "I could take you to this point," he assured them tapping his forefinger over the small dot. "The village of Porto Velho. This will carry us past the Jivaros and save you many miles of paddling. Also, the Caribe will give us a sturdy platform to defend if necessary and I can assure you it will most likely be necessary."

"How could you maneuver the Madeira with this boat? Aren't you concerned of getting stuck on a sandbar?"

"The Caribe is a shallow draft steamer that can maneuver in only four feet of water. The Madeira will give us plenty of draft… at least past Porto Velho to a point where the river turns south and becomes the Mamoré. I made that trip as far as the mouth of the Mamoré a few years ago and had no major problems except for a couple of Indian attacks we were able to fight off. The return trip is easier since we will be aided by the current."

"Sounds good to me. It sure would save our backs from a lot of miles to paddle."

"And probably save our heads," Roper injected.

"Captain Cadiz, how much would you charge to take us up the Madeira?"

"One hundred of your Yankee gold dollars should do it," Cadiz answered eagerly. He badly needed the money.

"Do we have that much money left?" Elijah whispered to his cousin.

Simon nodded and responded to Cadiz, "Agreed. You could reduce our travel time by several days…it will save us a lot of backbreaking work."

"And one more thing," Cadiz added. "If you should find the city of gold and return safely, I would like enough money to purchase a new boat."

Simon had to chuckle. "Agreed again, Captain…agreed. You will have your new boat."

The expedition members were all relieved that Cadiz offered to transport them the additional miles, especially knowing they would be a lot safer from the headhunters on the higher elevated steamer deck than in a shallow dugout canoe.

15

Aboard the Caribe

I# was the fourth day, just before reaching the town of Manus, when the Caribe made the southwestern turn around the tiny midstream island of Trinjdade and steamed through the entrance to the Madeira River. Like the Amazon, the water flowed brown and murky, not the type of water that would invite a good swim. Simon and Elijah were engaged in one of their frequent rail-side conversations when Professor Scott strolled up. "Follow me over to the port-side rail…I've something to show you."

The two men followed the professor across the deck where Patterson, Stafford, and Mann were gathered along the railing. Santos and Roper quickly joined them.

Scott pointed to a large sand bar protruding from the bank. Four large log shaped objects lay across the bar. Suddenly one started moving and slid silently into the water. "I know what those are," Elijah shouted. "One of those scaly bastards nearly grabbed Rosita and me for dinner in the Yucatan."

"Black caiman," Scott confirmed. "Those beasts are the largest and meanest reptiles in the alligator family. The normal adult is from 9-14 feet long and can reach a weight of 1,200 pounds. The big one to the right looks like he could easily reach 14 feet… maybe more."

"Actually," Captain Cadiz announced, joining the onlookers, "I have seen reports of caiman reaching a length of 18 feet and up to 2,000 pounds. One like that could devour a man within minutes. Not a pleasant way to die. The Amazon and its tributaries are full of them so swimming in the river is not advisable."

"We get the message," Elijah responded for the group.

As if on cue, the remaining three beasts slid off the bar and disappeared into the river.

The men dispersed and Simon and Elijah ambled back to the stern. Santos followed and spoke in a soft tone, "Don't stare to the rear but I believe we are being followed by a boat—looks to be about a half mile. I spotted it yesterday and it has maintained a steady distance behind us. Most of the boats stick to the Amazon, so it is very unusual for one to be trailing us on the Madeira, especially maintaining a steady pace. I borrowed the captain's glass and saw one of the men watching us through a spyglass."

Simon glanced toward the stern. "Who in the hell would be following us? No one knew of our plans."

"Except that guide shop owner—the one named Luiz," Elijah reminded him. "I'll bet the shifty bastard has something to do with that boat. Let's go assemble the group and alert them to potential trouble. We need to have a weapons check and pass out the three spare Winchesters to Patterson and his men." He sent Santos to fetch the captain—he wanted Cadiz informed about the possible danger shadowing them.

Simon spoke to the assembled group in the aft mess cabin, "We may have a problem. It appears we're being followed by another boat shadowing our rear. Santos spotted it yesterday and it has continued to maintain its distance. He saw one man watching us through a spyglass."

"Who could be following us?" Patterson questioned with concern.

"The guide shop proprietor, Luiz, arranged the deal for the boat and the dugouts and he knew our plans were to use the canoes on the Madeira. I have a feeling he is up to something."

Cadiz spoke up. "I've known Luiz for several years and I can tell you when he smells money, you can smell trouble. He cannot be trusted."

"Anyway, we want to be prepared. What weapons did you and your men bring along, Robert?"

"We have some old Sharps carbines from the war…not in the best of shape." Simon reached into a long duffle and pulled out a sleek looking rifle, holding it in the air for the entire group to see. "We brought along the latest rifles made by a company called Winchester Arms. They are introducing a new model repeater called the 'Winchester 73'. The army was able to get a few pre-release models. We test fired these guns at the Washington Arsenal and they are amazing weapons."

"You say they are repeaters?" Mann asked curiously.

"Yes. They're lever action weapons with a spring-loaded tube type magazine that holds up to fifteen .44-40 center-fire cartridges. The weapon is quite accurate. Professor Scott put fifteen shots into a six inch bull's-eye."

"Yeah…and I got twelve," Elijah proudly announced.

"Can you imagine how much destruction those rifles would have caused if both of our sides had them in the war?" Stafford injected.

"There was enough killing with the guns we had," Patterson reminded him.

"Anyway," Simon continued, "we brought along three spares for you and your men."

Patterson hefted the rifle and sighted down the barrel. "It feels comfortable enough—can't wait to test it. I'll take one and you can give the other two rifles to Stafford and Roper. I believe Mr. Mann prefers his Lorenz. It's pretty darn accurate at long distances and Mann is one hell of a shot."

Elijah laughed, "We'll have to let Mann and the professor here have a contest. That should be quite an interesting show."

"First things first…we have a boat chasing us we have to worry about." Simon wanted this point to sink in.

"And some very nasty headhunters ahead who will be most anxious to chop off our heads and shrink them," Roper reminded the group.

The Caribe had just passed by the village of Jenipapo when Captain Cadiz walked over to Simon and Elijah engaged in another conversation. "Excuse the interruption but I wanted to inform you we are now entering the lands of the Jivaros and they don't like outsiders invading their territory. I would strongly advise you alert your men and have weapons ready. I have already armed my crew. I'll try to keep the Caribe in the middle of the river but the currents can be tricky." Turning to Simon, Cadiz asked, "What is that boat behind us doing?"

"Still following us. If the guide shop owner is behind this, I suspect they're trying to find out where we're going."

"Let's keep a sharp eye on them. Luiz smells treasure and he knows some pretty nasty characters and I'm thinking one in particular named Marcel. Luiz has used him before and this killer would murder his mother for a single escudo."

Just past a bend in the river, a small midstream island was sighted where the river split and flowed around each side. The men aboard the Caribe had spotted a few Indians along the banks of the Madeira but here a large Jivaros village lined the south shore of the wider canal they were navigating. Santos was the first to spot the formidable barrier spanning across the island and connecting to each of the opposite riverbanks. He called for the group to come to the bow. "What the hell is that?" Elijah shouted.

"Looks like the Jivaros are trying to blockade us."

"Take the north fork…away from the village."

"Can't," Cadiz yelled. "That canal is too narrow and full of sand bars. We'll get stuck for sure—and it looks like they blocked that side as well."

Anchored from the island, the Indians had stretched a heavy net-like obstruction across the river, woven from vines, reeds, and tree saplings. Both sides of the river were blocked.

"Once they stop the boat, they'll use dugouts to attack from both sides and from the rear. You fellows better grab those guns of yours—it looks like we're getting ready to use them. The Jivaros are good with their pucunas or blowguns, and the curare poison they put on the darts will kill a man very fast. We can't let them get within range. We had better find a way to cut through that net or we'll be in real trouble. I have some machetes aboard and will get some of my men to start hacking through it from the bow."

From both sides of the river dozens of dugouts were pushed from the banks; each was occupied by three Jivaros warriors. Their strategy was to attack the boat from each side to get close enough to use their pucunas. "What are they doing?" Mann shouted.

"They're trying to hit us from both sides," Cadiz yelled back. "Mr. Murphy, I suggest you have your men cover the stern and both the port and starboard sides—my crew will cover the front. Take out the ones with the pucunas first."

The eight Americans, armed with their Winchester repeaters and Remington revolvers, quickly dispersed to each side of the boat with Simon, Elijah, and Mann covering the starboard and Patterson, Stafford, and Roper the port side. Santos and Professor Scott took positions at the stern to cover the dugouts fast closing toward the rear. Captain Cadiz and one of his crew stationed themselves at the windows of the second deck wheelhouse. The Caribe was dead in the water and could not move forward because of the heavy net blocking the channel. The strong current pushed the boat around into the barrier and firmly ensnared the anchor. They had no options but to stand and fight. With the dugouts closing in fast to their rear and both sides, a retreat was impossible.

Aboard the Amazonia

"What in the hell is going on up there?" Claudio asked Marcel who was watching through his glass at the activity up river.

"Looks like the Americans are being attacked by the Jivaros. Canoes are closing in fast. The Indians stopped the boat with a big net stretched across the channel."

"Maybe they will save us the trouble and kill the bastards," Claudio barked cruelly.

"Then how will we find out where they were going, you idiot? Go fetch Devereaux!"

The big man lumbered off to fetch the Frenchman.

"Why are we stopped?" Devereaux asked as he approached the bow.

"The Americans are being attacked by the Jivaros. What do you think we should do?"

"My instructions are to follow them and find out what they are up to. My government has a strong interest in knowing what they might be looking for and that might be hard to do if they are dead. I also don't want a hundred headhunters attacking our boat so I say let's wait a bit to see what happens."

Aboard the Caribe

The Americans and crew watched anxiously as the dugouts closed in within fifty yards. Elijah took aim at the man in the lead dugout that had risen to aim his pucuna. The slug caught him squarely in the upper chest, throwing him back to the side of the boat and tipping it over. The other two rowers were tossed into the muddy water. Simon's shot caught a middle rower in the second boat who sprawled back into the floor, but the boat kept coming. To the rear, Professor Scott hit another Jivaros standing in a lead canoe, pitching him heavily into the water. A second man stood to shoot his blowgun but Scott's second shot hit him as well. On the port side Patterson and Roper were firing and took out three warriors in two lead canoes. Cadiz and a crewman stood at windows in the wheelhouse taking random shots to either side. The captain saw one man fall in one of the canoes and tumble overboard. The dugouts kept coming.

In the bow a young Portuguese crew member grabbed a machete and begin thrashing at the net trapped on the starboard anchor. The blade was sharp and cut effortlessly through the vines—the sturdy sapling limbs not so easily. A lucky blowgun shot hurled a dart into the man's shoulder. At first he didn't notice the brief sting but within seconds, a dull numbness began to spread through his arm and he lost his grip on the machete handle, dropping it to the deck. The curare poison was quickly taking effect. His eyesight began to fade and his grip on the net began to weaken. Losing consciousness, he tumbled over the side into the water. Elijah, who was crouching toward the front starboard railing, saw the man fall and rushed forward to grab the machete—the net had to be cut—it was their only hope. Mann saw Elijah hacking at the vines and rushed to the bow to help. He grabbed a vine and held on to Elijah's belt as he leaned heavily forward to untangle the anchor. Some of the Jivaros in the closest dugouts spotted the Americans attempting to free the Caribe and turned their boats to thwart the effort. Elijah, holding onto the net with one hand took one final swipe with the machete and cut through the last vine holding on to the anchor. Suddenly freed from the entanglement, the boat lurched backward with the current and pulled quickly away from the net. The sudden movement jerked both Elijah and Mann from the boat and left them precariously clinging to the vines as they watched in horror as the Caribe swiftly drifted away. Sitting in the water before them were six Jivaros dugouts with twelve pucunas aimed directly at their chests. Elijah mumbled hopelessly to Mann, "This ain't looking too good. Don't move a muscle and smile…maybe they won't shoot and just take us prisoner.

Mann whispered back, "I'm not sure which is worse."

16

Aboard the Caribe

"What's happening?" Simon shouted to Cadiz, who had moved to the forward starboard railing watching the events unfold to their front.

"The Jivaros have captured Elijah and Mann. They have them in two dugouts rowing to shore. This doesn't look good. What do you think they'll do?"

"I suspect tonight they will have a big drinking celebration and in the morning conduct a ceremony to decapitate them and shrink their heads. That's the normal procedure with their prisoners."

"We have to rescue them," Simon responded in disgust.

Aboard the Amazonia

Marcel had pulled the Amazonia back at a safe distance, allowing him to observe the Caribe with his spyglass. He turned to Devereaux who was standing next to him. "The Caribe has pulled free from the net and I see the Jivaros' boats heading for shore. Looks like they've broken off the attack. I can barely make out two white men in the dugouts…they must have captured two of the Americans—hard to tell what's happening. The net looks like it is still intact though."

"Let's maintain our distance and see what they do," Devereaux suggested. "I'm sure they have seen us following them but have no idea who we are. But one thing is for sure, someone will have to cut through that net if our boats are going to get by those Jivaros and make it up-stream."

Aboard the Caribe

Patterson, Stafford, and Roper had gathered on deck with Santos while Professor Scott had joined Simon and the captain to assess the situation. Simon was angry. "The Jivaros have captured Elijah and Mann and carried them off to their village. If we don't rescue them quickly they will soon be dead."

"Do you have a plan?" Patterson asked. "They outnumber us ten to one."

"The first thing we have to do tonight is cut through that net and get upstream." Turning to Cadiz he suggested, "Why don't you move the boat back to a safe distance and Santos and I will take one of the dugouts and try to cut through the net. From what I could see, Elijah and Mann got a good start by hacking through several of the vines. We need to cut through that heavier top strand to break it apart."

"So we get through the net and move upstream, then what? How do we plan to rescue Elijah and Mann?" Patterson asked. "Even with our Winchester repeaters, a frontal attack on the village would be suicide…especially against those damn blowguns."

"I do know we have to attempt a rescue and we've got to figure a way to do it."

Santos offered a suggestion. "The Jivaros will probably have a big celebration tonight with heavy drinking so we need to wait until the early morning hours while most of the Jivaros are still sleeping. I might be able to sneak into the village and find out where they are keeping Elijah and Mann. I'll attempt to free them while the rest of you cover me with the rifles."

"Worth a try," Simon concurred, "and I'll go with you."

With the dugouts back on shore, a group of twenty Jivaros

roughly pushed and shoved Elijah and Mann along the well-worn path toward the village. Their wrists were tightly bound. The stares and expressions from the village inhabitants portrayed a mixture of curiosity and hostility. It was apparent the invaders were not welcome. As they approached the outskirts of the village, Elijah noticed the strange tall apparatus towering above them from a small clearing. "What's that thing?" he whispered to Mann.

"You don't want to know," he answered with alarm. "I'll tell you when we can talk."

The two Americans were pushed into a crudely made thatched hut backed up against the heavy jungle vegetation at the rear of the village. Two stoutly built guards took positions at the doorway.

With their wrists still bound, the captives tried as best they could to make themselves as comfortable as possible on the rough woven mats that covered the dirt floor. "What the hell was that weird looking structure we saw in the clearing? What's it used for?"

The structure Elijah was referring to was comprised of two parallel spaced medium sized tree trunks that were bent together until they touched at the top. The bases of the two trunks were spaced about twenty feet apart. Two sturdy strands of heavy woven cable were attached to two large reel-like objects positioned on the ground to either side of each tree. With the use of a heavy crank, the reels wound the cables that would pull the trunks together. Near the top of each trunk, two vertically spaced heavy rings were seen protruding from the wood.

Mann hesitated for a moment and then replied with a tone of despair. "I've never actually seen one before but I've heard several stories about them. That contraption is called a jebero. It's a very nasty device they use to execute a prisoner. A victim is lifted high into the air and bound to each tree trunk by his wrists and ankles… sometimes upside down. The cables are then released, allowing the trees to spring back to their upright position. The force will split a man apart or equally bad is the possibility that his arms and legs will be torn from his body, allowing the limbless frame to fall to the ground and bleed to death. That's when they cut off the head and shrink it."

Elijah groaned despairingly. "And I thought that wheel blade trap we encountered in the Yucatan pyramid was bad. At least it was a quick death. This damn thing makes that blade look like a child's toy."

The windowless hut was hot and stuffy and both men could not find a comfortable position with their wrists bound tightly behind their backs. "What a hell of a mess we're in." Elijah conceded.

Suddenly Mann let out a loud groan. "What's the matter?" Elijah asked.

"That hideous thing…hanging from the ceiling…above your head!"

Elijah looked up. "What is it?

There were three small objects dangling from the ceiling above Elijah's head. They were hanging by what appeared to be strands of human hair. "They're shrunken heads…and one of them…one of them looks like Radford's head."

"How can you tell?"

"It has lighter skin…and lighter hair. I'd swear it belongs to Radford."

"Oh, shit! If we don't figure out a way to get out of here soon our heads will probably be hanging next to them," Elijah groaned.

Even though darkness had descended, sleep was impossible as they sat in silence trying to figure a way to escape. From the outside they heard drums begin a steady rhythmic pounding and loud chants and screams started arising from the Jivaros. Elijah glanced at the doorway. "What's that all about?"

"Sounds like the savage bastards are starting their ceremony of victory. They'll start drinking and work themselves into a mad frenzy to celebrate our capture."

"And then what?

"When they're ready they'll probably string us up to that jebero in the morning."

17

Aboard the Caribe

SIMON AND SANTOS CROUCHED IN THE dugout using machetes to hack and slice through the remaining vines and saplings that held the net blockade together. The sounds of the drums, loud screams, and chants from the village muffled the sound of the machetes. Luckily, the Indians had not left sentries behind to watch the net. Santos stood on the seat and stretched upward as he swung the blade for a final cut through the top strand supporting the net. The sapling frame split apart and the net parted and then settled into the river, swinging downstream with the current. The river was now open.

They quietly paddled the dugout back to the Caribe where the deckhands retrieved the boat and secured it in the stern section of the steamer. Captain Cadiz throttled the engine and steered the boat upstream through the breach to a safe distance above the village. The incessant drum beats and chants from the village became louder and continued to muffle any sounds from the passing steamer, confirming the Jivaros were engaged in a huge celebration. Having reached a respectable distance upstream, the anchor was lowered and the Caribe held fast in the center of the river. Cadiz approached Simon and Patterson. "I know you want to rescue your friends, so what is your plan? My men and I will help anyway we can."

"By the sounds coming from the village, the Jivaros are having a hell of a party going on…hopefully, with lots of drinking. In a few hours they should be pretty well stoned and most of them soundly asleep. We'll wait until just before dawn, then Santos and I will slip into the village and find out where Elijah and Mann are being held. Robert, you, Stafford, Roper, and Scott will cover us at the edge of the jungle with your Winchesters. Hopefully, we'll find them quick enough and be able to get them back to the dugouts before they are discovered missing. Captain, I'll need two of your crew to guard the dugouts and help us paddle back to the boat. You'll need to have the Caribe ready to move up-river quickly when we return. I'm sure Elijah and Mann will be well guarded so Santos and I will have to use some stealth to dispose of any guards." He held up a sleek Bowie knife to illustrate his point. "This whole rescue operation will be very risky, but we've got no choice."

Just before sunrise, Simon and Santos slipped quietly through the jungle, working their way toward the rear of the village while their companions spread out and took concealed positions in the dense vegetation at the edge of the perimeter. It didn't take much searching for Santos to locate the hut where the prisoners were kept…the guards positioned at the opening revealed it. "What do you suggest?" Simon whispered quietly.

"I'll sneak around to the back of the hut and see if I can cut an opening large enough to enter. You keep an eye on those two Jivaros guarding the front. If they hear me I'll probably have to use my revolver and hopefully Patterson and the others can cover us while we free them."

The skies became lighter as dawn approached and streaks of light filtered through the trees. Santos prepared to move out when a big commotion erupted in the village—a group of four Jivaros approached the hut housing the prisoners. Santos stopped…big trouble, he thought. The men said a few words to the guards and then entered the doorway. Moments later they exited with Elijah firmly secured between two of the warriors and surrounded by the others. Simon raised his rifle but hesitated. He needed to find out their intentions. The Jivaros shoved and pushed Elijah toward the tall strange looking contraption in the clearing. "What the hell is that thing?" he whispered.

"I've never seen one before but have heard about them," Santos recalled. "Some of the Amazon Indians use these structures to execute prisoners. I believe they call it a jebero. They draw the trunks together and then fasten a man's arms and legs to those rings. Then they release the cables to allow the trunks to spring apart and rip a man's body in half…a horrible way to die."

Simon watched with intense alarm as four warriors pushed and dragged the struggling hostage toward the menacing looking frame. More commotion followed as four more Jivaros appeared and hauled Sergeant Mann from the hut and toward the clearing. Small knots of villagers began to emerge from the huts and gathered to watch the proceedings. The village was coming alive. Somewhere at the edge of the clearing a drum began a steady pounding and the onlookers began a soft chant. The macabre show was about to begin.

Elijah was hauled onto a small bamboo platform accompanied by two muscular Jivaros. Ropes extended from hooks at the top of the trunks and were attached to each corner of the scaffold. On the ground and from each side strong arms began to pull the ropes that started lifting the platform slowly into the air. Elijah's expression betrayed total resignation and distress as the crescendo from the onlooker's chants got louder. He knew he was about to die a horrible death.

Simon whispered, "We have to take out the ones pulling the ropes before that platform gets too high in the air. Elijah's hands are bound so we can't allow it to rise any further. I'll take out the ones to the left and you take the right…now!"

He sighted his Winchester on one of the Jivaros heaving the rope and fired. The .44 slug caught him in the shoulder and threw him to the side. A second shot hit another in the head, dropping him immediately. Santos fired at another man and hit him in the rib cage, spinning him to the ground and another was dropped with a slug through his hip and slamming down into his groin area. The ropes sprung free, causing the platform to suddenly tilt toward the ground. The two Jivaros holding Elijah slid from the scaffold and dropped to the ground with Elijah sprawled on top, breaking his fall.

From the edge of the clearing, Patterson, Stafford, Roper, and Scott opened up with their Winchesters, taking down three warriors holding Mann and two more rushing toward Elijah. Many of the spectators had rushed to the far side of the village to escape the fusillade of bullets from the repeaters. In the confusion that followed, Santos rushed toward Elijah to free his wrists while Simon sprinted over to Mann. One Jivaros swung a large axe at Simon, barely missing his shoulder. Simon was able to react by swinging the butt of his rifle upward, catching the man in the face. He fell to the ground with blood gushing from his nose and mouth. Simon reached Mann and quickly sliced through his bindings with the Bowie knife, freeing his arms. "Here, take my revolver!" Simon shouted. Mann grabbed it and turned in time to fire at another Jivaros charging them. He dropped with a bullet to the chest. As Santos was cutting Elijah's bindings, three Jivaros closed in fast. Simon and Mann moved quickly to their left to intercept them. Several small groups of the Indians had emerged from their huts with their pucunas poised, looking for a target. They spotted the four Americans in the clearing. One poison dart whizzed by Elijah's head and lodged into the tree trunk beside him. Another missed Santos by inches, burying into the ground next to his foot.

Patterson saw the danger and directed his companions to concentrate on the Jivaros with the blowguns. Six were dropped before they could aim their tubes. One Jivaros leaped onto Simon's back and pummeled his head with flying fists while two more dove for Mann's legs. The ensuing melee was a heap of entangled limbs swinging and pounding furiously at each other. Elijah and Santos quickly intervened and flattened one man with a rifle butt and another with the heel of his Remington. Another Indian kicked Simon in the stomach, dropping him to his knees, gasping for air. Before the warrior could swing his axe, Mann shot him in the face. Elijah, sensing a momentary pause in the fighting, pulled

Simon to his feet, and with Santos supporting his other arm, they began scurrying toward the edge of the clearing where the other Americans were located. Luckily, Santos had snatched Simon's rifle from the ground. While Patterson, Stafford, and Roper were concentrating on the men with the pucunas, Professor Scott happened to glance at one particular warrior pursuing the fleeing men. His axe was poised ready to strike the first victim he could reach—he was within an arm's length of Elijah's head, arm raised for the swipe. Scott calmly sighted his Winchester and pulled the trigger. The .44 caliber slug hit him squarely between the eyes, splattering part of his head to the side. He was dead before he hit the ground. The four men reached the safety of the forest, and with Patterson leading, quickly made their way back toward the dugouts at the river's edge. They knew the incensed Jivaros would not be far behind.

18

Aboard the Amazonia

"Mon Dieu! What's going on over there?" Devereaux shouted to Marcel as he approached the bow railing. "Sounds like a war with all the gunshots."

"I would imagine our American friends are in the process of rescuing their companions," the Brazilian answered as he lowered his spyglass.

"Do you think we should assist them?"

"Do you want to confront a couple of hundred angry Jivaros with those damn blowguns?"

"No."

"I thought not. We'll wait here and see what happens. I saw the Caribe pass through the barricade earlier and anchor up-river, so now I know we can pass through the breach easily."

It did not take the Americans long to reach the riverbank and the waiting dugouts. The shouts and screams behind confirmed a swarm of infuriated Indians trailing close behind. "Into the boats...quick!" Simon shouted. "The bastards are right on our heels!"

The eight Americans and two crew members piled into the three boats and began paddling frantically toward the waiting Caribe. Stafford, Roper, and Scott faced to the rear of each boat with rifles poised. The dugouts were forty yards from the shore when streams of screaming Jivaros spilled out onto the riverbank. Fortunately, the two Caribe crew members, Paulo and Fabio, who had been guarding the boats, had taken the precaution of smashing a hole in the bottom of the remaining twelve boats to prevent the Indians from pursuing the escapees across the water. Several Jivaros drew pucuncas to their mouth to release their deadly poison darts when Scott shouted, "The ones with the blowguns… take them down first!"

The three Americans opened up with the Winchesters and saw three Jivaros drop their pucuncas and fall to the ground. Several darts were released by other blowers and fell harmlessly into the water around the fleeing dugs. Several barbs imbedded into the sides of the boats but luckily no one was hit. "Paddle faster!" Elijah shouted. Slowly the distance increased. The men in the rear kept up their stream of fire, dropping several other assailants to the ground. Paulo felt a sharp sting in his neck and reached frantically to pull the dart from his skin. With an expression of total disbelief, the young crewman tried to stand but his legs wouldn't push him up. Numbness ascended over him and he quickly lost consciousness and tumbled over the side into the water. "Grab him!" Patterson shouted.

Stafford started to react and then stopped. "Too late…let him go…he's gone." The lifeless body drifted slowly away with the current.

Realizing the fleeing boats were now out of range, the Jivaros rushed to their dugouts to find the hulls smashed and unusable. The frenzied shouts and screams from the riverbank clearly communicated their rage and frustration. The Americans finally reached the safety of the Caribe and out of range from the deadly darts. Cadiz was poised in the wheelhouse as the remaining three crewmen assisted getting the escapees and dugouts aboard the steamship. The drive shaft was engaged and the paddlewheel began to move the Caribe forward, picking up speed as it steamed its way up the Madeira and away from the village. Simon, Elijah, Mann, and Patterson gathered in the wheelhouse with Cadiz who was anxious to hear more about the capture and escape.

"Hell of a close call," Elijah said. "I thought I was a goner on that ghastly tree contraption. Mann said it was called a jebero... will split a man in half...right up the middle. In another minute I would have been split in two like a cored apple and my head hanging from the ceiling like that other white man's head we saw."

"You saw a shrunken head from a white man?" Patterson asked curiously.

Mann answered for him, "Yes, we saw a shrunken head and I'd swear it belonged to Radford. I'm sure of it."

"Well, now I guess we know what happened to Radford. What about Dunn...was his head hanging with him?"

"No. There were two other heads...all natives with black hair. Dunn's head might be hanging in another hut though."

Elijah rubbed his neck gently, thinking about what might have been. "Thanks to all of you for saving our lives," he acknowledged appreciatively. Sergeant Mann echoed his remarks.

"Nothing to it...besides, we didn't want to have to carry you back to the boat in several pieces."

Elijah responded with a nervous but unconvincing attempt at a laugh. "Hope we don't run into those bastards again."

Aboard the Amazonia

Marcel watched through his spyglass at the bizarre scene taking place at the river's edge. The Americans had made it back to the Caribe and the steamer began to move forward. He turned to Devereaux. "It looks like they made their escape and now they're moving up river. It's time to crank it up." He rushed off to the wheelhouse with the Frenchman following.

"What's the plan?"

"The net is free so we'll let the Caribe get out of sight and then steam through as fast as this boat will take us. I don't want any confrontation with those damn Jivaros. Anyway, it looks like most of them have moved back to their village...probably to gather up their dead. We'll maintain our distance and keep following the Caribe. Those are our instructions."

On the lower deck, Claudio was furious. He kept screaming obscenities in Portuguese…none of which the Frenchmen understood. "Dammit ao inferno!" He bellowed. "I can't believe those American pigs got away. Those Indians should have killed them and saved us the trouble."

The two mercenaries accompanying Marcel were standing on deck and understood Claudio's blustering shouts. While somewhat amused, they were getting tired of his constant ranting and griping. One of the mercenaries, a hired assassin named Gustavo from Argentina, yelled, "Claudio, why don't you just shut the hell up and quit acting like an idiot. All you are doing is aggravating everyone. You'll have your chance for revenge."

Claudio knew of Gustavo's reputation and wanted no confrontation with him so he stopped his yelling and went off to the stern deck to sulk.

Aboard the Caribe

With Captain Cadiz at the wheel, the Caribe steadily streamed up-river past several small villages settled along the banks. Some of the inhabitants watched with a mixture of curiosity and hostility as the steamer passed by. A few unrecognizable shouts and screams were tossed their way, most likely warning the intruders they were not wanted. Some of the younger, more aggressive men threw spears at the boat but they fell harmlessly into the water. A couple even took their blowguns and blew darts toward the steamer. Two darts imbedded into the wooden hull but the rest disappeared into the current. Cadiz was careful to hold the Caribe to the middle of the river.

Simon, Elijah, and the guide, Raphael, were talking at the aft deck railing when Patterson approached. "Seen any sign of that boat that was following us?"

Simon glanced to the rear. "No sign of her yet. Maybe it turned around or maybe the Jivaros captured it."

"Don't count on it," Patterson countered. "Captain Cadiz said if Marcel is on that boat they would not have turned back. The man is a trained professional killer…a bad son-of-a-bitch. We'd better keep a watchful eye to our stern." His companions nodded.

"Raphael," Simon asked, turning to the young guide, "Captain Cadiz can only take us a few miles further up the Madeira. How do you suggest we proceed…do you have a route in mind once we leave the Caribe?"

"Yes, sir. The Madeira takes a sharp turn to the south then becomes the Mamoré River. It is much smaller. Here we'll have to leave the Caribe and transfer to the dugouts. We will need to travel south about fifty kilometers to a village called Villa Bella. Here, another river called the Madre de Dios branches to the west and several kilometers later it forks into two rivers, the Madre de Dios and the Beni. The Madre de Dios continues due west toward Peru and the Beni branches more southward into Bolivia. Here is where we have to make a big decision…to continue west or turn to the southwest on the Beni River and toward the La Paz Region."

Roper interrupted. "The Chibcha Indian told our guide, Mapi, that he thought the city was located somewhere in the mountains between the Madre de Dios and the La Paz region of Bolivia. It sounds to me like it makes more sense to continue west on the Madre de Dios that takes us to the mountains just to the south of Cuzco."

Raphael continued, "There is a small river that branches off from the Madre de Dios and moves in a southwestern direction toward the area we are probably looking for. I believe it's called the Tambopata. It should allow us a bit more travel time in the boats and put us out just north of Lake Titicaca.

"That sounds good to me," Simon concurred. "We'll paddle as far as we can then strike out on foot into the jungle."

"How much river do we have before we walk?" Elijah asked.

"From Villa Bella about 300 kilometers."

Simon replied, making the kilometer conversion to miles in his head. "Good grief! That's about 185 miles of paddling."

"The current is very light so the paddling won't be too bad," Raphael assured them. "About four or five days."

"Any hostile Indians on the river?" Patterson asked.

"We'll pass a couple of small villages but I don't expect any problem with the natives…most of the bad guys are behind us. It's the caiman and other animals we should worry about. Also, the stream is infested with devilfish."

"Devilfish?"

"Yes, piranha. It's full of red-bellied piranha and some black piranha. The black species can get up to 8 pounds. You don't want to fall into that stream and run into those guys." Elijah rolled his eyes.

The remainder of the voyage up the Madeira was uneventful and reassuringly, there was no sign of the small steamer following them. Perhaps they had turned back, they hoped…but most likely not.

The Caribe finally came to a stop near a small village called Abunã. They reached a bend of the Madeira where the little steamer could go no further and had arrived at the spot where the team would have to transfer to the three dugouts. The group now consisted of the eight Americans plus Raphael, the guide. Three occupants per boat would be manageable. With the equipment assembled and the dugouts in the water, Captain Cadiz met the team on the deck. "Gentlemen, it has been a pleasure working with you. I wish you a safe journey and should you find that city you are looking for—you know how I can be reached in Belém."

"Thank you, Captain, for taking us this far," Simon responded. "If we find it, we'll fulfill our bargain. I'm concerned about your return trip back down the Madeira. You might have a problem with Marcel and the boat following us."

"They have no quarrel with me—I am just a boat for hire," Cadiz reassured him. "If they question me I'll just tell them I could go no further than Porto Velho and had to put you ashore there. With my reputation in Belém, I don't think Marcel will give me much trouble."

Simon handed Cadiz a small bag of gold coins. "Here's an extra tip for bringing us this far up-river. We are in your debt, sir."

The captain nodded his appreciation as his passengers loaded into the dugouts. The expedition team could no longer rely on the safety of the steamer. With mixed emotions they sullenly watched the Caribe make its turn for the return trip back down river—they were now on their own.

Simon and Patterson were well aware the continuing journey would be very dangerous. They knew full well the Amazon jungle had claimed many lives over the years and held many lost skeletons within the bosom of her miles of dense forests and undergrowth. They were counting on Raphael to remember the correct routes through the jungle.

Captain Cadiz steered the steamer toward the middle of the Amazon to avoid any sandbars. He tensed as he watched another small steamer approach from the northeast. That murderer, Marcel, he thought with apprehension. As the craft came closer, Cadiz recognized it as the Amazonia. He knew the boat belonged to Marcel. He called his first mate and instructed him to arm himself and the remaining three crewmen…and stay under cover. Cadiz maneuvered the boat to the right side of the river hoping the Amazonia would pass by without incident, but he shuddered when he saw the opposing craft veer sharply toward him to cut him off. He would have to confront Marcel.

With the Amazonia blocking his progress, Cadiz shouted across to the dark skinned man staring at him from the bow. "Marcel, what the hell are you doing?"

"Sorry, Leandro," Marcel shouted with a sneer. "All I need is some information."

"What do you want?"

"Your passengers…the Americanos…where did you take them? And where are they now?"

Cadiz observed the two rough looking men standing beside Marcel, holding raised rifles.

"They were paid passengers who wanted to explore the river. Why do you ask?"

"I have no quarrel with you, Leandro. My employer has an

interest in the Americanos and wants me to find them and make them a bargain."

Cadiz saw through the lie immediately. "I carried them as far as this boat could go and put them ashore just past Porto Velho. They took the dugouts but I also heard them say something about a trek overland through the jungle toward the highlands."

"Which highlands?"

"They didn't say but I would guess the Madre de Dios and then probably up toward Peru…into the Ucayali region. They didn't tell me their plans. I think they were searching for something."

Marcel nodded. "Okay, Leandro, you may continue your journey back to Belém…but remember, if you are lying to me I know where to find you."

Cadiz was relieved to see the Amazonia pull away and pass by. He was intrigued to see four non-Hispanic men lining the rail watching him, most likely foreigners by the clothes they wore. Their expressions convinced him these were not men to anger.

19

As Marcel and his two mercenaries watched the Caribe disappear around a bend, Devereaux approached him with a concerned look. "What did the captain say? Where are the Americans?"

"He said he took them as far as the village of Porto Vehlo. They unloaded the dugouts so I would imagine they are paddling upstream as far as they can go and then plan to ditch the boats and then start walking. Cadiz told me he didn't know where they were going but guessed into the Madre de Dios region toward the Peruvian highlands."

"Do you believe him?"

"Not entirely, but I don't think they would have divulged their plans to him. I'm sure they are probably paddling up the Madeira in the dugouts and with our shallow draft I think we can overtake them." Marcel turned toward the wheelhouse…he would need to crank up more steam.

Well to the southwest and paddling down the Mamoré, Simon and his party pushed against the current trying to put as much distance as possible between them and the Madeira. With the light current and three men paddling in each boat, they were moving at a steady pace. Simon knew their pursuers would be in hot pursuit and steaming up the river as fast as the Amazonia would go. Captain Cadiz had mentioned the Amazonia had a shallow draft which meant they could easily steam to the mouth of the Mamoré and perhaps even further. Marcel knew the Americans had dugouts and was convinced they would have turned south on the smaller Mamoré when he saw that the Madeira terminated into a series of small streams and tributaries. Simon was also aware the pursuers had dugouts as well and would have to transfer to the smaller craft in order to continue the chase. He had observed them through his glass. His biggest concern, however, was the possibility they could navigate the Mamoré with the faster Amazonia and catch up to them.

Raphael occupied a seat in the first boat—his job was to spot the village of Villa Bella and the smaller Madre de Dios River that veered off to the west. Hopefully, this tributary would carry them many miles into the interior where they would find a spot to abandon the dugouts and continue on foot. Simon was satisfied that Raphael knew what he was doing…at least he hoped so. Their young guide insisted the village was no more than 75 kilometers from the Madeira. Sergeant Mann figured it would be about a forty-five mile paddle up the Mamoré until they hit the cutoff… not too bad of a run for the three dugouts and nine occupants. Luckily, the Amazon monsoon season prevalent for this time of year had not yet arrived and the current was relatively slow.

Professor Scott was in the second boat and motioned for the rowers to paddle gently but continue the forward momentum. He held his finger over his mouth conveying to the group to be silent. He pointed to an exposed sandbar next to the far bank. Three large dark logs were spread across the sand—one of them moved and opened his eyes. The beast slid silently into the water and the large wake revealed it was headed straight for the dugouts.

"Black Caiman," Scott shouted loudly. "They must be fourteen or fifteen feet long…huge reptilian monsters!"

Simon shouted. "Bend those paddles and move these boats! Quickly!" The dugouts coursed forward and the creature following them did the same.

The trailing dugout took the hard impact, pushing the craft nearly out of the water. The dug tilted heavily to the side but Elijah, Santos, and Mann managed to hold on, shifting their weights toward the impact to allow the boat to stabilize. The caiman rolled under the boat and turned to make another pass. From the sand bar the other creatures slid into the water and moved toward the disturbance. "Use your revolvers." Scott shouted from the second boat. "Try to hit him between the eyes."

The huge reptile approached the boat swiftly, intending to use his bulk to upend it and spill the occupants into the water. His head was barely above the surface, his rows of teeth slightly visible. While Santos and Mann used their paddles to stabilize the dugout, Elijah aimed his Remington at the reptile's eyes. The stillness of the river was shattered by booming gunshots as he pumped a half dozen .44 slugs into the caiman's head. It dropped below the surface and the three men frantically looked to each side. "Move those paddles!" Elijah shouted. "Get the hell out of here! I see his friends coming toward us."

The men dug their oars into the water and pulled with all their strength—the dugout surged forward. "Where the hell is he?" Simon yelled. "Brace yourselves and get ready for another collision!"

In their wake, close behind, a heavy turbulence of spray and froth erupted as hundreds of silvery darts engulfed the thrashing reptile. The blood from the bullet wounds had attracted a school of red-bellied piranhas that swarmed all over the beast, snapping and biting at anything their razor-sharp teeth could tear apart. To add to the melee, with gaping jaws displaying more deadly rows of sharp teeth, the other two reptiles lunged into the mass, tearing chunks of meat and tissue from the carcass and decimating scores of the devilfish as well. The churning, chaotic maelstrom was left behind as the three dugouts rounded a bend. "That was close," Elijah grumbled gratefully. "The scaly bastard nearly got us. This stinking river is the devil's playground."

Soon the young guide, Raphael, stood and pointed to a ribbon of smoke rising in the distance. He shouted, "Villa Bella... just ahead. And there is the Madre de Dios that forks to the west."

"Yes!" Roper confirmed. "I remember this is the tributary we took and it carried us well into the interior. This is the river that flows out of the Andes Mountains."

Raphael remarked, "And about 400 kilometers further is where the Tambopata River branches off to the south."

Professor Scott did some quick figuring in his head. "I hate to tell you but that is about 250 miles."

The village of Villa Bella was small and consisted of a few thatched huts and a small thatched roof long-house, most likely used by the natives for tribal gatherings. A few women were observed squatting over campfires preparing the evening meal while several children could be seen playing in the clearing. The scene looked harmless enough. The tributary cut sharply to the right, indicating another one of the hundreds of streams feeding into the Madeira and then on to the Amazon. Though small compared to the Madeira, the new river looked navigable enough with the dugouts. The paddlers turned the three boats into the stream.

Aboard the Amazonia

To the north, at the mouth of the Mamoré, Marcel slowed the Amazonia to get his bearings. Devereaux was standing next to him with the spyglass. "What now?" he asked. "It looks like the river takes a sharp bend to the south."

"It turns into the Mamoré here. They would have had to take this river south. Nothing to the west looks navigable."

"Wouldn't this take them further away from Peru?"

"Yes…but maybe they aren't going to Peru. Maybe more toward Bolivia…or the southern Peruvian border. I'm sure Captain Cadiz was lying about dropping them off at Porto Velho. He could have navigated much further upstream than that. This boat has a much shallower draft than the Caribe and I think I can handle the Mamoré…at least for several kilometers. We'll go as far as we can and then find a spot upstream to hide the boat and switch to the dugouts. The Americanos can't be too far ahead."

Claudio stood quietly in the background listening to the conversation. His cold eyes burned with hate and revenge. Marcel's last remark brought a cruel sneer to his mouth.

The small steamer steered around the bend and slowly began the journey up the Mamoré. The last thing Marcel needed was to get stuck on a sandbar. He proceeded cautiously.

The Americans made good time up the narrow Madre de Dios tributary, noticing the banks were lined with impenetrable jungle growth mixed with small marshes and bogs. The heat was stifling with clouds of swarming mosquitoes and insufferable bugs—not a good mix of terrain and conditions to attempt to walk through. They would navigate the river as long as possible and hope it would carry them to a higher elevation. As the dugouts rounded a bend they heard loud splashes and a funny squeal from in the partially submerged high grasses that lined the far bank. "What is that?" Patterson shouted.

Raphael laughed. "Water hogs! Capybara!"

"I see them. Two of them. They look like huge rats," Stafford yelled.

"Actually, they are kin to rats. I am told they are the largest animals in the rodent family. They can get up to two feet tall and weigh up to a hundred pounds. Those two you see are probably sixty or seventy pounds. They are normally shy of humans and won't bother us unless you corner one with their young."

Sensing the motion of the boats passing by, the large rodents disappeared under the water.

"We need to find a place to camp so look for some higher ground and one that has some partial clearing. We don't need any cats sneaking up on us in the middle of the night."

"What kind of cats?" Mann asked curiously.

"We have several wild cats in South America: ocelots, jaguars, and pumas, often called cougars. I believe in North America you call them mountain lions. The ocelots are small and probably won't bother us, but the jaguars and pumas are the big ones we need to watch for, especially at night. That's when they like to stalk for food."

Professor Scott couldn't stand it any longer. He interrupted. "Jaguars and pumas were revered by the Mesoamerican Indians, mainly the Incas, Mayans, and Aztecs. They even considered them sacred and included them in many religious ceremonies. As you remember, the city of Cuzco was designed and patterned in the shape of the puma. The head of the cat was represented by the fortress of Sacsahuaman, the heart by the main square of Huacaypata, and the tail by the convergence of the Huatanay and Tullumayo Rivers."

"Thanks for the reminder, professor," Simon remarked with a hint of annoyance in his voice. At the moment he wasn't in the mood for another history lesson. Then he thought, how the hell did he remember all of that stuff?

As they approached a series of bends in the river, Raphael pointed to a far bank. "Here is a good spot to camp. The ground looks slightly elevated and might be high enough to keep the caimans from climbing up the bank. Let's stop here."

There were no objections. The constant paddling had exhausted the group and they were ready for a break and decent night's sleep, if that was possible.

"As we have enough to worry about with pumas, jaguars, and oversized rats…now we have to worry about those damn big crocodiles crawling in our bunks," Elijah groaned.

"Actually, that's not all," Roper informed them. "This jungle is full of coral snakes, pit vipers, bushmasters, fer-de-lances, and twenty or so other poisonous snakes that can curl up in your bunk…not to mention the poison dart frog."

"What the hell is that?" Elijah asked.

"That's the nasty little creature that provides the natives the deadly poison they put on the dart tips for the blowguns. They also dip their darts in a deadly poison made from the curare plant. The jungles of Central and South America are full of poisonous things… so you have to be very careful what you touch, eat, or step on."

"I can see we're going to sleep well tonight."

Before turning in, Elijah turned to Simon and Professor Scott, and brought up the subject of their experience in the Yucatan and their first encounter with the alien space ship hibernating in the cavern near the city of Xepocotec. "Simon, there's something

I forgot to tell you about that flying ship we discovered in the Yucatan cave—the one we named the TOLTEC."

Simon looked at him, a surprised expression on his face. "What?"

"Do you remember that logbook we found in the command center...the one that had the strange metallic pages with all the strange writing and glyphs? It had those drawings of the Roman weapons and architectural designs?"

"Yeah, I remember it. It was lost when the Toltec exploded over the Atlantic."

"Well...not quite. I stuck it in my shirt when we were forced off the ship and I still have it."

"You what?"

"When I got home I put it in a drawer and forgot all about it. That's where it's been for the past eight years. When I left for Washington the other day I found it and put it in my bag and have it with me now. I thought it might come in handy."

Simon rolled his eyes in disbelief while Professor Scott muttered a funny wheezing sound at the prospects of another incredible discovery.

"We can't read the darn thing anyway," Elijah reminded him. "It's all written in that funny language with those weird symbols."

"Professor," Simon asked, directing his remark to Scott, "you know something about glyphs...maybe you can interpret some of the language in that logbook."

"I can't wait to see it. Maybe we can find a link between your logbook and the coin and scroll Mr. Patterson has. As you remember, I did finally translate the Atlantean scrolls that Elijah confiscated in the sunken city of Lythe, where we met Commander Ahular and the other explorers. Perhaps there is some sort of connection there. The Atlanteans were a great sea faring and advanced civilization. That logbook might reveal some connection to Atlantis as well."

Aboard the Amazonia

Marcel stopped his boat at the mouth of the Mamoré River...

he was certain this was the route the Americans had taken in the dugouts. He knew that the rivers located further to the south and branching from the Mamoré would head in a more south to southwesterly direction and away from the mountains and the coast. He was convinced this had to be the right river so he turned the Amazonia to the southwest and continued the chase. Surprisingly, the draft of his boat was shallow enough to continue navigating along the Mamoré —he would take advantage of this as long as possible to catch up with the Americans with their slower dugouts. The river took many sharp turns and bends and Marcel had to be very careful to avoid the sandbars that lined the banks. Although he had to slow his speed considerably, he would continue to push as far as he could. He was certain the Americans were not far ahead.

20

Early afternoon the Americans reached the fork in the Madre de Dios where it intersected with the Beni River. They were rounding a broad bend when the strange noise was heard. Elijah was the first to react. "What is that sound?" he shouted from the rear seat of the dugout.

The noise was coming from Simon's backpack stored under the front seat. He retrieved the pack and pulled out the small box containing the zenox. A green light was blinking rapidly and a small thin rod shot out from the porcelain-like surface.

"That thing is acting up again. What do you suppose is making it do that?" Elijah asked.

"I think it's trying to tell us something," Simon responded apprehensively.

He held the device to his front and moved it horizontally from left to right. The intensity of the sound decreased as he rotated it and then increased as he moved it back around to a northwesterly position. "I think it's signaling a direction. It gets stronger when you point it toward those trees."

Professor Scott, who through his experience and training in archeological digs, had a keen eye for the unusual. He pointed to a vague shape covered by dense vegetation. "That gadget of yours is pointing to the foliage surrounding that small clearing over there. I think it might be something of interest and we should check it out."

Aboard the Amazonia

It was late the third day when the Amazonia came to a point on the Mamoré where the river became too shallow to navigate. Through

Marcel's misjudgment, he steered the Amazonia too close to the left bank and became firmly stuck on a sandbar concealed just below the surface. The sudden stop sent Devereaux and several others sprawling to the deck. Marcel's voice boomed an obscenity that was heard throughout the boat as Devereaux pulled himself up and rushed to the wheelhouse. Marcel was frantically trying to reverse the engines in an attempt to back off the bar. His efforts failed—the Amazonia was firmly stuck. "What do we do now?" Devereaux shouted in disgust.

Marcel glared at him and roared back. "We get our asses into those dugouts and paddle!"

He knew the group of eight men would fit easily into three dugouts. Their equipment and supplies were assembled and three boats were lowered into the river. Marcel and his two mercenaries, Gustavo and Felipe, would occupy one boat, Devereaux, Allard, and Jacques the second, and Bruno and Claudio the third, mainly because the latter two were the largest and heaviest of the group. Bruno turned to Marcel and declared. "Tell that loud mouthed son-of-a-bitch, Claudio, if he makes one sound I'll tear his head off and throw him overboard."

Marcel laughed. "I'll let you tell him."

The boats reached the village of Villa Bella where the Madre de Dios split off to the west. The Americans would have most likely taken this fork but he was not certain—he needed proof. He turned to Gustavo in the rear of the dugout. "We need to know which way the Americans went. Let's paddle close to that village and you shout to one of the natives along the bank and ask which way the other dugouts traveled. I'm sure someone saw them." He reached into his backpack and pulled out a small flask of rum. "Hold this up in the air…this should loosen a tongue or two. I'm sure they must understand enough Portuguese to communicate… and throw the flask to the first one that gives us the information."

Several of the villagers stood along the bank watching the small boats when Gustavo shouted his request. He waved the flask high in the air. Two of the men must have known what the object was because they both frantically pointed to the smaller tributary. Gustavo tossed the flask toward the two natives and watched briefly as they both scrambled for it. He turned before he could observe the winner. Now with the confirming news, the boats turned into the Madre de Dios River.

As the Americans paddled their boats toward the bank, the obscure structure was vaguely visible at the far edge of the clearing. It was understandably covered with a thick matting of vines and other vegetation. The building was built of neatly laid stone blocks and the ruins appeared to be in relatively good shape, barring the crumbling effects of age. Scott, whose curiosity was normally aroused at anything smelling of antiquity, commented, "That building looks much like those constructed by the Mayans or Incas. It has to be very old. Let's find an entrance."

The boats were pulled from the water and beached on the higher ground near a tangle of bushes and vines. "Try to conceal them as best as possible," Simon instructed. "If we are being followed we don't want anyone to find the dugs and punch holes in them. We would really be in big trouble then."

The stone structure was an enclosed single story building without any signs of windows or open wall spaces. Santos found the small doorway near the center obscured by a heavy covering of vines. With the machete, he was able to cut an opening large enough for each of them to slip inside. Patterson left Stafford and Roper to keep watch on the outside while the remaining six men crawled through the doorway into the dark interior. To Professor Scott, it was if he had entered a stygian cavity…dark, damp, and emitting a heavy musty smell indicating that fresh air circulation had been absent for a very long time. This only aroused his curiosity even more.

"We need some torches," Patterson suggested. "We can't see much in this semi-darkness."

Santos looked at Simon. "We didn't think to bring torches. I can slip outside and make some but it will take a few minutes."

"I think I can solve that problem," Scott offered as he reached into his pack and retrieved two small metal objects.

"What are those things?" Patterson asked.

"These are oil lanterns that burn a refined mineral oil. I used these in Peru when Robert Drake and I explored a cavern behind a waterfall. They illuminate quite well from a single wick and small reflective mirror. I thought they would come in handy if we ended up in a cave somewhere, so I brought them along."

Simon chuckled. "I thought you lost those lanterns in that cavern beneath the old Inca fortress in the Andes."

"Nope, I was somehow able to hold on to them and brought them back with me.

"Well, let's light one and see what we have here in these old ruins," Elijah said, reaching into his pack and retrieving a match.

Scott's small lantern surprised everyone as to how well the single wick and mirror device illuminated and reflected light around the room. "Quite impressive," Patterson conceded. "I never saw one of those gadgets before."

"An archeologist friend of mine back at the museum built these lanterns. He said they would come in handy someday—an understatement, I might add. Each lamp will last about two hours before a refill and I did bring a can of extra oil along. Never can tell when you'll get caught in the dark."

The room was not large, measuring roughly sixty by ninety feet and, except for a few broken and crumbling slabs of stone scattered around the room, it was empty. It was an open space with no inner walls or separate rooms. Each man walked around the room, carefully examining the floors and walls for a possible opening or concealed doorway. Elijah was the first to spot them. Carved into the stone on the rear wall were six inscriptions etched into the stone, most likely hieroglyphs. They were spaced vertically in rows of two. "Come and look at this!" he shouted. "I found something."

Professor Scott held the lantern closer. "I've seen these hieroglyphs before."

The uncomprehending expression on Patterson's face revealed his total astonishment—he too had seen these inscriptions before. "General, can I see that gold medallion and scroll…the items you showed us the other day?" Scott asked.

Patterson retrieved the coin from the pouch and the scroll from the protective tube and handed them to Scott who compared them to the wall carvings. "Look! Four of the glyphs are identical to the bottom four inscriptions on the coin and in the same order, but the two on top are different."

"I thought I recognized those symbols," Patterson responded, boosting his curiosity further.

"Let's see," Simon said as he took the coin and held it close to the wall. "The bottom four glyphs are the same. How about the scroll?"

Professor Scott scanned the scroll as he glanced back and forth at the wall. He nodded. "Several of the same glyphs on the wall are scattered throughout the scroll. There is definitely a connection between the coin, scroll, and the inscriptions on this wall. How strange."

"Wonder why the top two glyphs on the wall are different than those on the coin?" Elijah asked.

"That just adds more to the mystery," Scott replied.

"What the devil could this mean, Robert?" Simon questioned the general. "You mentioned this coin came from the Confederate Treasury, yet four of the symbols are identical to those in this room in a remote jungle location several thousand miles away. How can this be?" he added, with a stunned expression. "How would the Confederate government get possession of these items? This is impossible...doesn't make any sense."

"Maybe not," Scott responded.

"How so?"

"The Confederates had close contact with the Mexican government during the early part of the war. A lot of British weapons were smuggled through Mexico. Perhaps a Mexican emissary or diplomat gave the artifacts to the Confederates for safekeeping. You may remember events weren't too stable in Mexico at the time."

"Interesting speculation," Patterson concurred.

"The hieroglyphs on this coin and this metallic scroll are perhaps Mayan, but I would guess most likely Inca. That means the coin might have come from somewhere near this area. The proof is with the identical glyphs we see on this wall. The runes have to correlate somehow—there has to be a connection. They must spell out the same thing. We just have to figure how to interpret them. The biggest mystery is the scroll." He turned to Elijah. "Do you have that logbook from the Toltec with you?"

"It's in my pack," Elijah answered, pulling the small bag from his back and retrieving the logbook.

Scott pulled out a small sketchpad and pencil and scribbled a copy of the glyphs from the wall carvings. He then held the scroll next to the book and sketching and then examined each of them carefully. "Several of the symbols and glyphs are the same that randomly appears in each document. The composition of the scroll matches the metallic feel of the sheets in this logbook, which means all of this could be a connection to our old friend, Commander Ahular. Somehow I feel there is a strong link to all of this. These runes might be some kind of a code that correlates to the scroll. This mystery is all of a sudden getting much deeper."

At that instant, a sudden loud vibration in Simon's pack resonated throughout the room, startling everyone. "What's that noise?" Patterson shouted.

"The zenox again," Simon responded, knowing he would now have to explain the device to his ex-Confederate companions. Retrieving the small apparatus from its container, Simon quickly added, "This is a communications device we retrieved from an ancient ship we found in the Yucatan. I'll tell you the story behind it later, but first let's find out what awakened it."

Simon held the zenox up and close to the inscriptions. A faint undistinguishable static noise was heard, and then the device abruptly stopped and went dead. "What was that all about?" Elijah asked.

"I don't know, but it sounded like it was picking up some sort of a signal and then quit."

About a mile downstream, Marcel, Devereaux, and the mercenaries had stopped for a brief rest. They had made exceptionally good time and knew the Americans had to be nearby. Claudio chose not to join the group but stayed near the riverbank, sipping from a flask of rum. With each swallow, his fury and anger increased. He wanted to get his hands on the American who had kicked him in the guide shop and smashed his face with the chair in the Belém tavern. His anger reached the breaking point so he slipped into one of the dugouts and began paddling upstream. He didn't need Marcel and the Frenchmen—he would find the hated Americans himself and extract his revenge. The thoughts of what he would do to them only spiked his adrenalin, allowing him to paddle faster with strong, steady strokes. He scanned the banks for any signs of the American dugouts. The scrapes in the mud along the right riverbank were recent—he easily spotted them and knew they had to be from dugouts dragged from the river. He then spotted the vague outline of a crumbling building hidden in the dense maze of vegetation. I have you now, you Americano bastardos, he smirked. The big man turned sharply toward the bank and knew he now had his quarry at bay. A cruel sneer revealed his rising anger. His hand brushed the handle of his knife to reinforce his intentions. In his haste Claudio had left his rifle behind, but with his Bowie knife at hand, he was ready to kill. The method was of no concern.

Resting under a thicket of trees, Marcel, Devereaux, and the others conversed quietly among themselves when Marcel realized Claudio was missing from the group. "Where is Claudio?"

"Haven't seen him since we stopped," Bruno answered irritably. "He must be down at the river guarding the boats. I'll go check."

The first thing that registered was the missing dugout. "That son-of-a-bitch," he growled. "The bastard has taken our boat and has gone after the Americans." He quickly jogged back to the group.

"What do you mean he stole a boat and left?" Marcel roared, his anger mounting like a raging firestorm.

"One of the dugouts is missing. Claudio was crazy about finding the Americans. That's all he talked about. Do you want us to go find him?" Bruno offered.

"Hell no…I hope he finds them and gets himself killed. It will save me the trouble."

At the ruins, Stafford and Roper sat quietly next to the building, talking, when the approaching boat caught Stafford's eye. "We've got trouble," he mumbled.

Roper turned in time to see the boat veer toward the riverbank. "Who the devil is that?"

As the dugout floated closer, they recognized the occupant. Claudio was unconcerned about stealth and also spotted Stafford and Roper in the same instant. He pushed the boat vehemently toward the bank; his face and expression was a mask of rage.

"It's that crazy drunk bastard, Claudio, the one we encountered at the dive shop and in the bar. Remember? He tried to take Elijah's head off. Looks like big trouble. This means those men in the boat that were following us are close behind. Go get the others while I see what he wants."

Stafford approached the bank while Claudio slammed the dugout into the soft sand and scampered up the incline to face him.

"Hello there, Claudio, what the hell are you doing here? Out for a leisurely boat ride?"

"You know what I'm here for…to kill Americanos…especially the one who hit me in the head."

"Sorry, Claudio, I don't think he's too anxious to see you. I suggest you jump back in the boat and tell your friends we know they're behind us. You just confirmed it."

"Where is he?" the big man screamed.

"I told you he's not interested in talking to you. Besides, he didn't bring any rum along for you to get drunk on."

This only infuriated the brute further. He lowered his head and charged Stafford like a raging bull.

The captain took the full impact in the upper body, throwing him to the ground like a sack of flour. The pain was horrific…he could feel two ribs crack. The giant balled his fists and pounded the southerner's head mercilessly. His fists felt like sledgehammers.

Claudio was too strong. All Stafford could do was to cover his face with his arms in a feeble attempt to ward off the unremitting blows. He tried to slam his knee into the man's groin but couldn't gain enough leverage. It was no use—it was a losing battle. Claudio pulled the lighter man to his feet by clutching his shirt. He reached behind his back, and grabbing the handle of his eight-inch Bowie knife, he plunged it deep into Stafford's chest, penetrating his heart. The man was dead before he hit the ground. Like a crazed animal, Claudio roared, "Come on out you American cowards…I want all of you dead like your friend here."

Santos was the first out of the doorway, followed by Elijah, Roper, and Mann. Right behind were the other three and the young guide, Raphael. Claudio saw Elijah and raised his arms, bellowing like a crazed beast. He pointed at him thundering, "I'm going to rip your heart out."

"What did he say, Raphael?"

"He wants to rip your heart out," the guide shouted back.

Santos circled Claudio then charged low into his legs. He wanted to get the thug onto his back. Claudio was too quick and sideswiped the charge and with his left fist he connected with the young Mexican's jaw, stunning him and sending him tumbling to the ground. With his right hand clutching the knife, Claudio took a sideswipe at Santos' back but missed by inches. Santos shook his head and slowly rose to face him again. Elijah bore in from the opposite side and drove his shoulder hard into the thug's abdomen. Claudio suddenly expelled a rush of air and fell to one knee. The thunderous curse word he shrieked was undistinguishable but the Americans knew his rage was boiling over the top. Elijah turned to face him again but the giant recovered and raised his knife for the downward thrust. It was time to kill his prey and get his revenge.

Professor Scott raised his Winchester to aim but couldn't pull the trigger. There was too much movement in the fray and he was afraid he would hit his companions. Hold still you animal…hold still.

Roper moved in toward Claudio's front to attract his attention while Mann slipped to his rear. They were hoping a coordinated attack would bring him down. Elijah moved in again and with a sudden thrust of his right leg slammed his boot heel into the man's knee. They heard the sickening crunch of a shattered patella and torn ligaments as the right knee gave way and the brute sunk to the ground kneeling, supported by his good leg. As Claudio fell, he grasped Elijah's wrist and pulled him to the ground beside him. He raised his knife preparing to plunge it into Elijah's chest and shouted with rage, "Now you die, Americano!"

Roper charged in from the blind side and grabbed Claudio's arm holding the knife. He forcefully twisted it downward and plunged the knife deep in to the brute's thigh, inflicting a terrible gash. Fully enraged, the big man bellowed another string of loud obscenities as he withdrew the blade and raised it again. He would take Elijah with him. It was at that moment a shot from Scott's rifle boomed across the clearing and the .44 slug hit him squarely in the wrist, blowing it apart and tossing the knife into the air, and then falling harmlessly to the ground. Elijah wrenched his arm free and pushed himself out of the man's reach. Claudio lay on the ground clutching his shattered wrist—he was bleeding profusely. He glared at the Americans with hate still raging in his eyes, although much quieter now as he slowly slipped into semi-consciousness with a huge loss of blood. "What will we do with the bastard?" Patterson shouted, knowing what the answer would be. "Why don't we just put a bullet between his eyes and be done with him?"

"That would be too kindhearted. I have another solution," Elijah answered. "Robert, grab one of his ankles and I'll take the other. We'll drag him to the river before he bleeds to death and throw him in." He turned toward Scott. "Great shot you made there, Professor…you saved my life." Scott smiled and nodded.

They dragged Claudio to the bank and rolled him down the incline into the water. A bit clearer than the Amazon, the water from the Madre de Dios River couldn't hide the blood flowing from his lacerated thigh and smashed wrist. The crimson cloud that arose and engulfed the body of the struggling giant drifted downstream to reach the alert sensors of hundreds of fish lying in their recesses and hiding places—they darted toward the source. Within seconds, swarms of piranhas hit Claudio from all sides, shredding his clothes like paper. He screamed. The turbulence in the water was explosive as scores of the devilfish tore hunks of flesh and muscle from his thrashing body. Raphael shouted, "Those are black piranha hitting him. For their size and weight, they are the most ferocious and ravenous creatures of any fish known."

It didn't take long for the devilfish to finish their meal and the water disturbance subsided as the exposed skeleton sank and settled gently into the mud.

Patterson was distraught about William Stafford. He had been a faithful soldier during their daring escape from Richmond with the Confederate treasure, the harrowing journey to the Georgia coast, and the desperate voyage to Brazil. They had become good friends while living in the South American country. Mann asked Patterson, "General, what will we do with Stafford's body?"

"You and Sam bury it over near the edge of the clearing…and deep enough so animals won't touch it. Be sure to cover the grave with some of that stone rubble we saw inside the building."

The burial process took less than thirty minutes. Patterson murmured a brief prayer about honor and duty and then the group gathered the boats and assembled at the riverbank.

"Let's punch a hole into Claudio's dugout and get the hell out of this place," Simon vigorously suggested. No one objected.

21

Downstream, Marcel and the Frenchmen boarded their remaining two dugouts and headed upriver. The Brazilian was still irate about the hot-headed brute, Claudio, and his desertion from the group just to satisfy a personal vendetta. In truth, he was much more frustrated about losing the third boat and the extra arms to paddle. Claudio was expendable—his incessant griping and complaining was an irritation to everyone and Marcel hoped the Americans had saved him the trouble of disposing of him. Good riddance, he thought.

The weight load was redistributed for the remaining boats with the heavier Bruno accompanying Marcel and Allard. "The man was an idiot," Bruno fumed. "Hope he got what he deserved."

The short trip upstream only took a few minutes. They floated by the clearing and spotted Claudio's dugout sitting on the bank. "Pull over," Marcel shouted, "it looks like one of our boats. I wonder what happened to Claudio. I don't see any activity or signs of a body."

Allard offered his assumption. "If I were the Americans and had killed him I wouldn't just leave him lying on the bank; I would toss his carcass in the river and let the piranha finish him off."

"Well, we can't use this boat," Gustavo shouted heatedly. "They chopped holes in the bottom—the damn thing is useless."

This infuriated Marcel even more. "Board up," he shouted. "We have some catching up to do."

Further upstream, the Americans paused to decide their directions. Simon turned to Raphael. "Which way now?" he asked.

"If we think the city lies further west toward Peru we have to stay on the Madre de Dios. I am inclined to believe this is the best way to continue. According to Mr. Patterson's map, the Beni River ahead would take us too far south. I think we should bypass the Beni and continue on until we hit the Tambopata, then we can branch off there." They all agreed.

The Americans continued paddling, trying to put more distance between them and their pursuers. "How much further, Raphael, before we need to start walking?" Simon asked.

"I have not traveled this river before but I would think we should paddle as far as we can then take the Tambopata branch until the river becomes too shallow to continue. Then we can hide our boats and start hiking inland. There is a large lake to the southwest called Lago Titicaca that borders Bolivia and Peru. We need to find a mountain range to the north of the lake. We will be looking for a range that contains three similar looking peaks called Os Três Diabos…just south of Cuzco. It is most likely the Cordillera Oriental Mountains that extend down from the Andes range and lies north of Lake Titicaca."

"The Three Devils?" Elijah repeated.

"Yes…three similar looking peaks. I think the lost city is located somewhere within a small valley near those peaks. I have never been there but this is what I have been told. In three or four days, we should be nearing the edge of the rainforest where the trees will begin to thin out and we can get a better view of the distant landscape. Further to the west the land becomes much more stark and barren."

The Madre de Dios was relatively wide and surprisingly navigable as it meandered in a southwesterly direction. In camp that night, Roper made an observation, "This stream is much bigger than I thought. We may be able to eat up a lot of miles before we have to ditch the boats."

Simon agreed. "I hope so. The more miles we can travel by river the less we have to walk through this accursed jungle."

Roper's opinion was accurate as they were able to continue the relatively easy float up the Madre de Dios for another three days.

Eventually, they came to a small stream that forked to the southwest from the Madre de Dios that shifted toward a more northwestward direction. The map revealed the stream to be the Tambopata. Raphael scanned carefully at the new tributary. "This is the one I told you about. The map shows it to be a pretty short distance before it plays out. The Madre de Dios would take us too far north into the Andes. I doubt if we are going to be able to stay on any river much longer before we have to start walking."

Everyone took turns looking at the map and then agreed with Raphael's assessment. The paddling was easy enough in the mild current and several valuable miles were eaten up before the river became difficult to maneuver. The Americans continued paddling, passing a small village lining the banks. It appeared to be abandoned. As Raphael had predicted, the Tampopata became shallower as they progressed southwest, forcing the paddlers to constantly push off partially exposed sandbars. "Like it or not, we're going to have to start walking soon," Simon declared. "We're wasting too much time keeping these boats off the bars. Besides, I'm getting tired of paddling." There were no objections.

After a couple of more miles, Raphael called a halt next to a small creek trickling into the river. "Let's walk the dugouts up this creek and cover them with brush. They should still be here if we return this way. Here is some higher ground for camp and we can strike out in the morning. I'll try to find us a usable path near the village." The tired travelers were ready to stop—welcome sleep was badly needed.

Roper was assigned first guard duty and positioned himself in a concealed spot near the river. If Marcel and the pursuers approached the stream, the Americans would need sufficient warning. Santos was assigned the next shift, then Mann to relieve him in the early morning hours.

A small fire was built and a meal of beef jerky and a yellow colored fruit was the meal for the evening. "What is that?" Elijah asked as Raphael handed him a slice.

"This is a tumbo or a passion fruit that tastes like a cantaloupe. They are very common in Belém…the natives grow them in their gardens. You will like it…they have a tart taste."

Elijah, who considered eating a refined art, bit off a chunk. "You're right, Raphael. It tastes pretty darn good…like you said, it has a sweet-tart taste. I hope you have a few more of those in the bag."

"There are two more. After these are gone I'm afraid we are going to have to rely on the jungle for food."

Patterson had remembered the strange object Simon had pulled from his pack back in the ruins they had visited. It had emitted a vibration and static-like sound when they were looking at the strange inscriptions engraved on the wall. Simon had not mentioned it again. Patterson was most curious and turned to Simon. "You said you would tell us what that weird device was you had in your pack…the object that started vibrating inside the old building. What the devil is that thing anyway?"

Simon opened his pack and removed the small box holding the zenox. He took the device from the case and held it up for the others to see. "You will find this hard to believe, Robert, but this little shell is called a zenox…we recovered it from a flying ship that came to our earth from another world…a planet from another solar system. It is a communication device."

Patterson, Roper, and Mann sat there with humorous expressions of total confusion and disbelief. "You're kidding, of course?" Mann uttered with a smirk.

"I know it sounds crazy but it's true. Elijah, Santos, and the professor here can back me up. We used it during our Peruvian expedition."

Simon explained how they had discovered the dormant spacecraft in the cavern in Mexico and how they had repaired it and instructed the craft to actually fly them to Washington. He further clarified how they got possession of the zenox that had been planted in the soil of the capital grounds by the Toltec before its departure and self-destruction over the Atlantic Ocean. His account of the expedition to Peru and subsequent encounter with the space battle cruiser, Cuzco, further confused his newest companions, but his story about their unexpected visit to the sunken continent of Atlantis and the city of Lythe left them totally dumbfounded. The final narrative explaining how they had encountered Commander Ahular and the other alien explorers in their underwater command center left his listeners speechless. The final blow was his explanation of how the laser guns from the Cuzco had saved the earth by welding the fault line together between the African and Eurasian tectonic plates as a catastrophic earthquake and volcanic eruption was about to split the planet apart.

"It this true, Professor?" Patterson asked, shaking his head in disbelief.

"Every word of it. I was with them on that ship and saw it with my own eyes. Elijah and Santos were also there and witnessed the whole thing." Both men nodded their affirmation.

"Then what happened?"

"At our request, Commander Ahular was kind enough to fly us back to Washington where we told President Grant the whole story. We even gave him some old coins and artifacts from the continent of Atlantis to prove it."

"What happened to the flying ship?"

"Commander Ahular told us they had been ordered back home…back to their world. I guess they flew the ship back to their home planet. He left this zenox with me and told me to hold on to it…said he would be back someday and be in contact. Since then, we haven't heard a sound from the device. Somehow, I think those inscriptions in the ruins woke it up and that's the first time we've even heard a sound, even though it was only a faint static noise."

Somewhat convinced, Patterson shook his head. "Craziest story I've ever heard, but somehow I believe you…I think."

Mann agreed. "I guess I'll have to believe you as well." Roper concurred and Raphael didn't say a word. All this weird space talk was way over the young Brazilian's narrow scope of normal understanding.

Patterson was still puzzled. "How could writing on a wall make it vibrate?"

"I don't know," Simon confessed.

"I have a couple of theories," Professor Scott offered. "Possibilities, mind you."

"Let's hear them, Professor."

"We know from our experiences in the Yucatan and Peru the zenox can hear sounds, like our voices. Remember when you first discovered the Toltec in that cavern in Mexico? You told me their data storage banks quickly communicated with you in English. The gadget was somehow able to assimilate and pass along the sounds of your conversations to their computers and from that, they were able to learn our language. I suspect the gadget can scan things with some type of invisible eyes or sensors and relay images. We know it can also sense and pinpoint locations and directions with precision accuracy. That little device is incredible… way beyond our technical understanding."

Elijah added his thoughts. "I think it's possible the zenox detected and recognized the location of the ruins and the inscriptions on that wall. I think it was reading those images. That might be why it started vibrating…it was either sending or receiving a signal. Once it had gathered the information it wanted, the vibrations stopped. Most important though, I believe the device is receiving signals from somewhere or someone that's controlling it and probably not too far from here."

Simon concluded, "Elijah has a point. Since it's a communication capsule, it would seem the zenox would need some kind of signal to wake it up. It's most likely receiving and sending signals back and forth from somewhere…back to the source. I know it sounds crazy but what else would wake the damn thing up but some kind of a remote signal?"

Simon and Scott answered at the same time. "Commander Ahular and the CUZCO!"

22

The American expedition group was able to get some much needed sleep except for a few moments during the night when they heard snarls from prowling cats roaming through the jungle. The next morning Elijah, whose imagination had envisioned unimaginable shapes running about, swore he saw the glowing, yellow eyes of a jaguar staring at him through the bushes. He said he tossed a stick in the apparition's direction and was convinced it was a big cat when the spots suddenly disappeared. He told Professor Scott that it was definitely a huge jaguar poised to strike, but he scared it away and most likely saved his hide from the cat's evening meal. While Elijah's mischievous grin revealed the obvious ribbing, Scott rolled his eyes and thought, the poor man must be losing his mind. Elijah enjoyed provoking the professor's serious disposition, but deep inside he wondered if those spots he imagined he saw might have actually been a real jaguar.

After securing their packs and a quick snack of unidentified meat jerky, the group followed Raphael through the underbrush in a westerly direction. The trek through the heavy vegetation was difficult and required continuous chopping through the incessant vines and low branches that constantly confronted them. "Shouldn't we be hitting a bigger trail somewhere around here? The natives in that village had to have made some paths to get around," Elijah shouted to the guide.

"We'll find one," the young guide assured him.

The most difficult part of the slog through the jungle was the dead and decaying tree trunks that lay across their path. Some were large enough to require added effort for the men to slide themselves and equipment over the trunks. The thick jungle and dense vegetation obscured everything around them and closed in like a shadowy curtain. "This damn place is spooky," Elijah mumbled.

"I think we have a trail," Raphael finally announced from the front of the column.

The track was a vaguely distinguishable footpath and one that suggested very little use, indicated by the undergrowth that spilled in from the sides and numerous hanging vines that bridged across it. Most likely it was only used by the animals that roamed the area.

Simon called a halt to rest and get their bearings. He turned to Raphael. "Where do you think this path will take us?"

"I don't know, but if it was used at all by the local Indians it should intersect with a larger trail somewhere. We need to be watchful though because some of the local tribes don't like outsiders…especially white men. White-skinned shrunken heads are a coveted prize to the Jivaros. They are worth much more than native heads when traded for food or goods."

"Oh, that's great," Elijah muttered, gently rubbing his neck. "Now I find out they want to use my head as money for food. Think I'd rather face snakes."

Simon laughed. "Just think Elijah, one of the Jivaros could trade your head for a stuffed jaguar and get two dark skinned heads back as change." This brought nervous laughter from the others as they imagined the same fate might happen to their own heads.

Although the narrow path was overgrown, constant hacking with the machetes cleared enough of the overhanging vegetation to allow the group to keep moving at a steady pace. They were on higher ground now where the undergrowth began to thin out a bit, allowing them a slightly better view through the trees. It also allowed two pairs of dark eyes to observe them through the foliage to follow the white intruders and stalk their movements. Santos, whose keen senses detected slight peripheral movement, turned his head but there was nothing but empty jungle. He had an uneasy feeling in the pit of his stomach that they were being watched. He turned to Simon. "I think we are being stalked. I saw movement to my right…near that clump of trees."

Simon turned to look. He saw nothing but underbrush. "It was probably an animal, but let's keep our eyes open. We don't need any surprises."

The two obscure figures following them through the bush were Shuar warriors, a separate sub-tribe of Jivaros. They were hunters and scouts for a larger group hunting game in the area. Having observed the direction the outsiders were headed, they silently melted away into the jungle and hurried off to warn their companions. Their village was located slightly north, deep in the Brazilian tropical rainforest.

The tribe that the Americans had encountered a few days earlier on the Madeira River were Jivaros but from a different sub-tribe called the Huambisa. There were four sub-tribes of the Jivaros, with the Shuar being marked as the most ferocious…they were fanatical headhunters. The Jivaros, named after the Spanish word for heathens, were described by the Spanish as the only race 'crueler than nature.' Their reputation for unconquerable ferocity was legendary, and they were the only native people of the Americas that were never defeated or slaughtered. In 1599, during raids on two Spanish settlements, the Jivaros killed 25,000 people in one day. Suspecting the viceroy of cheating them in some gold transactions, they poured molten gold down the leader's throat until his bowels burst. The Jivaros occupying the Amazon Basin were certainly a tribe of Indians to be avoided as the Americans learned from their previous experience on the Madeira River with the ghastly jebero execution contrivance.

Several miles to the northeast, as the mercenaries passed the tiny deserted village on the Madre de Dios, Devereaux turned to Marcel. "What do you think? I don't see any sign of their boats anywhere."

"They would have paddled as far as possible then ditched

them and headed out on foot. We should be able to spot their deserted dugouts a little farther upstream, but first let's pull over for a short rest. They can't be too far ahead because this stream is getting shallower and we can't paddle too much farther."

None of the group noticed the faint shadows that blended into the vegetation along the far bank nor did they detect the three pairs of dark shadowy eyes watching them through the leaves. Felipe stood up in the rear of the boat to relieve himself and was nonchalantly staring into the murky water when he felt a sharp sting on his neck. "Damn bugs, he grumbled as he slapped at the bite to smash the suspected insect. He was stunned to see a thin stick fall into the water with a small tuft of cotton-like material attached to one end. He stood silent, not realizing he had only seconds to live. He was transfixed as he stared at the thin object floating away with the current. The poisonous effect of the curare covered dart was quick. The venom fed through his carotid artery into his bloodstream and quickly into his nervous system. He suddenly felt a peaceful numbing sensation throughout his body as his sight became blurry and then suddenly there was only darkness. Felipe pitched forward and struck the water with a noiseless splash. The dugout lurched to one side causing Marcel and Gustavo to look up in time to see their companion tumble over the edge and float away. Another poison dart struck the side of the dugout and embedded deep into the wood.

"Indians!" Marcel screamed. "Grab those paddles…let's get out of here…and fast!"

"Where?" Bruno shouted, "I don't see any Indians."

"In the trees…let's move it!"

Another dart embedded itself into the stern of the second boat.

As the men frantically dug their paddles into the water, Allard fired a few blind shots into the dense foliage, hoping to hit something. The shadows suddenly faded away. It did not take long for the boats to cover a reasonable distance from the village and hopefully away from the poison projectiles hurled from the dreaded blowguns. "What was that?" Devereaux shouted to Marcel.

"Most likely Jivaros…those devils are all over this damn jungle."

"How about your man, Felipe? We saw him fall into the water."

"Poison dart got him. He is gone…nothing we can do about him. The poison on those accursed darts works fast."

They finally came to a place where the river branched off into two directions. They had reached the mouth of the Tampopata. "Which way?" Devereaux asked.

Marcel was silent as he viewed both rivers, trying to ascertain the most likely route.

"How do we know which direction they went?" Devereaux questioned again. "They could have headed either south toward Bolivia or northwest into Peru and the Andes. Remember, that captain of the Caribe told us they were heading toward Peru."

Marcel smirked with confidence. "All the more reason to go the opposite way. I think I know the directions they are going if the guide shop owner, Luiz, didn't lie to me. Apparently their guide told Luiz the general route he was taking and he passed the information on to me. All we have to do is find some mountain peaks called Os Três Diabos."

"What the hell is that?" Bruno grumbled cynically.

"The Three Devils. Luiz told me they are located somewhere near a big lake called Titicaca… between the borders of Peru and Bolivia. That means we take the left tributary that goes more to the southwest." They maneuvered the boats onto the Tambopata.

Marcel was surprised to find the river narrow but still navigable. "We'll travel as far as we can on this river…it should help us make up some time."

As the mercenaries progressed, they began to encounter shallower water, making it more difficult to paddle around the exposed sandbars bunched up along the banks and some extending across the river. Just past the tiny deserted village Gustavo shouted to Marcel. "That stream to the left looks like a good spot to hide boats. The opening looks just wide enough to drag a dugout through. I don't see how they could have paddled much further… water is getting too shallow. I'll wade up the creek and check it out."

Within minutes Gustavo emerged from the stream, a look of triumph on his face. "I found their boats…just upstream hidden in the bush. I know where they took off into the jungle…they left some branches on the ground that look freshly cut. They can't be too far ahead."

Marcel's cruel sneer displayed his feelings. His hunches had been right so far.

Devereaux and his three French companions were more than happy to abandon the dugouts and walk on solid ground again. Even the trained killer, Bruno, managed a slight grin.

Well in front, Raphael led Simon and the group along the worn trail a few kilometers and then veered off toward the southwest. They needed a suitable spot to camp before dark and found it in a small clearing bordered by heavy jungle growth. While Mann and Roper built a campfire, Raphael and Santos left the site to search for some game for dinner. The weary trekkers were tired of jerky and wanted a meal of fresh cooked meat after an exhausting day of walking. The two hunters briefly separated to cover more ground. Raphael rejoined Santos further up the trail and was pleased to see that he was dragging a medium-sized animal along the path. The bullet hole indicated Santos had made a clean shot just behind the shoulder blade and into the animal's heart. The mood at the camp became jovial when the two hunters returned with a large pig-like creature suspended from a long pole. "What the devil is that ugly looking beast?" Elijah shouted. "Don't tell me you're gonna cook that thing for dinner."

Santos laughed. "You'll love it. It is a tapir and tastes just like pig meat. You won't know the difference."

Elijah shrugged his shoulders and conceded. "Well…I'm so damn hungry I could eat a crocodile."

"Good…because that's what we might be eating tomorrow."

Santos and Raphael gutted the tapir and fashioned a makeshift rotisserie from a hardwood pole. The pole was inserted though the tapir's mid-section and placed over the bed of hot coals. With everyone pitching in to turn the spit, the animal started to roast and the aroma of fresh roasted pork began to fill the campsite. Santos was right—the meat was delicious and being famished helped the group to aggrandize the dining experience.

"That pig meat tastes great," Elijah admitted. "Almost as good as some of those hogs old man Gurley used to roast in his back yard."

Santos reminded him. "It's not a pig but a tapir. Probably in the same family though."

Elijah just grinned and nodded his contentment as he took another big bite carved from the animal's flank.

Concealed in undergrowth near the path, and being the last shift for guard duty, Mann carefully wiped the morning dew off his prized Lorenz, an Austrian made model 1863 sniper rifle. It was bored for a .54 caliber bullet and carried an English Whitworth scope. He had taken it from a Union sniper he had shot. He was immensely proud of this rifle and extremely proficient with it. The brightening light from an early morning sunrise began to illuminate the surrounding forest as his peripheral vision picked up movement farther down the trail. Several scantily clad figures appeared carrying spears and pucunas, the dreaded blowguns. His first thought was Shuar Jivaros. Mann picked up a stone he had placed next to him and tossed it toward his sleeping companions. It was a prearranged signal for pending danger. Santos had risen early and was preparing coffee when the stone skidded across the campsite. Quickly, he shook Simon and then Elijah and the others awake. "What is it?" Simon asked.

"Wake up…we got the danger signal from Mann. Grab your rifles quickly."

Mann quickly moved back to the camp. "What is it?" Simon asked him.

"A band of Jivaros headed this way."

"How many?"

"Looks to be about ten to fifteen…and some of them are carrying those damn blowguns."

The Indians had sensed the smell of smoke from the campfire and silently moved along the path looking for the intruders. The party had been warned by the scouts who had seen the Americans earlier. Mann, the closest to the path, observed one particular ferocious looking brute leading the column. He was adorned in a dark loincloth and painted from head to toe with crimson and black strips—surely ascended from the underworld. Mann held his Lorenz steady as he focused the crosshairs in the center of the man's face. Calmly he inhaled a deep breath and then slowly squeezed the trigger. The .44 caliber slug hit the Jivaros between the eyes, splitting his head apart and knocking him back into the men behind him. Two others stumbled to the ground as piercing screams from the rear column filled the air. The battle was on.

"Here they come!" Mann screamed, re-cocking his rifle. "Make your shots count!"

The rest of the group took the only cover they could find—a few stumps from rotted trees and clumps of thin bushes. The Indians saw the Americans and rushed headlong along the path brandishing short spears, battle axes, and pucunas. They wanted new white heads for trophies. Two of the Indians stopped to the side to take aim with their blowguns. One dart buried deep into the stump near Elijah's head and the other sailed harmlessly into the woods, barely missing Patterson's left shoulder by inches. One Jivaros threw his axe at Professor Scott but missed as the professor ducked. Scott raised his Winchester and shot the assailant in the chest. Another Indian reached the clearing and threw himself at Roper, knocking the big man to the ground. With the Jivaros on top, thrashing and flaying with his fists, Roper jerked a knee into the man's groin and pushed him off to the side. He grabbed the barrel of his rifle and swung it upward, the butt slamming the man in the side of the head. The savage dropped like a stone. Roper then fired a slug into his chest. Scott calmly stood to one side and pumped bullets into four unfortunate Indians, killing them instantly. What a great rifle, he thought.

Simon and Elijah dropped two more Indians, but took the full impact of three others as they charged into the Americans from both sides. Both went sprawling to the ground and dropped their Winchesters as they fell. One Jivaros jabbed his spear at Simon, grazing his arm and barely drawing blood. Another raised his axe for the deathblow when a slug hit the Indian in the side of the head. He was tossed to the side by the impact. Santos raised his rifle for another shot when a spear dug into the ground between his feet. He adjusted his aim and shot the thrower in the stomach then turned and shot the Jivaros straddling on top of Simon. Two more Indians fell as Patterson and Scott squeezed off more rounds. The few surviving Jivaros turned and scrambled for the woods and two more sprinted back along the path. The Winchester repeaters were too much for them…they were finished. One Indian turned and hurled his axe before disappearing into the trees. Raphael had turned to speak to Simon when he took the full impact of the axe—it buried deep into his back. He gasped and hurled forward into the grass. Elijah pulled the weapon out and flung it angrily to the ground. He gently turned the young guide over on his back and heard the soft words whispering from his mouth, "Lago Titicaca. Os…Três…Diabos…to the north." His head turned to the side and he went limp as he took his last breath. "Lake Titicaca…The Three Devils…to the north," Elijah repeated to himself.

"The Indians have disappeared," Patterson informed them as he approached and saw the prone figure of Raphael. "Is he dead?"

"I'm afraid so. What a damn shame."

Simon approached his kneeling cousin. "Let's bury him at the edge of the clearing…and we need to be quick about it. Those Jivaros are probably heading back to their village to gather up an army to come after us."

"Nasty animals," Scott commented.

"What did the young guide say before he died?" Patterson asked.

Elijah shook his head. "The last words he whispered to me were 'Lake Titicaca and the Three Devils to the north.' "

"What do you suppose that means?" Patterson responded.

"I guess it means we have to continue toward the southwest… toward the Peru, Bolivia border…toward Lake Titicaca, and then veer north to find those three peaks. I'm sure he was telling me where to go."

Roper spoke up, "I saw that lake on a map in the guide shop. If I remember correctly, it should be due southwest from us. Lake Titicaca is a huge lake and splits the borders of Peru and Bolivia. The way I figure it, we need to head southwest from where we are now."

"One thing we do know for sure," Simon remarked, "we're now on our own. But I agree with you, Sam. I remember Raphael saying the peaks are somewhere just northeast of the lake. We'll continue to stick with this path for several miles and find a suitable spot where we can travel cross-country. We sure don't want to veer too far south into the La Paz Region of Bolivia and miss that mountain range." He then asked Roper, "Did you get far enough to see the three peaks?"

"No. We only made it several miles down the Madre de Dios River before the Indians made us turn back. This is where Radford, Dunn, and I got separated and that's where they were probably captured by the Jivaros. I'm sure the shrunken head we saw in the Jivaros village was Radford and I'll bet Dunn's head was also hanging somewhere in that damn village."

The burial took fifteen minutes as a shallow grave was hastily dug for Raphael and covered with a few rocks found nearby. The Americans secured their equipment, checked their rifles, and briskly moved out on the trail in a southwesterly direction. The dead Jivaros were left for the animals.

23

Several miles to the east, Marcel, Devereaux, and the other mercenaries made good time along the path the Americans had previously taken. The trek was made easier by following the telltale signs of the cut vines and fallen leaves they carelessly left behind. It was unusual that Santos didn't notice this and caution his companions about leaving clues a tracker could easily follow. The excitement of searching for and hopefully finding El Dorado apparently clouded out their need for caution.

It did not take long for Marcel to reach the point where the path intersected with the worn trail that branched off in two directions. "Which way?" Gustavo asked, glancing both ways.

"We have to go left toward the southwest," Marcel answered. "That lake is toward the Bolivian border. I remember the map Luiz showed me indicated the lake was located more to the extreme southwest of the Amazon. We'll stay on this track and keep following any signs they might have left…and keep your eyes open for the Jivaros."

Devereaux was getting annoyed with Marcel and this whole arrangement. He didn't like the man and certainly didn't need the Brazilian thug giving directions and taking charge. He felt that he and his three companions could operate much better on their own. His mission had been explicit. Find and follow the Americans until they lead him to their secret weapon, the flying machine. French President, Adolphe Thiers, wanted that machine for France and he expected the agents to bring it back to Paris. For some reason he was convinced the Americans were looking for another hidden flying ship, not knowing they were now in search of El Dorado. Devereaux had been supplied a small map of the Amazon Basin by Le Guarde and had been secretly following their progress as they traveled westward. He knew the general directions to Lake Titicaca. He called a private meeting with Allard, Jacques, and Bruno. "We need to separate ourselves from those hired murderers. Any suggestions?"

Bruno spoke up. "There are only two of them left…we could cut their throats while they sleep."

"Too messy," Jacques offered. "I don't think those two ever sleep. Why don't we just disarm them and leave them tied to a tree. Let the jaguars or Jivaros have them."

Devereaux had second thoughts. "If we get into a fight with the Americans we might need their extra guns. Perhaps we had better tolerate them a little longer. We'll have plenty of time to dispose of them later." The others agreed.

The Americans moved along the path quickly—they wanted to put as much distance as possible between them and the Jivaros. "We should be leaving Jivaros country soon," Mann stated. "The trees are thinning out and the Indians would rather stick to the heavier jungle."

"Don't count on it," Elijah cautioned him. "Those devils are like grasshoppers…they can hop up anywhere."

The column stopped several miles farther up the trail to get their bearings. "Where do you think we are?" Patterson questioned. "We're lost without Raphael."

Mann posed a worrisome question. "What about Marcel and the band of cutthroats that were following us in the boat? We know they were still following us when that animal, Claudio, showed up at the ruins and attacked us."

Roper reminded them. "With what Captain Cadiz told us, I'm sure he's still somewhere behind us and probably not too far away. The captain said as long as someone was paying the greedy bastard, he would never give up the chase. Said he would cut his mother's throat for enough money. Yeah…you can bet he's still out there looking for us."

Elijah shrugged his shoulders. "Now we have to keep an eye out for Marcel and his merry band of murderers as well as our headhunting friends. This reminds me of our trip into the Yucatan. Everybody was chasing and trying to kill us."

"Yeah…that's what these are for," Professor Scott added, holding his Winchester high in the air.

Simon was trying to get some control over the rambling conversation. "The big question now is where are we and where do we go from here? According to Raphael we need to be looking for that mountain range with the three peaks, and I think we have it tabbed well north of the lake. Most likely the mountains block any view of Titicaca. I think we need to swing more to the southwest. That should put us just north of the lake. What do you think, Professor?"

Professor Scott stood there in deep thought, gazing toward the far distance. His mind was trying to assimilate the situation and put all the facts and clues together. He looked up at Simon. "I still think the key to all of this lies with that coin and scroll Robert has. Remember, four of the glyphs on the coin were identical to the inscriptions we saw on the wall in the temple ruins. I've been trying to figure out why that building was there in the first place. The local Indians didn't build it…it's much too old. It matched some of the Inca ruins we saw near Cuzco during our journey to Peru. There had to be a good reason they built that structure by the river. I think it was a religious temple put there to honor their sun god, Inti, and probably served as a resting place for hunting and warring parties traveling on the river to and from the interior. I think those inscriptions could be the key to directions to their city—the one we now call El Dorado."

"What about the similar figures we saw in the Toltec's log book? A few of those matched as well," Elijah reminded him. "And really, what difference does it make? We can't read the damn inscriptions anyway."

"That's the biggest mystery of all and still raises another

question I have about Commander Ahular and the Cuzco. I am convinced there is a strong connection between Robert's coin, the scroll, the logbook, and the inscriptions we saw in the temple and they all point to Commander Ahular."

"What are you getting at, George?"

"Do you remember the story I told you about the Inca king, Atahualpa. He secretly sent runners throughout the realm to gather the empire's gold, gemstones, and other treasure and move it to a secret place so Pizarro and the Conquistadors couldn't find it." Several heads nodded.

"The treasure was supposedly moved to a hidden city far to the south of Cuzco—to a remote place well hidden from the Spanish invaders. I doubt if the actual name of the city will ever be known but the place was cast into legend and named El Dorado by the Conquistadors. And I have another theory."

"Go on, Professor," Simon prodded. "You have our interest so we want to hear where you are going with this."

"Because some of the same glyphs from the coin, scroll, and temple wall were found in that logbook from the Toltec, I think the earlier alien explorers that preceded Commander Ahular visited El Dorado, just like his precursors did with the Toltec Indians in Mexico and the Incas in Peru. It is possible those inscriptions on the coin and walls might be directional signs to the lost city and it might be that Ahular's predecessors put those inscriptions on the coin and the wall. There may be more coins like the one Robert is holding. Perhaps we'll find them in the city."

"The big question now is how do we find the city?" Simon remarked. "We don't have a map."

Professor Scott pressed on. "Well, we need to improvise a compass. Think of directions on a compass as represented by a 360 degree circle with due north being 0 degrees and south 180 degrees. Let's say El Dorado is located in the dead center of the circle and we are standing due east on the edge of the circle. That means if we are standing at 90 degrees from the center and if we wanted to go to the city we would have to travel toward the 270 degree mark which would be due west." There were a few nods of comprehension.

Elijah pressed the issue. "But according to Raphael we are not due east but standing well to the northeast."

"That's true, Elijah. I was using 90 degrees and due east as an example. As we stand here facing the sunset due west, we have to shift our direction more to the southwest or the 225 degrees mark. Once we reach more open terrain, we can do this much easier to get our bearings than in the jungle. I suggest we travel on this trail a few miles farther and then swing toward the southwest. Hopefully we will be able to spot the Three Devils' peaks in the distance. Since Raphael told us the ruins of the city lie in a hidden valley near the three peaks and just to the the north of Lake Titicaca, we have to gauge our direction as close as we can to that point. To get our proper bearings we need to keep an eye on the sunset. At our campsite this evening I'll draw a circle in the ground and mark the sunset as due west and correlate north to the North Star. In the morning we can estimate our southwesterly direction by degrees on the circle. You'll be surprised how accurate this crude compass will work."

Scott turned to Patterson and Simon. "I have another theory. Robert, please get your coin and the scroll and hold it up. I want to see if Simon can get any reaction from the zenox."

Patterson retrieved the coin and unrolled the scroll. He held both artifacts to the front. Simon took the zenox and held it chest high facing the two objects. There was only dead silence. "Hold the gadget closer to the coin for a few seconds and then move it in a position to scan the scroll." A few more seconds passed. The silence was deafening. The coin produced no reaction but when Simon started scanning the scroll the zenox started a slow vibration and then increased in intensity. Simon nearly dropped it but managed to hold on. The vibrations became even stronger. The sound of static was faint but became louder as the device was moved across the lines of inscriptions. Abruptly a faint voice began to emerge, but in a strange language…nothing anyone had ever heard before. Everyone began talking at one time.

"That gadget is reading the scroll!" Roper shouted.

"What's it saying?" Patterson asked, with a look of disbelief.

Scott added, "I can't tell. It's talking in some strange language I've never heard before."

"It doesn't sound like ancient Quechua or any other of the native languages I've heard," Santos observed.

"It looks like the zenox is scanning the scroll and passing the information on to someone or someplace, wherever that is," Elijah noted.

The bewildered look on the Confederados faces were comical but openly conveyed their nervous curiosity and apprehension.

Suddenly the zenox went dead.

Scott spoke up with conviction. "I am absolutely convinced the information in the scroll was being conveyed to a higher intelligence and that would have to be someone like Commander Ahular."

That evening at their camp, Scott took a stick and carved a circle in the dirt. Luckily the clear horizon allowed a good view of the sun setting in the west, allowing the professor to mark the due west, 270 degree position on the circle. A brief view of the North Star confirmed the zero degree position. The compass was set and in the morning they would decide the proper course they would travel cross-country to the southwest. Scott knew it would only be an estimate at best, but hopefully they would eventually find the mountain range and identify Os Três Diabos.

Next morning the group gathered around the compass circle awaiting Professor Scott's assessment. Simon spoke up. "Okay, Professor, you are now our new guide. Where do we go from here?"

Scott glanced off to the horizon then down at the circle. He took a straight stick and scratched a north-south vertical line and then a horizontal line bisecting the center of the circle. He then scratched two diagonal lines through the center to divide the circle into eight quadrants. He explained, "The top of the vertical line represents due north or 0 degrees. The tip of the lines touching the outside of the circle is in 45 degree increments. This is our compass." He stuck a small stick in the center and continued. "This stick represents a calculated guess where the mountain range and the Three Devils might be located. We'll estimate our current position as here," he stated, pointing to the 45 degree position. "We follow this line toward the 225 degree mark. As we move along we'll keep an eye on the sun and try to adjust to the southwest along this line."

"Won't we get disorientated walking cross-country, especially if we encounter rivers, hills, or mountains?" Elijah questioned.

"At dusk we'll keep an eye on the sunset and at night the North Star. This should keep us going in the general right direction," Scott reassured him.

"And if we have a cloudy day?"

"Then we'll have to rely on some good guesswork. I drew a rough sketch of the compass on a piece of paper and marked the lines and degrees. As I said, we'll watch the sun and North Star and keep orientating our direction with the sketch. This will be our compass and I think we can maintain a fairly true direction."

Simon, who had been silent absorbing all of this speculation, finally spoke up. "Remember, all of this is a wild guess on our part. The main thing is we have to look for that mountain range and then spot the three peaks. We find those Three Devils we should be able to find the lost city or what's left of a city...that is, if there is even a city out there." He then turned to Scott. "Professor, you're the guide now...lead the way."

Elijah shrugged his shoulders and added sardonically, "And this is where the fun begins."

In a few miles the trail started bending to the right. Scott sensed the direction change and called a halt. "It looks like we're veering to the northwest and away from our target objective. It's time we leave the path and move off toward the southwest." He glanced up at the position of the late afternoon sun. "According to my dead reckoning and this compass drawing, we should be going that way." He pointed off to the horizon. There were no objections so Professor Scott deviated from the path and led the column into the scrub. There was no turning back now.

They were now approaching the far western section of the rainforest where the dense vegetation of the jungle and the trees and undergrowth began to thin out significantly. While some of the groves of vegetation were still thick, the size of the trees was definitely getting smaller. They were confident the trek ahead would lead them into more open terrain to allow for easier walking. The sun was dropping deep toward the west, spilling red and purple hues across the sky and resulting in an explosion of dazzling colors across the horizon. Scott called a halt. "It's time to set up camp," he shouted.

While the men were laying out their bedrolls, Professor Scott was aligning his compass drawing with the sunset. Continue to the southwest, he thought, satisfied they were hopefully on target. He looked at the 225 degree line on his rough compass drawing to ascertain the direction they would travel in the morning. When it got darker, he would get a fix on the North Star. So far, so good.

After a brief dinner of fruit and jerky dried from the left over tapir, the men turned in…it had been a long exhausting hike.

24

Marcel, Devereaux, and the other four mercenaries reached the spot where the Americans had encountered the Jivaros. Several startled vultures flew into the air as the men approached. Their presence was explained by the scant remains of the few body parts, not dragged off by the cats, lying scattered haphazardly on the ground. It was evident the scavengers and various hungry animals had been enjoying their fill of dinner. The stench was bad.

"What the hell happened here?" Bruno growled.

"Can't you see the bullet holes?" Devereaux shouted back. "Looks like the Americans were attacked but those Indians didn't have a chance against their guns. They apparently have repeaters like us."

Allard shouted from the edge of the clearing. "Hey, Paul, come and look at this!"

The men walked over to observe the faint remnants of the circle scratched in the dirt. He pointed to the ground. "Looks like someone tried to draw an outline of a compass. Look at the pointed arrow at the far edge of the circle. Now we know which direction they are heading."

That evening Devereaux and Allard slipped off and out of sight to look over their map. "Just as we thought," Devereaux said, tracing his finger across the chart. "To the southwest…we'll find them."

Next morning Elijah awoke with a start. His sixth sense told him not to move. He was certain he felt movement against his leg…

something smooth. He lay there like a stone, holding his breath. "Santos," he whispered to his companion preparing a fire close by. "Santos…over here… over here quickly."

Santos heard him and walked over to his bunk. "What is it?"

"Something in my bed roll…next to my leg. I'm afraid to move. See if you can move the blanket and see what it is. Very easy now…"

Santos was familiar with many of the jungle creatures…he did not hesitate. He kneeled down to one knee and gently removed Elijah's blanket and then he froze. "Elijah, don't move a muscle… don't even breathe," he whispered.

"Move…hell, I'm trying not to mess my pants."

The shifting of the blanket caused the long, slender reptile to move and it began to slither over Elijah's belly. With a lightning flick of the hand, Santos grabbed the creature's tail and snatched it into the air, and with a quick overhead motion, he cracked the five-foot snake like a whip, twirled it around his head, and slung it as far as he could into the trees. "It's okay…you can get up and start breathing now."

Simon, Patterson, and the others heard the commotion and scurried over to Elijah's bunk.

"Son-of a bitch!" Elijah shrieked at the top of his voice. "What the hell was that?"

"That, my friend, was one of the deadliest snakes in the world…a western green mamba. If he had bitten you, you would be dead by now. They are quite aggressive and their venom is very deadly."

Elijah was shaking like a leaf. "What was that creepy thing doing in my bunk anyway?"

"He was cuddling up to your body for warmth. Good thing you didn't roll over on him."

Simon couldn't resist. "Maybe he thought you were a girl snake and wanted to mate."

As the others chuckled, Elijah gave his cousin a very cold stare and then he roared, "Snakes…I hate those slimy, stinking bastards! They all breed in hell!" It took Elijah a few minutes to calm down.

Simon announced, "Let's get packed up and get ready to move out. We have a long walk ahead of us."

The route was still moderately wooded but thinning slightly as the column moved slowly away from the rainforest. Thankfully, as they journeyed southwest, the gradual increasing higher ground gave way to less dense undergrowth and scrub they would have to hack through. Although no one knew it, they were beginning the long trek toward the Yungas Foothills. The group was more than ready to leave the accursed jungle with its dreadful Jivaros and creature-infested rainforest. Maintaining their current route would hopefully carry them on a parallel course to the Cordillera Oriental mountain range, their intended goal. As Raphael had told them, this was supposedly the location of Os Três Diabos and the lost city of gold.

A few miles farther, the Americans broke out of the tree line and entered into a sloping grassy meadow giving them a good panoramic view of the horizon. Here the walking would be easier until they reached the mountains. Mann was the first to notice it in the distance…it stood out like a beacon located on the crest of a small hill. He pointed to his right and shouted, "Over there…on top of that hill…looks like the remains of a building." The group turned toward the hill.

The ruins were identical to those they had visited at the fork of the Madre de Dios and Beni Rivers. The unpretentious rectangular stone building sat in the crest of the hill with an overview of the meadow below…like a sentinel guarding the eastern approaches to the mountains. As usual, Professor Scott's archeological inquisitiveness burst forth with the idea of a new discovery. "We have to check it out," he shouted. "It looks identical to the other temple we explored on the Madre de Dios…most likely Inca or perhaps Mayan."

They made their entrance through the small front doorway and noticed the right portion of the ruins had collapsed and the pile of stones blocking a side entry would have required some risky climbing. Unlike the ruins they found on the river, this structure was relatively free of vines and other vegetation overgrowth. The building was roughly the same size as the other temple and luckily the collapsed east wall allowed enough light to enter to provide a dim illumination of the interior. Also, like the other ruins, the large room was empty except for a few crumbling blocks of stone scattered about the floor. Santos, with his inquisitive sense of caution, remarked, "We need to spread out and check the walls and floor for any signs of an opening or hidden door. Look for any lever or device that might trigger something."

Sergeant Mann was exploring the rear wall when he spotted something unusual. In the dull light he saw the inscriptions etched into the wall—glyphs similar to those in the other temple ruins. "Over here," he shouted. "Here on the back wall."

Professor Scott was ecstatic. "They're identical to the glyphs in the other temple, except the top two are different." He pulled out the penciled sketch he had made on the river to verify this. "I still think they might be reference markers since they're different than the others…perhaps leading to the lost city." He added a notation and sketch of the newest discovery.

As on cue, the vibrations coming from Simon's pack were heard throughout the room. He retrieved the zenox and was not surprised that it had awakened again. A red light was blinking and the thin rod shot out between his fingers.

"Hold it close to the inscriptions," "Scott instructed.

As earlier, in the other ruins, the device started making indistinct humming noises.

"What do you suppose the thing is doing now?" Elijah asked inquisitively.

"I think it's scanning the inscriptions like it did before." Scott speculated. "It's probably conveying the information to someone again…kind of like sending a telegraph."

He turned to Simon. "Why don't you see if you can make that little gadget talk to you…like it did before in the Yucatan and Peru?"

"Sure won't hurt." He held the zenox up and spoke. "Hello… can you hear me? Hello…hello? This is Simon Murphy, former commander of the Cuzco…can you hear me?" The humming continued. "The thing isn't responding."

"Keep trying." Elijah urged him.

"Zenox, this is Simon Murphy. Don't you recognize my voice?"

Suddenly a loud static erupted from the zenox then faint garbled words could be heard. They soon became clearer. "Yes… Commander Murphy. We can hear you now."

Patterson was totally dumbstruck and astounded by the voice erupting from the small gadget. "What the hell?" he stammered. "Is that thing really talking or am I losing my mind?"

Mann and Roper were equally stunned. "Did you hear that, Sam?" Mann asked.

Roper just shook his head, completely aghast.

"Yes, Commander Murphy," the zenox responded again. "Welcome back…we've been expecting to hear from you for some time."

Simon was ecstatic when he heard the familiar accented voice. "You have?" he finally uttered, trying to control his composure. "This sounds like Commander Nezar. Where are you calling from?"

"This is Nezar and I am calling you from our command center. Our sensors have been following you for some time now and keeping track of your pace along the Amazon River basin. We now register you entering the Yungas Foothills."

"Good grief, the thing knows where we are," Mann mumbled.

"Where are you calling from?" Simon asked, with as much authority as he could muster.

"We are unauthorized to provide this information."

"Is Commander Ahular with you?" he probed.

"That is an affirmative," the device responded.

"May I speak to him?"

"That is not possible."

"How can we find you?"

"Follow the inscriptions," the voice suggested bluntly. "The zenox can help." And suddenly the device went silent.

Elijah was getting irritated at the whole affair and spoke up.

"What does it mean? What inscriptions is he referring to? We've got inscriptions everywhere and we can't even read the damn things. What do you think, Simon?"

"I'm not sure," he responded as he held the zenox up to his mouth again and spoke. "Zenox, what do you mean by 'follow the inscriptions?' Which inscriptions? We don't even understand any of them." No response.

Patterson was perplexed. He turned to Simon. "What was that all about? Where was the voice coming from?"

"Good question, Robert. It's coming from a machine they call a computer and it originates from the alien's command center, most likely not too far from here. The voice you heard was one of the alien explorers we met three years ago in Atlantis."

"That's incredible," Patterson conceded. "So these alien people or things actually exist?"

"Yes, they do. I told you the story about the two spaceships we rode in. The Cuzco was commanded by an alien commander named Ahular. His second in command was Nezar. We met them in the city of Lythe on the sunken continent of Atlantis. He helped save our planet from a catastrophic earthquake by welding two tectonic plates together with their laser guns. We thought he flew back to his home planet, but he told us he would return some day. He also said for me to hold on to this zenox device and that he would contact me sometime in the future. Well, it seems like our friends are back."

"That is the most incredible story I've ever heard," Patterson confessed.

"But all true," Simon assured him. "And these men were with me and witnessed all of it," he confirmed nodding to his three companions.

Suddenly, a loud hollow thump was heard, followed by a piercing shriek. Turning toward the noise, Simon and the others saw a dark square hole in the floor close to the spot where Roper and Mann had been standing. Patterson's two companions had vanished.

25

Marcel and Devereaux arrived at the spot where the Americans had veered away from the path. They easily spotted the footprints and disturbed vegetation, indicating the new direction. "This is where we leave the path," Marcel announced pointing to the new route. "Just as I thought…they have changed their direction toward the southwest."

Devereaux pulled his map from his pack. At this point he had no qualms about displaying it to Marcel. "Where the hell did you get that map?" Marcel shouted irritably. "We could have used it on the river."

"Our employer gave it to me before we left France. I have been checking it since we departed Belém. Besides, you seemed to know exactly where we were going without it. Now it should come in handy to get our bearings."

The Brazilian shrugged with a hint of annoyance. "Let's take a look."

He spread the map out on the ground and aligned it with the direction of the trail, knowing it pointed due west. It was obvious that the new route for the Americans veered toward the southwest and in a general direction toward southern Peru. "These are the mountains where we should find the Three Devils' peaks," he suggested, confidently pointing to the map, "and most likely El Dorado. It looks like the Americans seem to know the correct location or they would not have veered from this path."

Devereaux smiled, knowing he now had his quarry in his sights. Soon it would be time to settle an old score with the one called

Simon, he thought as they veered toward the new direction…and perhaps the chance to bring home an incredible new source of wealth for me and France.

The Americans rushed over to the opening and peered into the ominous void. They could not see the bottom through the impenetrable darkness. Santos noticed fingers tenaciously clutching the rim of the hole and reached down to grab Mann's wrist just in time…he was losing his grip. "Help me, Elijah…grab his other wrist."

Although Mann was of medium stature, the two Americans were able to get a good grasp, and with the aid of Scott and Patterson holding each man's waist, they were able to haul Mann over the edge and onto the floor. He lay there a few moments in an effort to catch his breath and then looked up with an appreciative smile and mumbled, "Thanks, fellows…I was losing my grip…thought my arms were going to break off. He glanced to either side. Where's Sam?" he asked anxiously, peering back into the cavity.

"I'm afraid your friend Roper is gone…into the pit below. We can't even see the bottom. No telling how deep that damn hole is."

Patterson shook his head with a despondent look. "Sam was a good man and one hell of a fine soldier and friend. What a tough way to die."

Santos stared into the hole with curiosity. "Funny the Indians would put a trap in one of their temple outposts. These buildings were built to provide rest and worship to travelers, not to kill people. It also served the Indians as a storage facility. This trap reminds me of some of those we saw in Mexico. You can see the stone slab floor panel is attached to a spindle suspended across one end and it is released when weight is applied…the weight of a man will trigger it. It sure is a strange location for a trap."

Simon looked at Patterson and Mann. "I'm sorry about your friend but there's nothing we can do for him now. Check Roper's pack for anything we can use then toss it into the hole. We need to get loaded up and get out of this place. We have a lot more traveling to do."

Mann opened Roper's pack and retrieved a knife and some jerky and was about to throw it into the pit when Santos shouted, "Hold it...I thought I heard something."

Peering into the dark void again, the faint sound of rattling and movement was heard below, followed by a distinct groan. Simon turned to Professor Scott. "George, grab that oil lantern you have in your pack and shine it down in the pit. Something is moving down there. Roper may still be alive."

A match was applied and the light from the small lamp illuminated the dark pit enough to see the shape of Roper lying prone in a heap of rubble. The body was showing some movement. "He's alive," Mann yelled. "Sam, are you okay?"

"I...I think so...shoulder hurts like hell. I think I'm lying in a big pile of rags and bones."

"Hold on...we're coming down to get you."

"I'll do it," Scott volunteered with interest. The mention of ancient bones was all it took to arouse the professor's curiosity. "Get your rope, Santos. I'll climb down there and get him."

With the rope secured to Scott's waist, and four of his companions firmly holding the other end, Scott, with lantern in hand, was easily lowered into the pit.

With a few bruises and some aches and pains spread about, Roper seemed to be in decent enough shape, considering his ten-foot drop through the floor. Scott shone the light and to his astonishment, found that Roper's fall had been cushioned by a pile of mummies, or what was left of them. The bones had been shattered into small pieces but it was the scene around the chamber that caught Scott's attention. Piled throughout the room and against the walls were piles of weapons and more stacks of mummies. Scott also observed broken stone slabs, presumed to be the remnants of benches and tables. Some of the most interesting artifacts were broken pieces of potsherds scattered about the room. He assumed they were the remnants of clay containers once filled with foodstuffs to accompany the dead inhabitants on their long journey into the afterlife. The place was an archeological treasure trove. His reverie was broken by an inquisitive shout from

Patterson booming from the opening above. "What's going on down there? How's Roper doing?"

"He's a bit bruised but in decent enough shape. You won't believe what I found down here. The place is full of ancient weapons and stacks of mummies. I need one of you to come down here and help me haul Roper back up. I don't think he can make it by himself. It looks like we'll have to dead weight him up."

Elijah, whose curiosity was also piqued, was the man to first grab the rope and descend into the room below. Scott was standing near the wall with a short sword in his hand. He reminded Elijah, "Do you remember these swords in the Yucatan? It's fashioned after the famous Gladius sword of the Roman army. The foot soldiers used them in their battle lines when in close contact with their enemies. And that's not all… look at this particular stack of mummies over here…next to the wall. We saw mummies similar to these in the cavern in Xepocotec. They are over six feet tall and certainly much taller than the Indians of the day. I would guess they have been here at least a thousand years…maybe longer. This sure raises some interesting questions."

Elijah added his recollection to the mystery. "I recall Commander Ahular telling us the explorers before him had introduced the weapons to the Toltecs and Incas and taught them how to forge the swords as payment for their hospitality. If you remember the encounter we had with the Inca battle formations in the Sacred Valley, I noticed some of their warriors had these swords in hand. It looks to me as if the Incas brought them along as they traveled into other parts of South America. We still have the sketches of the weapons in the logbook I retrieved from the ship, Toltec."

"But this doesn't explain these taller mummies," Scott added. "They have to be from a different race…they certainly aren't Inca or other local Indians…much too tall…and they're certainly not aliens but a species of humans."

"You're right. They sure don't look like the mummies we saw of the alien explorers in that cavern in Peru either. They probably predate them...perhaps early Europeans or Vikings. It sure compounds the mystery."

A shout from Simon peering down into the cavity interrupted the conversation. "You guys get your butts back up here...we have a long way to travel."

Scott was the first to climb the rope to the upper floor while Elijah finished fashioning a crude harness for Roper's waist and shoulders. With four men tugging, he was pulled up to the surface. Elijah quickly followed him. "You okay, Sam?" Patterson asked with concern as Roper lay flopped on the floor trying to check for broken bones.

"A few bruises here and there and my shoulder sure hurts like hell but I don't think anything is broken. Believe I can manage okay. I can thank those fellows down there who cushioned my fall and whose bones are scattered all about. If it weren't for them, I would have probably been joining them."

Mann, now assured his friend was still in one piece, asked Scott the obvious question. "Did you see any treasure down there...like gold coins or precious stones?"

"No, I only saw mummies and old weapons. No gold or gemstones."

Elijah had strapped one of the swords to his back and now held it out for Mann and the others to see. "Damn fine looking weapon," he commented. "It's a Roman design called a Gladius and brought to the Incas by their former visitors who taught them how to forge the steel and fashion the blade and handle. We saw these in the Yucatan and also in Peru when we confronted the Toltecs and Incas."

Simon was getting impatient and interrupted all the rhetoric. "Okay you guys, enough chattering. We need to get out of here. I'm sure our pursuers are close behind and may show up any time. Santos, you need to reset that trap...maybe it will snare one of those goons who might be on our tail."

This brought everyone back to reality, prompting them to gather up their packs and weapons and prepare to move out. "Which way, Professor?" Simon questioned. "Since you're our new guide and seem to know where we're going."

"To the southwest," Scott shouted back, pointing in the general direction. "Based on the position of the sun, I'm pretty sure we want to travel toward those hills in the distance."

With packs and equipment secured, the Americans began their trek away from the temple and toward the distant horizon.

Marcel and Devereaux had no problem following the path of the Americans. Marcel was an excellent tracker and easily picked up the occasional footprints and distinct signs of crushed grass and weeds left by the trekkers before them. It didn't take long for the pursuers to break out of the trees and enter the less vegetated Yungas Foothills. *Now we can make faster time*, he thought.

The mercenaries reached the small hillock with the temple ruins sitting on top. Allard was the first to notice it. "I think we should check it out," he suggested to Devereaux. "The Americans might be in there."

"I doubt it," The Frenchman answered, "but I agree we need to take a look. They most likely visited the ruins. Besides we may find some clues as to their intentions."

The short climb up the hill was easy and the group ascended to the ruins and entered through the small doorway. They could see that the east side of the one-storied building had caved in, allowing enough light to enter to be able to see without the use of torches.

"The place looks just like that building we saw on the river… even about the same size," Bruno remarked.

Marcel noticed the inscriptions on the rear wall. "These look like the same etchings we saw in the other building."

"Any idea what they mean?" Devereaux questioned curiously.

"I have no idea unless they are religious engravings of some sort. Maybe they are directional markings."

"Where to?"

"Who knows…maybe to another temple or maybe to the city of gold we seem to be chasing after."

Suddenly a piercing scream erupted from the far side of the room. The men rushed over to discover a gaping hole in the floor.

Gustavo was the first to reach the dark cavity. "Over here," he shouted. "There is no telling how deep this hole is."

The group shambled over to the opening and peered down into the total darkness. Devereaux glanced at the group and was the first to notice Jacques, the French mercenary, was missing. He turned to Marcel, "Jacques was the one that screamed. The clumsy bastard fell into the hole."

It only took moments to assemble a torch and tie it to a rope. The torch was lit and extended down into the void. The flickering light emitted eerie shadows along one wall, creating apparitions of ghostly images dancing across the room.

The prone figure of the unfortunate Frenchman lay sprawled on the floor. Part of his broken femur was sticking through the leg of his pants, indicating he had sustained a compound fracture with his fall. He lay there motionless…he was either unconscious or dead.

"What is all that debris scattered about?" Bruno barked.

"Those are bones," Marcel responded. "This cavern is nothing but a tomb. Those heaps you see down there are mummies… most likely the remains of Indian warriors. No telling what tribe they belonged to. It is best we leave them alone," he added with a tinge of nervousness. Being a superstitious man, he had no desire to tempt the spirits of the dead. "We need to keep going so the Americans won't get too far ahead of us."

"What about Jacques?" Bruno asked, already anticipating the answer.

"Did you see that bloody bone sticking through his pants?" Devereaux reminded him. "His leg is badly broken and he isn't moving. He might be dead for all we know and if not, he sure as hell can't walk and we can't carry him. We'll have to leave him here."

"That opening was a trap. You can tell by the door hanging down suspended on that bar." Bruno added angrily.

"Let's get the hell out of here," Marcel shouted. "This place is only for the dead."

Bruno just shook his head. He had superstitions as well. "Yeah, let's go."

From the sloping plateau that housed the temple ruins, the Americans descended into a shallow valley that leveled out into a reasonably flat grassy plain. In the far distance the first distinct slopes of the foothills were visible, promising access to the higher mountain range beyond. These were the Yungas Foothills, leading to the rugged mountains that guarded Lake Titicaca—and hopefully Os Três Diabos. They were hopeful that somewhere ahead in the far distance was the destination of their search—El Dorado.

Professor Scott felt it in his bones. He had a sixth sense that told him they were headed in the right direction. He turned to his companions and grinned confidently as he pointed toward the hills in the distance. "The lost city is somewhere over there…beyond that range of foothills…I know it is."

Somewhat less convinced, Elijah retorted, "I hope you're right, Professor, because my feet are killing me from all this hiking." There were a few nods from the others, confirming their similar discomfort.

The next few miles were relatively easy walking through grass covered rolling countryside. As they topped the next knoll, Santos held up his hand and signaled for an urgent halt. "What is it? Simon asked. "Why the sudden stop?"

"Everyone down," Santos commanded quietly.

The Americans dropped to the ground. "At the foot of that ridge…to our immediate front," he said, pointing.

His keen eyes had picked up activity at the base of the escarpment. Numerous figures could be seen moving about in what seemed to be coordinated precision maneuvers and well-formed ranks.

"What is it?" Roper asked apprehensively. "It looks like an entire army."

"It is an army blocking our route." Simon confirmed with vivid recollections. "We've seen those formations before, just above Cuzco in the Sacred Valley."

"We sure have," Santos confirmed. "Based on their dress and movements, I would say we are facing another army of Inca warriors, and the thing I am most worried about is that it appears they are expecting us."

26

"Who are they?" Patterson asked as he moved up to kneel beside Santos who was scanning the ranks before them.

"They look like Incas. Their battle dress appears to be Inca and the tight formations look like they are well trained for battle. They have to be Inca."

"What do we do now?" he asked with a sense of dread. "There must be several hundred warriors over there."

"I would say nearly two hundred or more," Santos answered confidently. "They must have known we were coming and were sent here to stop us from entering their sacred mountains."

"How could the Incas find out we were coming this way?" Mann asked. "We were nowhere near Peru or any Inca territory during our trip up the Amazon and the Madeira."

Professor Scott was quick to assess the situation. "Either they found out from the Jivaros or they had scouts out scouring the countryside for intruders. The fact they are here in full force tells me they are guarding or protecting something really important and they probably think we're after it."

"Like El Dorado," Elijah added.

"Exactly. That lost city must be mighty sacred to them to send out so many warriors."

"What do we do now?" Patterson asked. "We can't fight off a whole stinking army."

"Maybe we don't have to fight them," Elijah suggested with a hint of uncertainty in his voice.

Simon picked up on this immediately. "Pocaca," he mumbled.

"What's that supposed to mean?" Patterson questioned. "What is a Pocaca?"

"It's not a what but a who."

"You're talking in riddles… who is Pocaca?"

"He was the Inca chief we encountered on our expedition to Peru. We did him and the Incas a huge favor and he told us he would welcome us back anytime. If he's still alive and their head chief, I'm sure someone in that army over there will have heard something about our finding and returning the golden Inti to the Inca Nation."

"Maybe we should turn back," Patterson suggested.

"Too late for that," Santos answered. "Ranks of Indians are already fanning out to our sides to encircle us. We wouldn't make it back to the temple ruins."

"They know we are here?"

"Yes, they know exactly where we are," Santos assured him. "I'm sure they have known for a while…at least when we left the temple. They most likely had scouts following us."

"We have these repeating rifles," Roper injected. "We could make a stand and maybe hold them long enough to make a retreat back to the jungle."

"And what do we use for cover standing here out in the open all exposed?" Elijah reminded him.

"No, we don't need to retreat," Simon announced with a feeling of more confidence. "We'll march straight to their center and appear totally unafraid. I want to speak to their chief. Santos, you speak some Quechua so you will interpret for me. I'm certain their chief knows of Pocaca and hopefully aware of our previous help to him and his people in Peru."

"And if the war chief never heard of Pocaca?" Patterson asked.

"Then Robert, our heads will probably be hanging on poles tonight."

"Oh, shit," Mann groaned in the background with a foreboding expression.

"Let's head out and make our way to the center of their ranks…and keep your rifles shouldered and the barrels pointed toward the ground. We don't want to appear hostile in any way. And while you're at it, keep big smiles on your faces."

Patterson and Roper just shook their heads in disbelief and Mann kept silent with fatal thoughts spinning through his head.

The column moved out in single file and steadily approached the line of warriors fanned out to their front and both flanks. Simon reasoned the single file approach would appear less threatening and hopefully signal peaceful intent. "Keep your rifles shouldered and pointed to the ground," he reminded the group, "but make sure they are cocked and ready to fire."

Professor Scott gazed at the well-formed ranks before him and marveled at the precision of their movements. As with the same scene he had witnessed three years ago, in the Sacred Valley near Cuzco, his mind drifted back into history and envisioned the figure of one of the great Roman generals leading the phalanx before them. To him it was as if the scene had been transformed to 197 BC when Titus Quinctius Flaminius and his Roman army defeated the Antigonid dynasty of Macedon led by Philip V. That was the great battle that brought Alexander the Great's once powerful Macedonian empire under Roman control. Scott was transfixed by the scene unfolding before him and suddenly oblivious to the pending danger. His thoughts of important events of antiquity usually transformed his mind into another dimensional state. He was now in his element. Elijah glanced at the professor and noticed his faraway gaze. He shook his arm. "Snap out of it, Professor…this isn't the Roman army standing there."

Scott shook his head and came back to the present. "Oh, my goodness," he mumbled warily.

"What do you intend to do when we reach their lines?" Patterson pressed Simon with obvious trepidation. "That's a whole damn army over there against our tiny group of seven. Even our Winchester repeaters wouldn't have a chance against those numbers."

"I intend to talk to them," Simon answered with some annoyance to his tone. "Santos speaks their language and can communicate with them."

Patterson couldn't believe what he was hearing. For lack of anything else to say, he kept silent and whispered a soundless prayer for their deliverance. His natural instinct was to tighten his hand around the stock of his rifle…at least he would take a few of the warriors with him. He glanced at both Mann and Roper and saw their expressions of anxiety. Both were also clutching the stocks of their rifles.

As the Americans approached closer to the warriors, the ranks begin to shift into a double-line battle formation with another wide rank of archers poised behind. Bows were drawn and arrows ready to release. Scott again imagined Roman ranks drawn up for a closed battle assault for close infighting. The short swords they carried would decimate their enemy's front ranks. His fascination of their precision totally intrigued him. These soldiers had to be trained by Roman centurions. They are so disciplined and steady in their positions.

"Steady men," Simon commanded. "Don't make any sudden movements and keep your rifles pointed to the ground…and keep smiling like these guys are your best friends."

Elijah rolled his eyes. You've got to be kidding, he thought. My cousin is going to get us all killed. Wonder if these guys shrink heads like those Jivaros savages.

The small procession stopped just yards from the assembled ranks and Simon extended both arms forward with palms facing upward…the universal sign of friendship. The rows of warriors held fast and watched with fascination at these strange intruders who showed no fear. Simon whispered to Santos, "Tell them we come in peace and friendship and want to talk to their leader."

Santos shouted out in Quechua and repeated the request.

A ripple of sounds arose from the ranks as they processed these words from the outsiders…still the archers held fast with their arrows.

"What are they doing?" Mann whispered to Roper.

"I think they're trying to decide if they want to shoot us with the arrows or attack us with those swords and spears they are carrying."

The ensuing silence was deafening as both sides stood facing each other assessing the situation. It was especially a tense moment for the Americans who knew a simple command would send hundreds of arrows raining down upon them. As if on cue, the ranks before them split apart and a stately looking figure strolled from the lines flanked by ten or more serious looking warriors. His bearing indicated he was a figure of importance and his elaborate headband adorned with multi-colors revealed him to be a war chief. He stopped within a dozen feet from Simon and Santos and eyed them cautiously. "For what purpose do you white men enter the sacred lands of the Inca? You are not welcome in our lands. My warriors would have killed you but you held out your hands as a sign of friendship and asked to talk."

Simon spoke to the Inca while Santos interpreted. "My name is Simon Murphy and my companions and I come from the great land to the north called America. We are friends of the Inca and to your great chief Pocaca. We were in your land of the Sacred Valley near Cuzco three years ago and we were the Americans who found and returned the Golden Inti statue to Chief Pocaca and your people."

The chief stood there in silence as he absorbed these astonishing words from the white man. "I have heard of you, Simon Murphy. You must be the same ones who saved the life of my uncle at the battle of the mists at the fortress of Machu Picchu. He is Capac, once a great leader of the Black Puma Legion?"

"Yes, we fought with Capac," Simon answered with a great sense of relief for the recognition. "That man saved his life," he said, pointing to Professor Scott. "Capac made him a blood brother after the great mountain battle."

"Yes," the young chieftain admitted, "My uncle told me about the great battle with the Yaquis. He told me you helped win the battle and drove the hated Yaquis from our land."

"Is Capac still leader of the Black Pumas?" Simon asked.

"No," the young man answered. "Capac was wounded in another battle…the region of Madre de Dios…an encounter with one of the warring tribes to the north. My name is Pahuac, now leader of the Black Pumas you see before you."

"The fact that you are assembled here tells me you knew of our arrival to your land."

"Yes, we knew you were approaching our sacred lands and our mountains to the south. Our scouts always know when outsiders enter into our lands."

"How about Chief Pocaca? Is he still the great leader of the Inca Nation?"

"He is still our great leader and protected by our gods, Inti and Quetzalcoatl. The golden idol, Inti, you returned to him has given him great power and abundance for our people. You are truly friends of the Inca Nation."

Simon nodded his appreciation and placed his left fist against his chest to show respect to the young chief.

The gesture was acknowledged by Pahuac who nodded approval and returned the gesture. "I must ask you, American chief, what brings you to our sacred lands again?"

Simon knew he had better come up with a plausible answer. He did not want Pahuac to think they were here to find the lost sacred city, El Dorado, if it even existed. The young chief would believe they were here to plunder and steal the treasures placed there by his ancestors. Other men had tried to find the city of gold and many men had died, including Incas. A more convincing answer was needed. "Pahuac, we are here to find another great flying bird that was once sent to your people from Inti, your god of the sun. It is the same flying bird we found at your mountain fortress…the same flying bird that returned the Golden Inti to Pocaca and your people."

Pahuac was silent for a moment, processing Simon's comments. "Yes, I heard stories of the great flying bird from the sun. I remember hearing that Pocaca and Capac both entered the mouth of the bird and walked out safely. Their courage is still celebrated by our people because they were not eaten by the sacred bird. They were protected and honored by our gods. My uncle and Pocaca thought you and your men had been eaten by the bird when it flew away. The fact that you are now standing before me tells us you were also honored by our gods. I look forward to telling Pocaca and Capac you are alive and back into the land of the Inca. They will be pleased. I hope you find the flying bird you are seeking. When you find it I know Pocaca and Capac would like to see you again in our sacred valley near Cuzco. You will be honored as our guests." Pahuac turned and shouted out several commands to the ranks assembled behind him. The archers withdrew and the ranks split apart. He then turned back to Simon. "You are free to enter our lands." With a similar salute of his fist across his chest, he turned and marched back to his army with his small cluster of protective warriors following him.

Professor Scott was enthralled as he watched the ranks close up and make a precision oblique turn to the north. He heard distinct commands being shouted as warriors of the Black Puma Legion began their march from the escarpment and back up the valley. He imagined, those movements are similar to the drills Roman generals would have given their legions as they maneuvered through their various battle formations. Remembering what he had learned from their previous expedition to Peru, he again thought, there is no doubt in my mind that the Inca's ancestors had extraordinary visitors before the Spanish Conquistadors invaded their lands. How else would they have learned those precise Roman maneuvers?

He was especially fascinated with the short swords some of the Inca warriors were carrying. They were replicas of the famous Roman Gladius battle swords so effectively used in close quarter fighting by the Roman soldiers and they were very similar to those carried by some of the Inca warriors they had encountered in the sacred valley three years earlier. He was equally fascinated to learn the technology for forging the steel and the Roman weapon designs were given to the Incas by the visiting alien explorers six or seven hundred years ago.

Patterson turned to Simon. "I am totally dumbfounded these Indians knew about you and remembered your previous visit to Peru. The fact that Pahuac was the nephew of that Inca leader, whose life Professor Scott saved, was even more incredible. It certainly saved our lives and gave us a pass to enter their land. My hat's off to you, sir," he added, with new found respect for his new nephew.

"We were damned lucky, Robert…but I had a hunch they would have most likely known what we did for them three years ago. Fighting at their side at Machu Picchu and returning that golden statue to Pocaca was a very big thing to them."

"Do you think you should have mentioned something about that bunch of murderers following us back there on the river? He and his army could have stopped them."

"We haven't seen them for days. They probably gave up the chase and returned to Belém or wherever they came from or maybe the Jivaros got them."

"Don't count on it," Roper added, hearing the exchange between Simon and Patterson. "I'm sure those guys are trained killers and don't give up easily…especially the one named Marcel. Remember what Captain Cadiz told us about him? He's a very bad hombre and the others with him are probably equally as bad."

"Let's make sure we keep an eye on our backs," Simon conceded.

27

Devereaux and Marcel were hastily making their way along the trail the Americans had made. The tracks had been easy to follow, especially since there had been no rain to obliterate them. Marcel's companion, Gustavo, was getting fed up with the whole affair and wanted to return to Belém. He felt this whole venture was a wild goose chase and the hope of finding El Dorado was totally ridiculous. His mind was soaring with negative thoughts. El Dorado is just a legend made up by a bunch of Spanish soldiers who tried to make themselves believe there was a city of gold somewhere in the Amazon. This whole senseless chase is going to get us all killed for no purpose.

"Dammit, Marcel," he shouted angrily, "this whole thing is crazy. Why are we trying to kill ourselves chasing some Americans when you know damn well there is no El Dorado out there? The story is a myth…a hoax. I'm ready to turn around and go back to Belém before we all get ourselves killed for nothing."

Marcel exploded. "Gustavo, you are a damn fool for wanting to turn back now, especially since we are so close. If you want to run home like a coward then turn back. You know you wouldn't last a single day by yourself in that stinking jungle. If a headhunter didn't kill you then a crocodile would. Maybe I should save you the trouble and shoot you myself."

Gustavo was steaming but knew Marcel was right. He wouldn't last a day trying to get back to the river and past the Jivaros. He mumbled something to himself and fell back in line.

Devereaux was also having mixed emotions about the pursuit.

The object of his mission had been made clear by the French president: Follow the Americans until you find that flying ship they are searching for then kill them and bring that ship back to Paris. On the other hand, he now felt they were in search for a more desirable objective, El Dorado, a lost city full of gold and precious gems and a treasure that would make him filthy rich beyond his wildest dreams. With a fortune like that he could escape to anywhere in the world and lose himself with a new identity. His mind was reeling with avaricious thoughts…this city of gold holds more rewards than chasing after some preposterous flying machine that most likely no longer exists on our planet. Why should I share any of the treasure with France…after all, I'm the one taking all the risks. He knew Allard and Bruno would agree with him. In any event, he decided he would continue the chase to see where it would take him as visions of an indescribable lost treasure filled his mind. Greed could be an overwhelming motivator.

The first line of ridges loomed to the front of the Americans. They had entered the upper region of the Yungas Foothills at a point slightly north of Lake Titicaca and were headed due west toward some placid looking hills. Simon glanced briefly at Scott's improvised compass and then gazed out over the landscape to find a line of ridges facing them. "I think somewhere on the other side of those hills are the Cordillera Oriental Mountains and the Three Devils' peaks we are looking for."

The visibility was good and the distant hills were assumed to be the Yungas Foothills. Santos, whose trained eyes were constantly scanning their surroundings, suddenly held up his arm and shouted, "Stop!"

Even Professor Scott who was leading the group didn't notice it. Santos pointed. "To our immediate front, just below the peak, I see something skimming along the ground…a silver-like looking object."

"What the heck is that?" Simon questioned, now spotting the shell-like object moving swiftly across their direct line of sight.

"I see it now," Roper responded excitedly.

"That thing looks like a silver-colored inverted shell and it's moving pretty darn fast," Simon observed. "Kneel down; I don't want whatever it is to spot us."

The vibrating noise coming from his pack was loud enough for the others to hear. Simon removed his pack and reached for the small box containing the zenox. It was vibrating and emitting faint audible static noises. He held the device in the air and immediately a thin rod shot out between his fingers and the static increased. Although Patterson, Mann, and Roper were still mystified with the zenox, they stared at it with fascination as the noise continued. "That thing is going crazy!" Elijah remarked.

Simon held it higher. "I think it's communicating with that object and the weird noises must be a code of some type. I sure wish they would speak to each other out loud in English."

Santos said, "The thing has stopped and is pointing this way." The loud static continued.

"That darn thing knows we're here," Simon presumed.

"What do you think they're saying?" Elijah asked inquisitively.

With an annoying look Simon responded. "How the devil should I know? I don't speak static."

Suddenly, the zenox went silent and the thin rod pulled back into the casing. In the distance the silver-like object made an abrupt turn to the north and continued speeding along the base of the hills. They soon lost it as it vanished out of their line of sight.

"What do suppose that was?" Patterson questioned apprehensively. "I didn't see any wheels or anything that supported it. It looked like it was just floating on air."

"I have no idea," Simon confessed. "The zenox and that object seemed to recognize each other. We need to get to those hills and maybe we can find some answers in the mountains."

The next three miles were easy walking and the level landscape of grass and scrub offered no obstacles. They finally reached the first ridge of the Yungas Foothills and at the base was a small village. "We need to avoid that village," Simon declared. "We don't need to be seen by the natives. We'll skirt around it and try to stay concealed."

Santos turned to the group. "I'll scout around the village and see if I can find an easy route over that ridge. From here it looks like there might be a small pass leading to the summit. Why don't you men move over to that clump of trees to the left while I check things out?"

Simon agreed. "Good idea. We'll wait for you there…and don't be long…we need to keep moving."

It only took twenty minutes for Santos to return. "There is a stream that cuts through a narrow pass behind the village. We can work our way around to the rear and catch a trail on the other side that leads up the pass. The trail up the mountain looks well-worn…pretty easy hike. There is some tall vegetation behind the village and I think we can get pass it without being spotted."

With Santos leading the way, the group maneuvered around the village undetected and located the path on the far side. The hike to the summit was relatively easy and the view on the other side revealed a spectacular panoramic scene of the sprawling valley below and the towering peaks rising in the distance. Santos was the first to notice and shouted jubilantly. "To the north…to the north…look beyond the valley!" Towering majestically in the distance the three peaks stood out like a beacon. "Os Três Diabos… The Three Devils," he shouted again, pointing triumphantly at the three majestic peaks across the valley. "We've found them."

The rest of the group was ecstatic and celebrated with a few handshakes, hugs, and back slaps.

"I don't believe it," Roper acknowledged enthusiastically. "The Three Devils actually exist. According to the guide, Mapi, the lost city is located in a small valley just on the other side of the peaks. If we find it there that would mean the Spanish Conquistadores and all the other explorers after them all miscalculated their directions. This would place the city much farther south."

Simon turned to Professor Scott and with a big smile. "You did a great job of navigating, George. Darned if you and that paper compass you drew didn't pinpoint it and lead us right here."

"Scott just stood there with a big smirk and proudly answered back. "Yes, I sure did."

Elijah shouted, "Well, let's don't just stand here gawking like a bunch of chickens in a corn field. Let's go down there and find El Dorado…the city of gold."

28

THE WORN PATH TO THE VALLEY floor was an easy hike bolstered by their exhilaration and anticipation of finding the legendary city of gold. Each man could envision gazing upon stacks of gold bullion, gold coins and artifacts, and mounds of gemstones. To Simon, Elijah, and Santos, visions of the vast treasures they had found in the ancient Toltec city of Xepocotec eight years earlier flooded their memories. To Professor Scott, the thoughts of confirming the truth about an enigmatic legend and uncovering a lost city and historic treasure made him ecstatic. Breaking the Atlantean scrolls had given him great professional credibility with his colleagues, but actually finding the lost city of El Dorado would make him famous worldwide. His adrenalin was soaring.

Strangely, they had encountered no natives during their trek over the mountain. The valley appeared equally absent of human habitation. Could it be that the valley was considered occupied by the gods and spirits of the dead and any intrusion was forbidden? Santos thought so. A small river wound its way through the valley and provided an abundance of fresh water. There were no signs of habitation—no boats or huts to be seen anywhere. Scott looked up to see the three barren peaks staring at him. Those Three Devils are watching me, he imagined. No wonder there are no signs of humans anywhere around here…the natives are scared to death of this place.

Using the map Devereaux possessed, Marcel and the Frenchmen were able to skirt the village and find the path leading over the mountain that marked the end of the Yungas Foothills. Like the Americans preceding them, they avoided contact with the village inhabitants and easily made their way to the summit. Also, like their predecessors, the pursuers were awestruck to see the valley spread out in the distance and the majestic mountain range that towered on the far side. Even to these trained killers it was an awesome spectacle. "Look!" Pierre Allard shouted excitedly, pointing to the far side of the valley. "Os Três Diabos…The Three Devils! Marcel, your information was right…we've found it."

The three inscrutable overshadowing peaks stood out dauntingly. It was as if they were overlooking the valley below, just daring anyone to enter their private sanctuaries. The men could even envision the three sinister devils' faces overlooking the valley. Devereaux mumbled uneasily, "I think we've found the valley of death."

Marcel hesitated and stared at something moving on the valley floor…near the meandering river. Something had attracted his attention. "Hand me that spyglass," he shouted to Gustavo. "I see some figures."

Gustavo pulled the glass from his pack and handed it to the Portuguese killer. "It's them," Marcel shouted anxiously. "The Americanos! They are wading across the river. I count seven of them." He handed the glass to Devereaux.

"Yes, I see them, too," he grumbled with a glowering sense of satisfaction. "Now we have them. Let's get down off this mountain and see where they are going, but we don't want them to spot us."

The river was shallow and the wade across easy. Just beyond the river they found themselves directly under the first of the Three Devils' peaks. The bare rock cliff soared into the sky with the top hardly visible…a climb up the face seemed impossible. The sheer vertical precipice was nothing but smooth bare rock…no handholds or outcroppings could be seen. Simon turned to Roper. "What now, Sam? What did the guide tell you about the city? You know darn well the inhabitants didn't try to climb up that monster cliff."

Roper laughed, "I don't think we have to climb up the precipice's face. Mapi said the city was located in a small hidden valley behind the Three Devils. Somewhere along these cliffs there has to be a passageway. It's the only way the Indians could get to the valley and much less build a city there."

Simon glanced up at the towering peaks. "Let's spread out along the base of the three peaks and see if we can spot an opening. Be sure and look for a path or anything that leads up to an overhang that might conceal an opening. According to the guide, the city lies just behind this mountain…there has to be a passageway somewhere."

The men split into pairs, except Santos who took off on his own to explore the third "devil." Simon and Patterson took the nearest, Elijah and Scott the second, and Roper and Mann followed Santos to the farthest peak.

The men scrutinized every piece of rock, every crevice, and every niche they could find—nothing. They searched for a hidden path or obscure trail but came up empty. They tugged at rock outcroppings, hoping to find a lever or anything that would activate a hidden door—still nothing was found. The men met at the base of the second peak, except Santos who had disappeared. "Dammit," Elijah grumbled, "we searched every inch of this rock and there is nothing here…not even a gopher hole."

"Same here," Mann added. "These stinking walls are nothing but solid rock."

Frustration was mounting as they were running out of options. Simon was beginning to show his aggravation as he turned to Roper. "I can't believe we've come all this way for nothing. If there is a hidden valley somewhere behind these peaks then it's damn well hidden. How did the Indians get there? Maybe El Dorado doesn't exist after all. Sam, did that guide say anything else that would give us a clue?"

"No. All he said was the city is located in a hidden valley behind Os Três Diabos." He didn't tell me how to get there once we reached the peaks."

Mann, who was glancing over toward the river behind them

saw what appeared to be tiny figures approaching from across the valley. "Over there!" he shouted pointing to his front. "We have some people coming this way."

"Looks like four or five of them. Those are not Indians but white men," Roper observed.

"It's Marcel!" Simon grumbled angrily. "Those killers have found us."

At the same moment, Elijah was the one to notice movement to his left. In the distance Santos was perched on a slight mound near the base of the mountain waving vigorously.

"What's he doing?" Patterson questioned.

"He's motioning for us to come over there. Maybe he's found something." The group quickly made their way along the path to the base of the third peak.

"What is it?" Simon asked anxiously as they approached their companion.

"I may have found the key to opening a door. Does everyone have full canteens?"

"We all filled them at the river," Simon assured him. "Why?"

"Follow me and I'll show you."

"I hope you found a passage because we just spotted Marcel and his men coming across the field. They may have seen us."

Quickly the Americans moved along the base of the cliff as Santos led them toward the far side of the third peak. He abruptly stopped when they reached a section that contained a small niche carved into the rock. Within the recess a small inconspicuous basin protruded from the wall with a hole apparently drilled into the side of the bowl. Santos grinned. "Does this look familiar?" he asked.

"Inside the lava tube…under the city of Xepocotec," Elijah recalled. "The water-lock."

"What is that?" Patterson asked with a puzzled expression on his face.

"Let's hope it's the key to opening a door. We saw one like this in the Yucatan under the pyramid. It was a trigger that opened a door inside the cavern we were in."

Elijah took his canteen and poured the contents into the basin. Nothing happened as the water was draining through the hole.

"I'll try another one," Santos said as he poured his canteen into the basin.

"Nothing is happening," Patterson shouted apprehensively.

"Give it time. It takes a little time for the trigger mechanism to work. The Indians who designed this lock were ingenious."

Suddenly, a faint rumble was heard deep inside the rock face. It progressively became louder as the sound moved closer. Then to their total astonishment, a stone panel started to rise and opened up into a recess concealed in the header above. "How did that happen?" Roper responded. "That stone slab must weigh a ton."

Simon explained. "The ancient Indians used an ingenious series of weights and balances to move heavy objects. In this case, the weight of the water trickling through that hole caused a lightweight trigger, most likely a small pebble, sand, or a small rock, to move or shift. This gradual shifting of weight distribution would cause a heaver rock or even more sand to move, causing progressively heavier stones to shift their weights until the slab was lifted."

Patterson was astounded. "What an amazing apparatus! Absolutely incredible! Who on earth could think up such a clever device?"

"Either very smart people or the devil himself."

The dark void beyond revealed a deep passageway.

"We need to move quickly," Elijah reminded them. "Marcel and his band of cutthroats are right behind us." The group needed no prodding as they passed quickly through the opening.

Much like a similar apparatus they had experienced in Mexico, just inside the entrance Santos found the recess containing the reset lever that deactivated the mechanism for the door. Santos pulled the lever and heard the distinct rumble of the rebalancing process begin. The sequence took a few moments but to their relief, the slab started the slow descent to the floor. "Let's hope Marcel and his cutthroats don't find the opening," Patterson commented. "We sure don't need those murderers coming up behind our backs."

"Yeah," Elijah agreed. "I'd hate to get into a fight inside this confined tunnel…no cover and no way to hide from ricocheting bullets."

29

Marcel, Devereaux, and the other three pursuers approached the peaks with caution, expecting a gunfight to erupt any second. There was only silence. "Where the hell did they go?" Gustavo growled.

"They have to be somewhere along the base of those mountains. I am sure they are looking for a trail or passageway," Marcel answered. "Stay low and be quiet. We want to take them by surprise."

Gustavo, besides being known as a hardened killer, was very superstitious of ancient spirits and phantasms. He looked up at the three peaks towering above them. All he could imagine was the three huge angry devils looking down at him. A sudden sense of dread and foreboding overcame him and filled his mind with an intense feeling of fear and panic he had not experienced before. Those devils want revenge for trespassing into their sacred land. We are all going to die for sure. He screamed loudly. "The Americanos have disappeared. The devils have eaten them and now we are next."

"Shut up, Gustavo…everyone for miles around, including the Americanos, will hear you."

The Portuguese assassin was enraged as he glared at Marcel with a twisted expression of disgust and fear. "Marcel, you are crazy," he shrieked. "There is no city of gold and you are going to get all of us killed for nothing. I'm leaving!" He turned and started back toward the river.

Marcel had had enough of Gustavo. He pulled his revolver

from his pack, calmly took aim, and fired three shots. The .44 caliber slugs tore into the man's back, dropping him instantly. Gustavo pitched forward to the ground before he realized what hit him—he was dead on impact.

"What the hell did you do that for?" Devereaux shouted.

"The man was a damn fool and a coward," Marcel shouted back. "We don't need him. Let's grab his rifle and clean out his pack. The animals will take care of him. Then we'll find the Americanos."

Inside the passageway, Professor Scott pulled the lantern from his kit and lit it. In the dark confines of the tunnel, the light illuminated the space well enough to allow a good view of the corridor and path that stretched before them.

Mann was curious. "Do you suppose this is the only entrance to the valley? Wouldn't you think the Indians would need a larger access to haul rock and materials through to the build their city? They would need wagons or some other way to haul materials in."

Scott had a plausible answer. "They didn't have wagons back then. There is probably an entrance from the other side that leads to the ocean. I would imagine rock was quarried from the cliffs surrounding the valley. They wouldn't have to move them far to shape the stones for the construction of their buildings."

"How would they have possibly carved this tunnel through solid rock?" Mann further questioned.

Scott had an answer for that as well. "Look at the smooth rock lining the walls and ceiling of this passageway. It had to be carved by water…most likely an ancient underground river. You can see some signs of chisel marks along the walls where they enlarged the shaft but most of the ceiling and floor is smooth. I'm sure this was a secret entrance that allowed them easy access to the valley we just left and it was apparently constructed in a way to prevent their enemies from entering the city."

"If there really is a city," Roper added with reservation. "Remember, El Dorado is a legend conjured up by Spanish

Conquistadors. I still think the city is most likely more myth than real."

The tunnel floor was smooth and allowed easy walking. Fortunately the ceiling height was sufficient enough to allow them to pass through without having to stoop over…just over six feet. It was no problem for the Indians of that day, who were shorter in height.

The group was well into the mountain with Mann leading the column when he felt a slight movement under his foot. Instinctively he hesitated…it saved his life. There was a loud rush of air followed by a heavy spiked door that sprang across the corridor at lightning speed, slamming into a recess on the opposite wall. Mann was pinned tightly against the door, his shirt impaled by three sharp wooden spikes. The points had missed his chest by fractions of an inch. Roper rushed to his friend's side. "He's alive!" he shouted.

Mann was too stunned to talk as Roper cut his shirt loose from the deadly apparatus. Santos spotted it…a small figure of a coiled serpent carved into the wall just above eye level. "What is that?" Patterson asked apprehensively.

"We saw these carved figures in Peru…inside a similar tunnel," Santos explained. "It's a marker to warn the friendly natives of a trap. It was also used as a trigger to retract and then reset the trap for unwanted visitors. This snake has his fangs exposed, which mean a trap is located close by. If there were no fangs it would serve as a directional signal pointing to the way the head was facing. In this case the serpent has its fangs showing and the trap was positioned just under the figure. It was activated when Mann stepped on that floor panel. He was very lucky he stopped in time. The ancient Indians loved to set traps like this and most of them were very clever. We learned this the hard way in Peru…the serpent saved our lives on several occasions."

Mann was still too stunned to speak.

Elijah agreed. "We encountered a bunch of these nasty traps under the Toltec pyramid in the Yucatan…and it was a miracle we were able to survive them. Thanks to the keen eyes of Santos, we avoided most of them. Now you see why I hate slithering snakes," he grumbled.

Santos reached and grasped the serpent figure and rotated it to the left. The spiked door pulled out of the recess and shot back into the opposite wall. When the men had safely passed over the floor panel, Santos rotated the figure back to the right. A loud click was heard and the trap was reset for another suspecting intruder. "If our pursuers find the tunnel maybe this trap will stop or delay them."

As the men proceeded, a slight movement of air was noticed flowing toward them. The draft seemed to become stronger as they moved forward. "Do you feel that?" Elijah mentioned to Simon. "Smells like fresh air."

"We're nearing an entrance and should be almost at the end of the passageway."

Faint traces of light appeared to be filtering through the tunnel and it became increasingly brighter as they continued walking. Suddenly a bright patch of light appeared ahead and they walked through an opening and found themselves on a protruding shelf of smooth worn rock. They were confronted by a panoramic view of a heavily wooded valley comfortably nestled between the precipitous cliffs. In the distance, a thin waterfall spilled effortlessly to the valley from an opening in the opposite cliff face. With an abundance of water and sunlight flooding the valley from the open sky, this explained the presence of the dense vegetation. A stone column positioned at the edge of the overhang marked the top of a long flight of stone steps that descended to the ground. The group stood there quietly gazing out at the spectacle before them when Simon broke the silence. "We found it…the hidden valley. Now let's go down there and see if we can find the lost city of gold."

30

Devereaux was getting annoyed as they searched along the base of the peaks. "I don't see any path or trail. Where have they disappeared to? It's like the mountain just swallowed them up."

"Maybe that's what happened," Marcel countered. "There has to be an opening or doorway somewhere. Spread out and look for any signs of a lever or something that might open a passageway."

The mercenaries spent over an hour searching for a key to an opening but only stared at sheer rock walls. The anger and frustration kept mounting when Bruno was seen trotting around the base of the second peak shouting something and motioning the others to follow. "I found something," he yelled. "Might be what we are looking for."

He led them to the base of the last peak and pointed to a shallow niche in the rock. "I removed some brush and found this shallow basin. There is a hole at one end and the bowl still shows a sign of moisture…like water was poured into it. It sure looks suspicious to me," he added.

Marcel took his water pouch and poured the contents into the basin. "Hand me your canteen," he said to Bruno. He dumped his water into the bowl and watched as he water drained through the hole.

"Nothing is happening," Allard growled.

"Give it time," Marcel shot back. "The early Indians had very clever ways to move heavy objects, so give it time."

After a few anxious moments, a soft rumble was heard, followed by a distinct grinding noise deep within the rock. They watched in amazement as a stone slab began to ascend into a hidden recess above. It exposed the dark passage beyond.

"I was right," Marcel pronounced smugly. "The Three Devils swallowed them up."

Reaching the base of the steps, Santos led the small band of Americans toward the edge of the woods. He was looking for telltale signs of a trail and remnants of man-made structures that might give hints of former habitation. The forest appeared to be more jungle-like with an abundance of vines and broad leaf fern or palmetto type plants covering the ground…unusual for this section of the country. "Why do these woods look so different than the vegetation we passed through in the foothills?" Mann asked curiously. "It looks like some of the jungle growth we saw in the Amazon."

"The abundance of light and water from the falls must give this confined valley plenty of moisture that contributes to all the growth," Scott answered. "You can feel the humidity…much like what we experienced along the Amazon and Madeira Rivers."

Elijah looked to one side and noticed something different in the pattern of vegetation along the edge of what looked like it might be an old road. He observed a stack of stones partly concealed by vines. They were arranged in an orderly pattern and stacked about three feet in height. "Over here!" he shouted. "I think I've found the remnants of a wall."

"It sure looks like a rock wall to me," Scott confirmed. "Or what's left of one."

Santos noticed a narrow track relatively clear of vegetation extending into the woods. "This looks like it might be an old road. Let's follow it."

As they advanced, more remnants of a wall lining the narrow corridor were observed. Although badly deteriorating, there was no doubt the rubble was the remains of an old stone wall. Soon more stone debris appeared on the opposite side of the strip giving further evidence that the track they were walking on was an old roadway leading into the center of the forest. Mann, Roper, and

Patterson fanned out to the right side and the others to the left. "Keep your eyes peeled for any signs of a structure or building," Simon suggested.

"I thought the streets of El Dorado were lined with gold," Roper jested. "That's what the legend says."

Elijah laughed. "I doubt if the Incas had that much gold to hide, especially to waste it on building a road."

Professor Scott had a thought. "The Inca chief, Atahualpa, wanted to hide all of the empire's gold from Pizarro and the Conquistadores, not display it for the world to see and find it. If this is the actual location of the city, I'm sure the treasure is buried and stored in chambers well beneath the ground and protected by more of those hideous traps."

The narrow track continued deeper into the interior as the low stone barriers on either side became more pronounced and intact. There has to be some remnants of structures ahead, Scott thought. His adrenalin was soaring with visions of an incredible discovery. I just know El Dorado is close by. I can feel it.

The professor's senses were correct again as the outline of a larger wall appeared to their right. It was the side wall of a building that connected with a decaying facade facing the road. The roof had long decayed and collapsed but the structure was remarkably intact. A little further, the remains of another structure appeared and soon even more remains of buildings were evident. This was definitely the ruins of an ancient habitat. Scott observed the stonework and design of the buildings were different from those they had seen in Peru. They seemed considerably more primitive than the structures built by the Toltecs, Mayans, and Incas. The stonework was more rudimentary and crude than others they had observed to the north. "I don't think this city was built by the Incas," he concluded. "I think much earlier tribes like the Chibchas may have been the occupants here. Many of these Indians migrated this far south from Columbia to get away from the Spanish invaders. When the original dwellers died out, the Incas most likely occupied the remains of the city to bury their treasures. Pizarro would have had a tough time finding this place."

"So what should we be looking for?" Simon asked.

"To protect their treasures for all time, they would have probably picked a sacred place guarded by their sun god, Inti, and other spiritual deities…most likely a pyramid or a temple."

"I agree," Simon concurred, as Santos nodded his agreement. "Let's look for a building that might fit that description. It is doubtful the early builders would have had the resources to build a pyramid, but a small temple would be more like it."

The road continued until it intersected into a small circular plaza with a tall column standing in the center. Perched on the top was a crumbling statue of Inti, the Inca sun god, referred by the ancients as Apu-Punchau. They noticed the small plaza was lined with similar paving stones set in an organized pattern. It was definitely the center of town.

Simon pointed to the carving—it aroused his curiosity. "That stone statue of Inti, the Inca sun god; it's very similar to the golden idol we returned to the Inca chief Pocaca three years ago."

Scott picked up on this. "That means the column and figure had to be built by the Incas when they occupied the city. They must have come here after the Chibcha occupants died out or maybe the Incas conquered them and took over the city for themselves. That statue proves the Incas were actually here and I'll bet it's the place where they buried their treasure. Now all we have to do is find it."

Marcel led the Frenchmen along the path that carried them deeper into the mountain. There was enough fresh airflow in the tunnel to keep the two torches burning brightly so visibility and maintaining a steady pace was not a problem. It happened so quickly that the three Frenchmen trailing didn't notice it. They only heard the sudden scraping sound and a heavy object slamming into the wall. A muffled moan escaped from Marcel's mouth…and then silence.

"What the hell was that?" Bruno yelled.

Devereaux cautiously approached the object and saw Marcel hanging limp, impaled against the wall. "This thing is a spiked door…a trap. Those spears went right through his body. The man is stone dead."

"It's a good thing we weren't walking the point or one of us would be hanging on those spikes," Allard commented. "Well… we wanted to dispose of Marcel but it looks like the Indians beat us to it. Now, the problem is how we open that bloody door. There has to be a trigger somewhere to deactivate it. The Indians would not have allowed this tunnel to be permanently blocked."

"Maybe this snake will help," Allard suggested, glancing up at the carved serpent mounted on the wall. "I'll try moving it."

The Frenchman reached up and grasped the snake figure and tried pulling it toward him, but it would not budge. He tried twisting it to the right…still nothing. He reversed the rotation to the left and heard a loud click. The spikes pulled from the wall and the door quickly returned to its recess in the opposite wall, resetting the trap. Marcel's limp body slid to the floor in a heap.

Bruno was aghast. "What do we do with him?"

"Devereaux glanced down at the prone figure with a total lack of remorse. The trap had done the job for him. "We leave him and get the hell out of this death trap." There were no objections as the three Frenchmen passed over the man's body and resumed their way through the passageway.

31

THE AMERICANS WERE ELATED THEY HAD actually discovered the lost city. At least this part of the legend seemed to be true. On the far side of the plaza a two-story structure confronted them with a small square building dominating the summit. A flight of stone steps had been constructed from the ground to the top level. The walls supporting the larger building had a few openings, most likely windows to provide light. It was the biggest structure they had seen so far. From their experiences and observations in Peru, Scott surmised the crumbling edifice on the top was most likely a religious shrine or perhaps a small temple. It was built much like those they had visited earlier on the Madre de Dios River and in the Yungas Foothills. "I think we've found the place we're looking for," he announced. "This must have been a communal gathering place used for religious or other social events. Let's check it out. We'll start with that smaller building on top. I want to see if it matches those other two temples we visited and see if it has similar inscriptions carved on the wall."

The stairway spanned the two stories to the roof and to an open doorway positioned through the front wall. The climb was easy and the Americans passed through the entrance to find a similar structure as the previous two temples. Small openings around the perimeter of the building provided enough light without the need for torches. The far wall immediately caught their attention. Carved into the stone were identical glyphs and inscriptions as they observed previously, with one exception…like the others, the top two were different. As they stood there looking at this startling discovery, the audible vibrations coming from Simon's pack were heard across the room. "It's that gadget of yours," Elijah shouted. "The damn thing is going crazy again."

Simon reached into his kit and pulled the small box out and retrieved the zenox device. He held it up and the familiar thin rod shot out and a red light began to blink vigorously. It was obviously reading the inscriptions on the wall and transmitting signals. Suddenly, a loud static resonated and a familiar voice filled the room. "Welcome, Simon Murphy, we see you have found the city and our command center."

"Nezar!" Simon shouted.

"Yes, this is Commander Nezar."

"Are you still serving with Commander Ahular?"

"Yes," the strange accented voice boomed out, "the commander is still with us and most anxious to see you again."

"Where are you located?" Simon asked.

"Our security protocol will not allow that information," Nezar answered back. "Just follow your zenox." Then the voice was silenced and the communication device went dead.

"Who was that?" Patterson asked, totally stunned.

Mann and Roper's funny expressions also betrayed their complete bewilderment.

Simon chuckled. "That was the voice of Vice Commander Nezar, from the alien space ship, Cuzco…the one we rode on in Peru and the ship that saved our planet from exploding into a million pieces three years ago."

"I can't believe this," Patterson said, shaking his head as if trying to dispel a bad dream. "That's incredible…Absolutely incredible. If that's someone from another planet, how come he speaks English so well?" he added.

"These people have incredible advanced intelligence and they were able to learn our language by listening to us converse in the cavern in the Yucatan. They told us the English language is composed of derivatives of ancient languages such as Latin, Germanic, Sanskrit, Saxon and several others. They also said they have many languages from other civilizations from other galaxies stored in their computers. Apparently, they were able to reconstruct and assimilate our language from these older dialects and by listening to us talk."

Patterson couldn't believe what he was hearing. "You mean to tell me that there are other people living on other planets?" he asked, symbolically pointing toward the sky.

Professor Scott cut in and answered for Simon. "When I was in their command center in the underwater bubble on the sunken continent of Atlantis, I asked Commander Ahular about the possibility of life in outer space. He told us there were thousands of other civilizations and living things out there ranging from most primitive to the far advanced. He said there are several hundred million suns in our universe that have millions of planets revolving around them within a temperate zone…planets much like our earth. That means an atmosphere that allows a climate and temperature environments that can sustain life. Ahular and his explorers are from a planet called Xeres located in a solar system millions of miles from here. It's very similar to earth. They are explorers that have visited many planets. For some reason they were assigned to watch and observe us humans like their ancestors have done for hundreds of years."

"In my wildest dreams I could not have ever dreamed up a story like that," Mann confessed, "not in a million years."

"We were just as stunned as you when we heard all of this," Elijah admitted.

Simon broke the rhetoric and shouted to his companions. "Their command center has to be close by so let's go find it and hopefully the city of gold."

All agreed.

It was reasoned that the command center would be located somewhere underground—perhaps under this temple. They also reasoned that the Inca chief, Atahualpa, would have instructed his warriors to hide the Inca gold and treasures in a secure place where the Spanish would not find it. "We'll start on the first floor of this building and see if we can find an opening to an underground passage. It will most likely be very inconspicuous."

They entered the first floor through a large doorway facing the plaza. The room was large and hazily illuminated by light filtering through small windows sparsely located around the perimeter walls. The first thing that attracted their attention was the large stone statue of the Inca god, Quetzalcoatl, towering against the far wall. The effigy was represented by a feathered serpent with its wings spread out, like in flight. To the Meso-American Indians this figure was worshiped as the god of intelligence and self-reflection. They also considered the winged serpent as the primordial god of creation and giver of life…they believed he created the world.

"Good grief!" Roper declared. "How could the Indians have worshiped a snake? It sure looks spooky to me."

"You can see why I hate the slimy bastards," Elijah concurred.

"This effigy is further proof that the Incas were here," Scott added. "It must have taken them months to carve that big statue… and more proof they occupied this city for a lengthy period of time. Like Machu Picchu, his place must have been a safe haven for the Incas who escaped from the Conquistadors who were slaughtering their fellow tribesmen to the north."

Santos had been scouring the walls for signs of an opening. So far he had found nothing but pieces of broken stone benches and a few pottery fragments lying on the floor. The walls were bare and no signs of niches, protrusions, or levers were found. There has to be an opening leading to some lower chambers, he reasoned. Santos' instincts were usually right. If this temple was the gathering place for the city and similar to other ancient temples they had visited, there had to be lower levels containing catacombs, corridors, rooms, and perhaps a large cavern. He knew there was a hidden trigger somewhere in this room.

"Over here, Santos. I found something…behind the statue," Elijah shouted.

Santos and the others rushed to the rear of the large structure and found Elijah pointing to a spot on the wall just above his head. It was located in a small depression carved into the stone. It was a small snake figure similar to the one they had discovered in the tunnel above the spiked door trap. "That's it!" Santos shouted elatedly as he reached up, grasped the lever and rotated it to the left. It wouldn't budge. He tried it again to the left and then to the right. He felt slight movement. He took a deep breath, and then with all his strength twisted the figure again to the right. The serpent broke its seal and sharply rotated 90 degrees. A familiar soft rumble was heard deep within the wall followed by a sequence of heavy scrapes and grinding noises. A stone panel began to slowly slide to the right and nest into a deep wall recess. The opening beyond revealed the threshold and a long flight of steps leading to a dark and sinister looking void below.

The vibrating noise sounded off again from Simon's pack. Retrieving the zenox he could feel the device as it swiveled slightly in his hand to point to the opening in the wall. "Well, it looks like we're on the right track. The zenox is pointing to the stairwell. This is what Nezar meant when he said for us to follow the zenox."

"Time to light your lantern, Professor," Simon said to Scott as the group of Americans paused anxiously at the doorway, waiting to descend to the depths and into another world.

32

Devereaux and his two companions emerged from the tunnel and stood on the shallow terrace overlooking the lush valley below. They were stunned by the panorama spread out before them. The valley was encircled by sheer cliffs that rose hundreds of feet and opened up to a cloudless sky. They were equally amazed by the distant waterfall that spilled from the sheer rock face on the far side of the valley. "No wonder this place has been lost for centuries," Devereaux commented. "It's a perfect hiding place. The place is impenetrable."

"I wonder if the tunnel we came through is the only way out," Allard questioned. "I can't imagine the former occupants would have allowed themselves to be trapped in here."

"There has to be another way, most likely a tunnel or path somewhere that leads to the other side of the mountain. The map shows there is a large range of mountains on the other side of this Cordillera Oriental Range then a fairly level plain that continues on to the Pacific Ocean. You know the Indians had to have access to the ocean or at least to the mountains on the other side. Right now our job is to find the Americans and see if there really is a city filled with gold like the legend says."

"What about our mission?" Bruno questioned. "Remember, you told us President Thiers wanted us to follow the Americans and find a secret weapon and bring it back to France."

"To hell with Thiers and France," Devereaux barked angrily. "They don't care about us. We are in this for ourselves now. If we find the gold, we can all retire to some lush place where no one can ever find us and if we find the secret weapon, we'll sell it to the highest bidder for millions of francs."

Both Allard and Bruno pondered his words for a moment then both nodded affirmably. The French Le Guarde agents responded. "Count us in."

"Good," Devereaux acknowledged. "Now, let's take these steps to the valley floor and find the Americans and the gold."

Inside the passageway, Santos found the familiar serpent imbedded in the wall and turned it to close and reset the heavy door. With the deep sound of grinding and grating, the stone slab slid back to its original position. Scott's oil lantern illuminated the tunnel as the Americans began their descent down the long flight of steps. They walked in single file with Santos leading the way. The wavering shadows cast by the lantern made the walls appear alive, casting ghostly phantoms along the shaft as they pushed forward. The appearance gave each man an uneasy feeling they were descending into a very unpleasant place…an underworld of death. Step by step they moved downward into the darkness until they came to a small landing that marked the point where the steps began a slight curve to their left. Santos abruptly stopped and held his hand in the air. Something was amiss…his senses registered a harsh warning. "Hold it," he shouted. "Something is not right." The young man's keen senses rarely failed him and had kept him and his companions from a fatal disaster on several occasions during their prior expeditions.

"What is it?" Simon asked.

Santos pointed to a shallow niche above his head, high on the wall. "Up there…a small round stone that looks suspicious." The projection jutted very slightly out from the wall. "It could be a trigger."

"How in the world did you spot that inconspicuous thing?" Patterson asked. "I would have never seen it."

"Mr. Patterson, let me show you what would have happened if you had stepped on the landing." Santos reached up and pressed the button. A sharp thudding noise resounded through the passageway as a heavy spike studded frame dropped from the ceiling, simultaneously followed by a floor panel that suddenly released downward. The frame plunged through the opening and came to a sudden stop. In a matter of seconds they heard another thump and a heavy metal shaft snapped back into the ceiling, pulling the spiked panel with it. The floor panel lay open, suspended on a bar, and the view through the opening revealed a huge black space below. "This is a very nasty trap and no telling how deep the cavity is…I would imagine several hundred feet."

Patterson was speechless, realizing the deadly consequences that could have occurred.

Simon was fascinated with the complicated sequence the trap's mechanism had to execute to initiate the plunge from the ceiling and then retract upward into its recess. "This thing is ingenious with all the series of mechanical stages it had to go through to activate it. Those spikes could have impaled two or three men at one time and then drop their bodies into that chasm below. We've seen some nasty traps but this has to be one of the worst."

"What kind of Indians would build this horrible thing?" Patterson mumbled, shaking his head in disbelief.

"This trap wasn't made by Indians," Elijah responded loudly. "It was probably put here by the devil himself."

Santos explained further. "It is a rather complicated device. I was able to trigger the trap by pressing the button, but had you stepped on the landing, your weight would have sprung it. The amazing thing is how the spiked panel was able to re-cock itself and quickly retract back into the ceiling. It would be interesting to look inside that wall to see all the parts that made this thing work. It took a lot of sudden and successive weight and pressure transfers." Santos then reached for the button and pressed again… nothing. He pressed it twice in succession and the floor panel rotated upward on the supporting spindle and snapped back into place. The trap was now re-cocked and ready for more unsuspecting victims.

Mann asked, "You reset the thing so how do we get across?"

Simon answered. "We jump over the floor panel."

Santos was the first to leap over the narrow space and land securely on the first step below the landing. Mann jumped next followed by Roper and then the others. The first jumpers were able to catch and stabilize their companions who followed to prevent some nasty falls. They all made it over safely and continued their trek to the lower levels.

"I wonder if that trap can be locked." Elijah asked Santos. "You know the Indians didn't keep it active all the time. They had to have a locking device built in so they could easily pass over it when they walked down the steps."

"I am sure it can somehow be locked with the trigger button," Santos reassured him. "I would have to play around with it a bit to find the sequence but we need to keep going. Maybe it will catch a couple of our pursuers if they are still following us."

The possibility of the trap eliminating some of the mercenaries was reassuring.

Devereaux and his companions had found the old road and followed it to the plaza located in the center of the town. The larger building facing them dominated the square and from his experience in Peru, Devereaux knew the small building on the top had to be a small temple or some type of religious structure. That meant the larger two storied building supporting it had to be used for social and spiritual gatherings. He and his two companions entered the front doorway into the large room occupying the space. They were stunned to find the large statue of Quetzalcoatl towering above them. "What is that thing?" Bruno shouted. "Looks like a huge snake with wings."

Devereaux laughed. "That's what it is you idiot…a winged serpent. The Incas thought this was a god that created their civilization. I was told they believed that winged snake flew their ancestors down from the sun and deposited them here on earth."

"How ridiculous," Allard retorted. "Snakes don't fly."

"Who knows? Anyway, that's what they believed."

Bruno spotted the tracks in the dust around the floor

surrounding the statue. "Over there," he pointed. "Someone has been walking around the statue."

The footprints were discernible, leading around to the rear of the large effigy. Devereaux bent down to take a closer look. "It looks like the Americans found something back there…must be an opening or door. That's how they disappeared into thin air." Moving quickly to the rear of the statue, they scanned the base of the figure and examined the wall behind it. "Look for a handle or lever. There has to be something here."

Allard spotted it first…a small inconspicuous shape of a snake embedded in a small recess in the wall. "Maybe this is it," he said. "I'll see if I can turn it." He pushed it to the left…nothing happened. He rotated it to his right and the distinct sound of a rumble emanated from the wall, followed by a heavy scraping noise. The heavy stone slab slid into its recess, revealing the dark passageway beyond.

"How many torches do we have?" Devereaux asked, turning to Bruno.

"I made six of them. Two for each of us."

"Go ahead and light one…you can lead the way." Devereaux had experienced shafts like this three years before in Peru and did not relish the idea of taking the point. It could lead to fatal results. He would stay to the rear.

"How about the door?" Allard asked. "Think we should try to close it?"

"No. Leave it open. We may have to make a quick escape out of here."

The three men started their descent down the long stairwell. The flickering shadows from the torch gave the passage an eerie feeling… an unnerving sensation. Bruno, being very superstitious, could sense the gaze from ancient spirits staring at him from the walls. What a sinister place, he thought, sensing a premonition of doom. "A landing ahead," he shouted, "and then the steps curve to the left."

"Keep moving," Devereaux replied. "I want to find those Americans."

Bruno stepped on the landing and it happened instantly. The heavy spiked panel plunged from the ceiling immediately followed by the floor panel that dropped and pivoted into the void. Bruno was struck by the heavy frame and brutally impaled by several spikes. He was dead before the sudden thrust of the panel plunged his body into the bottomless void and then retracted back into the ceiling. The whole process had only taken a few seconds. The floor panel stayed open, exposing the dark cavity below. Devereaux and Allard were totally aghast as they stood there staring at the ominous cavity below their feet. Bruno had vanished. "Let's jump over that damn hole and get the hell out of here…and fast!" Devereaux screamed. "This stinking place is the doorway to hell!"

The Americans reached the bottom of the stairwell and entered a long corridor. At the threshold there was another suspicious looking narrow panel embedded in the floor, similar to the one they had encountered on the landing above. Santos failed to spot any signs of the winged serpent activation device on the wall, but didn't want to take any chances. "Jump over the panel," he warned. "It could be another trap." It was an easy hop to the floor.

Several yards into the passageway, doorways appeared on opposite sides leading into two small rooms. Santos looked into the doorway to his left…it was empty. He then took Scott's torch and thrust it into the door to his right and peered into the room. The room was adequately illuminated by the flame. "Mummies," he announced curiously. "This room is filled with mummies."

Within the small chamber, there were stacks of mummies that appeared to be piled three or four high. The bodies had been coated in a dark resin meant to protect the occupants for their eternal journey into the afterlife. The mummies were definitely similar to others they had seen in the catacombs in Xepocotec and a cavern in Peru—the embalming coating was also comparable and provided a remarkable amount of protection from deterioration.

Professor Scott noticed something unusual at one side of the room. There were eight more mummies piled against a wall—they were different. "Simon, come over here," he shouted. "Take a look at these."

The group moved toward the wall. "These mummies are not like the others. They are much taller…I would guess six feet or more and they have different colored hair…much fairer and longer. These mummies are not Indian. They look more like European…like Vikings. They look similar to those we saw earlier in the temple ruins."

"They are different," Simon acknowledged curiously. "How do you suppose they got here?"

"Good question, especially since the Vikings existed about two to three hundred years before the Inca Civilization. The Viking Age existed generally from the ninth to the late eleventh century and the Incas came along during the thirteenth to sixteenth century. These mummies sure add more mystery to this place."

"Maybe they aren't Vikings," Patterson injected. "Perhaps they are European from another era."

"That's possible," Scott answered. "Whoever they were, they had to have a good knowledge of ships and the sea in order to get here. Maybe they were sea-faring explorers from the Mediterranean. I hope we can find some answers when we reach the end of this infernal tunnel."

There were piles of spear points and other assorted decayed weapons lying about, signifying they must have been the remains of distinguished warriors who had died in battle. As usual, Scott offered another observation. "These mummies could be Chibcha or a similar ancient tribe, most likely the original builders who once occupied this city."

Roper, who was standing in the door and partially in the passageway, heard a distinct sound to his rear and well above him. It sounded like a crash of something heavy. It came from the steps they had previously descended, most likely from the landing above. "We have visitors!" he shouted with alarm, "coming down the stairwell. It sounds like some poor bastard may have triggered that trap on the landing."

Simon peered around the door and saw a flickering light in

the distance moving slowly toward them. "Looks like our pursuers finally caught up with us," he whispered. "Have your rifles cocked and ready…we may be getting into a gunfight."

Patterson, Roper, and Mann moved silently into the opposite doorway with rifles poised while Simon, Elijah, and Scott covered the door of the mummy room. The torch was extinguished as Santos stood to the rear, ready to reignite it in an instant when needed. They would use the darkness of the passage to conceal their presence and the light from their pursuers' torch would enable them to assess the threat.

Elijah whispered to Simon, "Those guys are an easy target coming down the steps. They have no protection in that corridor—like sitting ducks in a barrel." The light moved closer and closer.

The torch Allard held above his head moved to the bottom of the steps and then stopped when the two Frenchmen saw the threshold leveling out. Simon shouted loudly. "Hold it right there or we'll open fire!" Allard was just in front of Devereaux and briefly hesitated. The Americans held their fire, knowing they were protected inside the doorways. Instinctively, the Le Guarde agent awkwardly raised his rifle as he took a quick step forward to assume a crouched position…his right foot stepped on the suspicious floor panel, the same panel Santos had spotted and the Americans had avoided. In an instant the panel rotated downward hurling the unsuspecting Frenchman into the black void below. His diminishing scream could be heard as he rapidly descended into nothingness. The light from his trailing torch became a mere speck then disappeared from sight. The corridor was plunged into darkness.

"Don't shoot!" Devereaux shouted as he dropped his rifle and heard it slide down the steps and into the hole. "I give up Americans… don't shoot."

Santos lit his torch and quickly moved to the doorway allowing enough illumination to see. "Jump over the hole," Simon commanded. "The floor is solid on this side."

The Frenchman did as he was instructed. "Where are the others?" Simon barked.

"They are all dead...I am the only one left."

Simon stepped out from the doorway to reveal himself. He was shocked to find himself confronted by his old adversary from the Peru expedition. "Devereaux!" he shouted. "What the hell are you doing here? We thought you had your head lopped off by your emperor. I'm sure he was pretty angry at your failed mission."

"Bonjour, Monsieur Murphy...we meet again."

"Yes, Mr. Devereaux. It looks like we meet again...and surprisingly with your head still on your shoulders."

"I was very lucky. I, too, thought the guillotine awaited me but it appears Bonaparte wanted to keep me alive for the valuable information I possessed about your discovery. Our current French president, Adolphe Thiers, sent me on this excursion to follow you and see if you still had the flying machine in safekeeping for your government. Like Louis Bonaparte, he wanted me to bring it back to France, but now it seems that my mission will not be realized."

"You are right, Devereaux, because my government does not have it. It was taken away by the original owners."

Devereaux was dumbfounded. "Original owners? I do not understand."

Elijah stepped in. "What do we do with this guy? He has been nothing but a pain in our side. Let's toss him into that hole with his buddy and be on with it," he added, grabbing the Frenchman's shoulder.

"Mon Dieu, Monsieur's...please don't do that. I no longer have any desire to work for France. The new president and our military leaders only want that machine for their own self interests. They have no concern for me...to them I am disposable. My only interest now is to smuggle my wife out of France and move to a remote place where I can live out my days in peace."

"So what would you have us do, Devereaux?" Simon asked suspiciously.

"I would like to join with you. I can be of help."

Simon pondered over this for a moment, scrutinized his adversary and then nodded. "Okay, Devereaux, you can tag along with us, but if you get out of line for an instant I'll personally save

France the trouble and remove your head myself." Elijah removed the Frenchman's revolver from his holster and handed it to Santos.

"Merci, Monsieur Murphy, I will not betray you. I lost my rifle into that hole and now you have my revolver. Can I keep it?"

"Not at the moment. We'll wait until I know I can trust you," Simon replied sternly. He then turned to Santos and pointed. "You keep the lead and let's see where this infernal passageway takes us."

33

The dark corridor revealed a few more rooms. All of them proved to be empty except one that contained pieces of broken shards of pottery. As they walked, Santos kept a sharp eye on the floor. He had spotted the floor panel at the bottom of the landing and was well aware one step could mean instant doom for another unfortunate victim…Allard's incident proved how fast that could happen. The column finally came to a stone barrier blocking the passageway. A thorough search revealed neither a lever nor any other protrusion that would open a door or move the obstruction. It was then that the distinct vibrating noise from Simon's pack sounded through the corridor. The zenox was alive again.

Simon removed his pack, retrieved the device, and then held it forward. The red light began to flash and it began a steady humming noise accompanied by faint background static—it was obviously communicating again. From behind the wall a similar noise was heard resounding through the barrier. "This is crazy. Something on the other side is talking to this thing. We've got to break through the wall," Elijah stated. The device suddenly went dead.

"There has to be a way to open it," Santos suggested. "The Indians would have provided easy passage to the other side."

They searched for a protrusion or a lever similar to the winged serpent but nothing could be found. The walls and floor were solid smooth rock. There was no niche or cavity in the walls that could conceal a trigger. Santos was stumped.

Mann noticed something different with the barrier blocking

the corridor. His close observation revealed an irregular pattern of slight cracks in the surface. "Take a look at this," he said, chipping off a flake of veneer. The wall wasn't a solid rock slab as it appeared but constructed of blocks of stone covered in a plaster coating. "This wall is man-made."

"I believe you're right," Simon concurred, taking his knife and chipping away more plaster, revealing an uneven pattern of joints reinforced with mortar. The old lime and clay stucco was very brittle and fell away easily. The wall they now faced was built of stone bricks. "This should be easy to break through," Santos remarked. "Hand me a shovel."

Santos began to chip at the mortar holding the brick joints together…the soft cement broke away in small chunks.

Professor Scott did not hesitate and took his own shovel and joined in the task. It only took minutes for enough blocks to be removed to allow enough space for the two men to peer through the opening. What they saw only inches away, was totally unexpected… another wall separated by a narrow cavity.

Scott took his torch and stuck it into the space to get a better view. The light from the torch illuminated the entire opening and revealed a small ledge built into the second wall. Looking down, he spotted the remains of a skeleton lying in a tangled heap with the leg and foot bones positioned to the top and the skull pressing against the floor. "Someone stuffed that poor soul down into this hole and then apparently repaired the outer wall." Scott surmised. "Sure is a weird place to stuff a body. Why didn't they just pile him in the room with the mummies? Unless…unless he was put here for a purpose. Maybe he knew too much."

"Like this?" Simon added, pointing to the small niche in the wall. Resting on the shelf lay two objects, a small rectangular box and a long slender item resembling a rolled up scroll. He gently removed the articles and handed the thin cylinder to Scott. Opening the box he was surprised to find a small oval shaped object the same size and configuration as Simon's zenox. When exposed, the strange device began to vibrate and emit a static-like noise. Immediately, the zenox in Simon's pack started making the same erratic sounds.

"These things are going crazy," Elijah said as he removed the communication device from Simon's pack and handed it to him. "They are talking to each other." Suddenly both devices went silent.

"What was that all about?" Patterson asked.

"They were communicating," Simon answered. "This little oval shaped thing is another zenox like ours and it's probably been sitting behind this false wall for hundreds of years. What do you make of it, Professor?"

"This is most curious. It opens up some very interesting questions. I would guess it means the earlier inhabitants in this area must have had visitors like our Toltec and Inca friends did… several hundred years ago."

Scott unrolled the metallic scroll, and to his delight it revealed lines of symbols and glyphs similar to the scroll in Patterson's possession and the one they had taken from the sunken Atlantean city of Lythe three years ago. "There seems to be a correlation between this scroll and the ones I deciphered from Atlantis. It seems like our alien friends visited a lot of different places in the past few centuries…and left a lot of unsolved mysteries from our past. Very interesting," he added, nodding his head with a tinge of excitement and curiosity.

Elijah was peering through the opening at the inner wall. "I found something else."

Embedded within the niche was a small inconspicuous stone lever. It appeared as it might be some type of activation device that could either open a doorway or spring a trap. Santos looked into the cavity and closely examined the small projection. It was apparent the object could not be rotated or pushed from side to side—it had to be pushed inward. Santos motioned the others to back away and then pushed the lever. It wouldn't budge—age had frozen it in place. Santos took his knife and used the metal butt tab to rap on the small projection. He felt it give slightly. He then positioned his thumb and gave it a hefty push. The lever broke free and depressed into the wall. Immediately a distinct thump and heavy grinding noise was heard…something was definitely moving. It was no surprise to Santos and the others to watch the massive wall slide slowly into a waiting recess and reveal another passageway through the opening. The tunnel continued on and disappeared into a corridor of darkness.

Enough blocks were removed from the outer wall to allow each man to slip through into the waiting tunnel, each one careful not to step on the scattered skeletal bones that lay beneath them. The path leveled out allowing easy walking, and in single file, the column moved on into the unknown.

As they proceeded, Santos scanned the walls and path carefully, knowing any unknowing step could trigger fatal consequences. Many of the traps the ancients placed into some of their sites were ingenious. They were deadly contrivances all designed to kill their victims and were placed in strategic locations to either prevent enemies from gaining entrance or protect the secrets of their hidden chambers. Most were designed to either impale or crush their victims or simply drop them into deep caverns to be smashed upon impact. The Americans were well aware of the risks as they continued a few hundred yards and encountered their first doorway…just another empty room. A little further, another room was reached and the light from the oil lamp illuminated a totally different spectacle. The glitter and explosive sparkles of light reflected off bright shiny surfaces…the brilliant reflection of gold and gemstones. They had found their first cache of the hidden treasures of the Incas. The group stood in awe as they gazed around the room at the stacks of carvings and ornaments made of gold and inlayed with precious gems… bright red garnet, topaz in dazzling shades of pink, blue, and honey, and vivid, bright green emeralds from the ancient mines of Columbia and Brazil. Various sculptures of deities were carved from clear crystal and masks made of jade and turquoise lined the wall. Professor Scott was exuberant. "It's true," he shouted. "The lost Inca treasure…we've found it…El Dorado!"

His excitement was infectious as the others released their

spontaneous shouts and cries of pleasure. Even the subdued Frenchman, Devereaux, was overwhelmed as he, too, voiced his enthusiasm and elation. "Mon Dieu, he cried…the legend is true…we have found El Dorado."

Simon broke the spell. "This is only the first storage chamber. I know this room is full of priceless ornaments and other valuable relics, but we've yet to find the remains of a city and the main cache of gold the Conquistadors were after. If we find that, it will prove this is really the lost city of gold and verify the legend. We need to continue on." Reluctantly, the men followed Santos from the room and proceeded through the passageway.

Three other small rooms were found. One contained more mummies and the other two were stored with more relics and the remainder of weapons…mostly remnants of spears and shields. Mann found the most interesting weapons of the cache…several more Roman Gladius-style swords and shields made of bronze. "Do you realize what this means?" Scott declared. "It proves the designs for this sword and shield had to have been given to the earlier occupants by the same extraterrestrials that visited the Toltecs and Incas. Remember what Commander Ahular told us in Peru? His predecessors taught the Indians the art of making steel for the swords, spear points, and shields in gratitude for their hospitality. These are identical to the weapons we found in Xepocotec and Peru."

"Most likely the Incas brought these weapons with them when they transported and hid their treasure here," Simon responded.

Elijah picked up a sword and strapped it to his pack as they filed out of the room to continue their search.

The dark corridor continued on for another several hundred yards and ended abruptly when they encountered another stone slab blocking the passageway. "Not another damn wall," Elijah moaned loudly.

"This should be easy to open," Santos announced, spotting a small figure of the familiar winged serpent projecting from the wall above him. He grasped the serpent and rotated it to the right triggering the complicated mechanism that started the process of pushing the barrier into the waiting recess. They were startled when they saw what awaited them through the opening…a huge cavern. Immediately they were immersed with a soft green light that flooded in from the chamber before them.

"This light looks familiar," Simon observed curiously. "This is the same green light we encountered aboard the Toltec and Cuzco, and in the dome covering the city of Lythe in Atlantis. I think we might have found our old friends Ahular and Nezar."

He was not surprised when a loud familiar accented voice boomed up from the ground below. "Welcome, Commander Murphy. I see you have managed to find our command center."

Patterson and his two companions were totally astounded. "Who is that?" the general shouted.

"It's the voice of our old friend Nezar, Vice-Commander of the ship Cuzco…the spaceship that we told you about. It was the one that carried us out of Peru then on to Washington and the same one that transported us beneath the Atlantic Ocean to the sunken continent of Atlantis. As I explained to you earlier, they saved our planet from total destruction."

The suspense was broken by the same accented voice filling the cavern. "Mr. Murphy, you will find the steps to your right that will bring you to the floor. We'll be awaiting you."

The group filed through the doorway and stood on a stone platform that overlooked the huge cavern. The scene that startled them the most was the remains of a small city spread out before them. It was centered by a circular plaza with narrow stone paved streets extending out like spokes from a hub. The streets were lined with small stone buildings that appeared to be in remarkably good shape. The concentric shape of the city struck an immediate bell with Simon. "It resembles the lost Toltec city of Xepocotec," he remarked. "Much smaller, of course."

"You mean the city you found in the Yucatan?" Patterson asked, remembering their discussion about their experience in Mexico.

"Yes!" Simon answered with excitement ringing in his voice.

"The shape of this city looks just like Xepocotec…circular like a big wagon wheel with spokes."

He was especially fascinated with the similarities and the questions it raised. "Well, I think we have finally found El Dorado. Now let's go down to meet our old friends and find the Inca gold."

As the group began their descent down the steps a strange object caught their attention on the far side of the cavern. The dull silver dome-like shape was large and sat close to the ground. The structure appeared to be supported by slender legs suspending the weight off the ground. Simon recognized it immediately although he couldn't believe what he was seeing. "The Cuzco," he muttered. "I would swear that is the Cuzco." He missed a step and nearly stumbled but Elijah was able to grab his arm and prevent a nasty fall. Mann and Roper brought up the rear of the file and were too dumbfounded to speak.

While Simon was regaining his balance, Patterson asked him, "Are you referring to that flying ship you told us about…the one you rode on in Peru…the thing that carried you to the bottom of the Atlantic?"

"Yes, the same one."

When the small column reached the floor, an unnatural shaped figure was seen walking toward them. The Xeresite was accompanied by two more figures with the same general features. All three were clad in shiny silver-like uniforms. Patterson, Mann, and Roper couldn't help but notice the strikingly different characteristics these figures displayed…the large elongated heads, the lack of hair, holes in place of protruding ears, and the large chests and slender lower extremities. Roper whispered to Mann, "These can't be humans. Those things look like freaks."

Mann laughed quietly. "I'm sure they think we're freaks. Well, one thing for sure, they have to be smarter than hell otherwise they wouldn't be here on our planet with that flying contraption Simon called a spacecraft."

The figure in the middle stopped, placed his fist over his chest and nodded slightly as a sign of respect and recognition.

"Welcome, Commander Murphy. We have been expecting you. And also welcome to you, Vice-Commander Walker, as well and your two companions from the Atlantis affair."

Simon and Elijah followed the same show of respect by placing their fists over their chest and nodding. "It is good to see you, Vice-Commander Nezar. It was reassuring to hear your voice on my zenox."

Nezar emitted a deep guttural sound followed by the other two aliens. Simon knew this was their way of verbalizing their pleasure and satisfaction. "Actually, Commander Murphy, I have been promoted to full commander and command the X326 battle cruiser."

"Is that the same ship we called the Cuzco…the one that carried us under the ocean to the city of Lythe?"

"Yes, it is. It is the same ship and the one you commanded for a short period of time."

"Is Commander Ahular here?" Simon asked.

"That is affirmative. He is in our command center. He is expecting you and will see you shortly."

Elijah couldn't hold it back. "Commander Nezar," he asked, "is this place the legendary city they call El Dorado?"

Nezar let out that same deep guttural sound as he replied, "There is no such city called El Dorado. That was a false name created by the Spanish explorers to create a legend to inspire their countrymen to seek the location where the Incas hid their treasures, but none of the Spanish ever found it. This city was built by an earlier Indian civilization called Chibcha and then later occupied by the Incas who hid their treasures from the hated Spanish Conquistadors. The original name of this underground city was Chimor, named after the Kingdom of Chimor located along the coast of Peru. The kingdom was once a rival of the Incas until they conquered it. When the Incas found this city they renamed it Yupauqui after the great Inca army leader who conquered the Kingdom of Chimor."

"Is this really the city of gold?" Professor Scott injected, his interest and excitement piqued to the breaking point. "And if so, where is the gold the Spanish and others frantically searched for all these years?"

Nezar let out another funny sound, perhaps a laugh for these aliens. "The Inca treasures are stored in all of these buildings you see before you and as you say in your language, tons of gold and works of their art creations are here. Later, you will able to explore the city but now Commander Ahular is waiting to see you."

As the Americans filed into the city they were able to peer into some of the buildings lining the narrow street. While the soft green light gave plenty of illumination, most of the building's interiors were dark. However, several large shops had large open windows and the shimmering reflections from within gave definitive evidence that something significant was stored inside… something dazzling and shiny…lots of gold and gemstones. Their exhilaration and anticipation rose as they were now convinced this was the place where Chief Atahualpa hid his empire's treasures from Pizarro. The chief knew the Spanish would never find it here. The different names didn't matter, but to Scott and the others, this was surely El Dorado…the city of gold.

34

A LARGER BUILDING DOMINATED THE SMALL plaza marking the center of Yupauqui, much like the dominate building in the small town above ground. It was obvious it was a temple built for religious ceremonies and community activities. Ahular and Nezar had established their command center in this building. Commander Ahular was standing at the front entrance awaiting their arrival.

He greeted Simon in the customary salutation gesture with his fist across his chest. "Commander Murphy, how good to see you. I told you your zenox would come in handy and we would meet again."

"Thank you, sir," Elijah responded, mindful that Nezar, and now Ahular, was addressing them by the former assigned ranks connecting them with the Cuzco.

"Yes, Commander Ahular," Simon acknowledged with a similar gesture of respect. "It is good to see you as well."

"What brings you back to Peru?" The alien commander asked.

"It's a long story, sir. Our President Grant asked that we travel to Brazil and bring our friends here back to America to retrieve a treasure from the vanquished Confederate treasury hidden after our great war. Events led us to travel up the Amazon River in search of El Dorado."

Ahular nodded. "You humans are a very complex species. You mention your war. It seems that all you humanoids do is fight wars and kill each other over senseless reasons. In our travels we have only encountered a few other planets where the species cannot co-exist. On the positive side, your wars seem to keep your populations in balance with your available food sources. You might say your wars help nature do its job."

Food for thought, Simon pondered for a moment but chose not to reply.

"As you now know," Ahular continued, "the name El Dorado is only a myth spawned by the Spanish Conquistadors, but this hidden city of Yupauqui does exist and is the place where the Incas hid all their gold and treasures from the Spanish." He hesitated briefly to discharge his funny guttural sound and then added, "I suppose to you humans, you can say you have found your El Dorado."

Simon nodded appreciatively knowing their search had been productive. "It seems like the legend was true about the Inca chief, Atahualpa, hiding their treasures from the Spanish although the legend placed the city far to the north. And, sir," he added, "we assumed you had departed back to your world three years ago after we left Atlantis and you saved our planet from destruction."

"We did return home briefly to restore our tracx fuel supplies and make some equipment repairs. Although our solar system is several light years away, our Vartz speeds allow for a short journey relative to your time measurements. We were ordered back to your earth and have been in this location for almost one of your earth years. This underground city was a perfect place to re-establish our command center since the underwater earthquake destroyed our former site at the Atlantis city of Lythe."

Patterson was completely amazed at these visitors from another world and totally perplexed at some of the conversation he was hearing. "Commander," he asked, "what does Vartz speed mean? Words like that are unknown to me."

Ahular was amused at the primitive technological knowledge levels of the human species. "I am afraid you humans cannot understand speeds like this and how they would relate to your primeval measurements of speed. Just try to think of light years… the distance light will travel in one of your earth years. Vartz is based on the speed of light and time relativity and our X326 is capable of exceeding that speed depending on the vacuum levels and gravitational variables from other celestial bodies. In other words, light is the fastest known element in the universe. In terms of your crude human measurements, light will travel 186,000 feet per second or in one year about 5.9 trillion miles."

Patterson turned to Elijah and whispered. "What does all that mean? I don't understand a blasted word he's saying."

"It means that sleek looking spacecraft sitting over there will get you where you want to go and damned fast."

Patterson just shrugged and looked at him with a perplexed expression.

Ahular continued. "We were ordered back here to continue our observations of your planet and study the inner core of earth as well as the effects of your oceans and tectonic plate shifts to your climate changes. Your planet is a very interesting and complex planet, much like our planet Xeres in the Scoros galaxy. By earth measurements, our galaxy would place Scoros about 3.5 billion miles from here."

"How long does it take you to fly home, Commander Ahular?" Scott asked curiously.

"By applying vartz speeds and under good conditions avoiding meteors, exploding stars, or black holes we can usually reach Xeres in about four of your earth weeks. We have sleep modules on the ship that allow us to hibernate most of the journey. But enough questions for now. I know you must be hungry so we will have some nourishment ready for you."

Elijah remembered the food the visitors had served them under the dome in the ruins of Lythe. He turned to Simon and whispered. "Do you suppose they still eat that slimy glop out of those tubes?"

Simon chuckled. "I remember you didn't complain too much and seemed to enjoy all that muck sliding down your throat."

"Yeah…and I was hungry as hell and would have even eaten a snake." He hesitated for a moment. "Well…forget that…anything but a stinking snake."

The Americans were ushered over to a long table and noticed

four of the alien crew-members eating and watching the strangers with curious glances. Each held short wide tubes above their faces and compressed a lever that allowed the congealed mixture to be emptied into their mouth slits. The substance resembled a stream of dark mud. Mann and Roper were appalled thinking they would actually have to put that ugly stream of paste into their mouths. Ahular saw their discomfort and assured them. "What you see here is actually a very delicious and nutritious mixture of food from your ocean. Today we are serving a combination of sea bass, shrimps, eel, and seaweed…all very tasty and quite nourishing."

Professor Scott assured them. "Try it…you'll like it." He remembered eating from the tubes in Lythe and how satisfying the food was to a hungry stomach.

Roper, who felt like he could eat a whale, took the first bite and nodded his approval. "Wow!" he muttered between bites. "This goo isn't too bad." He must have liked it as he emptied the tube and asked for another.

They all agreed the meal was pretty decent, acknowledging how the unappetizing looking sludge energized them and satisfied their hunger. Nezar stood up after the meal and spoke. "We know you are most anxious to explore the city, so you are free to do so. We ask that you return to this place soon for a briefing. At that time we have something very interesting to show you…something very unusual we found within the Inca treasures." Professor Scott was euphoric and deep into his element. He could hardly wait to see what Nezar had in store for them.

The Americans thanked Ahular for the meal and filed out into the street, anxious to explore the surrounding buildings and the vast hoard of treasure that awaited them.

The contents of the first three buildings they searched exceeded all of their expectations. Scott lit his torch and was stunned by the reflections of dazzling light glimmering back at him. The rooms were filled with a kaleidoscope of various blazing colors from stacks and boxes filled with gold bars, gold coins, and gems of every description. There were small statues of various deities formed of solid gold and glaring masks of jade and turquoise stacked around the rooms. The walls were lined with many artifacts crafted from gold, silver, crystal, jade, alabaster, and assorted gemstones. The fifth and sixth rooms were a bit larger and were the crowning blow. Each room was completely filled with stacks of gold bars, gold cubes, and many other solid gold artifacts. This was surely the main cache of the former Inca Empire's treasures. These rooms alone would pay for the war ten times over and fill the U.S. Treasury with enough wealth to completely rebuild an entire country devastated by the recent war. Patterson was especially enamored with a large box of various gems reflecting a multitude of sparkling colors while Mann and Roper hefted various objects of gold to test the weights. The most startling discovery of all was a large chest of gold coins Santos found in the corner of the room… they looked strangely familiar. He held one up and examined it. He motioned Simon over and showed him the coin. Simon shouted to Patterson, "Robert, would you come over here for a minute?"

"Let's see that coin you got from the Confederate treasury. I think we've found a match."

Patterson reached into his pack and retrieved the coin…it was identical to the coins in the chest…same size…same markings… same symbols and glyphs. "What do you make of that?" he asked, disbelievingly.

"Your coin is identical to these in the chest. It had to have come from here," Simon surmised. "We'll ask Nezar."

Devereaux was also overwhelmed at the vastness of the wealth around him but he had other thoughts in mind. He imagined himself living elegantly along the Rhône River, surrounded by manicured gardens, a huge mansion filled with priceless art, expensive furnishings, and with a host of servants catering to his every need. Any obligations and sense of duty to serve France were gone and Devereaux knew he must bide his time for the right moment to fill bags of gold and gems and escape from this place and the Americans. Greed overwhelmed his mind as he formed his plans. His chance would come.

Back in the command center the Americans gathered around a small stone table holding a round object covered with a silk-like cloth. Devereaux was in attendance. "We told you we had something very unique to show you," Ahular announced to the group, "Commander Nezar will give you the details."

The alien commander pulled the cloth away, revealing an elaborate crown of solid gold. On the front was carved a Chi-Rho symbol inside a wreath and on the back were the words inscribed in Latin, hac subcrobo victum followed by a name…Flavius Valerius Constantinus. Nezar explained, "As you can see, this is a crown made of solid gold."

The top was sculpted with an intricate pattern of decorative curves and the band filled with precise engravings surrounded by diamonds and rubies inset into the metal. One look revealed it was crafted by artisans who applied their finest skills to create a prize fit for a king. Nezar continued, "It is a very interesting and priceless piece owned by a very famous leader in your human history. The name on the back designates the owner of this crown." He hesitated for a moment to let the Americans absorb the exquisiteness of the object. "This is the crown of the Roman emperor Constantine I, the first Christian emperor of the Roman Empire. He was the 57th emperor and ruled from 306-337 AD."

Professor Scott knew something about Roman history and enough Latin to understand some basic words. He added, "I see the words on the back. They read Hac subcrobo nos victum. I believe this is translated as 'By this sign we conquer'."

"That is correct, Mr. Scott," Nezar confirmed. "This was a motto used by Emperor Constantine many times to refer to the larger carving on the crown's face…it is called the Chi-Rho symbol:

He discovered this image in a dream and had it imprinted on the shields of his soldiers. As you can see, the symbol is made of two letters overlaying each other—the letters P and X and in this case surrounded by a wreath. This is the oldest known monogram or letter symbol for the Christian messiah known as Christ. Constantine the First was converted to Christianity and was the first emperor to begin the transition of Christianity to the Roman Empire. For years the Christians were persecuted by the Romans but Constantine changed all that and forbid further suffering for these people. He strongly believed the Chi-Rho symbol gave his soldiers added strength and the great battle he won near Rome at the Milvian Bridge against his brother-in-law, Maxentius, confirmed his belief that this victory was attributed to the divine strength from the symbol. He was so moved by the triumph that he introduced a line of gold coins called the Solidus inscribed with various Chi-Rho symbols." Nezar reached under the stone table and with the help of Ahular, lifted a heavy container onto the surface. "This chest is full of the Chi-Rho coins that were released by Constantine in 312 AD in honor of his great victory. The crown and the coins are cast of solid gold and over 1500 years old. I'm sure the golden crown of Constantine the First would be honored by your chief back in your city of Washington. You may take it to present to your leader as a token of our friendship. You may also have the chest of Chi-Rho coins for yourselves."

"Thank you, Commander," Simon acknowledged, "He will be honored to receive this gift. How do you suppose these items from the ancient Roman Empire got to this isolated underground city across the Atlantic Ocean? I have to assume the Incas brought them here with their other treasures. That means someone had to have transported them from Rome and given them to the Incas."

"That is correct, Mr. Murphy. You may recall in Yucatan and Peru you learned our forbearers visited some of the pre-Columbian civilizations like the Toltecs, Mayans, and the Inca Empire prior to their collapse to the Spanish. You'll remember they gave these Indians the knowledge for making metal swords fashioned after the Roman designs and spear points similar to those used by the

Roman Legions in battle. We have to assume they also brought the Constantine crown and coins from the old Roman Empire as well and presented them to the Incas in reward for their kindness and hospitality. We have no firm knowledge of where and how our predecessors acquired the crown and Chi-Rio coins."

Simon pulled a handful of different coins from his pocket. "Commander Nezar, here is something else most curious. We found a chest full of these coins in one of the buildings and they are a perfect match to a coin Mr. Patterson found in a box from the old Confederate treasury in Richmond, Virginia." Patterson held up his coin. "Can you tell us where these coins came from?"

Nezar took Patterson's coin and compared it to those in Simon's hand. "The coins were actually struck by the Incas. Our earlier predecessors taught the Incas how to cast gold and form it into coins. The inscriptions you see are Inca and are references to their sun god, Inti. I would imagine those you found in the chest are the only Inca struck coins in existence. One can only imagine how this coin found its way to your country."

"May we have the Inca coins as well?" Simon asked.

"Yes, you may take that chest of Inca coins," Nezar responded. "We have no use for such items."

Scott brought up an interesting question for Nezar, referring back to the Constantine treasures. "The Roman Empire existed several centuries before the Toltecs, Mayan, and Inca civilizations. How could your forbearers have acquired these Roman methods and artifacts and passed them along to the Indians so much later in the timeline?"

"Our predecessors have been visiting your planet for many centuries, dating back even further than the Roman Empire. The knowledge they acquired has been passed down to many of our generations and stored in our computer databanks. Our historical information about your species is very detailed and precise. As you can attest by our current presence, our forbearers also visited in more current times, including the pre-Columbian civilizations."

"Have you visited many planets from other solar systems? Do other species like us humans exist?" Scott asked.

Ahular answered the question for his subordinate. "We estimate that there are over 8 billion stars within the universe that reside in millions of solar systems and galaxies. Of those stars, many are active suns with hundreds of millions of planets revolving around them. We have identified several million planets that revolve within a temperate zone much like your earth. This means the climatic conditions provide suitable atmospheres, temperatures, and elements to sustain forms of life. The odds are overwhelmingly huge that abundant life resides throughout the universe…we have already identified many planets that do support various life forms and some we have visited and confirmed it."

"Do they look like us humans?" Scott injected with probing excitement.

"In our travels we have found several species that do have similar forms as you humans, but you must realize species are developed and evolved through climate and environmental changes that affect cell growth and development over time. The intelligence development levels vary considerably depending how their brains and reasoning mechanisms have evolved. We are much like you in form, but with some very unique physical differences, as you can see. Our intelligence and technological development is much more advanced than you humans, but in time your brains and knowledge will develop and achieve incredible advances. Nature has a very unique ability to allow life forms to adapt and evolve to changes suitable to climate and temperature variations. Life forms have to do this for survival and procreation. For example, changes in the food chain have a very profound effect on cell growth and physical adaptation. However, there is one important similarity we have noticed from our visits to different planets and solar systems. The universe is a very violent place with exploding stars, celestial collisions, black holes, and other catastrophic events. But also, throughout the universe, there appears to be a very uniform harmony that allows changes to evolve in a consistent and orderly manner. It appears perhaps all of this is being controlled through a central source or a master plan. Like you humans, we too have similar views, much like your religions that believe events in the universe are being guided by a greater force far superior and even far beyond our comprehension."

Simon and Scott accepted this explanation and nodded their understanding while Elijah, Patterson, Mann, and Roper stood silent trying to absorb all of this bizarre conversation. Santos stayed in the background, oblivious to this information—it was totally out of his realm of comprehension, but growing up as a Catholic, he did agree with the part about a divine master hand at work.

Professor Scott was euphoric over the offer of the crown and coins and felt certain President Grant would eventually contribute these priceless articles to the national museum. They would be a huge public sensation and attract thousands of visitors while he, Professor George Scott, narrated their history. Unknown to the professor, Devereaux had other ideas.

There was one unanswered question that was addressed by Simon. He directed it to Nezar. "Is there another exit out of this cavern besides going back through the steps and long passageway and again through the other tunnel we passed through to get into to the valley above? Wouldn't the Indians have made an exit to the western side of the mountain?"

"Yes, there is," Nezar answered. "On the far side of the cavern there is a spring that provides fresh water to the city. Just to the right you will find an entranceway that leads to another passage through the west side of the mountain. It comes out in a large valley surrounded by another mountain range to the west. Just beyond that lies the Pacific Ocean. We neutralized the traps so one can pass through unobstructed. It is an easy passage with a gradual incline and with no steep steps to climb."

Devereaux was taking all of this in and tried to conceal the cruel smile on his face.

35

Although the soft green light that flooded the cavern was constant and denied the Americans the physical ability to determine night or day, their tired bodies knew when it was time to get some sleep. Nezar led them to a separate room in the rear where bunks had been prepared. They were exhausted and sleep came easily…except for Devereaux who kept his eyes open, waiting for the correct moment.

It wasn't long before Roper detected slight movement and opened his eyes in time to see a figure rise from the bunk and ease over to the stone table. Very gently, hands removed the golden crown and stealthily removed the coins from the chest and placed them in a backpack. The figure then hesitated and scanned the room before turning and silently moving toward the doorway. Roper nudged Mann and whispered for him to accompany him. Both men slipped out of the room and followed the silhouette as it left the building. The dark shadow moved toward the far side of the cavern and the gently flowing spring trickling across the rocks. The figure hesitated briefly and then turned to the entrance leading into a tunnel. "Hold it right there, Devereaux!" Roper shouted forcefully.

The Frenchman turned and saw Roper and Mann facing him. He turned and started to run through the passage but the weight of the gold laden pack slowed him down. Mann caught up to him easily and grabbed his arm while Roper slammed him from the side, knocking both he and Devereaux off balance. The Frenchman dropped his pack and turned to face the two Confederados.

Roper yelled at him. "Why are you trying to steal the Constantine treasure? You know damn well you have no place to run."

This didn't deter Paul Devereaux who pulled a concealed knife from his trousers and jabbed a thrust at Roper. The movement was so quick Roper had no chance to dodge the maneuver and took the full impact of the blade deep into his shoulder. At first he felt no pain and then suddenly a bolt of fire shot through his arm and down his back. A spreading red stain saturated his shirt. He staggered backward, grabbing his damaged shoulder. Devereaux was about to deliver another thrust to his mid-section when Mann thrust his boot forward and slammed it into his arm. The impact caused Devereaux to drop the knife. The Frenchman ran into the passageway leaving Mann, the pack full of gold, and the seriously injured Roper staggering in the doorway. Mann had to get help quickly or his friend would surely die from loss of blood. Removing his belt, he placed it around Roper's shoulder and fastened it as tight as possible to stem the flow of blood. He scooped up the pack by the straps and his friend by the waist and moved out toward the command center and his sleeping companions. Roper was about to pass out when they reached the building but they were able to make it to the bunkroom. Simon woke up from the disturbance, immediately followed by the others. Patterson, who had a respectable knowledge of first aid, saw the plight of his companion and immediately pulled out a spare belt to readjust the tourniquet and stem the flow of blood.

"Who did this?" Simon shouted, now realizing Devereaux was the only one missing.

Mann answered angrily. "It was that damn Frenchman. He stole the crown and coins from the table and was trying to escape through the passageway when we caught up with him. I retrieved the pack with the Constantine treasure but he escaped through the passage. I needed to get Roper back here quickly and had to let him go."

"We'll deal with him later."

Nezar, accompanied by two of his crew-members, had heard the commotion and entered the room. Simon turned to the alien commander and asked, "Do you still have one of those machines that generate quick healing rays from the green light tube? Our friend here is seriously injured."

"You are referring to the photosynthesis generator?"

"Yes...like the one we used to heal Mr. Drake's leg three years ago."

"There is one in the ship. Bring your man and follow us to the X326."

With Mann and Patterson on each side supporting Roper, the Americans followed Nezar and his crewmen from the building and to the far side of the cavern where the spacecraft was suspended on the landing pods. A quick command into Nezar's zenox opened a panel in the ship's hull directing a metallic-like ladder to extend to the ground. Roper was half carried and manhandled up the steps into the ship's first compartment filled with comfortable chairs and recliners—the reception room. The interior was just like Simon, Elijah, Santos, and Professor Scott remembered it. The ship was bathed in the familiar soft green light and Simon recalled the narrow corridor that branched off toward the fore section that housed the mechanical rooms and the tracx fuel containment and propulsion generator rooms. He also remembered the aft hallway that led to the rear of the ship containing the officer and crew quarters, mess area, and the laboratory where the photosynthesis generator was located. As they turned toward the aft corridor, Simon noticed the stairs leading up to the command cabin where all the operating and control instruments were placed. Memories of his previous harrowing experiences on the Toltec and Cuzco flooded his mind. It was like stepping back in time as he vividly remembered details of the ship's interior, and control instruments. He vividly recalled how they repaired the tracx propulsion turbine and power linkage to regenerate the power systems and enable the dormant Toltec to fly from the cavern under the lost city of Xepocotec. This saved their lives from a very probable and nasty demise from some very angry Toltec Indians who were descendants of the former occupants of the lost city. He also remembered how in Peru three years ago he had commandeered the Cuzco and flown it to Washington to the amazement of the president and other members of the Congress and military leaders. His most vivid recollection was how the ship's navigational controls were taken over by an unknown force that directed the ship to the bottom of the Atlantic Ocean and the sunken continent of Atlantis. This is where they first encountered the alien commanders in a huge watertight dome covering the remains of the ancient city of Lythe.

Roper was carried back to the rear of the ship and the laboratory that housed the photosynthesis generator. Nezar explained. "This machine consists of a large glass-like tube that contains a special lens that will magnify the green light into an intensity ray. The injured or affected area is bathed with the concentrated beam and will immediately begin to rejuvenate and reconstitute cell growth. It works quite well with human cells and will heal injured flesh very quickly. It also disposes of dead cells as well. I am sure each of you has noticed the rejuvenating effects of the green light that has surrounded you since you've been here in the cavern."

From their previous journeys on the Cuzco, Simon and his three companions had experienced the effects of the green light and understood the rejuvenating results to their bodies. Patterson and Mann also begin to feel a renewed sense of energy.

Roper's bloody shirt was removed and he was placed on the table directly under the tube. Nezar reached to the wall and activated a power switch. Immediately, accompanied by a soft humming sound, the tube filled with an intense bright green light. With Nezar moving a control device, the beam burst through the lens and onto Roper's deep wound. In minutes the discoloration around the gash began to fade and the puncture started to fill in with new flesh growth. The injured area beneath the skin also had the same rapid healing effects. Within forty-five minutes the laceration disappeared and the area appeared to be completely mended. Patterson couldn't believe his eyes. "This machine is a miracle!" he shouted. "I can't believe what I just saw."

Nezar was amused. "Actually, this is a very simple machine. Much like the regeneration of new growth of the leaves on your trees in the spring of your seasons, the light from the intensified ray creates a photosynthesis process for human cells as well. The green light provides the nourishment and chemical changes necessary for rapid cell growth. I suppose to your current human level of intelligence you might look at the machine as a miracle."

Scott couldn't figure out if that was a complement or insult. He let it pass.

Roper flexed his arm and felt his shoulder as he stood up from the table. "It feels pretty darn good," he admitted. "I don't feel any pain what-so-ever. That thing is amazing," he added, pointing to the tube.

Nezar broke the reverie. "We need to get back to the command center. Commander Ahular has summoned us for a brief meeting. It appears our sensors have picked up your Frenchman.

Hanging back in the shadows of the tunnel, Devereaux had watched as the Americans and alien commander carried Roper into the ship and closed the hatchway. He was angry that he had lost the pack filled with the Constantine treasure but was confident he could slip back into one of the storage rooms and retrieve more of the gold coins. Using his jacket as a bag by tying the arms together, he silently worked his way along the cobbled street and found the room he was looking for…the one filled with the Inca gold. Filling his jacket with coins and a small bag of gems, he made his way back to the tunnel. With the light from the torch he had confiscated, Devereaux worked his way through the passage and found the exit at the base of the mountain. Although his bootie would not bring the value of the golden crown and Chi-Rho coins, he was satisfied he had enough treasure to exile himself and his wife to a comfortable location. The exit from the passage was hidden between a rock outcropping. Stepping into the sunlight, he found himself overlooking a large valley. In the distance he saw another mountain range he would have to cross but took some comfort knowing that beyond that final obstacle was the Pacific Ocean. It was his plan to seek passage on a ship and sail around the Horn and back to Europe. Little did he know that concealed sensors placed along the roof of the tunnel had picked up his movements as he made his way through the passageway. The aliens had placed them there as a warning against any intruders.

Nezar led the Americans back to the command center where Ahular and three of his crew awaited them. Ahular addressed the group. "It now appears that your former companion, Devereaux, has passed through the passage and is now entering the valley beyond. Our sensors have been following him since he entered the tunnel."

"Where can he go from there?" Simon asked. "I'm sure he will want to escape to the ocean where he will look for a ship to give him passage."

"The Frenchman will have to cross the final mountain range but that passage will be difficult although there are a few accessible Indian trails he could use. Beyond the mountains his journey will not be easy as the land is very hilly and barren with very few water sources. His only hope is to head for the coast and there are very limited settlements in that area large enough to receive ships. I would say your Frenchman has placed himself into a very precarious situation. His greed will most likely be his undoing. "

Nezar offered a suggestion. "Why don't we take the dacidron and intercept him in the valley. We have our methods to deal with thieves."

"Dacidron? What is a dacidron, Commander?" Elijah asked curiously.

"It is a vehicle we use as transport over land mass. It travels on a cushion of air and is fueled by hydrogen we harvest from your air or water. Come, I will show you." Ahular nodded his approval.

36

The sleek little transporter was parked near the wall just beyond the X326, Cuzco. It was a dull silver-like machine that resembled a small inverted dome or a shell. It sat directly on the floor of the cavern.

Simon recognized the shape. "That thing looks like the same object that was skimming across the ground in the Yungas Foothills, near the base of the mountain." The others concurred.

Nezar observed the American's interest and offered a more detailed explanation. "The vehicle you see is called a Dacidron. Earlier, two of our crew members took the dacidron out into the foothills to observe the Indians that were massing there. Their army dispersed peacefully to the north so the vehicle returned to the command center. Interestingly, the dacidron picked up the signal from your zenox and transferred it to us. We were able to pinpoint your location. This is most likely when you observed it… just before it entered a special passageway through the mountain."

"You mean there is a larger passage through this mountain that will allow something this size to travel through?" Professor Scott questioned. "I was wondering how you got the Cuzco spacecraft into this cavern."

Nezar was amused at his curiosity. "Yes, there is. We constructed a passage large enough to accommodate both the X326 and the dacidron. This is the tunnel we use to transport both ships to and from the cavern and the outside. They both are able to transfer through the passage without the need for any mechanical lifting or conveyer devices."

Simon then asked, "Commander, we know the X326, or Cuzco as we call it, is fueled by your tracx fuel cells but you said the dacidron was fueled by a gas called hydrogen. How does this work? We are not familiar with hydrogen."

Nezar explained as simply as possible. "The air you breathe is an invisible gas called oxygen. It is a common element that makes up your atmosphere. Another element is called hydrogen. It is the most abundant and common element in the universe. It is an invisible gas that exists in almost everything, but most abundantly in the air you breathe. Also, oxygen and hydrogen combined together make up the water you drink. Pure hydrogen gas is quite flammable. We have a small molecule converter on board that can extract hydrogen from water or from the air and feed it into a simple fuel injection system that ignites the combustible gas and generates the power to turn the turbines. They generate the strong airflow that creates lift to cushion the dacidron from the ground and allow it to skim along the surface. The vehicle also has a series of lateral turbines that direct airflows to move the vehicle forward or backwards and from side to side.

"How do you extract this gas from the air or water?" Simon asked.

"The internal converter is quite simple. It is a small centrifuge type device that uses electromagnetic current and centrifugal force to separate the hydrogen molecules and feed them into the engine that powers the turbines. Do you understand any of this?"

"I'm sorry, sir…not a word of it," Simon admitted. "What is a centrifuge? I've never heard that word before."

Nezar emitted a deep guttural sound…an obvious chuckle. "Of course you have never heard of this. Your species has not evolved intellectually enough to know. A centrifuge is a simple device that is used to separate molecules from compounds. For example, water is comprised of both hydrogen and oxygen and the centrifuge can separate the molecules from both elements to harvest pure hydrogen and oxygen." The puzzled expression on the American's faces told Nezar that they had no inkling as to what he was talking about. He decided to drop the detailed technical explanation. These humanoids were just not ready for something this technical.

Professor Scott understood some of the explanation and had an inquisitive mind full of questions. "Is this hydrogen the primary fuel you use on your planet?" he pressed.

"For our smaller engines and land based vehicles we use hydrogen. The tracx fuel we use in our spacecrafts and other larger machines comes from non-radioactive nuclear ore we harvest from two specific planets within our own solar system. The ore is called tracx. One of our sources is the planet Aarnon and the other, Terchez Zen. In our travels they are the only planets where we have found the tracx fuel ore."

Scott was on a roll. "Is hydrogen the primary fuel we'll be using on earth as we advance into the future?"

Nezar considered this a fair question and was impressed with Scott's inquisitiveness and perception of a subject that would be essential to the future progress of the human species. Humans were now in the very early stages of technological growth. "Much like my species did in earlier days of our development, you humans will evolve through various stages of fuel and power sources. Today you are using steam power from coal and wood to drive your trains and steamships. This will change to fossil based fuels that will be used to power combustible engines. However, they are expendable resources and will be commercially depleted in time. Your species will attempt to use wind and solar power which will prove to be very limited and inefficient for extended use. You will even go through a period of using radioactive minerals such as uranium but will discover this is much too dangerous and expensive to refine for everyday usage. Your future generations will finally find a way to harvest hydrogen that is inexhaustible and very efficient as a fuel resource. Our ancestors evolved through these stages and I assure you your world will as well. And to answer your question, Mr. Scott, yes, hydrogen will be your fuel of the future."

Scott nodded his understanding and appreciation. "Thank you, Commander Nezar, that is very good information to know."

"Now," Nezar continued, "we will take a ride into the valley to find the Frenchman. I will navigate the dacidron and it can accommodate up to four passengers so which of you wish to accompany me?"

Without hesitation Scott volunteered. The next obvious choices were Simon, Elijah, and Patterson. Mann and Roper were content to stay back and Santos wanted no part of this contrivance.

To the south of the Cordillera de Apolobama mountain range where the lost city of "El Dorado" was located was the Bolivian town of La Paz. The settlement was just south of Lake Titicaca, split between the borders of Bolivia and Peru. The military garrison there housed three hundred soldiers from the Bolivian 2nd Army and were commanded by a harsh and ruthless officer named Colonel Arturo Suarez. With a very petulant disposition, he was known to be a strict disciplinarian even to the extent of hanging a few soldiers for minor insubordination. A career soldier himself, Suarez was not a man to cross or the consequences could be very unpleasant.

The Bolivian and Chilean governments were locked in an ongoing border dispute over the mineral rich coastal area of the Atacama Desert. This small section of land was seriously contested by each country as to whom it belonged to. Bolivia and Chile both vigorously claimed it, and aligned with Peru, Bolivia later declared war with Chile in 1879. It was referred to as the War of the Pacific. To Bolivia, it not only represented the rich minerals present, but just as important, the strip was their only direct access to the Pacific Ocean. Without this section of the coast, Bolivia would be a landlocked country. The Bolivian interim president, Adolfo Ballivián, sent Colonel Suarez to La Paz to reinforce their northernmost garrison and help enforce their country's interests in the northern region. Suarez had an assigned mission to patrol the northern borders to ensure Chile was not building a strong military presence in the area. This mission, with the approval of sympathetic Peruvian politicians, allowed him to take clandestine excursions around Lake Titicaca and even across the border to adjacent areas in Peru. The scouting assignment this day would take Suarez and a mounted detachment of thirty-two Bolivian soldiers past Lake Titicaca and into the Apolobama mountain region of Peru and into an obscure valley nestled between two mountain ranges. It had been reported that Chilean patrols had been seen in the area.

Devereaux made his way down the rock-strewn path to the valley floor below. Looming before him in the distance was another large mountain range. He was shocked to see snowcapped peaks at the higher elevations. Looking at the map from his small utility pack he had managed to save, his only consolation was to see this was his last big obstacle to cross as the barren rolling land beyond the range spilled into the ocean. Surely he could hail a ship along the coast, and with some of the gold coins he had confiscated in the city, he would pay for his passage around the Horn and on to Europe.

Deep in the cavern of the lost city, Nezar led the four Americans over to the dacidron and opened a small hatch that allowed him and his passengers to enter the vehicle. Nezar took the command seat with Simon in the seat next to him while Elijah, Scott, and Patterson occupied the three passenger seats behind them. A simple voice command turned on the power and the Americans were entranced as the alien commander pressed a screen on the instrument panel and watched through the front glass to see a large door moving laterally into a deep recess carved into the rock. The entrance led to a sizeable tunnel illuminated by a series of lights embedded in the ceiling. They could see where the height and width could accommodate easy passage by both the dacidron and X326 spacecraft. Nezar pressed another screen command and activated the turbines that generated a cushion of air—the vehicle rose and hovered three feet off the ground. A small lever activated the directional steering turbines and the dacidron begin to move forward into the tunnel. Scott couldn't believe what he was seeing. Nezar explained how the explorers had used the lasers from the command ship to carve the tunnel from solid rock. By using the correct combination of beam concentration and strength, the debris from the rock had been vaporized, thus eliminating the need to move tons of stone rubble to the outside. The dacidron's transfer through the passageway took less than three minutes when another large hatch was activated, allowing bright sunlight to spill into the dark cavity. The vehicle soared out into the valley.

In the south end of the valley, Colonel Suarez ordered his column to fan out to cover the width of the vale. He was looking for signs of any military activity to include any encampments or anything suspicious like discarded equipment or ration containers. The two scouts he had sent ahead was a precaution to prevent any unwanted threats. The colonel was a bit surprised when he saw one of the scouts galloping toward him. The soldier reigned in his horse, saluted, and reported excitedly. "Sir, there is a man ahead walking across the valley toward the mountains. He looks like a gringo and he is alone."

Suarez thought suspiciously of the lone figure. Why the hell would a gringo be out here walking alone in this remote valley in the middle of nowhere? He turned to his subordinate and gave a brief command. "Lieutenant Augulo, have the men close ranks and let's encircle this stranger and find out what he is up to. And have the men ready with their rifles. This may be a trap."

Devereaux was startled to see a column of horsemen riding toward him. He could tell they were mounted soldiers but had no idea who they were…he assumed they were Peruvian. He watched with a sense of apprehension as the horses fanned out to encircle him. Instinctively Devereaux reached for his revolver and then remembered the Americans had taken it and Murphy had refused to give him another weapon. He was helpless and totally at the mercy of these men. A slightly built man supporting a short beard and moustache appeared to be the leader…he trotted forward. With a resounding voice of authority he shouted, "Quienes son usted, gringo?" "Who are you, gringo?"

Devereaux, who knew enough Spanish to converse reasonably

fluent, answered, "Amigos, I am not a gringo. I am from France…I am a Frenchman."

Suarez was puzzled. "What are you doing walking alone in this desolate place?"

"Sir," Devereaux answered as politely as he could, "I am trying to make my way across the mountains to the ocean. I hope to get fare on a ship to carry me back to France." He heard some laughter in the background from some of the soldiers who thought the man delusional.

Colonel Suarez was suspicious of this foreigner and quizzed him again. "You failed to answer my question. Where have you been and how did you get here? Do you have accomplices?"

"Are you from the Peruvian army?" Devereaux asked.

"No, we are from La Paz…we are Bolivian soldiers on a routine scouting mission. Now, you must answer my questions or we will be forced to use rather harsh methods to loosen you tongue."

Devereaux knew he was in a hopeless situation and felt he had better cooperate fast or face some horrible torture. He had one thing in his favor. Devereaux knew where the lost city of gold was located and the mention of El Dorado and the incredible treasure hidden there was a strong bargaining chip he could use to his advantage. This knowledge could save his life. He hesitated for a moment then spoke. "Sir, my name is Paul Devereaux and I am from the country of France. I am no friend of the gringos and I was sent here by my government to follow some Americans who were in search of a vast treasure that was hidden by the Inca Indians many years ago. You have perhaps heard of the lost city of gold…more commonly known as El Dorado?"

This caught the colonel's attention fast. "You have found la ciudad perdida de oro, El Dorado?"

"Yes, and I can take you there."

37

Partially concealed nearby and hovering on a cushion of air, the dacidron sat motionless while the occupants observed the scene a few hundred yards away. The ultra-sensitive sound sensors mounted inside the vehicle's nose cone overheard every word spoken from Devereaux and Suarez. Nezar turned to Simon. "This is not good. The Frenchman knows where the underground city and our command center are located and we heard him tell his captors about the lost city of 'El Dorado' and the treasures hidden there. I also heard the soldier in charge tell Devereaux they were from the country of Bolivia. If Devereaux is allowed to take them to the underground city of Yupauqui they will most likely try to destroy our command center and confiscate all the treasure. These men are from Bolivia and have crossed the border into Peru. We are uncertain of their motives but once the word gets out that the Bolivians stole a vast Inca treasure from Peru it is most certain a great war will break out and thousands of innocents will die. It is most likely several counties will enter the conflict when the magnitude of the treasure's wealth is known. Greed will overwhelm the minds of their leaders who will all fight each other to acquire the treasure for themselves. This is the way the strange mind of the human species works. We cannot let that happen."

"What can we do, Commander Nezar?"

"We can make sure the Frenchman does not tell them exact location and we can prevent him from exposing any more information."

"How do we do that, sir?"

"The dacidron has a small laser weapon that will prove most useful. This laser is much smaller and less powerful than those you witnessed on the X326 battle cruiser but very effective for our intended use. I will show you how it works."

Nezar pressed a small green button that activated a tracking screen. He explained, "This armament operates much like the one you saw on the X326. I will use this lever to acquire the target within the small circle on the screen. Once acquired, it will lock on immediately. The lever also controls the beam direction and the small silver knob to your left will control the beam strength by turning it either right or left. Each click represents a five percent change in the laser power and exponentially increases or decreases the beam strength by ten times. The other silver knob controls the beam width. The wider beams would be used for larger targets."

Patterson had no idea what all of this meant, but he was very fascinated with the instruction and target screen. He watched intently as the circle traversed across the landscape and scanned the group of horsemen in the distance. Simon assured him the laser weapon was much stronger than all the Civil War weapons combined. "Robert," he said reassuringly, "we witnessed the power of the lasers on the X326 or Cuzco, as we called it. These weapons have incredible power. It was Elijah's suggestion that Ahular synchronize all the lasers to get the power needed to weld the rock together from the underground earthquake. Those lasers saved our planet from totally splitting apart and exploding into oblivion."

Patterson nodded at Elijah to show his appreciation for helping the aliens save the earth.

Nezar observed Devereaux pointing to the eastern mountain range that indicated he was in the process of divulging the location of the lost city. He maneuvered the dacidron toward the Bolivians and raised the craft high enough to allow an unobstructed field of fire. The commander nudged the lever to capture both the Frenchman and Colonel Suarez within the target circle and heard the distinct tick indicating both figures were firmly locked. He made a slight adjustment to the strength setting and then pressed the red button. Instantly a blinding bright flash of light erupted from below the dacidron and within a split second Devereaux and Suarez ceased to exist…they were vaporized along with the colonel's horse. Most of the mounted soldiers, stunned by the instant flash, instantly turned their mounts and spurred them back toward the south end of the valley. Several soldiers paused long enough to fire their rifles at the strange object, but had no way of knowing the bullets bounced harmlessly off the dacidron's impermeable hull. They quickly turned and fled. Professor Scott was so enthralled with the whole scene that he was content to sit quietly and just watch.

"You could take them all out with just one more flash of the laser," Elijah remarked.

"No, Mr. Walker," Nezar answered. "Those men are mere soldiers just following orders. They can do us no harm…they are free to go."

As Nezar and the four Americans watched the mounted men disappear from view, he turned and commented, "I have just received orders from our command center. Commander Ahular has summoned us back to our base. He has just received an urgent message with disturbing information."

Back inside the lost city the Americans noticed the alien crew was dismantling various pieces of equipment and transferring it to the X326. Santos, Mann, and Roper were helping. Nezar and Commander Ahular stepped to one side and were noticed to be conferring about something. The expressions on their strange looking faces and the noticeable downturn of their mouth slits indicated a look of great concern. Nezar glanced over to the four Americans then turned and walked their way. "I have some very alarming news." He hesitated for a moment to accentuate the gravity of the situation. "One of our ships exploring another solar system located in your neighboring Andromeda galaxy has discovered a huge asteroid currently located at the outer band of your solar system. It is hurling at a trajectory directly toward your sun. It is reported the object is a section of an exploding star and is comprised of substantial materials such as solid rock, metals and ice. It is several hundred miles wide and if it strikes your sun, the results to your solar system could be catastrophic."

"What do you mean by catastrophic?" Patterson asked with apprehension.

"It means your sun would explode and totally break apart and obliterate all of your surrounding planets with superheated air and radioactive debris. In other words, your earth and the other planets would be instantly incinerated."

"What does radioactive mean?" Professor Scott asked. "Is it harmful?"

"It can be very harmful when administered in strong doses. Radiation from your sun is basically sunlight, a mixture of electromagnetic waves from infrared to ultraviolet rays within the electromagnetic spectrum."

Scott was so perplexed that he just shook his head with bewilderment. There was nothing to say…a rare occurrence for the professor. He didn't have a clue what Nezar was talking about, nor did the other Americans.

"What can we do?" Simon asked.

"Nothing you can do, I'm afraid," Nezar answered. "But we can call on our sister ship, the X354 to assist us and use our combined lasers to attempt to break the asteroid apart in smaller pieces. Hopefully, if we can accomplish this, the smaller chunks might bypass your sun and continue beyond your solar system. I suggest you gather your belongings and prepare to board the ship."

Scott was devastated. They had discovered El Dorado…the discovery of a lifetime and he couldn't imagine leaving all of this behind. With a feeling of despair, thoughts of the museum and his reputation were foremost in his mind. For some strange reason the idea of the total destruction of the solar system eluded him for the moment. "Can we take some of the treasure with us?" he asked sheepishly.

Nezar answered with a tone of urgency. "You make take the Roman Constantine crown and Chi Rho coins along with the chest of Inca struck coins if you wish, but you must move quickly and board the ship so we can return you to Washington. We will need to depart as soon as possible so we can rendezvous with the X354. Our signal has already been sent to establish an assembly point just within the outer band of your solar system."

Patterson turned to the other three and remarked, "I don't think it's necessary to divulge this news about the asteroid to Santos, Mann, and Roper until we find out more details."

The others agreed.

The Americans gathered the Constantine treasure, the chest of Inca coins, and their belongings and boarded the X326, Cuzco. The aliens had loaded their equipment and the dacidron was raised into a dedicated hatch under the spacecraft. The Cuzco was ready to depart. The sleek ship transported itself through the tunnel passage and exited the mountain into the serene Peruvian valley, and as sunlight spilled through the viewing ports, the X326 swiftly rose into the sky.

The Cuzco followed a general course along the Pacific Coast where the flight plan was programed to veer to the northeast. When they reached the Isthmus of Panama, the ship would continue on a direct flight to Washington. Santos, who had an inherent fear of heights, especially sitting in a giant shell commanded by aliens from a planet millions of miles away, decided he wanted to stop in California. He approached Simon. "I do not want to continue on to Washington. Would you ask the commander if he will set me down in California? They can drop me off in San Juan Capistrano where they picked me up three years ago or at Rosita's Del Viejo ranch nearby. I know my sister needs my help so I will stop there and resume my duties of managing the ranch."

"Are you sure?"

"Yes…very sure."

"I'll ask Commander Ahular."

The commander had no objections since Southern California was in close range and would not cause any noticeable delay. He would take Santos to the ranch.

With Santos's help, the ship settled over a large field near the house and eased down over the extended pods that had been activated. Rosita was in the kitchen when she saw the sleek looking craft land nearby. Having been on the Toltec back in sixty-five she knew exactly what it was…her hopes soared. She threw a towel to the floor and rushed out of the rear door, hoping to see her brother and Elijah emerge from the craft. Santos came out of the hatch first and walked down the steps to the ground. Simon was next, followed by Elijah. Rosita was overjoyed as she gave her brother a big hug and then with tears streaming down her face, she threw herself into Elijah's arms. "You came back," she cried. "I knew in my heart you would come."

Elijah gave her a passionate kiss and held her tightly. He whispered, "Santos wanted to come home so our friends agreed to let him do so."

"And you are staying here with him…aren't you?"

"No, Rosita, I am very sorry but I cannot stay this time. I wish I could but I have something very important to attend to with Simon and the others…something vital to our country and perhaps the world."

"Will I ever see you again?" she asked sobbing.

"Yes…I promise to return as soon as our job is done…I promise." He gave Rosita another lingering kiss and then walked back to the hatch. As he turned to wave goodbye, he saws tears streaming down her cheeks and then he watched as the silent words formed on her lips…I love you. Before he ascended the steps he shouted, "I'll be back…I promise." The hatch closed and then they were gone.

Commander Nezar made a slight adjustment with the controls and turned the X326 toward the Arizona territories for their flight across the country to Washington. They were somewhere over Texas when Mann and Roper approached Simon and Patterson who were engrossed in a conversation about their war experiences. "Simon, could I ask a favor?" Mann requested. Roper was nodding, conveying it was his question as well.

"Sure, Parks, what is it?"

"Sam and I have talked it over and want to ask you if this ship will drop us off near Atlanta. Both of us would like to go home and find our families. The war was very hard on folks in Georgia and we just know our families desperately need our help. Besides, there is no need for us to travel all the way to Washington then turn around and travel back to Georgia."

"You agree with that, Sam?" Patterson asked.

"Yes, sir...I want to go home as well."

"I'll ask Ahular and Nezar," Simon responded.

The two alien commanders agreed to the request and slight adjustments were made in the flight path to divert the two men to Atlanta. Patterson whispered to Simon, "Good thing we didn't mention that asteroid thing streaking toward the sun. All that would do is cause a general panic when those guys started telling folks."

Simon agreed.

The craft descended to an elevation of ten miles high as it glided over Mississippi and then across Alabama. Their destination was located just north of the city of Atlanta, a city that had been devastated by General Sherman in July 1864. The war had left the city and surrounding area in ruins. As the X326 passed over the city, several wagons filled with lumber could be seen in the streets indicating a great rebuilding effort was underway. A landing site was picked slightly to the northeast in a large field near a small railroad station named Norcross. The ship landed gently on the extended pods and came to rest. As the hatch opened, Patterson accompanied the men to the ground and said appreciatively, "Parks and Sam, both of you have been of great service to me and your country. Simon and Elijah have asked me to give you a few of these to help you get re-established with your families." He held out his hand and handed each man twenty golden Inca coins. "Thank you, General," each responded as the men observed the brilliant coins they held. "These will surely help."

"There is one more thing you need to remember. Both of you must never divulge the location of the Confederate treasure we hid in that cave in North Carolina. Our deal with President Grant was to give him and the country the Confederate treasure in exchange for our return to the United States and a full pardon and citizenship. I am going to try to convince him to allow some of the funds to be used to help rebuild the south, especially cities like Atlanta that were hit the hardest. You must not breathe a word of this to anyone."

"We understand," Mann replied. Roper concurred.

"And while you're at it, I wouldn't mention anything about our finding El Dorado. This would only incite a gold rush fever and most likely a stampede to Peru."

"You have our word, General.

Patterson shook hands, turned and climbed the steps back into the ship as the two men stood back and watched the hatch close tightly into the hull. With the pods retracted, the X326 quickly rose from the ground, became a speck in the northern sky, and then disappeared from sight. Mann and Roper turned toward the small town of Norcross where they hoped to catch a wagon headed a few miles east to the Snellville area where their farms were located, and hopefully their families.

As the X326 streaked toward Washington, Simon, Elijah, Patterson, and Scott gathered in the assembly room to discuss their prospects. Simon asked Elijah, "I'm surprised you didn't stay in California with Santos…you told me you wanted to go to California and back to Rosita."

"I know," he answered sheepishly, "But…" He hesitated.

"Well…what?" Simon pressed.

"I've decided I want to accompany Commanders Ahular and Nezar and destroy that asteroid. It would be an experience of a lifetime to travel with them to outer space to see what it's like out there."

"You're kidding, of course."

"No…I mean it." Elijah retorted. "We've been on this ship before and know it is safe up here, especially with the guys who built this damn thing at the helm. We'll never get this chance again. You and I were aboard the Cuzco when they used the lasers to weld that underwater fault together and save our planet. Maybe I can be of some help again. According to Nezar our whole solar system is in danger of totally incinerating if that big hunk of rock isn't stopped and it plows into the sun."

This was all Professor Scott had to hear. "I want to go as well," he offered, enthusiastically. "This is a scientific opportunity I can't miss," he added, with thoughts of the speeches he would make and scientific journals he would write. He would offer all of this information and his experience to the world's scientific and academic community. Visions of fame and fortune bombarded his head and the mere idea of the dangers involved and unimaginable idea of the sun and earth being obliterated escaped him. There was no way Scott could miss this chance to travel into outer space where no man had been before.

Simon pondered the situation but thoughts of Maggie and the new baby he had not yet seen troubled him greatly. He could not bear the idea of not being able to ever see her again. The idea of his wife and baby being reduced to instant ashes was unthinkable. Patterson broke his train of thought when he announced, "I would like to go, too. This would be an experience I could share with my grandchildren. This opportunity will never happen to me again in a lifetime. How about you, nephew, are you with us?" he asked, turning to Simon.

Simon's deep-rooted sense of adventure and vivid memories from his recent experiences in discovering the lost continent of Atlantis, the earthquake affair, and El Dorado overshadowed his emotions. He was confident in the two alien commanders and the crew and knew he couldn't let his companions go without him, especially after all they had been through together. A big grin formed on his face as he nodded affirmatively, "I'm in. Let's go talk to Ahular."

38

COMMANDER AHULAR WAS DEFINITELY SURPRISED WITH the unusual request from the Americans but felt it might be prudent since it was their earth and solar system they would be trying to save. He and Nezar had grown to like these humanoids and reflected that these men were the only members of the human species they had ever befriended, and for that matter ever had face to face contact and personal communication with. Ahular also considered the fact that Simon had once commanded two of their former ships, the Toltec in Mexico and briefly the Cuzco during the Peruvian expedition. Simon and Elijah had earned their respect as capable crew members. Ahular willingly consented to the four Americans request to stay and face the difficult and dangerous task ahead. He understood their desire to participate in the attempt to save their planet from total destruction. The Americans were elated when Ahular, as a sign of respect, placed his fist over his chest and announced, "You may accompany us."

Nezar made a few adjustments to the computer and reset the X326 on a course to rendezvous with the other ship, X357. He had been advised the asteroid had entered the outer band of the solar system and already passed by a huge orbiting sphere of ice and rock currently in a position at 3.7 billion miles from the sun. In later years, this orb would be discovered by humans and named planet Pluto. Communications between the two ships calculated the necessary point of contact to be 2.79 billion miles from the current position of earth. They wanted to catch the asteroid before it entered the stronger gravitational influences of the inter-solar system where the earth and the other sister planets, especially Jupiter, revolved around the sun. The race would be close but Ahular and Nezar were confident the vartz speed capability would get them to the connection point with X354 at the designated time. They knew the combined strength of the six lasers from both ships would have to be utilized in a coordinated attack to break up an asteroid of this size.

Gathered in the assembly room, Ahular gave the Americans a briefing as to the plan. In addition to the two alien commanders, the ship had six crew members aboard. Nezar and one of the crew attended the control room while the other five attended the briefing. Ahular started by explaining the flight procedure. He wanted to make it simple so the four Americans could easily understand—he hoped they might prove useful in some diminutive way. "It is our plan to rendezvous with X357 at a designated position between your planets Uranus and Saturn. Our intercept point is currently calculated at 2.79 billion miles from our present position. Our intent is that the demolition effect of the asteroid will allow the smaller pieces of rock to be caught in the gravitational influences of the planets Neptune and Uranus and fall harmlessly to their surfaces while other pieces burn up and disintegrate in space."

"How long would it take for us to reach the asteroid?" Professor Scott asked.

"With our Vartz speed capabilities, in earth time we calculate the journey will take us 75 hours, 22 minutes to linkup with our sister ship. Commander Nezar and I, along with two crew members will take turns manning the control room while the rest of you will hibernate for three days during the journey."

"I assume you mean sleep?" Scott asked curiously. "How can we sleep continuously for three days?"

"You will be placed in an incubator capsule for the journey. The containers have the proper instruments to allow feeding and waste elimination for normal body functions and will allow you to sleep throughout the flight. You will be well nourished and rested when you awake."

Professor Scott was a bit perturbed that he might miss

something during the journey but kept the thoughts to himself. He would sleep like everyone else.

Ahular continued. "Once the ship passes the gravitational influence of your sun, we can convert to vartz speed and cover the vast distance required to make our rendezvous."

The inquisitive professor had to ask the question. "Commander, exactly what is vartz speed and how do you manage to reach it?"

Ahular knew any explanation to these questions would be difficult for these humanoids to understand but he would try. "Speed is a variable of time and distance. In other words, how fast can an object travel from one point to another? The fastest known speed in the universe is the speed of light within a vacuum. When our ship travels beyond any gravitational influences from planets and other celestial bodies, we have a special piece of equipment on board that allows us to bend light waves and enable the X326 to reach a speed equivalent to seventy five percent of light speed or approximately 139,500 miles per second. At this speed we can achieve time warps that will enable us to travel incredible distances in a relatively short time. We call this vartz speed." Ahular knew by the blank expressions on his visitor's faces that he had completely lost them to the point that no questions would be forthcoming.

Professor Scott started to say something but thought it best to keep quiet even though his mind was racing with questions.

Ahular broke the reverie by commenting on a forthcoming event soon to happen. "Shortly, we will be approaching your planet Mars. You will be able to get a brief glimpse through the starboard porthole and you will observe the red cast from the planet. This indicates an abundance of iron oxide minerals in the soil. Mars is uninhabitable although we think millions of years ago microorganisms most likely inhabited much of the planet. We will be circumventing your sun soon and then we will begin our acceleration to vartz speed. Before we initiate the command sequence, you will be placed into your incubation capsules and drift into a somniferous induced sleep where your body will remain dormant until awakened. I assure you the time will pass quickly. When you awaken, you will feel very refreshed and will be very far out in space and close to a designated coordinate within an inner band of your Milky Way galaxy. This is the area where we want to rendezvous with the X354 and initiate our attack on the asteroid."

The incubation capsules were housed in two cabins in the stern section of the ship with each room accommodating five glass-like chambers. Nezar, with the assistance of another crewman, would commence the sleep process by placing the four Americans in separate containers in one room and the remaining four crew members in the other. Passing through the laboratory, Simon noticed the large liquid filled containers that had previously contained the suspended bodies of incarcerated workers bound for the sunken city of Lythe during the Peruvian expedition. He was relieved to see the tanks were now empty.

Once in the incubation room, Elijah couldn't believe he was going to climb into one of those translucent tubes for three days. "Damn things look like glass coffins," he anguished to Simon. "I'd rather stay awake and catch some naps for three days. How am I supposed eat and go to the bathroom?"

"Ahular said they have a way to feed you and let you relieve yourself inside the container. Maybe they'll pump some of that slimy glop down our throats from those food tanks they eat out of," Simon ribbed.

"You've got to be kidding me. Let's hope they have some fried chicken, mashed potatoes, and gravy to stuff down those tubes. As far as the bathroom is concerned, I'll probably get so damned stopped up I'll explode all over the place and have to sit in a bathtub for a week to clean myself up."

Simon chuckled aloud. "Good grief, Elijah. You'll only be sleeping for three days and that's nothing," he said, accepting the fact they had no idea what to expect. They just had to trust Ahular and the knowledge this is how the aliens endured the long journeys they made—in a dormant state of sleep. Nezar and the crew member came into the room and announced it was time for the four Americans to enter the incubators. A small platform was placed to the side of each container and with Simon going first, each man entered his chamber and lay face up while in succession Nezar and his helper fastened the straps, electrodes, and tubes necessary to sustain them in a dormant state throughout the three day journey. Wow…this cocoon thing feels like a feather bed, Elijah thought as a thin fog spread across him and filled the tube. The gas was relaxing and with a few deep breaths, he drifted off into a deep sleep, as did the others. The real journey had begun.

Back in the control room Ahular and one of the crew named Quapuac took the controls for the first shift while Nezar and the other crew member slipped off to get some needed sleep. The commander made a few adjustments to the computer and then took a seat and watched through the front ports as the vartz speed took over and hurled the X326 through the vacuum at an unimaginable speed. He watched as Jupiter flashed by. The commander sat back in his confortable command seat, satisfied all the controls and instruments had been properly programmed and confident they would make the rendezvous with X354 at the designated time. The flight preparation had been easy, but the most difficult task would come in three and a half days when they were faced with a very challenging job of saving the earth and her solar system from total destruction. Failure was out of the question.

The time passed quickly and the Americans awoke inside the incubator chambers. Simon was astonished he felt no negative effects from the long sleep. He actually felt refreshed, just like Ahular had told them, but had to wonder how he was fed or how he disposed of the waste from his body. He had no intention of asking but the thoughts were filed away as just another mystery of these aliens from a far off world. Nezar and his assistant walked into the room and punched in a command on a small screen to allow the lids to rise up and open each incubator. In only took seconds to remove the straps, tubes, and electrodes and help each man to exit to the floor. Elijah let out a big yawn and long stretch to awaken muscles that had lay totally dormant for so long. With a surprised look he announced, "After all that I feel pretty good."

Professor Scott replicated his thoughts. "Me, too," he said with a stretch. "It's amazing."

Passing the other room, Simon observed the other four crewmen had already been awakened and were most likely already at their stations preparing for the events to come. Nezar ushered the Americans up to the control room where Ahular was waiting. The upturned slit on his elongated face was conveyed as a smile as he greeted his visitors. "I trust you feel rested and refreshed after your long sleep?"

"Yes, Commander," Simon responded. "It certainly doesn't feel like we've been down for three days." He glanced out of the command porthole and saw total darkness with numerous specks of light in the far distance and asked, "Might I ask where we are?"

"We are approaching an intermediate band of the Milky Way galaxy and those bright spots you see in the distance are stars. We have reduced our speed and are only four hours from our rendezvous point with X354. Once we link up with it, we will observe and analyze the asteroid and have some time to prepare our plan of attack. I have been in communication with Commander Xedoc and he informs me they have been following the asteroid and confirmed its direction. As we thought, it is on a direct impact path with your sun."

"How large is it?" Simon asked with concern.

Commander Xedoc told me the object is irregular in shape and measures 457 earth miles at its widest point. This particular body is actually the largest one we have ever seen. For an asteroid this big, it is traveling very fast…246,500 miles per hour. That would be nearly 70 earth miles per second.

"What is the thing made of and where did it come from?" Patterson asked inquisitively.

"This asteroid is part of the remains of a collision between two planets or other planetesimal bodies in space. It is mostly composed of rock and tempered metal."

"When do you think it could reach our sun?" Scott added.

"It depends on gravitational influences from other celestial bodies. We estimate our contact point with X354 to be 1.1 billion miles from your sun. At the current velocity, our computer would estimate the asteroid would cover a distance of 2.062 billion miles in one year so we could expect an impact to the sun in earth time in one hundred eighty-five days, a little over six months. The closer it gets to the sun the more unpredictable it will be and more difficult to manage. This is why we need to neutralize it before it gets too far into your galaxy. Shortly, Commander Xedoc and I will calculate a strategy of where and how to organize our attack. Meanwhile, I ask each of you to have a seat while we coordinate our plans.

39

SIMON AND HIS THREE COMPANIONS COMPLIED and took the seats provided at one side of the control center. Elijah turned to Simon and whispered, "What the hell have we gotten ourselves into this time? I have a bad feeling about all of this."

Simon just glanced at him with an ominous look. "Beats me. Maybe we shoulda jumped off this ship in Washington after all."

They observed Ahular talking in his strange language on a zenox. In a few moments he placed the device on the command console and turned to Nezar and crew members to give them a briefing. Since all of the aliens spoke fluent English, a language they had learned during the Mexico encounter, he spoke in this language to explain the plans so the Americans would be included and understand the situation. "I have just conferred with Commander Xedoc and we will now be making our rendezvous in five hours and fifteen minutes."

To the Americans the time passed like an eternity. Several of the crew received instructions from Ahular and scurried off to other parts of the ship while three remained in the control room to attend different stations. No doubt a couple of the crew would be in the tracx power room where the energy that controlled the ship and the multitude of instruments could be constantly monitored. Simon recognized one familiar monitor station dedicated to the target acquisition screen and the lever controlling the lasers. Another was devoted to navigation and another to the ship's power devices. Simon knew the X326 was totally controlled by the computers but also knew a crew member had to be on hand to make any adjustments or corrections if an emergency arose or mishap occurred. The waiting and silence was unnerving as they sat quietly observing Ahular, Nezar and the three crewmen attending to their duties. Suddenly, Commander Ahular stood up and looked out of the window to his right. He turned to the Americans seated against a wall. "If you will join me, you can see the X354 to our starboard."

Anxious to finally stretch their legs, the Americans stood and rushed over to the window. In the distance, cruising parallel to the X326, an identical ship was spotted…the rendezvous was successful. Against the darkness of empty space, the dull silver hull of the alien ship was remarkably visible. Although the matching speeds were extremely fast, the distant ship seemed to be hardly moving. Scott reasoned it was because there was nothing but an empty void in the background to distinguish any discernable movement.

Ahular approached the Americans and explained the plan of attack. "We are now positioning ourselves where both of our ships will be directly above the asteroid and we will be matching the same speed of 246,500 miles per hour. There is one slight obstacle we will have to deal with. The target is showing a noticeable rotation that will make it difficult to concentrate our combined lasers on one spot."

Elijah remembered three years ago how, over the Atlantic Ocean, the ship had adjusted the lasers to full strength and then concentrated the three beams into one single stream to weld the two tectonic plates together and cover the expanding void that was splitting the earth apart. He asked Ahular if that was the plan for the asteroid.

"Yes, Elijah, that was the intended plan, but it now appears the asteroid's rotation might not allow a coordinated stream. What we will have to do is for each ship to operate independently and blast chunks of the rock away to reduce the size. Hopefully we can eventually blast enough splinters away where the small pieces will burn up when they contact friction resistance as they pass through an atmosphere."

As if on cue, the two ships made a wide circle and maneuvered into positions on each side of the asteroid. The revised plan was to use the concentrated beams of each ship's lasers to break off small chunks of the huge rock to reduce it to a more manageable size. Each commander knew this huge 457 mile wide rock would take numerous blasts to split sections away. The crewman, Quapuac, was assigned to the laser controls and Simon watched with interest as he moved a lever to raise and position the three lasers to merge into a single concentrated stream of energy. A few clicks of the left silver knob reduced the beam to the narrowest width and he turned the right knob five clicks to adjust to the maximum power. He then nudged the tracking circle to lock on a large outcropping near the edge of the asteroid. A distinct click confirmed the target was locked in. When Quapuac saw his commander give an affirmative nod he pressed the red button. A brilliant flash spilled through the portholes as if a thousand lightning bolts had been simultaneously discharged. The concentrated beam of light struck the asteroid with a vengeance, blasting huge chunks of metal and stone apart. The Americans watched in awe as a large slice of the rock mass broke away and tumbled to the side, falling harmlessly away toward empty space. Several more laser blasts were repeated, knocking off more fragments of rock, but it was apparent the bombardment was only making a dent in the huge asteroid. Quapuac adjusted the laser to attempt to dislodge a larger slice and pressed the firing button. The beam of light energy cut deep into the rock causing another large section to break loose. Fragments flew in all directions but one huge boulder was propelled directly toward the ship. Nezar saw the imminent threat and shouted, "The port thrusters! Full power…Now!"

The crewman handling the power console was slightly slow to react and for an instant it appeared the huge rock would collide with the ship causing instantaneous destruction. Patterson and Scott looked on in total shock and horror at the annihilation about to happen. In a split second the thrusters responded and discharged a sudden burst of tracx energy and instantly hurled the ship laterally away from its position. The collision did not happen as the boulder hurled past and barely missed the X326 by only a few feet. While Simon and his companions had to sit down to get control of their shock, Ahular calmly gave a command to return the ship to its normal course. He now realized it would take something much different to reduce the asteroid…something much more powerful…a tracx thermo- fission bomb.

Simon watched as the commander picked up his zenox and talked briefly in his strange language. He assumed it was the commander of the X354. Ahular then motioned to Nezar and spoke a few words to him. Nezar nodded his understanding. The Americans sensed something big was happening and glanced at each other with uncomprehending concern. Elijah whispered, "I wonder what these guys are up to now? I smell more trouble brewing."

Nezar walked over to a monitor and projected a picture on the screen. It was a wide-angle view of the asteroid below them. He entered a few calculations and watched as strange looking symbols flashed across the screen. Nezar then turned and approached the Americans. "Conditions make it necessary that we change our attack strategy. The rotation of the large asteroid makes it impossible to concentrate our laser power in one spot to achieve any noticeable damage. It will burn too much of our tracx energy to break the rock apart piece by piece. Also, the body is composed of a variety of metals that have been subjected to intense heat. This has tempered the metal into an extremely hard and resistant composition. In order to neutralize it we will have to resort to a much more powerful weapon… one that will shatter the asteroid into small and harmless pieces."

"What could be stronger than those lasers you have?" Elijah questioned.

"We have a much stronger weapon aboard that will have to be used. It is our tracx thermo-fission device…a bomb so powerful it will shatter the asteroid into a billion pieces and hopefully vaporize most of the pieces of rock and metal into dust."

Simon couldn't imagine something so lethal. "If this bomb is so powerful, how can you deliver such a weapon to the asteroid's surface and detonate it without destroying both of your ships and all of us on board?"

"That will be no concern as we will be far away from the explosion."

"Then how will you deliver the weapon?" Simon pressed.

Nezar hesitated for a moment to gauge how his answer would be received. "We will use the dacidron to land on the asteroid's surface and manually plant the device deep into the rock. Since our crew is so limited and assigned to specific functions managing the ship, they cannot be spared. Two of you will have to accompany me and walk out on the rock's surface while I navigate the vehicle and keep it stable in a hover position just off the ground. One of you will use a laser drill to bore a hole in the rock while the other will implant and secure the thermo-fission bomb into place. We will detonate it electronically from a safe distance. I will give you a few moments to select two volunteers."

40

THE ARGUMENT OVER WHO WOULD GO became a bit heated but Simon took the lead and announced he would be the first to volunteer. Patterson immediately objected. "No, Simon, I forbid it. You are a married man to my niece and have a new baby to take care of. I'm the oldest so I'll go instead."

Simon thought of Maggie again and the son or daughter he had never seen. He relented.

Elijah spoke up. "Robert, you are forty-one years old and too damn old to go. I'm going to be the first volunteer and that's final."

With some relief Patterson didn't put up an argument. Professor Scott jumped into the fray. "I am going with Elijah," he announced convincingly. "I am most curious to see what that big rock looks like up close. Perhaps I can even grab a sample rock to carry back to the museum. When I get home and start my lecture tour, can you imagine what those scientific fogies and academia fuddy-duddies are going to say when I tell them I actually walked on the surface of a speeding asteroid out in deep space?"

Elijah laughed aloud. "Yeah, they're going to say you are as crazy as a loon and suggest the authorities lock you up somewhere."

This lightened the mood as Simon motioned over to Nezar who joined them. "Well, Commander," he revealed, "Elijah and Professor Scott will be accompanying you. You have your team."

Nezar seemed pleased with the choices and began to explain the procedure for the landing and placing the bomb. He was prepared to answer any questions, anticipating there would be several. He was right as Scott offered the first. "Commander, how are we to get to the surface of that asteroid?"

"We will launch the dacidron and drop it to the ground where you will step out onto the surface."

"What will keep us from blowing off the surface with that tremendous speed it's traveling and tumble out into space?" Elijah asked.

"Remember there is no atmosphere on the asteroid. You will be working in a vacuum and will be traveling at the same speed. You will be able to complete your work just as if you were on earth. You will be provided with a special insulated suit and helmet that will feed you oxygen and provide a normal atmosphere within the suit. It will also keep you warm in the extreme cold temperature."

Scott jumped back in. "Operating in a vacuum? What will prevent us flying into the air when we take a step? There will be no gravity to hold us on the rock. In a vacuum won't the force of inertia push us upward when we take a step?"

"The asteroid is comprised of rock and dense metals. In this particular case the target area we have selected has a very high density of hardened metal on and under the surface. You will have special electromagnetic boots that will be activated to provide you a solid adherence to the metallic rich surface. In other words, both of you will have a firm magnetic attachment to the ground."

"Can you explain how that works?" Scott pressed curiously.

"The boots have a mechanism that can be adjusted to provide a positive or negative electromagnetic field. Like any magnet, two positive polar fields pushed together will repel each other and a positive and negative field will attract. The metal composition of the object's surface will provide a negative polar effect and the boots will be adjusted to positive. This will allow you to magnetically adhere to the surface. The adjustment will have to be set to the correct positive polar strength position to allow you to be able to walk normally over the surface. The setting will have to be calculated to the intensity and type of metal you are walking over. Our sensors indicate a strong presence of iron and cobalt along the surface. The danger here is to make sure the boot is not adjusted to full positive, as to do so will cause your feet to be firmly attached to the surface making it difficult or even impossible to take any steps. The opposite is worse…a full negative polar field will most likely propel you high above the asteroid's surface."

Elijah and Professor Scott were uncertain that they understood all of this but they did comprehend the fact that to over-adjust the boots in either direction was bad…very bad.

Nezar glanced over to Ahular to see his nod indicating he had positioned the X326 to the center of the asteroid at a suitable location to plant the fission bomb. He then turned to his two new volunteers and announced, "The ship is in place and it is now time to go. I will take you to the dacidron hatch where we will suit up and I will show how to operate the control knob on the boots to adjust the electromagnetic polar fields. Before we board the vehicle, I will also show you how the laser torch is operated and how to set and activate the fission bomb."

Elijah and Scott gave each other a despondent look and shrugged. They were now committed.

Simon and Patterson wished their companions luck and watched with ominous feelings as Nezar led them from the command center to the ship's belly below where the dacidron awaited their fate."

The docking compartment for the air-powered vehicle was located in the lower center section of the X326. The cubicle had an airtight hatch that would extend laterally to allow the dacidron to float out of the ship on a cushion of pure energy inertia. Since they were in a vacuum void of heavy air, the vehicle relied on internal thrust from the turbines to create an inertia force to manipulate movement in harsh airless environments such as this. Nezar at the controls had a skillful way of doing this. From a small locker the commander pulled two insulated suits and helmets from their supports. He explained how the suits were self-sustaining and would provide good warmth and protection in the airless vacuum they were about to enter. The electromagnetic boots took more instruction but the positive and negative control knob was easy to understand…turn toward the right for the positive polar field and left for negative. The magnetic field for the metallic infested surface they would be walking on was calculated at forty-two percent negative. The dial was marked from a neutral setting of zero to a maximum positive setting of ten either way, positive and negative. Nezar showed them the markings on the dial that displayed the settings and explained how to adjust them. He then adjusted the setting to five positive to correspond with the surface readings. "Don't exceed the designated setting on the boots or you might get permanently stuck on the asteroid and get vaporized by the thermo explosion," he warned them. "And also watch that you do not reverse the setting from zero to the negative polarity field. You would lose magnetic attraction with the surface and this would produce some very unpleasant contrasting results."

"One other thing you need to know," he added, "the helmets have a two way wireless headset transistor that will allow conversation between the ship's control center, the dacidron, and each other. We will all be in constant touch by voice communication. I'll be wearing a suit and helmet as well because when we open the hatch, the dacidron will lose its atmosphere and I'll be working in the same vacuum as you."

The laser drill was also easy to understand. A strong preset concentrated laser beam would cut a seven inch diameter hole through the rock at a depth of ten feet, large enough to accommodate the five foot tubular shell containing the tracx fission bomb. Elijah was selected to manage the drill and the professor would arm the electronic signal regulator and implant the tube into the hole. Elijah would complete the process by using the laser from the drill to remove enough rock and debris to tightly refill and tamp the hole. Elijah thought the final step would be the easiest to remember…Get the hell outta there.

The team entered the vehicle and took their positions, and on cue from the X326 control room, the hatch opened, the turbines were engaged, and the dacidron smoothly floated out of the ship.

Nezar maneuvered the vehicle to a position about 200 yards from the hovering spacecraft. A spot was selected just below a jagged outcropping to drill the hole. The dacidron touched the surface and the hatch opened to allow the two Americans to exit the vehicle. The whole operation would commence in two minutes.

Elijah carried the laser drill strapped over his shoulder and helped Professor Scott carry the fission bomb. Even though the bomb and housing weighed over 200 pounds, the weightlessness in the airless vacuum made it much lighter and easy to carry. Both men found walking on the surface rather easy although Elijah noticed the magnetic boots tightly adhered to the ground with each step. With a little effort he was able to lift his boot and continue trudging forward. Through the headset Nezar confirmed their arrival at the target location. This was where they would start drilling the hole. The bomb was gently placed on the ground and Elijah activated the laser switch and positioned the drill over the selected spot of smooth rock just under the outcropping. He pressed the drill trigger and watched as the intense beam of light energy sliced into the rock like it was butter. Molten rock and metal poured out of the hole as the beam dug deeper and deeper. He was thankful the beam width and correct power level had been preset as the diameter of the hole appeared to be the seven inches they needed to plant the tube containing the fission bomb device. It only took a few minutes before the depth sensor attached to the drill registered the prescribed depth of ten feet. He turned off the beam and helped Scott activate and maneuver the bomb housing into place to lower into the hole. Positioning the nose of the tube into a small fabric hand held sling, they slowly lowered the bomb into the hole and played out the thin cord handles until it stopped at the bottom. The fission bomb was now in place and armed. Elijah relayed the progress of the mission through the headset to Nezar and the command center. "The bomb housing has been lowered into the hole and now I am initiating the tamping stage with the laser."

As instructed, Elijah readjusted the laser drill to the lowest power setting and ignited the beam to strike around the edge of the hole. The lower setting allowed the laser to fracture fragments of rock around the opening and spill into the hole. Satisfied it was full, he shut off the laser and turned, ready to return to the dacidron. While Scott moved out ahead, Elijah hesitated a moment to step on the hole to compact the debris tighter and ensure a good tamp. Somehow the top of his right boot scraped a small protrusion under the outcropping and somehow twisted the control knob to the right and toward the positive magnetic setting. The sensors in his boot transferred the new command, synchronizing both boots to the higher positive polarity field. Satisfied the bomb was securely in place, he turned to see Scott almost to the vehicle's hatch and took a step to follow. A feeling of panic hit him when he realized his feet wouldn't move. He was firmly stuck to the ground.

41

Professor Scott turned when he realized Elijah was not behind him. He spoke into the headset, "Elijah, where are you?" His reassuring voice in Elijah's ear calmed him a bit. "I'm stuck back here at this damn hole. My feet won't move."

"Hold on. I'm coming back for you."

The professor could see his friend tugging at his leg as he approached the site. "What's wrong?"

"My feet won't budge. I'm stuck to the ground."

Scott grabbed Elijah's right leg and pulled with all his strength but he could not dislodge it.

Nezar, who could hear the conversation, recognized the problem and broke in. "This is Commander Nezar. I believe the positive force field on your boots is turned much too high and holding you to the surface. You have to move the setting toward the negative field to break the magnetic attraction to the metal you are standing on."

Elijah was magnetically and firmly bonded to a boulder of cobalt with a strong negative and positive magnetic attraction.

"I can't budge your leg," Scott shouted frantically, forgetting the instructions and details from Nezar about the boot settings.

"You have to break the magnetic bond," Elijah yelled back.

"How do I do that?"

"Turn that control knob on the top of my boot to the left. We have to change this boot from positive to negative to break the magnetic connection."

In the ensuing confusion, Scott wasn't sure what Elijah meant but he knelt down and turned the knob counterclockwise as far as he could. Big mistake…

Elijah, not realizing what Scott had done, felt the connection suddenly break loose. He was relieved that he could now return safely to the ship. At that instant, he didn't sense the magnetic setting on the boots had been radically changed to negative positions as he took a step toward the dacidron. The strong repelling inertia from the two identical magnetic force fields hurled him head-over-heels upward and about fifty feet above the asteroid's surface. An earsplitting scream blasted out of the X326 speakers and Nezar's and Scott's headsets… "Ohhhh SHIT!"

Back in the control room, Simon heard Elijah's shriek and knew something terrible had just occurred. He hurried over to Ahular and shouted, "What's happening?"

"I am afraid your companion has been hurled into space… away from the asteroid. He is now somewhere above our craft and floating away fast."

"Can't Nezar grab him with the dacidron?"

"The dacidron is only designed to operate close to the ground and cannot maneuver in free space."

"Well, Commander Ahular, what can we do?" Simon persisted anxiously. "We can't let Elijah just float away and die."

"First, we will retrieve the dacidron and then attempt to rescue him with our ship. It will not be an easy task as he is moving away fast. I fear you should prepare for the worst."

Professor Scott had hurried back and entered the vehicle, not exactly certain what he had done to cause this terrible mishap to happen. Nezar closed the hatch and engaged the thrusters to return to the ship.

"What happened?" Scott asked with alarm.

"It appears you reversed the boot settings to identical magnetic poles. This repelled Elijah from the surface and into space."

"Oh my God!" Scott shouted. "What can we do?"

"We can't retrieve him with this vehicle so we need to get back to the ship and dock and then we can attempt to find your friend with the X326."

With a complete sense of hopelessness, Elijah found himself free-floating into space. He could easily see the huge asteroid sliding below him and the small image of the X326 drifting further and further away. He tried to control his nerves as best he could but the situation appeared to be getting more desperate each moment. This is no time to panic, he thought.

"Commander Nezar, Simon…anybody…can you hear me?" he yelled into his headset. "This is Elijah," No response.

He shouted again. "Can anybody hear me? I'm floating away from the ship. Helloooo!" Still no response. Things were getting critical. He was trying to think. I must be drifting too far away from the ship for the signal to get through…Somehow I need to propel myself forward to move closer. Good grief…how can I flap my arms and legs to move myself…there is no air to get any resistance and I sure can't blow out any air through this helmet. There isn't any damn air to blow anyway and get any inertia to move me. Looks like I'm in a heap of trouble.

Elijah knew his oxygen was limited and would not last much longer. He tried to imagine what it would be like to die floating around in space. Maybe my body will be hit by a meteor or maybe I'll just float into the sun and burn up in a flash. I could close my eyes and go to sleep and not wake up but I'll never see Rosita again. All sorts of weird thoughts flashed through his head and his feeling of despair was getting worse until suddenly it hit him like a hammer…The laser torch!

He reached to his side and thankfully felt the device still strapped to his back. Removing the torch from his shoulder he held it firmly with both hands trying to figure how to use it to get some thrust of motion. His mind was racing. Better hold on to this thing. If I point it behind me, maybe the energy force of the laser will push me forward. Sure worth a try. It's the only option I've got.

Elijah activated the ignition switch and shifted his body where the nozzle of the torch was facing to his rear. He adjusted the control switch to full power and then pulled the trigger. A narrow burst of light surged from the barrel and streaked a dazzling bright beam across the sky. In the airless void he could not feel any sense of movement but he persisted and kept the energy beam flowing. This is hopeless, he thought, I don't think I'm going anywhere. Just when Elijah was almost at the point of giving up he noticed something different…the asteroid appeared to be getting closer. He kept his finger on the trigger.

Suddenly a faint burst of static filled his ears followed by the intermittent sound of a familiar voice. He responded with a shout. "Hello…hello…this is Elijah. Anybody there?"

His signal was picked up by the X326 receivers and broadcast through the speakers. Simon could not believe his ears. Miraculously the energy and inertia from the laser had pushed Elijah through the airless void and through a rare ionization energy field that blocked the signal to and from the ship's transmitter. A familiar voice filled his ears. "Mr. Walker, this is Commander Ahular. Our transponder receiver and locator sensor picked up your signal and we have your current position at 223 miles and 146 degrees from our present position. We observed the laser beam streaking across the sky and know you are still in possession of the drill device. In approximately three minutes, on your count to two-hundred, fire another laser beam from the torch directly to your front and we will be able to visually pick up the light and get an exact fix on your position. Our target locator will pinpoint your position and we will be there to get you."

"Aye, aye, Skipper," Elijah shouted euphorically. Ahular's voice was the most gratifying sound he had ever heard.

The commander turned to Simon with a bewildered look on his face. "What is that language? I do not understand what he is saying."

Simon chuckled. "That is a nautical term we use on Earth. It means he understands what you said and he will comply."

Nezar had successfully docked the dacidron and Professor Scott and he made their way to the control room. "We heard the transmission. Have you secured him on the locator?"

"Yes, we should arrive at the contact position in exactly eight earth minutes and twenty-three seconds." To Simon the eight minutes seemed like two hours but he was elated when he heard the crewman manning the locator screen announce, "Target in sight...we have a visual."

Elijah saw the X326 approaching and he was so excited he urinated in his pants and was embarrassed to see beads of moisture misting on the glass of his helmet. He had to chuckle, oh what the hell, it coulda been worse. Wait until Simon hears about this.

As the ship maneuvered into position, Elijah watched the hatch open from the dacidron's docking compartment and a helmeted figure floated out tethered to a cable. With a small thruster attached to his back, the crewman drifted swiftly toward Elijah. He couldn't be sure but the upturned slit on his rescuer's face was most likely some sort of an alien smile. The crewman reached the American, snapped a towline to his belt, and then turned and maneuvered back to the ship. He pulled Elijah into the hatch, closed it, and re-pressurized the chamber. With his feet firmly planted on the deck Elijah mumbled a brief prayer. He removed the helmet and damp pressure suit and then followed the crewman to the command center.

Simon, Scott, and Patterson were overjoyed to see their companion and each gave him a big bear hug to express their relief. "We thought we would never see you again," Simon said to his cousin.

"Oh, it was nothing," Elijah lied. "Just a little side trip I took to see the sights."

Patterson and Scott laughed while Simon rolled his eyes. Only Elijah...I can't believe he's my blood cousin, he thought humorously...but damn sure glad to see him in one piece.

42

NEW COORDINATES WERE ENTERED INTO THE computer as the X326 made preparations for the return to earth. "Where is your other ship, the X354?" Simon asked Ahular. "Will it return with us?"

"No," the commander answered, "it will be returning to Andromeda and to a planet they have been monitoring...one that is very earthlike and inhabited by an intelligent species."

"Are they like us humans?" he questioned.

"Their brains have advanced to a higher intelligent level but Commander Xedoc tells us that evolution has shaped their bodies into a slightly different shape than your species."

Professor Scott was taking all of this in and the conversation piqued his imagination and curiosity. "This planet you speak of, does it look like our earth with oceans and land masses?" he inquired.

"We have not visited the Andromeda Galaxy but we are informed the planet exists in one of Andromeda's inner bands, within a solar system designated as ZTX 383. Much like your solar system, it has eight revolving planets around its sun. This particular planet, designated Sorius, is 94.65 million earth miles from their sun as compared to your earth's 92.96 million miles. The sun is a little larger and provides adequate warmth to allow similar earthlike climatic conditions to exist. We are informed Sorius does have adequate water and atmosphere to sustain intelligent life forms."

Scott's curiosity was soaring now. "Can you take us there?" he asked, disregarding thoughts of the harrowing incident they had just experienced.

This question brought harsh looks from his companions. Elijah thought, How the hell can you ask such a ridiculous question when your carelessness nearly blew my ass into another galaxy?

Scott, realizing the foolishness of this request, could only shrug with an 'I'm sorry' expression.

Ahular picked up on this and answered with some amusement, "No, that is impossible since we are assigned to monitor your solar system and specifically your planet, Earth…some other time perhaps. Due to the gravitational effects from your planets, our return time will be a little shorter. With vartz speed our flight time will be three days, two hours. You can dispense with the incubator chambers and get periodic sleep on the assembly room couches if you prefer."

After the events involving their encounter with the asteroid and near disaster with Elijah, the four Americans were wound up like banjo strings and couldn't dream of a three day nap. "Thank you Commander, we would prefer to do that."

Much to the gratification of his guests, Ahular nodded his approval.

New coordinates were entered into the navigation console and the computers locked in the coordinates for the return trip to planet Earth. Nezar tuned to the four Americans. "We are going to achieve vartz speed within the next few minutes and reach a safe distance before Commander Xedoc detonates the tracx fission bomb. It will be a catastrophic explosion and we want to achieve a safe distance from the shock waves the bomb will generate."

"How far will we be from the explosion?" Patterson asked with some apprehension.

"We plan to be at least 225 million miles from the asteroid when it blows."

Patterson nodded with an irresolute sense of relief, although in his mind, thoughts of the speeds and distances Nezar was talking about were incomprehensible. He reasoned his best option was to keep quiet and refrain from any more questions.

"How long will it take us to go that distance?" Scott asked.

"Our calculations indicate at our vartz speed of 139,700 earth miles per second we will arrive at our designated distance in 36.8 minutes. This should eliminate any threat to us from the asteroid. Now, I suggest you find a place to relax and enjoy the ride."

They left the control room and gathered down in the assembly room to discuss Elijah's ordeal and wait for the big light show.

Patterson turned to Elijah. "Did you understand any of that explanation about the speed and distance we will be traveling?"

"Sure," Elijah answered frivolously. "Nezar said the same thing we used to say in the cavalry. We'll be hauling ass."

That brought laughter from everyone and seemed to loosen the tension in the room.

Simon was most interested in finding out what went through Elijah's mind as he floated out in space. "What happened out there and what went through your mind as you were drifting?" Simon asked him.

"Are you kidding me?" his cousin responded. "I was scared shitless."

"I mean what were you thinking about?"

Elijah hesitated a moment and then answered, "When I saw the ship and asteroid drifting further and further away I thought I was a goner. All I could imagine was running out of oxygen or slamming into a meteor or landing on some remote planet somewhere."

Professor Scott had kept a low profile and was embarrassed at the mistake he had made when he turned Elijah's magnetic boot control knob to a full negative polar field and propelled him from the asteroid's surface. "I'm really sorry about my mistake, Elijah. I was overly excited and wasn't thinking." Trying to add something positive to the conversation he added, "How did you think to use that laser torch to propel you back toward the ship? That was brilliant."

"I tried flapping my arms and legs but that didn't work. I was about to give up and just go to sleep. In that airless void I knew I couldn't get any movement or thrust without something to help me. That's when the idea of the torch hit me. Good thing it was still strapped to my back. I was hoping the sheer force of the laser beam shooting out of the nozzle might produce some push so I tried it. I wasn't even sure it was working until I happened to look down and see the ship and asteroid getting closer. The damn thing was actually working and pushing me along."

"How did you make contact with the ship?" Patterson asked.

"Commander Ahular's voice boomed into my headset… prettiest sound I ever heard. Can you believe I got so excited I actually pissed in my pants and covered the faceplate on the helmet with beads of moisture?"

"That's the funniest thing I've ever heard," Simon shouted with a big laugh followed by an explosion of laughter from the others.

"Remind me not to put on your suit if I have to jump out into space," Simon joked. More laughter erupted as Elijah gave his companions an annoyed look.

The time passed quickly as Nezar approached them with an announcement. "We have reached our designated point and the vartz speed converter has been turned off to allow us visual contact with the explosion of the fission bomb. On a coordinated command, the X354 will initiate the detonation in a few minutes so we will be able to see the flash of light. We will monitor the pressure waves and record any effects they might have to your solar system. Please follow me back to command center where you will have a better view through the forward viewing ports."

When they arrived in the control room, the ship had come to a standstill and turned so the ports had a good view of the asteroid's general location. At that distance they couldn't see anything but dark empty space filled with specs of light reflected from distant stars. A crewman locked in the locator screen and manipulated some control dials to allow the ports to expose a magnified view of the horizon. The countdown began…ten…nine…eight. The count hit zero and the target acquisition operator announced, "Detonation initiated."

Patterson commented, "I don't see anything. Where are are the fireworks we are supposed to be watching?"

Ahular reminded him, "Remember, we are 225 million miles from the explosion. We have to give the light time to reach us… about twenty-six minutes."

Precisely at twenty-five minutes, forty-two seconds, a small sphere of blazing light flashed in the distant horizon and spread a dazzling luminosity across the dark endless sky. The fission bomb had exploded.

The communication from Commander Xedoc confirmed the asteroid had been destroyed and no longer posed a threat to the sun and solar system. Planet Earth had escaped another catastrophe thanks to these alien friends from a far off world.

Nezar turned to Elijah and Professor Scott. "Your mission was successful and the fission bomb you planted vaporized the asteroid. I think it is time we return you to your home. At vartz speed, we will have you home in three days."

Elijah thought a moment and then spoke up. "Commander, this whole experience has really worn me out. I am exhausted and hate to sit around for three days doing nothing. I've changed my mind about the incubator. I feel I could use the three days of sleep."

Simon agreed and thought it would be a good idea after all. It only took a few moments for Patterson and Scott to relent and also agree to enter the incubators. They all concurred that the whirlwind journey through space and tensions from the asteroid experience had thoroughly drained them. Nezar informed Commander Ahular of their decision and then led the Americans to the stern of the ship and the incubator capsules.

43

THE FIRST THING SIMON REMEMBERED WHEN he was awakened was the wild dream he had about Maggie and his son on a treasure hunting trip to Peru. He smiled with the thought, I don't know yet whether it's a son or a daughter. The hatches lifted from the incubators and Nezar and an assistant removed the tubes, electrodes, and straps, allowing the four Americans to emerge from their hibernation.

"Where are we, Commander?" Simon asked as he stretched his sluggish muscles.

"We have reduced our speed and have entered the earth's gravitational field. Our destination is your city of Washington." They were finally coming home.

In the control room, the Americans watched the earth appear larger and larger as the ship descended from the sky. It was still dark throughout the western hemisphere when the X326 reached Washington in the early morning hours. A landing spot was selected in a vacant field close to the Potomac River and the ship slowly settled onto the landing pods and came to a stop. It was just before daybreak.

Simon and the others had assembled their packs and other belongings and gathered in the assembly room. The Constantine crown and the two chests filled with the Chi-Rho and Inca coins were ready to carry off the ship. Commanders Ahular and Nezar met them at the hatch. Simon placed his fist across his chest as their customary gesture of respect and said, "We are very grateful to you for saving our planet again. On behalf of the leaders of our world I wish to say thank you."

Ahular nodded to acknowledge the gesture and responded with a similar salutation. "You humanoids did very well assisting us by placing the bomb."

"Where do you plan to go when you leave us?"

"We have orders to soon return to our planet for necessary refurbishments to our ship and take on more supplies. We also need to regenerate our tracx energy cells and replenish some components to our anti-gravity and vartz mechanical systems. But first we must return to Peru and the underground city of Yupauqui to complete some unfinished work there, and then we have one more project to complete in your northern ice belt before we depart."

Simon reached into his pack. He retrieved the zenox and handed it to Ahular.

"No, my friend," the commander said. "You keep the device. You may find it useful again.

"Does this mean you'll be back?"

"We never know where our explorations will take us but there is always that possibility. We can always be reached by a signal from the zenox. The signal will transmit great distances."

The Americans gathered up the two chests containing the crown and coins, the Winchester 73 rifles, and their packs and personal belongings. They departed the ship and turned just in time to see the steps retract and the hatch close. The X326 lifted from the ground, hovered for a moment, and then slowly rose for a final glimpse in the dim light of the early morning sky.

"What do we do now?" Elijah asked. "We can't just stand here all day."

Simon had the perfect answer. "I suggest we go over to the Burlington House for breakfast. I'm sure Miss Whittington is up by now making biscuits and gravy."

That's all Elijah had to hear. "No argument from me…let's grab those chests and go."

Simon added, "After breakfast we'll get a buggy over to Maggie's parent's house. I want to see my wife and baby. She probably thinks I'm either stuck somewhere in Brazil or dead."

The walk to the Burlington House covered several blocks, normally an easy stroll. They were hindered by having to carry the two exceptionally heavy chests—it required the arms and backs of all four men to lift them. Luckily, daybreak was still several minutes away when they reached the front door of the boarding house. After a knock and long pause, they were pleased to see Miss Whittington's pleasant face open the door. She displayed a complete look of disbelief and surprise as she gazed at the four men standing at her front porch.

"Oh, my goodness," she shouted. "Why it's Mr. Murphy and Mr. Walker. Pray tell, what are you gentlemen doing here at this hour?"

Elijah answered. "Well, ma'am, we have just returned from a long journey and thought we'd just stop by for breakfast."

"By all means," she answered. "You are just in time for my biscuits, hot out of the oven. The ham, gravy, and country style potatoes should be ready in a few minutes. You'll have the dining room all to yourself because none of the guests are up yet."

Just like her mother used to do, Fannie Whittington knew how to prepare a meal that would please any guest. To Elijah, she was a gourmet chef sent down from heaven. He soused his ham, potatoes, and biscuits with enough gravy where they were unrecognizable. Simon couldn't believe his cousin's eating habits. "Why do you use so much damn gravy? You could float a boat in your plate."

With a full mouth he mumbled, "Where I come from gravy is the staff of life...makes the food taste better, chew easier, and go down smoother."

Simon just rolled his eyes and muttered, "Oh, what's the use. You should live in a pig pen."

The foursome was just finishing up when the first two guests arrived for breakfast. One look at the disheveled diners was a bit unsettling so the couple selected the table furthest away. "How are we going to pay her?" Elijah questioned. "We don't have any money."

"I have the solution," Simon answered, reaching under the table. "With this," he declared triumphantly.

The gold Inca coin glittered in his hand from a reflected band of light streaming through the window. "This should cover breakfast plus a healthy tip," he said to Miss Whittington as she approached the table.

"My goodness boys, this more than covers the meal. I'm not sure I have enough money in my box for the change."

Simon explained, "There is no change…it is all yours for a wonderful meal. This is an ancient Inca solid gold piece and worth much more than an American double eagle."

"Thank you, Mr. Murphy. You boys are welcome here any time."

"Elijah whispered to Simon on the way out. "You remember what I told you about her mother? Well, Fannie Whittington could also kick those alien asses anytime in a cooking contest. That breakfast will beat any of that slimy goo we ate from the tubes…any day."

Simon wholeheartedly agreed.

Lugging the chests and baggage, the men left the boarding house and pondered their next move. Elijah brought up a good point. "Weren't we supposed to report to President Grant as soon as we returned from Brazil with Patterson?"

"Yeah," Simon acknowledged. "But no one knows we are even here and before we do that I want to see my wife and baby. I'm sure Robert would want to see his brother and niece as well. We'll stow the chests at Maggie's parent's house and then we can take Robert to the White House and pay Mr. Grant a visit in the morning. Now let's go hail us a buggy or wagon to the Patterson house."

Professor Scott had other ideas. "No need for me to go with you fellows. I think I'll just walk over to the museum and look up Robert Drake. It's only a block away. He won't believe me when I tell him my phenomenal story, especially about the ride on the Cuzco into outer space to blow up a giant asteroid streaking toward us."

Elijah laughed. "Yeah, I'm sure he'll love the part about you walking out on the asteroid and planting a bomb. He'll probably commit you to the nearest insane asylum."

Scott gave him an exasperated look and countered, "You forget that Mr. Drake also rode on the Toltec during our episode down in Mexico. He'll believe me."

"Hate to see you go, George, but there is no need for you to be with us to see the president," Simon acknowledged. "We'll give you a bag full of the Chi-Rho and Inca coins for the museum… and make sure Drake keeps the part about the asteroid and El Dorado confidential for now. We don't need to create a worldwide panic or stir up a frenzied gold rush to Peru."

"Oh, by the way, George," Patterson remarked as he reached into his pack and retrieved the metallic scroll. "I want you to have this scroll for the museum. Maybe you can interpret some of the glyphs and symbols and find out where it came from. I don't know how it got into the Confederate treasury but maybe you can figure it out. Simon told me about the work you did with the Atlantean scrolls so perhaps you can do something with this."

Professor Scott was ecstatic. "Thank you, Robert…thank you. I'll get on it right away," he acknowledged as he took the bag of coins, tucked the scroll under his arm, and elatedly trotted off to the museum. After several steps he turned and shouted, "Thanks again, Robert—wait until the old fogies and stuff-shirts hear about this."

Elijah laughed. "With all the gold and diamonds he could have grabbed at El Dorado, I don't know of anything that would have made the ole boy any happier than that scroll. It should keep him busy for a while."

It did not take long to hire a driver to transport them to the Patterson house on top of a wagon full of lumber and hardware items. The gold Inca coin offered as fare was convincing. Simon directed their 'chauffeur' to the house on Wellington Street.

Lugging the heavy chests and assorted luggage, they deposited the load on the front porch. Simon rapped the door knocker. After a few moments they heard a latch being turned and a medium built man opened the door. He stood there for moment in total shock…his expression betraying his complete surprise and bewilderment. "Robert...is that you?" he stammered to his brother apprehensively.

"William, it's really me."

The two brothers embraced in a sincere show of emotion. "My God, Robert!" he shouted. "I thought you were dead somewhere in some godforsaken jungle down in South America. The captain of the ship that was supposed to bring you home from Brazil said you and your party had decided to travel up the Amazon. We had all given up on you but here you are alive and well."

"Yes, sir, William, we're alive and here all in one piece."

Turning to Simon he said, "You actually brought my brother back home." William glanced down at the chests and bags and added, "Good grief man, let me help you with your baggage and come on in. I know a young lady that can't wait to see you."

Elijah was briefly introduced and the unexpected visitors entered into the house. Depositing the chests and luggage in the hallway, William led them to the kitchen where Maggie was engaged in idle conversation with her mother. When Simon entered the room she stopped in mid-sentence, her expression frozen with disbelief and astonishment. "Simon!" she shouted, "You're back and you're alive." Jumping up from the table, her hand swept the coffee cup, knocking it to the floor. The sound of breaking glass was muffled by a loud sob as she flung herself into his arms. Maggie acknowledged her uncle Robert with a brief hug and Elijah with a brief smile and then grabbed her husband by the hand and whispered, "Come with me, Simon…I want to show you something."

He followed Maggie up the steps to a small second floor bedroom located at the rear of the house. Simon's emotions nearly burst over when he saw a baby sitting in a small protected bed. A reflexive smile crossed the baby's face when he saw his mother and

Simon. Maggie announced passionately, "I would like for you to meet your son, Thomas Murphy, named after your father."

"Wow! I have a son," he shouted as he swept Maggie back into his arms. "I have a little son!"

"Yes, we have a beautiful baby boy and he looks just like you."

"Can I pick him up?" Simon asked.

"Of course you can…he's your son."

Simon picked Thomas up and gingerly held him to his chest. Simon thought this was the proudest moment of his life…he was euphoric. Looking at this little baby in his arms brought back a brief reflection of the experience they had endured with the asteroid. It gave him a shudder when he briefly thought of the pending horror and devastation the huge block of stone and metal could have caused if it had hurled into the sun. The realization that the destruction of the asteroid had saved this beautiful woman and baby boy justified all of the hardships they had endured over the past few weeks. Soon, he would tell Maggie the full story, but for now he would cherish holding her tenderly in his arms all night long and release his pent-up tensions by making passionate love to her… long overdue.

44

THE MORNING CAME MUCH TOO EARLY as Simon awoke and strolled into the kitchen. Maggie was still asleep. Elijah, Robert, and William Patterson were already sitting at the breakfast table having coffee.

"Morning, Simon," William greeted him. "The boys were telling me about your amazing trip up the Amazon. Sounds like you had quite a harrowing experience and lucky to be alive with all those headhunting Indians, man-eating fish, and crocodiles down there."

"It's sure not a place you'd want to take your family on a vacation—got to be one of the most dangerous places on earth," Simon responded pensively.

"Speaking of the Amazon," Elijah reminded him, "what are we going to tell President Grant when we see him today? I don't think he's going to take kindly of us taking that little side trip up the Amazon when we were specifically ordered to bring the general here directly home. He might throw us all into jail, or worse, string us up on the gallows for disobeying a presidential order."

"I think when we hand him that Constantine crown and a handful of the Chi-Rho and Inca gold coins and explain where and how we got them, he won't get too upset. Then when we tell him about the journey we had on the Cuzco and throw in the asteroid story as a bonus, we'll have him eating out of our hand. Just think, Elijah, he might declare you a national hero and schedule a parade when he hears how you and the professor walked out on that big space rock and planted the fission bomb."

The bewildered expression on William's face revealed his total confusion. "What in the world are you talking about? What's all this nonsense about a Constantine crown and space rocks?"

"It's a long story, William. I'll tell you all about it when I get back. It's going to take a couple of hours and a bottle of fine whiskey to explain it. But first we have to get ready and go make an unexpected call on the president…and I hope you don't mind if we borrow your horse and buggy for a little while. And by the way, we need to secure those two chests full of coins in a safe place while we're gone."

"I can handle that," William assured them. "I have a secret compartment in my basement."

The sergeant posted at the North Portico gate of the White House was perplexed to see the three unidentified men standing there with a request to see the president. He immediately went to a mental state of alert and positioned his rifle in a ready position. "What business do you have with the president?" he demanded with some apprehension. "Do you have an appointment?"

"Sergeant," Simon responded with a tone of authority, "President Grant will be very pleased to see us. Please inform him that Simon Murphy, Elijah Walker, and General Robert Patterson are reporting in from our mission to South America."

At the mention of a general in his midst, he came to attention and gave a salute to the strangers, not knowing which one was a general. Simon laughed silently to himself and thought, wonder what he would do if he knew Patterson was an ex-Confederate general? The soldier summoned a lieutenant and explained the situation and the officer left hurriedly to deliver the message. In a matter of minutes he returned. "Sir," he said with a tone of urgency, "The President asked me to bring you with all haste. He seems most anxious to see you gentlemen."

Ironically, President Grant was in the midst of a meeting with Secretary of State, Hamilton Fish and the newly appointed Secretary of the Treasury, William Richardson. Grant could not believe what he was hearing when the young officer delivered him the news and identity of the visitors waiting to see him. He had given his emissaries up for dead. "Bring them to this room immediately, Lieutenant," he ordered. Turning to his secretaries he said, "I want you to stay and be in on this. It seems as if our two treasure hunters have returned from the dead."

While the officer was ushering Simon and his companions through the hall, a servant happened to recognize Simon and Elijah from earlier visits to the White House. The servant, who was being paid a handsome sum by a pro-southern group to observe and report important matters from the White House, thought this must be important. He remembered these same two men had been here before and were somehow involved in treasure hunting. His first thought was, I need to report this to my contact.

Hastily the unanticipated visitors were ushered into the meeting room to face the president. Simon noticed Mr. Grant looked much the same as when he last saw him; black suit and vest, chin whiskers and hair a little grayer. Between his fingers he held the ever present cigar. "Sir, we wish to report to you upon the conclusion of our successful mission. May I present to you former Confederate General Robert Patterson," Simon announced boldly, unsure of the reception they would receive.

Grant looked them over with a stunned expression and then with a booming voice barked, "My God man, where have you been these past weeks? We had all given you up for dead. Mr. Murphy, you were supposed to have returned from Brazil with the general on the Halifax but instead, Captain Whitmore told us you had decided to go on some wild goose chase up the Amazon River. He said you told him the Confederate treasure was buried somewhere up river. According to Mr. Patterson's letter, we assumed it was hidden somewhere in one of the southern states. Mister, you have a lot of explaining to do."

Grant's outburst even put his two secretaries' nerves on edge. Fish and Richardson gave each other a cursory glance relaying the silent message, the boss is really mad.

Elijah and Simon were also stunned at the president's angry reaction. Elijah looked briefly at Simon as if to say, Okay buddy, you got us into this mess now let's see you talk your way out of this one.

Simon took a deep breath and replied as calmly as possible. "Mr. President, the Confederate treasure is hidden in the Appalachian Mountains in North Carolina and Mr. Patterson is prepared to show you where it is, just like his letter explained."

"Then why the hell did you have to detour up the Amazon River and take two months to come home?"

"Sir, what if I told you we found a treasure of gold and gemstones far grander than a thousand Confederate treasures and what if I told you what we found was the legendary Inca gold hidden in the fabled lost city of El Dorado."

Secretary Fish was still dubious of these visitors and had to voice something. "Mr. Murphy, what you are saying is preposterous. I think you have lost your mind."

On cue, Elijah handed Simon the large bag concealed behind him. Ignoring Fish's remark, Simon held up the bag. "Perhaps this will convince you, Mr. President."

He placed the bag on the table, retrieved the gold crown, and then laid it in front of Grant. "Mr. President, this is the solid golden crown belonging to Emperor Constantine the First… fifty-seventh emperor of the Roman Empire who ruled from 306-337 AD. He then tilted the bag allowing coins to spill out on the table. "And these gold coins are Chi-Rho coins first issued by Constantine to depict his conversion to Christianity and the first emperor to convert the Roman Empire to the Christian religion. They are over fifteen hundred years old."

A second bag was produced and emptied onto the table. "These gold coins were cast by the Inca Empire of Peru. The unusual visitors we just met in El Dorado said their predecessors taught the Incas the art of melting gold and casting coins in appreciation for their hospitality during earlier visits."

"What visitors are you talking about?" Grant questioned.

"Do you remember three years ago when we encountered the explorers from another world in the sunken city of Lythe on the continent of Atlantis? And do you remember the story where they used their laser guns and saved our planet from splitting apart by welding the tectonic plates together from the huge Atlantic underwater earthquake?"

"Yes, I do remember," Grant admitted, recalling the bizarre events of three years ago. "I still have the obelisk you gave me as a token of respect from their leader."

"Sir, if you will permit me, I have an incredible story to tell you about those same alien visitors and our ride into outer space to assist in destroying a huge asteroid that was streaking on a collision course toward our sun. Such a catastrophic collision would have totally incinerated and destroyed our planet and most of our solar system. Elijah, here, and Professor Scott assisted the aliens by walking out on the asteroid's surface and planting a fission bomb that destroyed it deep in space."

Uncomprehending most of what Simon was talking about, the president commented, "I noticed the professor is missing. Where is he?"

"He is at the museum right now, most likely telling this same story to Robert Drake, the curator."

Simon and his two companions spent the next two hours explaining the details of their harrowing adventure to the three men sitting across the table. Each man was spellbound and completely speechless with this phenomenal story.

President Grant remembered the events of 1870 and how Simon and Elijah had flown the Cuzco back from Peru and landed it in Washington. He remembered his brief ride on the ship and the destructive power of its laser weapons. "Where are our alien friends now?" he asked inquisitively.

"Right now they are back at their command center in Peru but said they would soon return to their home planet. They left me the zenox communication device in case I ever needed it again. The commander did not tell us they would return, but somehow I have a gut feeling they may be back someday."

Reaching into his pack he removed the small box and held up the zenox for emphasis. "Our space explorer friends have saved Earth twice and, you never know, this device may come in handy in the future if we ever need to contact them. And by the way, Mr. President, Commander Ahular from the Cuzco, asked me to give you this crown and these coins as his gesture of friendship and respect."

Grant picked up the heavy crown and turned it in his hand. "Thank you, Mr. Murphy. I hope I have the chance to meet him someday."

"I'm sure you will, sir…I'm sure you will."

The president continued. "As you know, we made two unsuccessful attempts to retrieve the Toltec treasure you found in the Yucatan back in sixty-five. General Kirby's first attempt was a disaster with the loss of several men and the second attempt last year was no better. Perhaps in the next few months we will call upon you and Mr. Walker to lead an expedition back to Peru and retrieve some of the treasure from El Dorado. From what you have described, we can dock a ship nearby along the coast to transport the treasure back to the United States."

"Yes, sir, Mr. President," Simon replied as he gave Elijah another glance, only to see a slight shrug and a 'you've got to be kidding me' look across his face.

45

The White House servant, a man named Henri, slipped out of a side door and made his way along Pennsylvania Avenue to a nearby bar located on an obscure side street. A heavyset man named Bernard was the bartender and Henri's immediate contact. Henri pulled him to the side and revealed his information about Murphy and Walker's visit to the White House. Bernard recognized the names from the newspaper publicity the two treasure hunters had received from the strange events that had occurred in Washington three years ago. "Good information, Henri. I'll pass it along to my connections," the man whispered, as he handed the servant three American gold double eagles. Henri nodded and left the bar and made his way back to the White House.

Back in the meeting room, President Grant turned and addressed his remarks to the ex-Confederate general. "Well, Mr. Patterson, in accordance with your letter, I believe we made an agreement to provide you and your former comrades residing in South America a full pardon and restored citizenship provided you disclose the location of the hidden Confederate treasure."

"Yes, sir," Patterson answered. "I am prepared to do that."

"Does anyone else know of the location?" Grant asked.

"Two former soldiers from my detachment know of the location. They were with me when I cached the treasure and they accompanied me to Peru and also on our journey up the Amazon. We dropped them off in Georgia before we departed with our alien friends to confront the asteroid."

"What will prevent your men from trying to retrieve the treasure for themselves?"

"Sir, they can be trusted. They are devoted friends and one of the men, Sergeant Mann, was once attached to Mr. Walker's command before he was transferred to me in Richmond."

"Very well, Mr. Patterson, I want you to accompany an armed detail with wagons to travel to your hiding place and retrieve the cache and bring it back to Washington where we will place it into our Department of the Treasury vaults under Mr. Richardson's protection. We will assemble the detachment to go with you. I wish to expedite this mission so I want you to prepare your detail to depart day after tomorrow."

"I will be happy to do that, sir."

"And Mr. Murphy and Mr. Walker," he added turning to both men, "I want both of you to accompany Mr. Patterson as my advisors and see to it that he accomplishes his mission."

Back at the Patterson house Maggie was livid. "What do you mean you and Elijah have to leave for another trip?" she shouted angrily at her husband. "You just returned home yesterday."

"I know that, Maggie, but this will only be a very short journey down to North Carolina and back. It shouldn't take more than two weeks."

"You don't even know your baby son yet. Why did you agree to do this?"

"I didn't agree to anything. The president told Elijah and me to accompany your Uncle Robert and make sure we retrieve the hidden Confederate treasure. It's hidden in the mountains near a town named Asheville. I sometimes think President Grant considers Elijah and me as members of his staff. It wasn't a request but an order and I couldn't refuse a presidential order."

As a former newspaper reporter, Maggie had been around Washington long enough to understand how the political establishment worked. Her husband happened to be in good favor with the president and she knew he couldn't abuse that relationship. She unwillingly relented and gave Simon one of those female despondent looks that told him she wasn't too happy about him leaving again. "Okay, Simon, you go with Uncle Robert but you had better hurry back to Thomas and me…and in one piece." A big hug and a less-than-passionate kiss told Simon he had her unenthusiastic permission.

Standing in the shadows next to a small harness shop, Louis Cantrell watched the stable attendants harness four sturdy perchrons to two wagons. Cantrell knew enough about draft horses to realize the use of these hardy animals could mean the wagons were to be used to haul something heavy. His suspicions were further aroused when the White House servant standing beside him, Henri, pointed out the three men talking to an army officer standing near the wagons. He quickly identified Simon, Elijah, and the other man as the recent visitors to the White House and briefly defined the reputation of the first two as being successful treasure hunters for the government. Receiving another two gold double eagles for his services, Henri turned and quickly made his way around the back of the building and then disappeared.

Cantrell, a former Confederate soldier, turned to the man next to him. "Since Murphy and Walker are standing next to two heavy wagons surrounded by a unit of cavalry it appears to me something big is brewing. What do you think, Alan?"

"I don't see anyone loading the wagons with anything but food, blankets, and essential supplies so I think those fellows must be planning to take a trip somewhere away from town to transport a heavy load of something."

"Our employers have instructed us to follow them and find out what they are up to," Cantrell advised him. "What weapons did you get for us?" he asked.

"I was able to get some late model 1866 Winchesters from our supplier over in Maryland. Each will hold seven .44 caliber rimfire cartridges. They should be adequate enough for our mission."

"Go assemble the men and have them meet me behind Morgan's Tavern on Thirteenth Street in thirty minutes. I expect the wagons will pass by there. Tell them to have their weapons and supplies prepared and ready to go immediately. We might have a long ride ahead of us."

Alan Quaid was another southern sympathizer who had been involved in clandestine activities and unauthorized raids against Federal installations in the Maryland and Virginia areas. He was a ruthless man possessing all the skills of an experienced assassin. Earlier in the war he had once briefly served some time with Quantrill's Raiders, referred to as the Bushwhackers, who had been an independent group of self-proclaimed Confederate guerillas. They had conducted murderous raids along the Texas and Missouri borders and as far north as Iowa. He bragged about briefly serving with Frank and Jesse James, who were now notorious bank and train robbers in Texas and the Midwest. He was equally proud of the fact the two outlaws had thus far eluded capture by Pinkerton agents and were still robbing banks. He also bragged about his participation in the Lawrence, Kansas massacre where innocent women and children were slaughtered like sheep by the Quantrill raiders. Like the other mercenaries, he was a cold-blooded killer. The other five men assembled and waiting nearby were pro-southern mercenaries who would slit anyone's throat for a single Yankee dollar. Although all of them had a deep hatred of the north for winning the war, the primary motivation for their work was money. The fact was they were mercenaries and an unscrupulous collection of spies, assassins, and murderers.

One man named Edward Joachim even boasted he had killed his commanding officer and deserted from a Confederate infantry unit during the battle of Antietam. The man had all the traits of a first-class psychopath. Cantrell needed his skills but knew he would have to keep a wary eye on the man.

Simon, Elijah, and Patterson mounted their horses and led the troopers and wagons in a westerly direction down Pennsylvania Avenue toward Georgetown. Once there, they planned to cross over the Potomac River Bridge and skirt around the west side of the town of Arlington. Patterson's intended route would take the small caravan in a southwesterly direction to the west sides of Culpepper and Lynchburg where he chose the general route his detachment had followed in sixty-five. He hoped to cross the North Carolina state line near Mount Airy, bypass the town of Blowing Rock, and find the small river leading to the treasure cave. Once the cache was loaded, he planned to use a similar route back to Washington.

Close behind and just out of view, the hired pursuers followed the convoy. The instructions from their contacts specifically stated they should avoid any engagement unless absolutely necessary. The mission was to follow the two treasure hunters and see what they were up to. The presence of the wagons and military attachment proved that the Americans were after something very important and most likely involving money, something most needed and useful to the organization that employed them. After all, Cantrell reasoned, treasure seekers don't use men and equipment like this to haul peanuts.

The journey south was uneventful as the convoy bypassed Culpepper and Lynchburg and made its way through the small settlement of Bedford. It was here Patterson converged into their original route he had followed from Richmond in March of sixty-five. As they maneuvered around the small town of Rocky Mount, Simon had a chance to converse with the officer in charge, Captain John Morgan.

Striking up a conversation, Simon divulged, "I served as an officer in the 14th Michigan Cavalry, mostly western campaigns including Shiloh and Vicksburg. How about your assignments?" he asked the young captain.

"I was assigned to the 9th New York Cavalry, 4th Division," Morgan replied pensively. "I saw some action at Antietam and Fredericksburg... real horrible battles...lost a lot of good men there. Lee and Longstreet really kicked our ass at Fredericksburg. General Burnside led us into a stinking hellhole there. Rebs stood behind a stone wall and had our boys pinned down in an open field. We didn't have a chance. How about your friend over there?" Morgan asked curiously, nodding toward Elijah.

"He was also a captain in the cavalry, just like me."

"And the other man?"

"His name is Patterson and he was a brigadier general."

"Oh, I see." The captain acknowledged with a renewed feeling of respect for his new companions and their previous military positions.

Simon divulged the rankings without mentioning what side they fought for. He wanted to avoid any details but he knew as soon as Elijah started talking and spilling all of that southern syrup out, suspicions would arise. Captain Morgan didn't press the issue, assuming Simon and Elijah had served in the same unit and that Patterson was perhaps a former commander of a Union regiment or division. The eight-man detail consisted of seasoned Union veterans, some who had served at the battles of Antietam, Gettysburg, and Cold Harbor. One of the soldiers, Sergeant Morris, had even been at Appomattox when General Lee surrendered to General Grant. They were all adequately trained to drive wagons. Ironically, none of the men had been told they were being guided by an ex-Confederate general. The high command felt it was in the best interest of the mission to withhold that information.

Simon looked down at the sleek rifle suspended in the saddle scabbard beside him and gently patted the stock. It gave him a feeling of assurance. Good thing Elijah and I held on to these Winchesters, he thought. Sure hope we don't have to use them.

Not far behind, the six mercenaries followed within a safe distance, designating one man to move far enough ahead to keep the wagons in sight. Cantrell was most anxious to find out what the detail's intentions were and what they were after. The presence of the two renowned treasure hunters made the pursuit all the more interesting. He envisioned the returning wagons filled with gold, just ripe for the taking.

The detail crossed the border just west of the sleepy town of Mount Airy and then swung toward the southwest. This was familiar terrain to Patterson who picked up the track that would carry them to Grandfather Mountain. The cave and hidden Confederate cache was located just beyond and near a pristine waterfall. Patterson knew all he had to do was locate the small river that would lead him to the falls. They finally reached the abandoned field that had once been a thriving cornfield before the war. The heavy growth of high chickweed, quack grass, and cockleburs revealed that the land had not been replanted in several years. "What are you planning to do when these wagons get past this field?" Elijah asked. "Looks like nothing but dense woods surrounding it. Those trees are so thick it looks like a man would have trouble walking through them."

Patterson stood up in his stirrups and pointed to a spot across the field. "There is a narrow track on the other side that we can pass through. We did it before so I know these wagons can get through. On the far side of the woods we'll pass through another big meadow and from there you can see Grandfather Mountain. The cave we're looking for is just beyond that."

Just as Patterson had said, they found the narrow overgrown path at the edge of the trees. The two ruts depressed into the soil was an indication that earlier wagons had passed through but certainly none recently. "I'll bet our wagons were the last ones to use this old road in the past eight years," Patterson assumed. "It looks like it has been taken over by the undergrowth but we can get through with a little hacking and chopping. Good thing it hasn't rained or we would be in a hell of a mess trying to negotiate muddy ruts."

Surprisingly, with the help of the strong percherons, the men were able to coax the wagons through the narrow road and finally the procession exited into another large field. On one occasion a wagon became stuck between two trees but the sturdy horses were able to wrench it through despite the heavily scraping of both sideboards. Patterson pointed to a large string of hills in the distance with one prominent peak that stood out. "There she is boys…Grandfather Mountain. Now let's go find that river."

46

From the other side of the field Cantrell and his men watched from a grassy knoll as the last wagon disappeared into the dense forest. Quaid remarked, "Wonder how those wagons got through those thick trees over there. I sure can't make out any road...looks like they just disappeared into thin air."

"There has to be a road because wagons just don't vanish like that," Cantrell assured him.

"Spread the men across the field in case they left a rear guard covering their rear."

The pursuers quickly discovered the obscure overgrown track and worn wheel ruts extending through the woods. They cautiously entered the narrow access. "Still can't believe those wagons can actually get through this tight opening," Quaid mumbled cynically. "And how the hell did they ever find this road anyway...unless one of them has been here before?"

Cantrell completed the sentence for him. "And that someone knows exactly where he's going and what he's looking for...right, Alan? This little chase is getting more interesting by the minute."

About halfway across the new clearing, Patterson spotted what he was looking for. He pointed to his right and shouted, "There it is running along that grove of trees over there...the river I told you about. All we have to do is follow it and it will lead us to the waterfall and the cave. A decent enough track follows along the river and it should be no problem getting the wagons through."

The road was in relatively good shape and allowed the teamsters to make good time through the second stand of trees. They passed the old dilapidated barn Patterson and his detail had encountered on the previous trip and overheard the sound of splashing water just ahead. He only hoped someone had not accidently discovered the cave and cache of gold stashed inside. They soon reached the falls and small clearing where the wagons were quickly moved into position and the horses were corralled nearby in a makeshift enclosure made of branches and brush. Captain Morgan quickly assigned three troopers to sentry duty and instructed them to spread out in a loose semi-circle to provide perimeter security. The others would stay within the enclosure and safeguard the wagons. Morris and four soldiers were delegated to help carry the heavy boxes from the cave while Morgan elected to stay with his men to guard the wagons. Simon and Elijah, with Winchesters in hand, followed Patterson up the path to locate the entrance to the cave. Once located, the designated soldiers would follow and assemble at the cave entrance to transfer the boxes back to the wagons.

John Morgan was a capable officer who had learned many lessons of survival during the war. He was a cautious man and one of his personal attributes was an ability to calculate and anticipate unforeseen predicaments before they occurred. He turned to Morris and gave him a simple order. "Sergeant, I want you to follow them to the cave entrance to see where it is located. When you get there, just turn around and count the exact number of steps it takes to return to this spot." Morris nodded and turned toward the path to follow Patterson to the cave.

Memories flooded Patterson's mind as he reflected back to March of sixty-five when he and his detachment hastily departed Richmond with the Confederate treasure in tow. He remembered the harrowing escape circumventing various Federal checkpoints as he led his detail and the wagons southward. The firefight at the old Virginia barn site came back to him with the unpleasant thoughts of having to bury so many of his men. Reflections of the five companions who escaped with him to Peru coursed sadly through his head when he considered the only two remaining survivors from this original group were Mann and Roper. He thought back to the preposterous statement made by President Jefferson Davis when he assigned him this mission and when he informed the newly promoted general that he and his fading government were going into exile. His most outlandish statement was when he said the money would be used to rebuild the Confederate army and continue the war at a later date. Patterson was now aware that Davis had been captured by Union soldiers in Georgia in May of 1865, spent two years in prison at Fort Monroe, and given a pardon by the U.S government in 1867. He could picture the old boy sitting in a rocking chair right now, somewhere down in Mississippi, wondering how he could find and recover the hidden money from his diminished treasury. Patterson smiled, knowing for certain that Mr. Jeff Davis would not be using any of this money to rebuild an army or anything else for that matter.

Simon broke his reverie when he asked, "How far to the cave, Robert?"

"Oh…just ahead," he answered abruptly, disrupting his reflection of memories.

The entrance was just as he remembered and the stones piled up to conceal the entrance appeared untouched, a good sign that the cache had not been discovered. As the sergeant returned for the hike back to the wagons, the three men pitched in to remove the rock barrier that revealed a narrow opening in the side of the hill. "How did you ever find this remote place?" Elijah asked curiously.

"You remember Captain Stafford who was killed on the Amazon by that Portuguese maniac, Claudio? He knew of this cave and showed it to me. We figured it would be a good place to hide the gold."

They lit the prepared torches, and with Patterson leading, filed through the opening into a narrow passageway. "The storage chamber is just ahead," Patterson assured them as he led them deeper into the cavern.

The three men passed through the corridor and into a larger chamber. To Patterson's relief, the boxes were stacked against the far wall just as he remembered them. To dispel any doubts he rushed over and opened one of the top crates and felt relief when he saw the bright reflections of gold radiating from the torches. With a big grin he turned to his companions. "It's all here," he shouted with exuberance, "just like we stashed it eight years ago."

To assess the wealth sitting before them, each man opened and examined the containers to evaluate the contents. Some of the boxes contained a mixture of U.S. Liberty Head gold coins… quarter and half eagles, and several separate boxes of $10 gold eagles and $20 double eagles. It was most curious that they also uncovered four strongboxes of French gold francs of different denominations and seven cases of assorted Spanish gold escudos, doubloons, and Mexican gold pesos of mixed denominations. Three small boxes contained assorted gemstones, two cases of silver coins, and four crates of 50 ounce gold bars. Simon marveled at the immense wealth sitting before him but his thoughts were tempered somewhat when he realized all of this gold was but a mere fraction of the treasure hidden in El Dorado.

Elijah was rummaging through some of the Mexican coins when he pulled a leather bag from the bottom of the case. He spilled several of the gold coins into his hand and gasped, "Good grief! I can't believe it."

"What is it?" Simon responded, glancing at Elijah's open hand.

"These coins…they're the same as the coin Robert showed us in Peru…same inscriptions and symbols. I think they are the same as the Inca coins Commander Ahular gave us."

Patterson retrieved the 'good luck' coin from his pocket and compared it with the coins Elijah was holding. "Yeah, they are the same…no doubt about it."

"Wonder how they got into the Confederate treasury?" Simon questioned. "I doubt if even the Mexican government had access to these coins since they were hidden by the Incas several hundred years ago."

"It sure adds to the mystery of El Dorado, doesn't it?" Patterson acknowledged. "I can't even imagine how they would end up in Richmond unless some Mexican emissary gave them to President Davis."

"If that's the case, some earlier explorer must have stumbled on the lost city, found the coins, and brought them back to Mexico City," Simon reasoned. "If someone had actually found El Dorado it's amazing word didn't get out about the location. Obviously he must have remained silent because all the treasure was still intact…or perhaps he died before he could tell anyone."

The speculation was suddenly broken by the sound of distant gunshots booming through the cavern.

47

"What the hell was that? Sounds like a war going on out there," Simon shouted as he grabbed his rifle and rushed toward the entrance with Elijah and Patterson close behind.

Cantrell and his band of mercenaries had followed the river and spotted the wagons parked in the small clearing. He dispersed his men to take up concealed positions around the bivouac area. Against Cantrell's orders, Edward Joachim, the psychopathic killer, allowed his irrational instincts to cloud his brain and opened fire on one of the sentries standing against a tree, killing him instantly. Their cover blown, the remaining pursuers began firing at the soldiers guarding the perimeter, killing the other two. Cantrell glared at Joachim and mumbled to himself, "You crazy bastard, you gave our position away. I'm going to have to put a bullet through your brain yet."

Captain Morgan, Sergeant Morris, and the three remaining soldiers were milling around the wagons when the firefight broke out. With the waterfall behind them they had nowhere to retreat so they jumped for the only protection they could find...the wagons. Their assailants were concealed behind trees so the soldiers could not find visual targets in which to return the fire. The tall wagon wheels elevated the wooden sides well above the ground, offering very little protection to the men crouched behind. They were sitting ducks. Morris detected movement to his front and snapped off a shot from his 1873 Springfield 'Trapdoor' carbine, hoping for a lucky hit. Ironically, the .45-70 caliber bullet sped across the clearing and struck one of the attackers high in the chest, standing him up like a stalk of corn before hurling him backward into a patch of undergrowth.

In the fading light, one of the mercenaries slipped through the brush to a flanking position with a clear view of the soldiers crouched behind the wagons. He took careful aim and hit a soldier in the side of the head. The unfortunate man dropped like a rock. Two troopers immediately spotted the man and fired off two rounds in his direction. They missed but drove him away from their flank. Another soldier, a corporal, made a dash for the trees vacated by the mercenary but was struck within ten steps by two .44 caliber slugs from the Winchesters held by the attackers concealed in the foliage.

Sergeant Morris turned to his captain. "Sir, we have to vacate this exposed spot or they'll cut us to pieces. We don't have a chance here."

"I agree," Morgan responded. "It will be dark in a few minutes so we'll try to slip away then. We sure as hell can't retreat to our rear and we can't move to our right flank into their line of fire so that narrows our options down to one direction. Pass the word to the others. On my count we're going to make for that path along the mountain and see if we can reach the cave. Grab any extra ammunition you can find and distribute some to each man…and as much food and water as they can carry."

Morgan knew without the use of torches the escape up the path would be treacherous with the possibilities that someone could take a misstep and tumble down the side of the mountain. They would have to take that chance because to stay here and try to fight it out would mean certain death for the entire unit. Turning to his sergeant, Morgan asked, "How many steps did you count to the cave entrance?"

"I counted four hundred sixty-three steps," Morris answered.

Morgan did a quick calculation in his head. That's about a quarter mile hike, he thought. "You take the point and let's move it out. Tell the men to be quiet so our assailants won't hear us leaving. It's going to be dark going up that trail so tell them to put their hand on the shoulder of the man in front to help guide them.

We sure don't want anyone to expose our position by walking off that damn mountain."

The men assembled and silently moved out in single file with Sergeant Morris leading the way and counting each step in his head. At one point one man slipped on a loose rock that tumbled over the edge and down the embankment. The column froze, hoping no one on the opposite side would hear a splash when it hit the river. No sounds of alarm were heard so the hike continued. To Morris, each step seemed like an eternity but he continued to push forward as he slowly and deliberately counted each step…230…231…232. Halfway there, he thought as he groped for the side of the hill for balance in an effort to keep the column away from the edge of the path. Just behind, Morgan was furious not knowing who the attackers were and what they were after. The Confederate treasure was a top secret and even his men knew nothing about the mission. They only knew they were there to recover something important and return it to Washington. He was especially incensed about the loss of five men. Who the hell are these killers? He pondered.

Elijah was guarding the entrance when he heard the faint sounds of movement on the outside. He peered around the edge but saw nothing but darkness. He retreated to the cavern and aroused Simon and Patterson. "Bring your guns…sounds like somebody is coming up the trail."

Quickly they rushed to the entrance expecting their pursuers to rush through the opening at any moment. A muffled voice was heard coming from outside. "Mr. Murphy…Mr. Murphy…this is Captain Morgan."

Simon peered around the opening and nearly bumped into Morris who had reached the cave. Morgan and three remaining soldiers were right behind him. "What are you doing here? I thought you were guarding the wagon?"

"We were," Morgan answered furiously, "but we had to evacuate the clearing. We were attacked by a group of men and too exposed to hold our position. I have no idea who they are but we have already lost five good men to those bastards. They blocked us on three sides and this was our only escape."

"Did you have a chance to grab any food and water?" Patterson asked. "All we have are two half full canteens."

Morris did a quick inventory. "I count four full canteens, some beef jerky, and a few hardtack biscuits. That's about it."

With the two soldiers posted at the entrance as sentries, Morgan and Morris followed the others into the chamber where the treasure was stashed. The dazzling reflections of gold from the torches stopped Morgan in his tracks. Patterson enlightened the captain. "This is what's left of the Confederate treasury."

"So this is what we came down here to get. Hard to believe the Confederate government had this much gold in reserve."

"I understand they were hoarding the gold to rebuild their army and re-start the war at some later date," Patterson carefully explained, trying not to reveal his true identity. "This is what President Grant is expecting us to bring back to the Treasury Department. The question is how we get it down the mountain and loaded on the wagons with those murdering bastards waiting to shoot us down. Makes me wonder how they knew there was a treasure here in the first place?"

Simon came up with a plausible theory. "With the publicity we got from the newspapers back in sixty-five and seventy, our faces are pretty well known in Washington. The word got out about the Toltec treasure we found in the Yucatan back in sixty-five, so most likely someone recognized us and tipped off somebody about our visit with the president… maybe an informant inside the White House or maybe even the Burlington House. I have an idea that somebody thinks we were there to see the president regarding more hidden treasure and they want it real bad."

"Most likely an informant in the White House," Elijah speculated.

"It's bad enough to kill five of my soldiers," Morgan remarked bitterly. "Those killers are going to pay for this," he added with conviction, "if it's the last thing I do."

Alternating for sentry duty every three hours, the group slept fitfully in the cave, trying desperately to get some needed rest. It was very difficult to sleep knowing the next morning could be their last.

48

Protected by darkness, Louis Cantrell moved his men closer to the wagons so he could get a better assessment of the opposing strength. At daybreak he wanted to eliminate the soldiers huddled there and take control of the wagons. He needed to confirm what Murphy and Walker were up to, convinced in his mind that money was at stake…a great deal of money. He and Quaid had privately talked about it and decided their personal financial welfare was more important than their employers. Greed and illusions of great wealth bolstered their imaginations. They agreed that before turning over any treasure to anyone, each man would ensure they get their healthy cut.

As daybreak approached, early morning light began to filter through the trees, offering Cantrell a better view of the wagons and encampment. No movement was detected so he ordered his mercenaries to move in closer to the wagons… still no movement or sounds. One man darted over to one of the wagons with the intention to swing around and catch the soldiers by surprise. Once engaged with the defenders, the others would rush the camp from two sides. Carefully, the assailant made his move and discovered the camp and wagons were deserted. Cantrell was enraged. "Where the hell did those men go?" he roared. "They can't just disappear."

"They didn't disappear," Joachim yelled back. "They escaped up this path."

Cantrell rushed over the edge of the clearing and saw the obscure trail heading along the side of the mountain. He turned to Quaid, "Take two men and make your way back along the river while I take Joachim and Lacour with me. We'll try to find them and flush them out and you try to get some clean shots from the other side."

The three men carefully moved up the path looking for signs that would reveal the whereabouts of Murphy, Walker, and the soldiers while Quaid and the other two mercenaries followed a parallel route along the riverbank. Quaid kept a careful eye on Cantrell moving along the opposite side and prepared his group to rapidly swing into action when their adversaries were spotted. From the path Lacour nudged Cantrell on the shoulder and pointed. "I saw some movement just ahead."

The soldier guarding the cave entrance caught a glimpse of the three men approaching and quickly aimed his rifle. He fired and watched with satisfaction as the slug caught Lacour in the midsection. The man let out a loud groan and then recoiled over the edge and tumbled down the steep embankment to the river below. Quaid and his two companions observed the action from their concealed positions and fired simultaneously. Two of the three bullets smashed into the soldier and hurled him back against the hillside and then propelled his body forward and over the ledge. Simon and Elijah grabbed their Winchesters and vigilantly made their way to the entrance with Patterson close behind. Elijah peered across the river and saw movement. He fired off two quick shots from his repeater but missed. The target had ducked behind a tree. There was a brief moment of silence as they pulled back into the cave to assess the situation and consider the options. The stillness was broken by a loud voice booming through the opening. "Mr. Murphy, we know you are in there. Throw down your weapons and come out peacefully and we won't harm you or your men."

Simon hesitated for a moment before he responded. "Who the hell are you and what do you want?"

The voice roared back. "We represent the KGC and dedicated friends of the south. I believe you have something we want."

Elijah remarked, "Who the hell are the KGC? I've never heard of them."

Patterson was somewhat familiar with the organization and explained. "The KGC is a secret organization of pro-slavery discontents that formed during the Civil War. It stands for Knights of the Golden Circle. I heard they once tried to carve out and annex some territory and form new states along the Mexican border. They were going to designate the area as the new Confederacy. Here it is eight years after the war and I thought the group had disbanded and disappeared. Apparently there are still some of these diehard insurgents around still trying to fight the war. Those guys out there must have been hired by the KGC to grab the Confederate treasury so they could start the war all over again."

Simon was outraged and shouted back. "We've got nothing here for you. I suggest you get back to your horses and get out of here while you can."

He was answered by a volley of shots from across the river that ricocheted through the entrance and forced the men to throw themselves to the ground. "A man could get himself killed in here," Elijah grumbled. "They have us boxed in this stinking hole."

The same menacing voice again reverberated through the entrance. "We have you and your men surrounded and trapped inside that cave. I suggest you throw out your weapons and surrender the gold to us or the buzzards and wolves will soon be dining on your carcasses."

"Why the hell do you think we have any gold in here?" Simon yelled back indignantly.

"Because we happen to know you and your companion are treasure hunters and you wouldn't be in that cave picking cotton. We can either starve you out or you can come out peacefully."

"What now, Mr. Murphy?" Captain Morgan asked." There are six of us and we could try blasting our way out of this mess if you give the word."

"I'm afraid if we crowd out on that narrow ledge they'll cut us to ribbons. We don't know how many men they have and they could easily overwhelm us with firepower. We need to think this through."

Thoroughly incensed, Cantrell shouted again. "Have it your way, Murphy. We have plenty of time and plenty of food and water. You better hope you have enough in there to last awhile."

Cantrell turned and he and Joachim retreated back down the path where they would take up positions with Quaid and the others to watch and cover the cave entrance from across the river. He would instruct two men to hitch up the percherons and move the two wagons and the American's horses back to the vacant field to deny the trapped men access should they somehow escape. They would burn one of the wagons and release the American's horses but secure two of the percherons. Cantrell's intent was to keep one wagon to haul the gold when the standoff ended.

Taking inventory of the available food and water, to his dismay Simon counted only three canteens left and only enough jerky for a quick snack. "We won't last long on these meager rations," Patterson remarked. "Maybe we should try to slip out of here while it's dark but I sure would hate to leave all of this gold for those rotten killers."

"That's too risky," Simon countered. "The bad guys are sitting just across the river watching the entrance and I'm sure they have lookouts just waiting for us to try an escape. Any other ideas?"

"I have one," Elijah offered with a slight hint of enthusiasm. "Morning is fast approaching so let's use your zenox and see if we can reach Commander Ahular. Remember, he told us we could contact him anytime we got in a jam…and I'd say we're in a hell of pickle right now."

"This is no time to be joking, Elijah. The Cuzco is probably a couple million miles away by now, on its way home."

"No, I'm serious. Ahular told us he was going to return to El Dorado to finish up some work there and then complete some type of project they were doing at the ice belt…most likely the Arctic. Maybe they are still here. I'd say we should at least give it a try."

Patterson thought for a moment and nodded his head in agreement. Captain Morgan, Morris, and the young corporal named Peters didn't have a clue what they were talking about. They were content to just keep silent.

Simon reached for his pack. "This is probably a long shot but under the circumstances I guess it's worth a try."

With the zenox in hand, he turned it on and spoke into the mouthpiece. "X326…Cuzco…this is Simon Murphy…please come in. X326, can you hear me?" Only silence.

"X326, this is Simon Murphy and Elijah Walker calling. Come in please." Still silence. With a despondent look, Simon turned to his cousin. "Just like I said, they're probably heading home and out of range."

The grim expressions in the cavern betrayed both disappointment and apprehension when suddenly a burst of static erupted from the small communication device in Simon's hand. He flinched and then spoke as calmly as possible. "X326…X326…Can you hear me? Please come in. This is Simon Murphy calling."

Morgan, Morris, and Peters stared at the little contraption in complete shock and astonishment. Morris whispered to his captain. "Sir, I think I heard that thing make a noise."

Captain Morgan nodded in agreement…he heard it, too.

49

At that moment, the Cuzco was hovering over Prudhoe Bay and the Beaufort Sea. The Polar Ice Cap was of particular interest. Commander Ahular and Nezar were experimenting with a project involving ongoing movements in the geomagnetic field of the magnetic North Pole. They knew the process was caused by the earth's axis rotation and the effects of the magnetic shifts were of special interest to the aliens. The immediate study was broken when the sound of Simon's voice suddenly burst through the speakers. Nezar reached for his zenox and responded. "Yes, Mr. Murphy…This is Commander Nezar…we can hear you."

Simon nearly dropped the zenox when Nezar's voice came flowing from his hand. "They heard me!" he shouted. "Commander, I am glad you answered. We need your help. Where are you?"

We are currently over your Arctic Ocean conducting some experiments with your planet's magnetic shifts. What is your status?"

"We are trapped in a cavern by hired assassins in our Appalachian Mountains in eastern North Carolina. We are trying to fulfill a mission assigned by our leader but unable to move. Can you provide some assistance?"

"We have just completed our research and can be there within the hour," Nezar answered.

"How will you find us?" Simon asked.

"Keep your zenox turned on and we can receive a signal from the device that will allow us to vector to your exact location. Our computers are plotting the coordinates as we speak."

"Thank you, Commander. We will be awaiting your arrival." The speaker went silent.

Captain Morgan glanced at his sergeant and corporal and noticed their dazed expressions. He shared in their bewilderment. He didn't have a clue as to what had just occurred.

Morning arrived quickly and the skies became brighter as sunlight slowly filtered through the trees. The attackers, waiting in concealment across the river, watched for any movement from the cave. They were prepared to concentrate their weapons on anyone who tried to exit. The familiar voice boomed out again and through the cave opening. "Time is running out, Murphy. Toss your weapons into the river and we'll let you live. We want access to the contents you have in that cave. We're sure it is the remains of the Confederate treasury that disappeared at the end of the war."

"That's ridiculous," Simon shouted back. "Why would you assume such a crazy thing as that?"

Cantrell responded. "Because, our employers discovered a journal written by former Confederate Secretary of the Treasury, George Trenholm, detailing a substantial hoard of gold and silver coins that were removed from the Richmond banks just before the fall of the city to the Yankees. A military detail was picked to transport and hide the money somewhere in the mountains in one of the southern states. We are certain now it is the Confederate treasure you have hidden in the cave and we have been compensated to return the money to its rightful owners. If you and you men value your lives you will surrender and allow us to take possession of the treasure. If not, you will certainly die in that cave before the day has ended."

Elijah gave the first response to his companions. "If we do as that rotten bastard says they'll kill us anyway. They have no intentions of letting us out of here alive." There was no argument from his companions. Surrender was not an option.

Cantrell was irritated that there was no response from the cave. He ordered Quaid to fire a coordinated blast of gunfire into the entrance. On his signal, five rifles discharged a fusillade into the opening. Sergeant Morris was watching the entrance and flinched as a bullet barely grazed his arm. The rest of the slugs shattered harmlessly against the rear rock wall. "How much time left?" Elijah shouted.

"Nezar said they would be here within the hour. My watch shows about fifteen minutes to go. With that speed device they have on the Cuzco, they could show up any minute," Simon assured him as he held the zenox in the air and toward the entrance to ensure the best possible reception. The minutes ticked away but it felt like an eternity. Suddenly Nezar's voice broke the silence. "Hello, Mr. Murphy. This is X326…come in please."

"I hear you, Commander," Simon shouted into the device. "What is your status?"

"We have pinpointed your exact location with the signal from your zenox and the X326 is hovering above you. Unfortunately, the heavy foliage prevents us from landing so we will have to launch the dacidron to assist in your rescue. I will personally operate the controls and maneuver to your location."

"Commander, we are located in a cave situated on the side of a steep embankment. I'm afraid there is no place for you to land."

"The dacidron does not have to land. I will hover next to your location and you can enter through the portside hatch."

"We have several heavy boxes of gold to carry back to Washington plus six of us. Will you be able to accommodate this?"

"It depends on the total weight load but that is an affirmative. It might take more than one shuttle back and forth to the X326."

"I counted twenty-six boxes…mostly gold coins and some bullion," Simon informed him.

Nezar did some quick calculations in his head. "Without knowing the size and volume of the containers I estimate the dacidron can easily accommodate your cargo and six of you humanoids in two trips."

Simon figured it was up to him to make some choices so he glanced at his companions and offered the decisions. "This means three of us will have to remain and guard the cave until the shuttle can make the return trip. Robert, you, Sergeant Morris, and Corporal Peterson will take the first trip with half the boxes and I'll remain with Elijah and Captain Morgan and wait for the second pick up. We need to start moving these boxes to the front where we can load them on the shuttle as soon as the dacidron arrives."

Commander Nezar carefully steered the dacidron just above the trees and settled in the clearing where the wagons were recently parked before Cantrell's men moved them. He hovered for a moment looking for a clear route to approach the mountain. The clearance above the river appeared to be the most likely approach. A light touch of the controls rotated the vehicle to begin its movement forward. The constant signal from Simon's zenox was being monitored by the dacidron's receivers and the locator transponder had the cave positioned slightly upriver.

Alan Quaid glanced to his left and saw the strange object drifting toward them. "What the hell is that thing?" he screamed to Cantrell seated a few yards away.

The mercenary leader stared at the suspended metallic looking disk and shouted back. "Hold your fire until we find out what it is!"

Nezar spotted the opening to the cave and applied slight pressure to the power control that raised the vehicle to the level of the path. With the portside edge of the dacidron positioned on the edge, the vertical thrusters provided the cushion of air needed to keep it hovering in a level position. Nezar spoke through his zenox. "Mr. Murphy, I am opening the portside hatch so you may start loading your cargo and allow three men to board the vehicle for the first run back to the X326."

Simon and the other five men crowded to the entrance to find the dacidron hovering just in front of the opening. The hatch was already open and waiting to be loaded. With two man teams, they began to move the boxes through the hatchway and into the vehicle.

"What is that flying shell doing?" Quaid yelled.

"It looks like it's trying to evacuate Murphy and the Confederate treasure. Tell the men to start firing and see if we can bring it down."

Cantrell and his team of mercenaries opened up with their Winchesters, concentrating on the hull of the dacidron. The heavy slugs pelted the vehicle but bounced off the skin like raindrops. The vehicle's impermeable hull was composed of a hardened ceramic-like material fused with a tempered metallic compound much harder than the known earth metal, titanium. The materials used to manufacture the hulls were indigenous to the alien's planet Xeres and were utilized in all of the skins of the spacecraft they used to explore the galaxies.

Simon and his companions were protected by the vehicle's bulk, allowing them to move freely across the path to load the boxes of gold coins and bullion. Fourteen of them were secured in the hold and Patterson, Morris, and the corporal scampered aboard. As the hatch was closing, Simon could see the head of Robert sticking out of the hatch shouting. The only audible words he could hear were… "Maggie is waiting for you…be careful!"

As the dacidron lifted into the sky, Cantrell was furious and snapped off a final shot from his rifle but with no effect. He called to Quaid. "Tell Joachim to get his ass over here. He and I are going to hit them from the path. You'll stay here with the other men, and on my signal, start firing at the entrance. Murphy and the others may have already escaped but maybe they abandoned the gold. If there is still anyone left in that cave maybe we can flush them out by pumping enough bullets through the opening."

Quaid nodded his understanding as Cantrell and Joachim backtracked along the river to pick up the trailhead back at the clearing. Unspotted, they made good time and began the short hike up to the cave.

Elijah was in the passage watching the entrance when the sound of gunfire erupted from across the river. Simon and Morgan were protected standing in the treasure chamber but Elijah, crouching in the passageway, caught the full fusillade of bullets pinging off the walls. He threw himself to the ground and instinctively covered his head with the butt of his Winchester, trying to flatten his body deep into the rock floor. Miraculously he escaped being hit, but when he looked and saw a .44 caliber slug buried into the rifle stock, Elijah realized that one little protective reflex saved his life.

The fire from across the river ceased and Simon and Captain Morgan rushed into the passage to find Elijah picking himself up off the floor. "Are you okay?' Simon shouted.

His cousin just nodded and held up his rifle. The flattened bullet sticking out of the wooden stock answered his question.

50

Edward Joachim took the lead as he and Cantrell carefully made their way up the path. The entrance lay just ahead. Joachim was an impetuous man whose impulsive actions were triggered by reckless assumptions that clouded his ability to reason things through. At this moment, the fact that he had overheard Cantrell talking about treasure made him snap. He bolted toward the opening. Joachim wanted the gold and he would kill anyone who stood in his way. Cantrell frantically shouted at him to stop but his words went unheeded.

The madman flung himself through the entrance and collided with Morgan who was crouched just inside, peering across the river. The two men tumbled to the ground with Joachim landing on top. He began pummeling the captain with flying fists. All Morgan could do was to cover his head with his elbows to ward off the blows. A bloodlust sensation filled the mercenary's head as he shouted incoherent words in the air. Simon heard the commotion and rushed into the passage with his rifle in hand and saw the captain getting the worst of the melee. With all his strength, he slammed the butt of his rifle into the killer's jaw and heard the harsh crunch of bone shattering. This was enough to free Morgan as his assailant went sprawling across the floor. Joachim was badly hurt but not out of it. He raised himself from the floor and drew a Bowie knife from his belt. "Now you die!" he screamed, charging at Simon with the knife raised for a slashing stroke.

Morgan rolled and thrust his foot at the charging man's ankle. The timing was perfect as the mercenary's foot rolled out from under him, causing him to slam into the wall. Morgan grabbed the knife from the floor and plunged it to the hilt into his belly. Joachim let out a loud groan and stood for a moment in shock. Captain Morgan then turned his assailant, grabbed him by the collar and belt, and with a forward running motion, hurled him through the opening, across the path, and over the edge. His fatally wounded body tumbled down the hill and sank into the river. Then at the top of his voice, Morgan shouted, "That's payback, you murdering bastard, for killing my men."

Cantrell pulled back against the slope to assess the situation. Moving silently behind him, Nezar was maneuvering the dacidron back up river on his second run. He saw the man crouched against the hill and knew he had to be one of the assailants. He began to inch the vehicle closer to the path with the intent to use the nose of the craft to crowd Cantrell and nudge him into the river. Cantrell turned to see the strange object moving toward him and thinking he was about to be crushed, flung himself against the hull and grabbed a small antenna, enabling him to gain a slight foothold on a narrow stabilizing fin. Nezar saw Cantrell from a port window and hit the vertical thrusters. The dacidron shot upward into the air with Cantrell holding on for dear life. Nezar quickly elevated the vehicle to a height of 10,000 feet. Cantrell was terrified, not realizing he was dangling nearly two miles high when Nezar retracted the antenna and fin, releasing his passenger into thin air. The mercenary's piercing screams went unheard as he plunged toward the ground at one hundred-twenty miles per hour. He was mercifully rendered unconscious just before he plunged into the trees and rocks below.

Dropping back to the ground, Nezar maneuvered the dacidron back to the river and toward the entrance to the cave to retrieve the three remaining defenders and their cargo. Quaid and the other two men jumped up from their concealment and ran out into the open, firing their rifles at the sky demon. Nezar calmly pressed a control button to activate the target locator screen and quickly acquired his targets with a click. Another handle turned the laser gun to lock onto the assailants shooting from the riverbank below.

He pressed the firing switch and watched as a sudden dazzling bright ray of superheated energy burst from a hidden nose port and lit up the three mercenaries like a torch. In a split second they were gone in a thin swirl of vapor.

The retrieval of the remaining three Americans and treasure chests went smoothly and Nezar guided the dacidron back to the X326 and into the dedicated docking station in the belly of the ship. With the help of their companions, the remaining treasure was transferred up to the assembly room awaiting delivery to Washington and the hands of the Treasury Department officials. Simon and Patterson gathered the group into the room for a final briefing. Simon was the first to speak. "Gentlemen, I am pleased that we have successfully completed this mission although not without tragic loss of life to six of our dedicated soldiers." Turning to Captain Morgan he continued. "Captain, you, Sergeant Morris, and Corporal Peterson have served us well and we would like to express our appreciation and reward you for your services."

Patterson and Elijah handed each man a heavy bag. "In each of those bags are fifty gold U.S. Double Eagles for each of you from the three of us."

Morgan was stunned. "Thank you, sir, but we would all get into deep trouble by accepting government property without proper authorization from our superiors. I'm afraid we can't accept this money."

Patterson replied, "Mr. Morgan, I must remind you the treasure is not yet official government property but still belongs to the Confederate treasury, even though it no longer physically exists. Since this is the case, I am authorized to give you this reward for your services."

"I don't understand," Morgan responded, thoroughly confused.

"You see, young man, I was a brigadier general, but not in the Union army like you thought. I was the former commander of the 5th North Carolina Mountain Brigade, Confederate States of America, and Captain Elijah Walker was a commander of a cavalry unit from Alabama. It was my detachment and me that was ordered by President Davis to move the treasure from Richmond and cache it in the cave. Therefore, I am still officially in command of the Confederate treasure. We are all Americans now and citizens of the United States. The money is officially yours to keep."

Morgan looked over at Morris and Peterson and saw expressions of approval. Then suddenly, as a gesture of respect, he barked out a command… "Attention!"

Captain Morgan, Sergeant Morris, and Corporal Peterson jumped to a rigid stance and rendered a stiff military salute to the three men standing before them. "Thank you, sir. We will be pleased to accept your gift and I wish to say it has been an honor to have served with you."

All being former military officers, Patterson, Simon, and Elijah came to attention and returned the salute.

Nezar came into the assembly room and summoned Simon and Elijah back upstairs to the control room. Commander Ahular was looking through the forward ports and turned to greet them. "We are now approaching the city of Washington. Where would you like me to land the X326?"

"Commander," Simon responded, "why don't you put it down in the large back yard of the White House, at the same location you used three years ago. I want President Grant to see the ship and it will give us a more secure location to unload the treasure boxes."

Ahular nodded and instructed his navigator to initiate the landing sequence.

President Grant had just sat down to the dinner table with his wife, Julia, and their four children to enjoy the first course, a delicious looking fish bouillabaisse placed before them by two servants. An aide rushed into the room shouting, "Mr. President! Mr. President! Please come quickly. A strange looking object has just landed in the back yard."

Grant jumped up from the table and followed the young lieutenant from the room, trailed closely by his wife and kids.

The aide led him to a back door where he could see the Cuzco's hatch opening and figures moving just inside the entryway. Several of the staff had gathered on the lawn, including the servant, Henri, the paid informant, and a few of the security guards.

Simon was the first to descend the steps, followed by Elijah, Patterson, and the three soldiers. The captain and his two other men stopped long enough to express their farewells and with the bags of gold double eagles in hand, Morgan led them across the lawn to seek a ride back to their headquarters.

President Grant, who had previously ridden on the Cuzco three years prior, knew that the ship presented no threats and strolled across the lawn to greet his visitors. His three sons followed behind him with four security guards. Julia and their daughter, Ellen, were content to stay back next to the protective wall of the White House. Most of the staff felt the same apprehension and lingered with them. Secretary of Treasury Richardson, and Secretaries Belknap, Fish, and Robeson, were attending a nearby meeting and joined the growing throng of spectators.

Grant greeted his unexpected guests warmly and turned to Simon. "Well, Mr. Murphy, I assume you and your companions have successfully accomplished your mission and I notice you were able to hitch an unexpected, and I must say, an unusual ride home."

"Yes, sir, Mr. President. The crates of the Confederate Treasury are just inside the door waiting to be unloaded."

"And your friends," Grant continued, "Am I to assume they are the same people who have managed to save our planet from destruction on two occasions?"

"Yes, sir. Although they are not exactly what you would describe as people, they are the same aliens who saved planet Earth and recently our whole solar system."

"Is it possible to meet their leader and express my gratitude on behalf of all our world leaders?"

"I believe we can arrange that, Mr. President. If you'll assign some men to help us unload the treasure chests, Mr. Walker and I will take you up to the control cabin to meet Commanders Ahular and Nezar."

Secretary of War, Belknap, who had moved to the president's side, whispered, "Sir, are you sure you want to climb aboard that thing without a military escort?"

"Heavens yes, William, I've been on this ship before and I'll be fine. You can organize some men to help unload the boxes."

Simon turned to the president and quietly said, "Mr. President, someone tipped off some assailants who followed us and attacked us in North Carolina. They knew about our mission to retrieve the Confederate treasure. They represented a dissident pro-Confederate group called the Knights of the Golden Circle. We think it might have been a spy within the White House who recognized Elijah and me during our meeting with you in your office the other day."

"Interesting," the president replied. "I will ask Mr. Pinkerton and his security group to check out the staff. Pinkerton is very good at rooting out spies."

While the treasure crates were being unloaded to the ground, Grant followed Simon and Elijah up the steps into the assembly room and then up to the control center where Ahular was preparing the X236 for launch. Simon instructed the president. "When you meet the commander, place your right fist over your heart and nod your head. This is the greeting they use for introductions and a sign of respect… and don't worry, they speak perfect English."

"Commander Ahular," Simon announced, "I would like for you to meet our President Grant. He is the leader of our country and wanted to meet you."

As Simon had advised, Commanders Ahular and Nezar placed their fists to their chests and nodded. Grant did the same. Ahular spoke first. "Mr. Murphy and Mr. Walker have told us a lot about you and your country, America. You are the leader of a large land mass and have our respect. We and our predecessors have been observing yours and earlier cultures for a very long time and find the evolution of your development is progressing much the same as ours did on our home planet, Xeres."

"Thank you, Commander. I know your time is short so on behalf of myself and our world leaders, I wanted to thank you for saving Earth and millions of human lives."

"We are glad we could be of assistance." The crewman sitting at the navigation console whispered a few guttural sounding words to his commander. "I am sorry, Mr. President, but one of my assistants advises we must make final preparations to depart. We have a very long journey ahead of us." Turning to Simon he added, "As you might remember, we have to first travel to the Hydrox in your country of England to recalibrate our navigation instruments and navigation coordinates for the journey back to our solar system."

Elijah whispered to Grant, "He's referring to Stonehenge. We'll explain that to you later."

"Will we ever see you again, Commander Ahular?" Simon asked.

"Probably not," he answered. "But you never know what fate will bring. You will have the zenox and the means to communicate with us if necessary." Then directing his remarks to both Simon and Elijah he added, "Farewell my friends… we will not forget you."

Ahular turned back to the command console indicating the meeting was over. Simon, Elijah, and President Grant left the ship and turned just in time to see the hatch close, the ship slowly lift off the ground, and the pods retract. A strange feeling of sadness engulfed each of them as they watched the Cuzco zoom into the sky, become a distant speck, and then disappear.

Epilogue

MAGGIE WAS OVERJOYED TO SEE HER husband when she opened the door of her parents' home. She led Simon into the house with Elijah and Uncle Robert trailing close behind. Softly crying, she threw herself into her husband's arms and gave him a huge lingering kiss. Elijah watched with satisfaction as similar emotions flooded his mind... emotions that thought of someone at a little ranch located all the way across the country.

William came into the room and grabbed his brother by the arm and led him back to his study where they agreed to open an expensive bottle of fine brandy and catch up on memories, beginning with their childhood. It was going to be a very long night for the two Patterson boys.

Simon turned to Elijah and motioned him to the front porch. "What are your plans now?" he asked.

Elijah hesitated for a moment to organize his thoughts and then answered. "I'm going to go directly over to the Baltimore and Potomac train station and catch the first train going west. I'm heading out to California. There is a beautiful girl waiting for me at a ranch near San Juan Capistrano that loves me very much and I love her as well."

"You're kidding me aren't you?"

"No, I'm not kidding and I would appreciate it if you would borrow Mr. Patterson's horse and buggy and drive me over to the train station."

"What about your share of the gold coins in Patterson's basement? You don't want to leave them here."

"I will stick enough of the coins in my pack to pay for my tickets and expenses and I can get the rest some other time. Now, how about that ride to the station?"

Elijah said his goodbyes to the Patterson brothers and gave Maggie a big hug. With his pack filled with clothes, a bag of gold Chi-Rho and Inca coins, travel essentials, and his Remington revolver, Elijah climbed aboard the buggy, confident the trip to the B&P station would only take about an hour.

During the ride the two cousins had plenty to talk about. "I have always thought there was something between you and Rosita," Simon remarked kiddingly. "And I suspect it all started when we were in the lost Toltec city of Xepocotec. There must be something pretty darn special about her to make you want to go all the way out to California."

"I've never met anyone like her," Elijah admitted. "She does something to me I've never experienced with any other woman."

"You told me you had a girlfriend you wanted to marry and some farmland you own down in Alabama." Simon remarked.

"Yeah, Matilda is a decent enough girl but doesn't light a fire in me like Rosita."

"What about your land?"

"I doubt if I'll ever get back to Gurleyville so I might just deed it to her. On the other hand, Rosita has several thousand acres of land on her Del Viejo ranch and several hundred head of cattle. That's enough to keep me busy." Elijah reversed the conversation. "How about you?" he asked. "I thought you owned half interest in a hardware store over in Michigan."

"Yeah, I do, but I have no interest in running a hardware store in Battle Creek, Michigan. I have two partners, the Fox brothers. One of them is a decent enough fellow but the other, Howard Fox Jr., is an idiot and I can't stand to be around him."

"Why don't you sell them your half?"

"They've offered to buy it, so I think I will."

"Then you can travel with me as far as Michigan," Elijah suggested.

"Hell no... Maggie would kill me if I left her again. I'll just send Sam Fox a telegram and work out a deal and they can send me the money. Besides, I think I'll buy a little place nearby out in the country and settle down with Maggie and my son. It will be a good place to raise Thomas and maybe a couple of more kids."

Elijah brought up a forgotten subject. ""We've been so occupied with our expedition to Brazil and Peru we've forgotten something."

"What's that?" Simon asked curiously.

"Do you remember the fifty thousand dollars in Yankee gold coins we buried down in Mississippi... when we were on the run to Mexico? I believe we named the location Cockelberry Hill after a creek nearby."

"Good grief. That was eight years ago. I had forgotten all about it."

"I'm sure the gold is still in the ground where we buried it. What do you think we should do about it?"

Simon chuckled. "Well, I'm sure not going to ride all the way down to Mississippi and I know you're not either, especially if you're going all the way out to California. Why don't we just give it back to the army? I can reveal the location to President Grant and he can send a detail over there to dig it up."

"Fine with me... it was their money anyway."

Simon reined the horse in close to the train station. "I'm going to miss you, cousin. We've sure been through a lot together. I know it sounds crazy, but with all the adventure and close calls we've experienced and wild places we've visited, I'll probably go totally stir crazy sitting around raising kids. I'm sure I'll find something to do to keep me busy though."

Elijah lifted his pack from the buggy and reached into a compartment retrieving a small bulky leather pouch. He looked his companion in the eye and grinned.

"What are you up to now?" Simon asked suspiciously. "I've seen that look before and it spells something fishy going on."

Elijah laughed. "Simon, there is something I haven't told you," he confessed as he opened the bag, allowing some small intriguing baubles to spill into his hand. Some of the pieces resonated bright bursts of fire and others, brilliant shades of green effervescence. "I have something very old, very expensive, and quite dazzling for you." His hand was filled with an assortment of finely cut diamonds and emeralds.

Simon was mesmerized at the brilliant display in his cousin's hand. "Where did you get those?" he gasped.

"Do you remember when we were in El Dorado getting ready to go aboard the Cuzco and Commander Nezar allowed us time to go back to the storage rooms to get the other two chests of Chi-Rho and Inca gold coins?"

"Yeah, I remember that."

"Well…I found another chest filled with these diamonds and emeralds so I stuffed both of my pockets full and transferred them to my pack just before we boarded the ship. I carried these stones all the way to outer space and back."

"Elijah, you are one of the most incorrigible thieves I have ever known."

"I can't help it if I love the smell of gold and diamonds," he chuckled as he handed his cousin the bag. "Anyway, here is your share and I'll keep the other. Guess I'd better get moving… I don't want to miss my train."

"Good luck, my friend," Simon replied. "I'm sure I'll see you again someday. I might even bring Maggie and the kids out there to visit you and Rosita on that ranch of hers."

Elijah smiled and turned toward the station but stopped for a moment. He turned back and shouted. "Hey Simon, let me know if you get bored with raising kids and I'll meet you somewhere and we'll go back down to El Dorado and fill up a wagon with Inca gold."

Their laughter was drowned out by the shrill sound of a train whistle rolling in.

Acknowledgments

Writing novels, such as ZENOX, the third novel from my Toltec Series, takes a great deal of support and encouragement from many people. My first thanks go to my dear wife Diane who provided me support and encouragement while I typed away and poured my wild fantasies into my computer. Her support and pre-editing skills are greatly appreciated.

A special thanks to my daughters Laurie and Shannon, and son Scott, who offered me helpful suggestions and encouragement along the way.

I also extend my sincere appreciation to Leanne Polsue who performed an initial proof editing of the novel and helped me correct many pesky grammar and word errors that plague all authors. Her keen eye for word usage and correct grammar was an invaluable help.

Special thanks go to my publisher and friend Bob Babcock, CEO of Deeds Publishing, who embraced my novels and agreed to edit, publish, and help market them. I look forward to a continued fine and productive relationship with Bob, his wife, Jan, his son, Mark, and other members of his staff.

To my good friend George Scott, official book seller for the Atlanta Writer's Club, Books for Less Bookstore, and Director of the Books for Heroes Charity Foundation, I owe my sincere appreciation for his constant encouragement and overall knowledge of authors, publishers, book readers, and the overall book business in general. George inspired me to keep writing and putting my wildest fantasies to paper. In gratitude, I named one of the main characters after George in the second novel, *Cuzco*, and extended the same character in this novel, *Zenox*.

It has been a wild and enjoyable ride to put this adventure together and now, thanks to this incredible group of family, friends, and professionals, another journey begins.

About the Author

WILLIAM (ALEX) WALKER WAS RAISED IN Knoxville, TN and graduated from the University of Tennessee, majoring in Business Administration, Marketing and Traffic Management. Walker spent eight years in U.S. Army Reserve with an honorable discharge and the rank of captain. He spent a long career with United States Gypsum Co. in various marketing and sales management positions. He is currently retired.

For several years he operated a small company, Executive Fly-Fishing Services, that organized and conducted fly-fishing trips for corporate managers and key clients to various rivers in the western U.S. and Canada.

The author wrote several fly-fishing articles published in an international fly-fishing magazine, *Rackelhanen Fly-fishing*.

Walker wrote the 30-chapter historical documentary *From Our Past* published on the Gurley, Alabama website, www.contactez.net/gurleyalabama/, now sponsored by the Gurley Lions Club.

He wrote magazine articles for *Lost Treasure Magazine* titled *The Lost Gold of Keel Mountain* published in the December 2006 issue, *Criner Treasures Found*, July 2012 issue, and *An Unlikely Treasure Found*, in the May 2013 issue.

He has written three historical action/adventure thriller novels titled TOLTEC, CUZCO, and ZENOX (Part of a three-book series) published by Deeds Publishing, Atlanta, GA.

Walker currently lives in Peachtree Corners, GA with his wife. His interests are writing adventure thriller novels, photography, fly-fishing, golf, and acoustic guitar.

CPSIA information can be obtained
at www.ICGtesting.com
Printed in the USA
FSOW01n2024210417
33430FS